13/, 1197

D0262460

Darrell, E.

WE WILL REMEMBER

WE WILL REMEMBER

Elizabeth Darrell

MICHAEL JOSEPH
LONDON

MICHAEL JOSEPH LTD
Published by the Penguin Group
27 Wrights Lane, London w8 5tz
Viking Penguin Inc., 375 Hudson Street, New York, New York 10014, USA
Penguin Books Australia Ltd, Ringwood, Victoria, Australia
Penguin Books Canada Ltd, 10 Alcorn Avenue, Toronto, Ontario, Canada m4v 3b2
Penguin Books (NZ) Ltd, 182–190 Wairau Road, Auckland 10, New Zealand

Penguin Books Ltd, Registered Offices: Harmondsworth, Middlesex, England

First published 1995

Copyright © E.D. Books 1995

Typeset by Datix International Limited, Bungay, Suffolk
Printed in England by Clays Ltd, St Ives plc
Set in 10.75/12.5 pt Monophoto Times

A CIP catalogue record for this book is available from the British Library

ISBN 0 7181 0077 8

The moral right of the author has been asserted

The quotation on page vii is reproduced by permission of Mrs Nicolete Gray
and The Society of Authors on behalf of the Laurence Binyon Estate

The Sheridan novels are for Ken,
to whom I owe everything

Brilliance lasts but a short while
The afterglow remains forever

They shall grow not old, as we that are left grow old:
Age shall not weary them, nor the years condemn.
At the going down of the sun and in the morning
We will remember them.

From 'For the Fallen' (September 1914)
by Laurence Binyon

CHAPTER ONE

As David Sheridan drove his sky-blue MG towards home on that January morning in 1946 he thought the Dorset country-side looked superb. Fields spread out below Wey Hill in a green and brown patchwork glittering with frost beneath pale sunshine. Here and there pheasants pecked in vain at the hard earth, and rabbits frolicked enjoying the gentle warmth after a night's freezing temperature.

On impulse, he pulled up and left the car to walk across turf that crunched beneath his shoes. His cheeks grew cold and his breath vaporized in the chill zephyr: he felt invigorated. Reaching the vantage point he knew so well he stopped beside the lone tree, gazing into the distance. It was too hazy for the view of three counties today; the succession of grassy ridges over to the west vanished into the misty horizon. In the valley lay the villages of Tarrant Royal and Tarrant Maundle. For a hundred years or more there had been friendly rivalry between Royal stalwarts and Maundle men. The war had put an end to that. Too many sons and husbands had been lost, too many alien elements had intruded on their simple farming lives.

David's gaze moved to the rise above Tarrant Royal village. The lovely grey stone mansion was just visible between trees bare of leaves. In the earlier world war his home had been used for convalescent officers. From 1941 until three months ago it had housed the officers of whichever squadron happened to be based on Longbarrow Hill. Pulling the collar of his sheepskin flying-jacket up around his ears, David's thoughts drifted to the occasion when his own Spitfire squadron was forced to land there because their airfield had been destroyed by bombs. There had been no more than a small runway then, and they had all bunked down in the clubhouse. Later, Tarrant Hall had been constantly shaken by the roar of fighter-bombers from the enlarged base, and the greater part of the Sheridan home had resounded with the laughter and bravado of those who had flown them.

It was good to see the back of those compulsory lodgers, although restoration of that part of the Hall had not yet been undertaken. David guessed it would be many months before that happened. There were so many things to put to rights after a war and, after all, his mother and sister could manage a little longer with the few rooms they had retained. He turned back to the car, shivering slightly. When he left the RAF at the end of June he would want to use more of the house. He could not expect his bride to move in like a guest in his mother's domain. Pat must have space of her own . . . and so must he.

Driving slowly in order to appreciate the peaceful beauty around him, David yearned for the day when he would abandon the blue uniform for ever, and start his new life as landowner and Squire of Tarrant Royal. He could then see all this whenever he wanted. He could gallop flat out over Wey Hill with Pat so that clods of earth flew up from the horses' hooves. He would be his own master for the first time in his life, he reflected, entering the long, steep drop leading to Tarrant Maundle. From public school he had gone to Cranwell, then to his first official posting. For around twenty-six years – he had been five on entering prep school – he had been obeying rules and orders. From July onwards he could please himself totally.

Cruising with care through the village where wood smoke drifted from chimneys of thatched cottages, David waved greetings to people he had known since boyhood. He did not stop at Wattle Farm. Pat would have already gone up to the Hall with her parents for pre-lunch sherry. He had been unable to swear that he could get away early enough to pick her up. As it happened, the delay this morning was due to an encounter which had produced an unexpected and exciting outcome. He could not wait to tell the girl he loved.

Out on the open road between the villages optimism bubbled up within him. The war was over, Pat was in love with him, and soon he could set the wedding date. Leaning from the car he yelled, *'Tally Ho!'*, scaring sheep standing disconsolately on the frozen slopes. He laughed and called out to them, *'Smile, you woolly mutts! Everything in the garden's lovely.'*

His exuberance was reflected by his speed as he roared through his home village, scattering the ducks by the pond and bringing to the windows of the George and Dragon men old enough to remember another Sheridan, also a flier, who had roared his merry way through the lanes on a motor-cycle until he had taken to the air one day in 1918 and never came down again. The people of Tarrant Royal were proud of their distinguished premier family. The Sheridans were gifted, handsome and irresistibly charming. What was more, they were the hub of the village life, unlike many similar landowners who took no part in the activities of those who worked for them.

David was so eager to see Pat he did not feel the usual sadness on passing the war memorial bearing the names of his two uncles, but not that of his father which rightly belonged there. He turned on to the long upward drive bordered by chestnut trees, and came to a skidding halt on loose gravel outside the side entrance used by the family for the past five years. Although he had been home for Christmas it seemed an age since he was here. Pulling his grip from the back seat he turned to find Robson at the open door. David grinned. 'I swear you have built-in radar.'

'Nothing like that, sir, merely good enough hearing to track your progress up the drive. The family is about to sit down for luncheon. Shall I ask Cook to delay it for half an hour?'

He shook his head. 'I'm ravenous after that chilly drive. Give me five minutes, that's all.'

'Very good, sir.'

Following the manservant inside, David reflected that although the Hall had served a wartime purpose which was no longer needed, it would only be the end of an era when Robson retired – unless he died at the helm! Walking into the small sitting room he found everyone there.

Pat came to him, her face aglow with love. 'Only you could create such a noisy arrival,' she teased. 'We even heard you race past the George and Dragon without stopping for a pint.'

'Cheeky wench!' He gave her a long, lingering kiss which left her in no doubt of his mood. When she finally pulled away to look up at him with questions in her large silver-green eyes, he murmured, 'There are more where that came from, believe me.' Then he glanced across to the others in the room, and smiled. 'Sorry I'm late. Some of us have to work for a living.' Cradling Pat in his left arm, he walked across to his mother who was clearly put out by his uninhibited greeting of the girl he was going to marry. She approved, she already loved Pat like a mother, but she had an aversion to public demonstrations of affection. The light kiss on her cheek David gave did not count as such in her eyes, and she softened up. 'Did you have a good journey, dear? Shall I delay lunch?'

David was treating Pat's mother, Tessa, to a filial kiss, so said over his shoulder, 'I told Robson to serve in five minutes.' He shook Colonel Chandler by the hand. 'Hallo, Uncle Bill. Still in retirement?'

'The day Daddy "retires" I'll eat my hat,' declared Pat, still happily cuddled against David's side. 'We're only too glad to get him out from under our feet three days a week.'

'Little do these females guess I'm only too glad to *get* out,' confided the silver-haired neurologist who had never lost his Australian accent. 'You look very chirpy, David.'

'Who wouldn't be on a day like this?' Releasing Pat, he turned his attention to his sister, Vesta, and took her hands in a warm clasp. 'Sorry I'm late on your special day, Vee. Have I mucked it up for you?'

'Don't be silly,' she said with a fond smile. 'I can just as easily unveil it after lunch. If you're ravenous, as you always seem to be, you'll appreciate it more when you've eaten.'

'Bless you.' He gave her a bear hug. 'I really am keen to see it, though.'

Robson announced that lunch was served, and they all went to the dining room while David made a brief visit to the cloakroom. When he rejoined the others he gave a sigh of pleasure. The polished table was set with starched linen edged by heavy lace. Cutlery gleamed and crystal glasses sparkled in the cold sunlight. In the centre stood a silver bowl containing yellow and white chrysanthemums among glossy holly sprigs. This was home as he had always known it. Although his mother had never accepted her role as wife of Sir Christopher Sheridan, brilliant linguist, classical scholar and tireless advocate of world peace, she had run the estate for him and turned Tarrant Hall into a place of distinctive beauty and comfort. Her touch was in every room. It gladdened the eye and relaxed the weary brain.

He studied her as he ate pâté and conversation flowed around him. Marion Sheridan looked exactly what she was: a county squire's widow. Her greying brown curls framed a face which bore an echo of sadness on its healthy complexion, and her brown eyes still contained a hint of incomprehension over the loss of a man who had seemed the most unlikely one to desert her. David supposed there was no reason to keep the truth about his father from her now the war was over. Yet the right moment had to present itself. It was not something he could broach by saying, 'Oh Mother, by the way . . .' In any case he suspected that the truth would only make things worse for her. Once he and Pat were married and living here, the responsibility of the estate would be considerably lightened. His mother might then branch out a bit; take a holiday. The Chandlers were forever talking about going on an extended visit home; she might go to Australia with them. It would do her good.

'A penny for them,' offered Pat softly, breaking into his thoughts.

He turned to her, murmuring in her ear, 'I want a damn sight more than a penny from you before the day's out.'

She kicked his foot and deliberately broke the intimate moment by attracting Vesta's attention. 'Tell David about your latest commission, Vee. He'll be terribly impressed.'

'Another one?' he exclaimed. 'You haven't even had your exhibition yet.'

Vesta laughed with pleasure. 'I know. With all this work coming in it won't matter so much whether or not the exhibition is a success . . . but don't tell Reynard Chase that.'

'*Reynard!*' he said in disgust. 'What a damn silly name. He should call his establishment the *Fox* Gallery.'

'Don't tell him that when you come,' his sister begged, giggling. 'He's terribly sensitive and superior. I'm awfully lucky to be granted the premises to myself for the whole week.'

David said nothing about not being able to attend the exhibition. He must give the news to Pat first. 'So what's this impressive commission, Vee?'

She paused while Robson removed her plate and replaced it with another containing rabbit. Then she leaned forward

5

eagerly. 'I've been asked to do a massive canvas of the desert campaign to hang in the ante-room of the Cavalry Club.'

'The old boy who approached her is a belted earl,' put in Pat just as eagerly.

'His grandson was something of a hero in the campaign,' said Tessa.

'And he remembers Vesta speaking over the intercom during a tank battle when she took over from a bloke with fever,' added Bill.

David turned to his mother with a grin. 'Your turn to continue the story.'

'Oh, dear! Well, the young tank-commander's grandfather wants to present the painting as a gift to the club in recognition of all who fought in the desert.'

'And are you all going to help the artist paint it?' he asked slyly. 'Congrats, Vee. A real feather in your cap.' He helped himself to vegetables. 'Do you remember the earl's grandson? Who is he, by the way?'

'The Honourable Jeremy Stanstead. No, he would have been just one of the voices reaching me through the earphones.' Vesta grew pensive. 'It was incredible, you know. I was receiving and passing on instructions from men in the thick of battle way, way off over the sands. They were speaking to each other as well as to me, and I . . . I felt so privileged yet so helpless as I followed their progress. I shall never forget that day.'

'The war's over now, dear,' said Marion brightly. 'You should put all that behind you.'

'Can *you*, Mummy? Can any of us?' Vesta cried.

Bill intervened in his usual easy manner. 'Of course we can't. It's far too soon. What your mother means is that you must use all your experience to enhance your future rather than dwell in the past. Everything points to a pretty *rosy* future, my girl.'

'I'll say,' put in David, making short work of his rabbit and heartily agreeing with Bill. He, himself, dared not dwell in the past. By the end of next month he would have freed himself of the last remaining ghost. Then there would be nothing standing in the way of his golden future. 'Will you have to go back to North Africa for inspiration, Vee?'

His sister had returned from her memories, but she pushed

away her plate without finishing her meal. 'No, I've enough recollection of desert terrain for the setting. I'll probably have to visit the Hon. Jerry's regiment to make a few sketches.' She smiled across the table at David. 'It's exciting, isn't it?'

'Not half as exciting as this present you've got for us. You've been so mysterious about it.'

'She forbade me, on pain of death, to peep before she was ready to show us all,' said Marion. 'If you had been much later coming, David, I swear I would have looked.'

'You'd have caught me doing the same, and it isn't even *my* present,' confided Tessa.

'Shame on you,' said Vesta and Pat together, then they laughed. 'Of course, I shall have to borrow it for the week of the exhibition, but it won't have been hanging here long enough to leave a mark on the wall,' Vesta added.

'I do envy you being given a *painting* as a present,' said Pat. 'What a family the Sheridans are!'

'You never know, I might give you and David one as . . . later on,' Vesta finished tactfully, flashing a glance at her mother.

David was annoyed. 'As a wedding present? That would be wonderful, wouldn't it, darling?'

Pat nodded but kicked his foot once more, increasing his anger. It was so ridiculous not to mention something everyone knew was on the cards, but his mother preferred to ignore their plans until such time as David had traced his wife in Singapore. God knew he had been trying almost from the day the island had been recaptured but there were much higher priorities and all his efforts had been in vain. Now he had been offered an opportunity he had never expected, and frustration would be at an end. It nevertheless annoyed him when everyone around the table pandered to his mother's attitude by embarking on a new topic of conversation.

As soon as the meal was over they all went to the wood-panelled study where Vesta had placed an easel covered with a sheet. She now appeared rather nervous. Her career had really begun when, as a war artist, she had covered part of the desert campaign against Rommel and produced some very unusual pictures of tank warfare which had captured the public imagination. She had then moved to Italy and worked alongside

American war correspondent Brad Holland. Together they had produced some stunning words and pictures of the desperate fight for command of the Mediterranean, which had sealed Vesta's future as an artist of unique talent. Commissions, an exhibition in a prestigious gallery ... so why was she slightly nervous of unveiling this gift to her family destined to hang at Tarrant Hall?

'Come on, girl, don't keep us in suspense any longer,' urged Bill from beside the log fire.

Vesta gave them all a swift apprehensive look, then folded back the sheet with care. The large painting showed their own seventeenth-century village church as it used to be before a German bomber had crashed on to it. The hands of the clock pointed to twelve. Midnight. The heavy door stood ajar to give a glimpse of the congregation wrapped in thick coats and scarves. Holly boughs and mistletoe decked the ancient walls. The churchyard lay beneath snow, the curves and ledges of gravestones magnified by an additional layer of white. Light streamed through the stained-glass windows to put pale echoes of colour on the glittering spread, before illuminating a grave that stood alone in a far corner. The vase contained Christmas roses dusted with snow. At the foot of the mound a single candle burned in the chill air.

Entitled *The Afterglow*, the picture was stunning. As David studied it he could feel the frosty stillness of that Christmas night, hear the lusty voices rising in praise within the church, sense the impact of what was happening there. He had taken part in it all so many times. His throat tightened as he stared at what Vesta had created. The combination of sadness and hope was inexpressibly moving, but most poignant of all was the single set of footprints in the virgin snow leading up to where the candle burned.

There was a long silence until Bill broke it in typical manner. 'My word, that's bloody brilliant. *Brilliant!*'

'Yes, it is, Vesta,' echoed Tessa quietly. 'I have a lump in my throat.'

'And I have goose bumps,' said Pat. 'Oh Vee, it's the best thing you've ever done. You've captured the church exactly as it was. Gosh, it takes me back to all those Christmases when we were young, before everything was spoiled.' She gripped

8

David's hand with emotion. 'It's the most beautiful present anyone could ever give ... but, honestly, it should be on display to the general public, not hidden away here.'

'I didn't paint it for the general public. Here is where it's meant to be, Pat,' Vesta told her friend, her voice thick.

David saw that his sister was on the verge of tears. He was himself. Their mother was not similarly affected, however. She went across to kiss Vesta. 'Darling, it's absolutely lovely. It'll be our first family heirloom.' With her arm around Vesta she studied the painting once more. 'You've captured the church as it used to be, there's no doubt of that. Such a lovely old building. Despite what they're trying to do with it, it'll never be like that again. We must take this down to the village hall one day so that everyone can see it, and we must ask the Rector and Marjorie up for sherry before we show anyone else. They'll be so impressed.' She hesitated momentarily, then added gently, 'Before we do you must correct an oversight, dear. You've shown footprints leading to Laura's grave, but none coming away from it.'

Vesta's expression was almost agonized as she said, 'There are not meant to be any coming away.'

As David mentally willed his mother to drop the subject, Marion made the situation worse. 'But whoever lit the candle couldn't have vanished into thin air.'

Dangerously close to shedding her hovering tears, Vesta murmured raggedly, 'It's symbolic, Mummy.'

'Oh ... I see,' came the response in tones that showed she did not.

Bill Chandler saved the moment, as he often had in the past. 'Well, folks, knowing what a special occasion this was to be, I've brought along something rather appropriate.' From behind the chair where he had hidden it he brought out a bottle topped with gold foil.

'Champagne!' cried Marion. 'However did you get your hands on it?' She walked to a bell-push near the door and pressed it. 'I'll ask Robson to bring glasses. My goodness, a family heirloom and a bottle of bubbly on the same day. Put a red ring on the calendar around the date.'

David released Pat's hand and crossed to his sister who was still looking upset. 'It's a magnificent tribute, Vee. He'll be immensely proud of you.'

Vesta gripped his arm, searching his face with eyes framed by wet lashes. '*You* know who it's really for?'

'Of course. And I understand about the footprints. He always used to say Aunt Laura's grave represented all the male Sheridans who died in foreign lands. Yes, *I* understand about the footprints, Vee, dear.'

'Grandfather in the sea off Madeira. Uncle Roland in France, Uncle Rex in mid-air over there, and then Daddy in the English Channel. There has to be *somewhere* here for them. The uncles are at least mentioned on the memorial, but Daddy . . .' She broke off to glance back at her painting. 'You know why it's called *The Afterglow*?'

David nodded. 'The words he put on Aunt Laura's headstone. "Brilliance lasts but a short while/ The afterglow remains forever".' He fought an inner battle then decided on a compromise. 'There's something I have to tell you about Father one day soon. When we're alone.' Putting his hand on her shoulder, he said, 'Don't take her remarks too much to heart. Mother's no artist. I suspect the only other person who saw what you're saying here is Uncle Bill. He's a canny old devil.' He smiled. 'Come on, let's have some of his bubbly. I have something to celebrate, as a matter of fact.'

'You've heard from Singapore?' she asked swiftly.

'No, the next best thing . . . but I must tell Pat first.'

'Oh, David, I'm so glad for you. Yes, let's have some bubbly.'

An hour passed before David was able to have Pat to himself. They put on coats and walked in the grounds as the sun began to be swallowed by the mauve mists of oncoming darkness. They strolled arm in arm past the lily pond to the sunken garden beyond. Birds were racing back to their roosts to face another cold night, and dogs in the village barked at closed doors to be allowed in for the comfort of hearthrugs. There was an immense air of peace which increased David's yearning for the day when this would be his for all time.

Beside the ornamental fig he stopped and pulled Pat into his arms. 'I thought I'd never get to this,' he murmured, kissing her very thoroughly. 'The three weeks since Christmas seemed an *age*. I'm ravenous.' He kissed her even more thoroughly until she struggled free of his arms. 'They can't see us here,' he pointed out, reaching for her again.

'It isn't that.' She stepped away from him. 'I'm ravenous too.'

He closed in on her joyfully. 'Tally ho!'

'No, David. That isn't an invitation, it's a plea.' She kept him at arm's length with her hands on his chest. 'Under other circumstances I'd have become a wanton woman long ago. You know that.'

'Under other circumstances I'd have *married* you long ago.' He seized her wrists and moved in closer. 'I want you so much it's becoming a real problem, darling.'

'I know, I know,' she cried softly, 'but I just can't . . . she's always there, coming between us. I want you, too, but only when I'm certain you're mine to have.'

Releasing her he leaned back against the tree trunk, marvelling that he had only seen the truth about his feelings for her after years of treating her like a sister. He now wanted to spend the rest of his life with her and could not wait to start.

'I was late arriving this morning because I had to make an official detour to another squadron,' he told her carefully. 'I met a chap I knew at Cranwell but hadn't come across any time since. He's in Transport at present. We caught up on what each of us had been doing over the last six years. That took a while, as you can imagine. I told him about Singapore and so on, and he then said he was flying some civvy bods there next week for an official investigation into atrocities.' He straightened up, excitement returning. 'I explained about the difficult job I was having trying to trace a girl I married before the Japs invaded, and he said, "Why don't you wangle some leave and come out there with me?"'

Pat stared at him across the luminous dusk. 'You're going back?'

'Yes. Next week. He's offered me a lift.' As Pat continued to look at him with a mixture of apprehension and concern, he began to grow tense. The prospect of settling his future had obliterated the shadowy side of what he was proposing to do. It now darkened his mood. 'A lot has happened since then, and it's the only way to find out about Su. All else has failed. We can't go on like this, wanting each other desperately and suffering because of a Chinese girl who's probably dead anyway.' He gently drew her against his chest. 'Darling, I want more than anything to marry you this summer when I leave the RAF, and live here on the estate as we planned. You refuse to sleep with me because of a cold-hearted bitch who took me for a ride, and you don't know what that's doing to me. The thing's *got* to be resolved. I must grab this chance to do it, for both our sakes.'

Pat rested quietly against him for a moment or two, then she said softly, 'You could have lied when you returned from the dead three years ago; told us she was killed in an air raid before you got away. We'd have believed you.'

He stroked her hair gently. This girl he wanted so much did not know the truth about what had happened to him between leaving Singapore as the Japanese invaded and arriving in Australia. Nobody did, apart from those few who had been with him. He had been in no state to consider any kind of future, much less pretend Su was dead in case he wanted to marry again.

'My only concern at that time had been how to survive each day back in civilization. I'd been away from it for seven months, and I was a different man from the one who had left England.'

They stood close for a while, both remembering his dramatic return, then Pat asked, 'How long will you be here?'

'Only tonight. I'm due to take an evening flight to Düsseldorf tomorrow.'

She tilted her head to look at him. 'A room at a local inn is out of the question. We're too well known and the news would be all over Dorset by morning, but if you can devise a way we could cuddle up together for a couple of hours, I think we should before we both go crazy.'

Darkness and ghosts fled as he took in what she was saying. Tightening his hold, he murmured, 'You're bloody wonderful! I'll definitely put a red ring around the date. A family heirloom, a bottle of bubbly and *you!*' But even as he kissed her, doubts crept in. He had visited a woman prepared to take on any client provided he paid enough, just to prove he could still function. That had been a year ago, and there had been no more sessions since then. He hoped to God he could still do it. With his lips against her hair, he said, 'I'm so glad you've stopped fighting for your honour, darling. I just hope I haven't forgotten how to thrill a girl.'

'Not you,' she responded warmly. 'Just make certain it's a bigger thrill than you've given any other girl.'

Pat arrived at six a.m., tiptoeing across the gravel from the stables to where David waited with a torch by the door. He drew her inside and gave her a hug to warm her up, then they both crept through the hall to where a door led to the main part of the house. David had taken the key from his mother's office and he locked the door behind him once they were through. It was unlikely that they would be disturbed at this hour, but he was guarding against any unexpected intrusion. Despite his sense of excitement he was feeling ridiculously nervous. It was his own damn silly fault for precipitating this test of virility. There was a vast difference between proving himself to a whore who could do the most amazing things to provide a client with his money's worth, and taking a virgin who loved and trusted him. Pat had surrendered with reservations, he was certain. What if he now made an almighty fool of himself?

It was hardly the best atmosphere for seduction: chilly, unlit rooms empty of furniture. It was the only place they could be alone, however. They still moved stealthily, hand in hand, until they reached the room where he had put pillows, blankets and an eiderdown along with two candles in saucers. He went straight to them and lit the wicks, making the surroundings come into soft focus. From his squatting position he turned to find Pat gazing at plum velvet curtains, dove-grey walls and an old polished oak fireplace where logs burned.

'The CO's bedroom,' he explained. 'It has the thickest carpet and the added advantage of being the furthest away so no one will hear me chucking more logs on the fire.'

'It's very posh. Better than a draughty room in a pub.' She giggled. 'Remember that awful place called the Crook and Fleece where I came to fetch you after you'd crashed your car following a disgusting drinking party that first Christmas of the war? It should have been called the Crook and Fleas.'

His confidence took a further plunge at this reference to the womanizer he used to be. 'That was six years ago. The fleas probably don't bite any longer.'

'And this is much, much better,' she said hastily. 'So are

you, darling.' She came to kneel beside him, a lovely young woman who was his for the taking right now. 'You were terribly arrogant in those days, which is why I thought I was in love with Uncle Chris.'

'He was more worthy of it.'

'I don't think so.'

Going on to his knees he drew her against him and kissed her with gentle deliberation, afraid to do more. When they drew apart they simply gazed at each other in the light from candles and leaping flames. Her hair lay darkly against ears and neck gilded by firelight. Her face was soft with the love which also glowed in eyes more green than silver in this semi-darkness. She had always been part of his life. David wanted her to stay that way for ever.

She whispered, 'I've grown shy of you all of a sudden. Isn't it silly.'

He shook his head. 'It's natural. You've never done this before.'

'I . . . I wish you hadn't.'

In that moment, so did he. He wanted this to be so very special. Knowing he must take the lead he murmured a silent 'Here we go', and reached for the buttons of her coat. Fingers that had once done such things with ease now worked slowly on the task. Beneath the coat she wore a red sweater. Sliding his hands under the wool David slowly lifted it over her breasts, then her head, tumbling her curls. Excitement began to override his nervousness. Four years had passed since he had touched the body of a young, beautiful girl and his own was reacting more than satisfactorily. Bending his head he kissed the soft swell above the lace, and reached behind her for the fastening. He fumbled a little with the tiny hooks and eyes but, by then, Pat was trembling with anticipation and his doubts slipped away.

'Oh God, you're beautiful,' he breathed, tugging off his own sweater and drawing her against his warm skin.

Her palms moved over his back, putting fire in his veins, and he lowered her to the pile of blankets while he removed the rest of her clothes and discarded the trousers he had pulled on to greet her. For a few moments he feasted his eyes on her naked perfection which no other man had yet possessed, then the pain of his desire had to be eased. As he initiated her, gently at first but with greater and greater insistence, he became again the man whose smooth, strong body had thrilled so many in the past. The wartime scars across his face and body, the misshapen hands were forgotten as, for the first time in his life, there was true love between himself and his partner. His spirits soared as she responded eagerly. It was as if David Sheridan was reborn in that empty room bathed in golden light.

The minutes flew past as they revelled in expressing feelings they had subdued for almost two years. Pat was delightfully generous and David was greedy to take all she would give. They spoke, as lovers do, of the ways in which they adored each other, believing themselves, the first pair to have discovered such overwhelming ecstasy.

Finally spent, they lay arms entwined beneath the eiderdown while David felt tears gather on his lashes. The virile aviator he had once been had failed to find what Pat had just now given him. He would value it all his life.

Pat stirred eventually and tilted her head to kiss his throat, murmuring, 'Hurry back from Singapore and make an honest woman of me, darling. Now I know how wonderful this is I shall want a lot more of it from you.'

Vesta and her mother walked across Longbarrow Hill after David drove off. The sun was shining again, but a chilliness in the wind hinted at snow before long. Distant clouds echoed that possibility. Marion was always restless after David had been home. She had suggested the walk before the sun went in, and Vesta was agreeable because she also felt restless after the special event of the previous day. In her heart she wondered whether it had been wise to make such a fuss over unveiling the painting. Yet it had been so important to her, it had seemed right to make a ceremony of giving it to her family. The Chandlers were counted as such.

They walked briskly, the dogs racing ahead. Vesta was always surprised by her mother's fast pace, but Marion had lived in the country all her life and was hardy despite her slender build. Striding beside her with the wind whipping the ends of her long scarf, Vesta still felt the curious ache of her mother's incomprehension over the missing footprints in the snow. The omission conveyed so much; how could anyone who had known her father well *not* see the poignancy of what she had created? *The Afterglow* was the result of many months of despair and anguish as she had struggled to transfer her inner visions to canvas so that it would be worthy of the man she so much wanted to honour. On completion, she had known it was better than anything she had yet done, so exactly what she yearned to capture, that she did not immediately want to share it with anyone. For some days she had kept silent about it. Then, when Reynard Chase had agreed to give her an exhibition, she realized *The Afterglow* must be hung publicly before taking its place in the Sheridan home, so the picture had had to be brought out of hiding. She now could not wait to exhibit it in the Chase Gallery, where connoisseurs and other artists would surely acknowledge its subtle power.

Glancing at her mother stepping out energetically, Vesta suddenly knew that the brilliant Chris Sheridan would not have expected his wife to understand the message of the footprints. Neither should she. On impulse, she tucked her arm through Marion's, causing her to smile.

'Was I dreaming? Sorry.'

'No, Mummy, I was miles away, too.' Vesta smiled back. 'You go so fast I thought I'd hang on to you to avoid being left behind.'

They reached the barbed wire surrounding the airfield and stopped for a while to gaze at the view they knew so well. The low temperature produced the clarity that had been missing yesterday. Hills rose in ranges as far as the eye could see; gentle green hills where sheep grazed and Dorset men and women lived in peace with their neighbours.

Gazing across the still, wintry landscape Marion said, 'Did you know David and some of his squadron landed up here late one afternoon when it was only a club airfield?'

'No, he never told me . . . but we didn't see much of each other during those days.'

'Of course.' She gave a light chuckle. 'He didn't let me know he was so close because he thought I would come up here with food and blankets to fuss over him.'

'Well, you would have,' said Vesta.

Marion nodded, still gazing ahead. 'I suppose so.' After a pause, she added, 'I wish he weren't going back there.'

It was a moment or two before Vesta understood. 'To Singapore? But it's the most wonderful opportunity for him to settle the business about his wife. All the official sources he's tried are inundated with enquiries about missing people. The Japs never kept true records of casualties and death, so it'll take *years* before the fate of some can be traced. Going there independently means that David can do in a week what officialdom will take months to achieve.'

When Marion turned, her expression was distressed. 'Suppose she's still alive?'

'David's almost certain she isn't.'

'But what if she is?'

'Then he'll arrange a divorce so that he can marry Pat.'

Marion looked away again. 'It's so . . . *sordid.*'

Vesta tried to sound calm. 'Brad is getting a divorce from *his* wife so that he can marry me. There's nothing sordid in it. Gloria wants to be free.'

'That's slightly different. His wife is American.'

'And David's is Chinese. Is *that* what makes it sordid in your eyes?' Vesta said sharply. 'Daddy never agreed. He did his best to trace her when Singapore first fell, and would have done all he could for her.'

Marion chose not to comment on Chris's tolerant regard for all peoples of the world, for she had never condoned or understood it. Vesta took advantage of her silence to speak frankly.

'You can accept Gloria Holland's existence because she's American, but not Su Sheridan's. Yes, Mummy, that *is* her name, if she's alive. David's divorce will be "sordid", but not Brad's. Yet you approve of David marrying Pat, and avoid mentioning my intention of marrying Brad. Isn't your reasoning mixed up somewhere?'

'I think we should start back. Those clouds have almost reached the sun. When they do it's going to get very cold.'

Vesta refused to attempt to keep up with her mother's even faster pace, and made the return to the Hall at her own speed. What she had said was the truth. So far as her mother was

17

concerned Su Sheridan had no legal claim on David and should be forgotten, but he could not do that. Whatever madness had caused him to take the Chinese nurse as his wife in 1941 tied them together until death or divorce. She had apparently wanted only his money. Even if she had once loved him, it was unlikely that she would now. Vesta sighed. She had grown so used to her brother as he now was, he looked a stranger in old photographs. His experiences in the East had turned the golden-haired, handsome athlete into a man with deep blue eyes holding an echo of suffering and a face bearing the physical evidence of it to overshadow the finely drawn features. Any girl who had married him with stars in her eyes would be totally disillusioned on meeting him again. Pat, on the other hand, loved only the person beneath, whom she knew so well.

Poor Pat had been waiting so long for fulfilment, unable to grasp happiness because that girl in Singapore had stood in the way. Pat had explained to Vesta that it was not because Su was David's wife, or that she was Chinese, but because no one knew what she had been suffering under Japanese occupation. 'Honestly, Vee,' she had said on several occasions, 'whenever I find myself surrendering I suddenly freeze and feel such a traitor. All through the war I worked on a farm in reasonable safety, with plenty to eat and a lovely home. I had *freedom*. Who knows what that poor thing went through? I just can't have David until the wretched girl has been traced and he's free of her.'

Plodding along behind Marion, with the wind now biting into her face, Vesta reflected that she had not once considered Gloria Holland while making love to the woman's husband. Thinking of Brad brought the usual yearning. Pat was unhappy because she could not 'have' David yet. Once she did, she would realize that it was then even worse when she could not. Brad Holland was charismatic and unforgettable. They had met in the desert at a time when Vesta was hurt, distrustful and uncertain of herself. The encounter had been explosive until she discovered he was married. Months later, Brad had secretly arranged for her to be sent to Italy on an assignment with him, and the fireworks had begun again. But, on the verge of surrendering, Vesta had recalled her bitter experience with a married Polish pilot, and walked away. It had cost her more than she knew to do it, because she lost artistic inspiration and all her new personal confidence fled.

In that state, and coming to terms with her father's unexpected death whilst flying to a conference, Brad had walked up to her outside Tarrant Royal church to tell her Gloria wanted a divorce and *he* wanted the girl who had got under his skin so much he could not live without her. After that punchline, he had asked Vesta to go back to Italy with him to cover the final campaign. That was Brad all over. Sock 'em between the eyes with the irresistible approach, then bring out the million-dollar question. *Come with me to Italy and sweeten my nights while I chase an exclusive.* And she had gone. And the nights had been sweeter than she had imagined. And she longed for more of them.

They had made plans. Brad would go to America, get his divorce, settle his affairs, then take up residence at Tarrant Hall until they found their ideal home nearby. Their civil wedding would be blessed in the church that was being repaired with financial help from Sir Christopher Sheridan's estate. Vesta wanted to concentrate on embracing new subjects in her career that must change and broaden now there was peace. Brad was keen to write a book on his experiences as a war correspondent. He had covered so much of the action and had narrowly escaped death on more than one occasion owing to his compulsion to get the story no one else dared to chase. It would be a bestseller, without doubt. He already had a publisher's contract, with lucrative magazine rights. Together with Vesta's recent commissions and almost certain sales at the coming exhibition, the Hollands' future looked extremely rosy.

Brad had cabled that the loose ends of his former life were almost all tied up and he had booked passage on a ship docking at Liverpool next week. Vesta planned to travel there to meet him. The thought of even one additional day of waiting was unbearable. Unlike Pat, she knew what she was missing.

After tea Vesta went to her studio to review her selection of paintings for the Chase Gallery. They would have to travel to London on the day she would be in Liverpool meeting Brad.

She was studying these in artificial light, as they would be in the gallery, when she heard her mother come in. Without looking around, she murmured, 'I've made my selection three times already. I should have packed them up the first time and not looked at them again.'

'I guess you should have. You never could make up your mind, Vic.' Just the sound of his voice was enough to fill her with excitement. Brad was standing just inside the room and, even in its spartan, working atmosphere, his charisma was overwhelming. It was as if virility personified had entered. Bronzed by Californian sun and wearing that familiar, slightly cynical, smile, his physical impact was impossible to resist.

'I wasn't expecting you for another week,' she murmured in his arms. 'I had it all planned: straight from ship to hotel room. How did you get here so soon?'

'Guy I knew in the old days runs an airline now. Told him I couldn't wait to get over here. If he could see you, he'd know why.'

'I was going to wow you with a stunning outfit when I came aboard at Liverpool, and you have to walk in to catch me without make-up in a paint-smeared smock, you wretch.'

He laughed. 'Hell, I've seen you in every situation a woman hates to be in with a guy she wants to impress. Remember that first day in the desert when you smothered yourself in cologne and soon resembled a dancing flypaper? Or that storm just outside Anzio when we threw ourselves flat in liquid mud because the column was being machine-gunned? I'm still hanging around, so it must be because of something other than your snappy dressing.'

She was back in those situations he had mentioned, when each day had been so vital. 'It's so wonderful to see you! I've been only half alive since you left me.'

Smiling down provocatively, Brad said, 'Your mother is preparing a room for me. Is it OK to take you there as soon as it's ready, or would it be *frightfully bad form*? Seduction in an ancestral home is new to me.'

'Heavens, I thought you had exhausted all possible locations.'

'I had until I met this crazy, upper-class female lootenant in a pith-helmet, who made me forget all those other times,' he replied smoothly to counter her slightly caustic reference to his womanizing, and kissed her again with some force. 'That's what you'll get each time you go all prissy on me about my past,' he breathed. 'I meant it when I said from now on it's just you and me, Vic.'

Vesta sighed with contentment. It was exactly what she wanted to hear. 'When are you going to stop using that silly name?'

'When you stop rising to the bait. That little spark which flies each time reminds me of your expression when I told you I'd only been asked to escort the war-artist *Victor* Sheridan, not some woman looking like an eccentric Edwardian explorer, then prepared to drive off leaving you in a deserted oasis.'

'Remind me one day to describe *your* expression when that drunken fool in Cairo declared he had met your glamorous wife upstaging uniformed women in London, just as you thought you had me eating out of your hand,' Vesta retaliated.

'You were, admit it.'

She veered away from that. 'How *was* Gloria?'

'Greedy. She has a millionaire on ice but still wants all she can get from me.'

'Will she get it?'

'I guess.'

'But you're finally free of her?'

F/409385.

'As a bird.' On the verge of another embrace, Brad caught sight of something over her shoulder and stepped aside. 'That's it? *The Afterglow*?'

Turning towards her painting, yet watching his face, she asked if he liked it.

'It's sensational,' he murmured, studying it intently. 'That's got to be the best piece of work you've ever done. There's something about it that makes the hairs on the back of my neck rise. I'm no sucker for sentiment, but this really gets to me the same way a great piece of copy does.' He glanced at her. 'You shouldn't hide it away. It should be in a public gallery.'

'It will be, for a while.' She slipped her hand in his. 'You know why I want it here at home.'

'As a tribute to your father. He must have been quite some man.'

21

'He was. You would have found a lot in common with him, Brad.'

He grunted, still intent on the painting. 'A cynical newspaper hack and a brilliant linguist and Greek scholar? Fat chance!' He pointed. 'There's only one set of footprints.'

Vesta felt badly let down because this man she loved so much did not understand. Yet why should he? *He* had never met her father, or heard him declare that Laura's grave represented all the Sheridans lost abroad, as her mother had. Even so, there was hollowness in her voice as she explained that the omission was symbolic. As she moved away, Brad stopped her.

'Whatever it is, honey, it really gets to me,' he insisted. 'If a hard-drinking, world-weary guy like me can react this way, just wait until the entrepreneurs see it.'

A discreet knock prevented what would have followed. Marion entered to tell Brad that his room was ready if he wished to unpack and dress for dinner.

'Heavens, is it that late?' cried Vesta, thinking of how long it would take her to become the alluring vision she wanted to be for Brad's first night back. 'I'll never be ready in time.'

'You doing the cooking?' Brad asked, all mock innocence.

Vesta smiled angelically. 'Had we known the renowned Bradford Holland was arriving we'd have hired a cook for the evening. As it is, you'll have to make do with one of Lord Woolton's recipes for absolute beginners.'

'In that case, Vic, there's no need to pretty yourself up,' he retaliated. 'That smock will do just fine.'

'I'll show you the way, Mr Holland,' said Marion, already in an elegant black wool full-length dinner-gown. 'We dispensed with the gong several years ago,' she added over her shoulder as Brad grinned at Vesta, winked, then followed his hostess. 'When the whole family lived here it was necessary because our rooms were some distance from each other. Once I was left alone I told Robson to serve dinner at seven-thirty each night unless told otherwise, so a resounding summons was no longer needed. Here you are.' She stopped to throw open a bedroom door. 'It's next to mine and used by all our guests since the house was commandeered by the R.A.F.' She gave a polite smile. 'Once David comes home we can open the rest of the house again and make our visitors more comfortable.'

'I've slept in more foxholes than you have around your village, ma'am, so this room will be pure luxury . . . and please call me Brad.' His smile should have had any woman melting beneath its charm, but this one was proof against it.

'If you care for sherry, Robson usually serves it about twenty minutes before dinner in the sitting room.' As an afterthought she added, 'And if there's anything else you would prefer, he will do his best to provide it, naturally.'

Having witnessed this exchange Vesta hurried to her room vowing to speak to her mother about her stiff attitude towards someone soon to become her son-in-law. She had no chance before dinner. Brad had so little to unpack he was already downstairs when she descended, having washed her short light-brown hair and ransacked her wardrobe for the right dress for this occasion. It did not appear to exist, so she had to settle for deep blue crêpe studded with rhinestones.

Brad turned as she entered the room where a huge log fire gave out much-needed warmth. He looked tough, assured and excitingly masculine in that atmosphere of chintz, chrysanthemums and expensive porcelain. '*Wow!*' he exclaimed, causing Marion's mouth to tighten.

'If you had been considerate enough to let me know you were coming I could have bought something *really* special,' Vesta said.

'That's special enough for any man who's been travelling for almost two days non-stop.' He raised his glass to her, and his murmured '*Salute*', plus the look in his eyes, revived all the excitement of Italy.

CHAPTER TWO

DINNER was a plain meal. There had been no time for Cook to change the menu planned by Marion for just two people after the celebration of the previous day. Robson clearly did not approve of guests who ate lamb cutlets and garden vegetables with only a fork, and who drank wine faster than the manservant considered polite. The elderly man's expression showed his disapproval, and Vesta smiled across the table at her lover. Robson would have to grow used to American ways. Brad would be living here until they found a suitable house. It would be as well to begin looking right away because they would be inhibited by her mother's presence before their marriage, and possibly after it. In any case, David would soon return for good. There was not enough room in the only part of the house presently habitable for two newly married couples and a widow.

Conversation was polite and slightly stilted at first, but Marion began to relax towards the end of the meal as Brad drew her out on the subject of Tarrant Hall during the two world wars. He was skilled at coaxing facts from people he interviewed, and Vesta soon realized what he was up to. Her mother was unwittingly giving him what he called 'a good heart and soul story'. She was certain he already had the headline.

'I've been given an exciting commission to paint a large picture of the desert campaign,' Vesta said deliberately, letting him know she was well aware of what he was doing. 'It's to be hung at the Cavalry Club.'

'Will that get you free life membership?' he asked. 'What's the story behind it?'

'Ladies aren't allowed to become members,' Marion explained, thinking he was unversed on such things.

'And the story behind it is that the handsome grandson of

one of our most distinguished earls won a VC during the campaign against Rommel, and he recalls hearing my voice over the radio when I substituted for the operator during a battle. He's been searching for me ever since and all the earl's money will be mine if I marry this hero.'

'*Vesta!*' cried Marion.

'So what's stopping you?'

'My heart belongs to another,' she declared histrionically, then laughed. 'Oh, Mummy, you've forgotten Brad's a newspaper man first and foremost. He'd turn *anything* into a "scoop" if he thought he could sell it.' Then, seeing Marion's face, she added, 'It was a joke; he knew that.'

'But you *have* been given the commission, haven't you?' he asked.

'Yes, of course.' Vesta told Brad the details of it and of two others which would be more of a challenge because of the subject matter. 'War I know, but these are different. The four children of a banker at play in their nursery, and a Scottish glen which was the scene of a tragic hunting accident some years ago. The glen should be easier than the other. Beautifully dressed children in a nursery filled with expensive toys won't have the appeal of ragged Italian urchins scrambling for sweets as we passed through the villages, will they?'

Brad was looking thoughtful. 'Is that what you *want* to do?'

'No . . . At least, I don't think so. But I have to try various ideas out before I can specialize.'

'And then what?'

Vesta laid down her spoon and pushed her dish away, slightly irritated. 'We've discussed it enough times. You know the answer . . . or the probable answer. *You* can always sell a hot story, or a topical one. *I* now have to change direction to survive as an artist.'

'And become just another landscape or portrait painter?'

Vesta's irritation increased. His first night back and he was skipping the honeymoon hours to pin her down on a subject which needed time to resolve. Flinging down her napkin, she said, 'Let's have coffee and talk about something else.'

As they walked to the sitting room, Brad murmured, 'This is the Vic I know and love. Cut out the sweet-talking and get mad!'

She flashed him a fiery glance and whispered, 'If I do, you'll be sleeping alone tonight.'

'Wanna bet?' came his tantalizing reply.

Dispensing coffee Marion asked Brad about his home in America, and listened with apparent interest to his description of a boyhood vastly different from David's. A country-raised boy, certainly, but on a farm in the middle of nowhere. The only amusement for a lonely child was reading, so he was soon keen to write his own stories.

'I guess I must have used every scrap of paper in the place,' he said with a smile that appeared to complete Marion's surrender. 'On Saturdays I'd jump a freight train into Malcolm – that was the nearest town – and hang around the office of *The Mercury* until old Pa McKenzie gave me something to do. Usually it was sweeping out the printing room or fetching tobacco from along the street, but I felt part of the place.' He chuckled and threw his arm along the back of the settee to put his hand on Vesta's shoulder possessively as he confided to her: 'More times than not I'd get a strapping from my pa when I got home because I'd left my chores undone. After the third time I'd been stranded all night in Malcolm because there was no train back, I was forbidden to go there again.' He looked back at Marion. 'When I was fourteen I talked McKenzie into giving me a job. As nothing much happened in Malcolm I made up news items.' With another chuckle, he added, 'They were so sensational one eventually reached a national news agency, and poor old McKenzie was besieged by hacks from as far off as Chicago who wanted to interview the people in my fictional account. Oh boy, that put an end to my career with *The Mercury*.'

'But not to your ambition?' asked Marion, clearly fascinated by a story which could have been the opening chapters of a Hemingway novel.

Vesta knew Brad. He was certainly dramatizing the bare bones of his early life told to her during those hectic days in Italy. He was a newsman able to wring the most out of any situation, and he was very definitely set on winning Marion over. Vesta listened in silence, prepared to accept anything he said but longing for the moment when the evening ended and he would come to her room.

26

The story continued in the same rollicking vein. He could have been describing life in another world, so alien was it to a woman who had never been to America. Only when he reached the part about fighting in the Spanish Civil War did Vesta wonder if it might all be the truth. They had met someone in Italy who had been there with Brad, so she knew that as fact.

'I was on the losing side, so a number of us went home. The libellous novel I'd written was into its sixth impression, but still no newspaper would employ me. The men I had offended with it were very, very powerful. It was during those weeks of bitterness and unemployment that I began a novel about the Spanish War. It was corny, but the daughter of my landlady believed it all. She thought I was a hero. When you're beat and wondering what to do next, any kind of praise is like wine. It went to my head and I married her. Two months later I was approached by a London news agency and asked to write copy about the situation in Spain. When they offered me a place on their payroll I knew I'd finally made it. We settled in London, but I was off all over the world and Gloria was alone in a foreign city. End of marriage, pretty well.'

Marion said nothing. An intriguing story had become uncomfortable fact. Before Vesta could speak, Brad continued his theme along quite the wrong tangent for her mother, at a time when David was about to go in search of a wife Marion had never, ever accepted.

'There'll be broken marriages all over the States in the next couple of years. Many of our guys are turning up in small conservative home towns with Polynesian, Philippine, Hawaiian or Chinese wives they met while serving in the Pacific. These hapless women find themselves insulted and rejected by their husbands' families. Pretty soon the men are doing the same. What seemed natural enough out East is all wrong back home. War leaves a hell of a mess, especially if children are involved.'

Marion glanced at the clock and got to her feet. 'I have some correspondence to attend to so, as I'm sure you must be tired after your long journey, I'll leave you to have an early night, Mr . . . Brad. I hope you will find your room comfortable. When we open up the rest of the house . . .' She kissed Vesta's cheek. 'I'll see you at breakfast, dear.'

The door closed behind her mother and Vesta went over to Brad who had stood up when Marion left. 'You put your foot in it with your talk of East–West marriages, I'm afraid. Until then you were weaving your usual magic.' She slid her arms around his waist. 'How much of that engrossing tale was true?'

'Every last detail. I *swear*,' he insisted, seeing her doubt. 'Didn't I warn you I had a chequered past?' He kissed her swiftly. 'Let's go to bed and start on my chequered future.'

Being lovd by a man highly talented in the art, who cared for her deeply, was all Vesta knew it should be. She had experienced it in tents and huts; in tiny *pensioni*; once in a haystack and once in a bomb-damaged Roman palace. They had indulged their desire beneath the stars on sweltering Italian summer nights, and they had made hilarious love on a fishing boat after a particularly Bacchanalian wedding. Being possessed by Brad was the most exhilarating sensation on earth. She surrendered to it greedily now.

There were several lulls between passion during which they both lay rediscovering with gentle hands the texture and shape of each other's body, but they finally settled back wonderfully exhausted. 'What a start to your chequered future,' she murmured sleepily. 'I can't wait for the rest of it.'

'Stand by for tomorrow, then. We're flying to Japan at twenty-two hundred.'

It was as if the last few hours had never happened. They faced each other angrily as they had on many occasions during the early days when Brad had put the pursuit of a story before everything, and Vesta had been determined not to fall beneath his spell. Kneeling on the bed, now wrapped in a pink woollen dressing-gown, she reminded him of their plans.

'You *agreed*,' she said hotly. 'We'd get married as soon as you were free, look for a house here, then get down to our new careers. You would write a book. Couldn't wait to get started, you said. You had a fat advance, with magazine rights all sewn up. No more sleeping rough or helter-skeltering around the trouble spots of the world, you said. All you wanted was me and a profitable partnership with a publisher who would give you a contract to write more hefty stuff. *You said*.'

'OK. So we've established what I said,' he told her calmly, 'but this is something we're going to do *before* we do all the rest.'

'*I'm* certainly not doing it,' she flared. 'Apart from "all the rest", as you so dismissively call our future, I have an important exhibition next week and three major commissions to fulfil.'

'They'll wait, and the exhibition will be all the more impressive with an artist who is absent on the other side of the world on an assignment hundreds would give their eye-teeth for.' Brad lunged from the bed to grab up his bath-robe. 'I worked damned hard to get them to include you on this trip.'

'Then your damned hard work has been wasted. I'm not going . . . and neither are you.'

Brad swung round. 'Now, see here. No woman has ever dictated what I can and can't do.'

'This is your chequered future, remember? Time to try something new.'

He resorted to familiar persuasion. Dropping to the bed beside her, he let his hand rest on her half-exposed thigh. 'Honey, can't you see this is the chance of a lifetime for us? To hell with a banker's pampered children in a gilded nursery. This will be real heart and soul stuff, the kind of thing you do better than anyone. You're a *war* artist, for God's sake.'

'The war's over,' she told him, throwing his hand from her leg.

'You've too much intelligence to believe that. It has spawned a dozen or so smaller ones. All your precious colonies are bidding for freedom, and areas you annexed during the Victorian land grab have already signalled their determination to break away. The world's been turned upside down. Nothing is going to be the same as it was, and every nation is out to capitalize on the fact. Communism is spreading alarmingly. Starvation and statelessness are making people desperate enough to kill.' He took hold of her upper arms and spoke with earnest urgency. 'Before we know it the whole shebang could start up again. Doing this thing on Hiroshima six months after the bomb will remind the world of the horrific weapon now available. It'll be the most significant and constructive work we've ever done. This time, we could be *altering* events rather than merely recording them as helpless observers.'

Vesta drew away from him and left the bed. She did not want to hear what he was saying. The war had taken up six years of her life. It had claimed her father; it had changed her handsome, carefree brother into a white-haired, scarred, haunted young man not yet free from nightmares. The war had killed so many: girls she had known in the ATS; desert warriors; British and American soldiers she had mixed with in Italy and grown fond of. Sandy, her father's personal assistant, with whom she and David had grown up. Brad had almost died in her arms when an aircraft crashed on their jeep. She, herself, had had a lucky escape from a flying bomb dropped on the London apartment. The rosy future was what she desperately wanted, not more dying and suffering.

'I don't want to go to Hiroshima,' she told him emotionally. 'David was glad, *glad* when the bomb was dropped.'

'So were millions of others like him, I guess,' came his thoughtful reply. 'But the world has to know the consequences of dropping it. It ended the war, but no one surely wants it to start the next.'

She had to make him understand, but all the time he looked at her the way he was it was impossible. She switched on another light and sat in a chair near the window. 'I've always tried to show the human side of war in my pictures, you know that. It wasn't always easy to find hope or humour in what we witnessed. While you wrote the chilling facts I looked for signs of physical or spiritual survival in the midst of destruction. Now I want to find joy in what I do. I want to find a new outlet which has beauty and colour. Don't, *please* don't, ask me to go to a place that's been horrifyingly devastated, that's inhabited by disfigured, suffering people. It isn't fair, Brad. I've had my share of war. Now I want peace.'

'At any price?'

'What does that mean?'

He got to his feet and walked around the bed restlessly. 'Jesus, I could do with a drink.'

'You'll have to go downstairs for that. The days of sleeping with a bottle under your pillow are definitely over, you said.'

He swung round to face her. 'Do you remember every goddam word I've ever said?'

'Every one I believed you meant.'

Perching on the side of the bed he appealed to her: 'This assignment is very important to me.'

'And our plans aren't?'

'I didn't say that.'

Hurt, and feeling curiously sick, Vesta hit out again. 'Why didn't you tell me right away?'

'Your mother was there.'

'Not when you first came up to my studio.'

'Oh, yeah! I walk in after three months away and straightaway announce to a girl with a come-to-bed look in her eyes that we're off to Hiroshima in twenty-four hours? In any case, *The Afterglow* hit me between the eyes and I forgot everything else for a while.'

'So do you recognize that *I* have things that are very important to *me*?'

'I'm not expecting you to give them up – just postpone them.'

Sensing that she was being inexorably drawn into something she did not want, Vesta challenged him. 'To persuade me, you thought you'd reduce my resistance in the way that comes so easily to you. That's typical of your methods. You use bed as a weapon.'

'Doesn't everyone?'

Scrambling to her feet, she turned away from him to look from her window over familiar ground. The night was moon-washed and cold. Frost whitened the lawn and low shrubs directly ahead; moonlight whitened the chestnut trees bordering the sloping driveway down to the village. The stars were particularly brilliant tonight, and the distant sound of a dog-fox barking added to the call of home. She had been here so infrequently over the last six years. She wanted it now with a longing that was almost an ache.

On the edge of tears, she asked, 'What about the wedding?'

'We can have that out there. There's bound to be a missionary, or some sky-pilot with the occupying forces, who can marry us.'

That really hurt. She gripped the windowsill hard. 'I don't want to get married in a place of non-Christian devastation. Pledging my life to yours actually means something to me, believe it or not. I want to do it here in the church that is so associated with the Sheridans.'

He moved swiftly to come up behind her. 'OK, honey, we'll

still do that if it means so much to you. We shouldn't be out there much more than three or four months. It'll be summer then. A better time for weddings than February.'

The quick flare of hope died as Vesta turned to him. He took instant advantage by kissing her with all the persuasive skill he possessed, convinced of victory. For once, his physical impact failed.

'So what relationship would we have on this assignment?'

He grinned. 'The same as we had in Italy, Vic.'

'*Stop using that damned silly name!*' she cried. 'The joke's over, Brad. And you can forget the rest, too. I'm not going *anywhere* with you as your mistress.'

Drawing in his breath he began to lose some of his assurance. 'It didn't bother you in Italy.'

'I had no choice. You were married to Gloria. Now you're not.'

'So I've offered to marry you out there. Hell, I'll marry you on the aircraft if there's a parson aboard. What more can I say?'

'You can say that for once you'll put the wishes of someone else before your own. For once, you'll give up a "scoop" for something that will last longer than a nine-days'-wonder news story. We made plans, Brad, plans for our life together. Do they mean so little to you you can turn your back on them?'

Losing patience, he walked away, running his hand through his hair. 'How many more times must I emphasize I'm *not* abandoning our plans? I *want* to make you my wife. I *love* you like hell. All I'm saying is three to four months' delay isn't going to change anything. We can have all you want. You're not going to lose it by doing this assignment first. And it's big,' he said, turning back to her. 'We may never get a chance like this again. It could put me up there among the giants.'

'And what of my exhibition and commissions which could put *me* among the giants?'

'We've been over that. We'll be doing this thing in Japan *together.*'

Deeply hurt, bewildered by the joy in his unexpected arrival which had turned sour, and feeling that the passion they had just shared had, in reality, been a carefully calculated move on his part, Vesta said quietly, 'I don't want to do it, Brad. Leaving aside all other issues, I truly have no wish to paint pictures on this subject or to go to Japan. David has never spoken about those months following the fall of Singapore, but if you had known him before then you'd realize he didn't become like he is now without severe ill-treatment. There have been enough stories about Japanese atrocities since we released their prisoners to know why David still cries out in his sleep. If you're determined on this, you'll have to do it on your own . . . and then I'll know exactly where I come on your list of priorities.'

Taken aback by her unexpected stance, Brad gazed at her, lost for words. Eventually, he said, 'You've known all along that I'm not a nine-to-five guy who'll plant out the garden at weekends and help around the house. I'm a newsman. A *good* newsman. We made the perfect team in Italy. I thought that's what we'd always be.'

'So you had no intention of buying a house here and writing a book?' she demanded tautly.

'Sure I had, but this came up. I'll do the book later.'

'Something will always come up, admit it.'

'And if it does, I'll sure as hell do it,' he replied, angry at last. 'You're starting to sound like Gloria.'

To someone who had chased all over Italy with him, dodging shells and mortars, sleeping rough, washing in streams, and eating spasmodically, that comment was the last straw.

'I'm beginning to understand her. Your bloody ambition comes before anybody or anything else. Go to Japan, then, but don't be surprised if I find a doting millionaire while you're away. Now kindly get out of my bedroom.'

The camp was on Salisbury Plain. Vesta borrowed her mother's car to drive there during the second week of February to meet the Honourable Jeremy Stanstead, who was to be the subject of her desert-warfare picture. The day was overcast and dreary after several days of torrential rain. The gloom matched her mood, even though her exhibition had been hugely successful and profitable. *The Afterglow* had caused a sensation. It had been photographed for newspapers and magazines, enormous sums had been offered for it, more than a few galleries had requested it on loan. In short, the painting designed to honour her father had done so overwhelmingly. More commissions were offered and she was presently on her way to make a start on a most important one. Yet none of these things now mattered. Brad had gone; the light of her life was out.

David had flown to Singapore last week and the tension at Tarrant Hall added to her general unhappiness. As well as her mother, the Chandlers were edgy and preoccupied. Pat, to whom she had always been so close, had shown no sympathy over Brad's going and more or less implied Vesta was entirely in the wrong. She had tried to make allowances for Pat's short temper but, after a third sharp comment on women who did not know when they were well off, Vesta returned an equally sharp one concerning those who had gone through the war living off the fat of the land safe from danger. They had not been in contact since then.

At the first sight of Nissen huts, khaki uniforms and whitened edges to doorsteps, Vesta immediately felt at home, mentally stepping back into a life she had only relinquished four months before. The guard at the gate, visibly surprised to see an attractive young woman when he had clearly been expecting an ageing eccentric artist, showed her where to park and informed the sergeant on duty that Miss Sheridan had arrived. Jeremy Stanstead raced up in a jeep to collect her within a very short time. Although they had talked on the telephone this was their first meeting. He was tall, very thin and bespectacled. No Errol Flynn, she thought, knowing she would have to get round that problem somehow if he were to appear heroic in the painting, although she knew from experience that heroes seldom looked the part. More often than not they were men who would go unremarked in a crowd. This one had spontaneous charm, however.

'I've been nervous all morning,' he confessed with a smile that made one forget he was not Errol Flynn. 'When you telephoned last week, the sound of your calm voice brought back memories of that day we suddenly heard it over the intercom in the thick of battle. You've no idea how it affected us.' He held the jeep door open for her. 'I was so afraid I'd be disappointed when I saw you, but I needn't have worried. The lads will be frightfully jealous when we walk in to lunch.'

Vesta smiled back. 'It won't compare with the sensation I caused on arrival at that desert oasis. Because of a typical botch-up they were expecting someone called Victor Sheridan.'

Not some crazy upper-class female lootenant wearing a pith-helmet, added Brad's silent voice to dismiss her smile.

Jeremy climbed in behind the wheel and let in the clutch. 'Knowing how starved we were of female company, I'm amazed you survived in one piece.'

'Safety in numbers, perhaps,' she murmured, seeing so clearly Brad in very brief shorts with khaki shirt open and flapping in the breeze. 'Each one guarded me against the others. I made so many friends out there. I often wonder where they are now.'

'Some have gone on to higher things,' he said nonchalantly. 'You must have met up again with a few of them in Italy. The rest of us were in Europe after Normandy.' He drove fast along the tarmac between rows of huts until he neared a substantial building which was clearly the Officers' Mess. 'I'll give you coffee and biscuits to warm you up while you tell me what you want to see and do. I'm entirely at your disposal.'

Once they were sitting before a large log fire, drinking the best coffee Vesta had tasted in a long time, her companion made another confession. 'I know Grandfather wants you to paint me in full fig beside a tank, but I'd rather you didn't. An awful lot of chaps were given medals for what they did – some received *no* recognition for their efforts – and I'd be most terribly embarrassed to be hung in the Cavalry Club alongside our great heroes of the *armes blanches*. You were out there in North Africa, so you'll know *everyone* deserved a medal. Tanks turned into ovens in that heat, and the flies alone nearly drove one crazy.' He gave his irresistible smile. 'Can you please paint it without me?'

'Not really,' she said, helping herself to more coffee. 'Your grandfather is paying me a great deal of money. He's extremely proud of you. However, his letter stated that he wants the picture to commemorate all those who served in the desert. I hadn't thought of you posing heroically beside your tank – that would be too static for words. I had in mind an action picture with your head and shoulders showing through the hatch. Wearing a tin hat and looking through binoculars, no one would recognize you.' She pointed to his wrist. 'Have you always worn that watch?'

He unstrapped it and held it out, looking relieved. 'Unusual, isn't it? It was a coming-of-age present from Grandfather; an antique French pocket watch which Garrard converted. Some crafty little urchin in Tobruk tried to pinch it, but I caught him at it and gave chase. Thanks.' He took it back from her.

'Good thing you caught him. That watch is going to solve our problem nicely. I can make you anonymous with binoculars, but the exact detail of what's on your wrist will identify the man to your grandfather.' Vesta set down her empty cup. 'I can please you both.'

His gaze was full of admiration that soothed her bruised spirits. 'Not only calm in an emergency, very pretty, and extremely talented, you're also a diplomat, Miss Sheridan.'

'Please call me Vesta. We're going to be spending some time together on this painting. What I'd like to do today is make some preliminary sketches of you in your tank so that I get your position right, and also the exact details of the tank itself. Then, perhaps next week, you could put on your desert gear and pose seriously with the binoculars.' She got to her feet. 'The idea may not work. I normally paint exactly what I choose as subject matter. This will be my first attempt at something chosen by another person. You're a sort of guinea-pig, I'm afraid.'

'There's never been a more delighted member of the species,' he said, leading the way outside. 'I see you've come dressed in workmanlike fashion.'

'I didn't cover three campaigns without learning what to wear in military situations,' she told him, climbing back into the jeep. 'I may need to clamber all over your tank before we're through.'

He drove off towards some tall, tin-roofed workshops. Vesta sensed that he was talking, but she was somewhere in Italy in a different jeep with a very different driver. They spent about an hour and a quarter with the tank, provoking much curiosity from soldiers working nearby. Jeremy was very patient while she made rough sketches of him in the vehicle, but they grew cold in the open air and Vesta was glad to head back to the Mess for lunch. There, a surprise awaited her. After tidying her hair and adding fresh lipstick, she walked in to a crowded ante-room with her escort to be met by enthusiastic applause from everyone present. Feeling her colour rise she glanced up questioningly at Jeremy.

36

'They all remember your voice in that battle. This is their way of saying "thanks",' he said.

A rush of warmth spread through her and she found herself close to tears. The hollow sense of rejection she had known since Brad left was suddenly banished by these men whose voices she had also heard on that unforgettable day from far away across the desert sands. Men who had fought in the heat and dust knowing they could be trapped within a burning tank with no escape; men who had managed to joke with her or apologize for their bad language even while battle raged. How foolish of her mother – or anyone – to think she could put all that behind her just because the war was over.

When the colonel approached with a spray of deep pink roses, made a brief speech of appreciation, then kissed the back of her hand, Vesta was so emotional she was unable to make any verbal response. Seeing her problem, he put a glass of sherry in her hand and began to talk about art.

'I dabble a bit myself in a very amateurish fashion,' he confided. 'A bowl of apples, string of onions hanging on the wall, jug of cream and a few luscious strawberries. My wife always says thank God none of my subjects ever move or I'd be right up the creek. She's right. It's all very boring and useless, really, but I enjoy it and it's marvellously relaxing.'

Recovering slightly, Vesta smiled. 'Every artist paints static subjects, which is why poor Jeremy got a stiff neck this morning holding a pose for so long. One has to give an *impression* of movement by adding things like exhaust trails behind an aircraft or, as I shall, tracks in the sand behind the tank. Painting is total illusion, because everything is merely a blob of paint on perfectly flat canvas. Artists are confidence tricksters. We make people believe in something they're not actually seeing.'

The man smiled warmly. 'Shame on you, Miss Sheridan! I hope Jerry gave you every facility this morning. We're all tickled pink about this picture, you know.'

The lunch had clearly been chosen for a female palate. Vesta enjoyed it, slipping back into a regime she knew well while she chatted about the ATS and her years as an official war artist. If anyone noticed that she used 'we' rather than 'I' they did not ask about her companion. Only when lunch was over and they all returned to the ante-room for coffee did Vesta remember that 'we' had become 'I', and feel a return of that sense of rejection during a few moments when those grouped around her were arguing over the merits of the radio programme ITMA.

A hand slid beneath her elbow to draw her gently aside. 'I've been awaiting my chance to get you away from their monopoly. Not being a member of the regiment I have to take my turn. How are you, Vesta?'

She studied him closely. Sensitive features, light-brown hair shining with health, attractive blue-green eyes. All vaguely familiar. He smiled, which increased the sense of familiarity.

'Paul Gaynor,' he prompted. 'I was attached to the desert group you were with, but I wasn't there much. I was usually up ahead clearing mine-fields, or *attempting* to.' He allowed time for that to sink in. 'You don't remember me.'

'There were so many and I wasn't with them long. That awful Colonel Villiers sent me packing as soon as he possibly could.' She tried to soften her non-recognition of him. 'I knew we'd met before, but quite where escaped me. What are you doing on Salisbury Plain, Paul? Not clearing mines.'

'I'm having a bit of a rest as an instructor. Rather nice to be in a lecture room this time of year instead of defusing unexploded bombs in London.'

'And safer.' She thought of Jeremy saying many men received no public recognition for their efforts. Here was a case in point. No hero-figure this, just a soft-spoken, pleasant young man whose everyday work involved the risk of being blown sky high six months after the war had ended.

'I took a day off to visit the Chase Gallery. I'm sure *Victor Sheridan* couldn't have bettered your enormous talent.'

Vesta laughed. 'Thank you. If you run into Colonel Villiers do tell him.'

'He was killed trying to take Caen. He was actually a very good man. I expect he was overtired, worried and concerned about your safety. We all got a bit edgy out there.'

They sauntered away from the main groups and stopped by a square bay window to look out over the small triangle of grass towards rows of huts. 'I'm sorry about Colonel Villiers,' she said. 'I was very intent, at that time, on establishing the

38

fact that women were valuable members of the armed forces; that we could do a great deal more than cook and sweep floors.' She smiled up at him. 'I used to get on my soapbox rather a lot.'

'I hope you still do. All those wonderful girls like you who were in Signals, Ack-Ack, and so on, are going to find themselves back at home wearing an apron with no more expected of them than cooking and sweeping floors. They're certain to feel unsettled and unwanted unless someone speaks up on their behalf. Your talent could be your soapbox. Captured on canvas their invaluable contribution would be there as a reminder for all times.'

Vesta looked at him speculatively. 'You're a most unusual man. Very few would give a thought to such things.'

Amusement lit his clear, bright eyes. 'I have two sisters who have lectured me so often on that theme, I can't fail to give more than a thought to it.'

'Were they in the ATS?'

'Didn't think khaki very flattering, so they joined the WAAF. One was in Communications, like you. The other worked on aerial photographs. They're very disgruntled at home, particularly after being turned down for civilian jobs on the grounds that priority has to be given to men being demobbed. All that propaganda at the cinema about women getting back to domesticity and bringing up a new, healthy generation makes them livid.'

'I'm not surprised,' she said heartily. 'They sound delightful.'

'You should meet them. Our home is near Dorchester, not far from your village. I could pick you up next weekend. It's Hazel's birthday – her twenty-first – and there's to be a swanky party. Will you come?'

Surprised at the ease with which he had led her towards the invitation, Vesta caught herself accepting. It might be a pleasant weekend; prevent her from wondering who would console Brad in Japan and what would happen when his assignment was completed. At that point, a thought struck her. 'How do you know my village?'

Paul took her coffee cup to place it on a low table. 'My father worked with yours at Beaulieu Manor. I know a lot more about you than you suspect. Colonel Sheridan was very proud of your war paintings, as any father would be.'

Vesta was bewildered. 'Beaulieu Manor? Daddy worked at the Ministry with Lord Moore – translating documents and acting as interpreter at conferences. He could speak over thirty languages fluently, you know.'

Paul was looking at her curiously. 'He never mentioned Beaulieu? Oh, of course, he was killed before the war ended, so he probably wouldn't have done. But your brother knew about it.'

'About what?' she asked, beginning to feel uneasy for some unfathomable reason.

Her companion frowned and hesitated momentarily. 'Perhaps you should ask him.'

'He's in Singapore.'

'Wasn't he one of the last pilots to fly out before the Japs overran it?'

'You *do* know a lot about us.'

'Yours is the kind of family that is talked about.' He smiled with considerable warmth. 'I've been ticking off the days until I could renew my acquaintance with someone who has remained in the forefront of my mind since those desert days. I hardly stood a chance then. I was forever being sent ahead, and you seemed to be unofficially guarded by that heftily handsome American correspondent. Didn't you cover the Italian campaign with him?' She gave a taut affirmative, and he continued. 'Well, he's no longer around, so I –' He glanced behind her. 'Oh, damn! You're about to be whisked away by Jerry Stanstead. However, I'll be at Tarrant Hall at about eleven next Saturday morning. We can lunch on the way to our place and talk about old times. Goodbye until then, Vesta.'

Although she and her model spent another hour and a half with the tanks, Vesta could not forget her conversation with Paul Gaynor. He knew far too much about her and, it seemed, something her brother would know but she did not. She suddenly recalled David at the viewing of *The Afterglow* saying that he must tell her something about their father one day when they were alone, but he was presently in Singapore and she would be seeing Paul next weekend. She would demand to be enlightened about the curious reference to Beaulieu Manor which everyone but herself appeared to understand. On one thing Paul was ill-informed, however. Brad might no longer be around, but he still dominated her every thought and hope for the future.

CHAPTER THREE

ANOTHER night awoken by his own screams. His neighbour began banging on the wall again, but the dull thuds merely continued the thunder of waves on a beach that he had heard in his nightmare. David lay sweating and shaking uncontrollably, until the urge to vomit had him clawing his way to the bathroom like a drunkard with no control over his movements. He sat on the tiled floor, feeling icy cold and ill for a long time. When he was able to move he stumbled to where he had hidden a bottle of whisky and drank lengthily from it. The twitching slowly subsided, but the terror did not.

He moved to the window and opened the blind. Palm trees wherever he looked; no sign of the sea. The incessant shrill chorus of cicadas bombarded his ears and the unmistakable smell of the aftermath of a monsoon wafted to him across the darkness. There were no men screaming at him in Japanese preceding further torture, no stench of blood and urine, no agony. Yet his nerves and sinews still jumped with pain. His thudding heartbeat gradually quietened as he recognized the view outside as the garden surrounding the Officers' Mess.

He drank some more whisky, slowly growing warmer. It was 1946, the war was over and he was among his own countrymen, yet his terror would not be banished. He had not expected such a violent reaction to this return to Singapore. It had not been a trip he welcomed but he had underestimated the strength of his memories from four years ago. At the first sight of green tropical jungle below the aircraft, fear and loathing had flooded through him. The moment he had stepped into the sweltering humidity of mid-morning the unique smell of the East had made him want to throw up. The swarm of Oriental faces before him had aroused overwhelming revulsion and fear. It had not diminished after seven days.

Sinking into a cushioned cane chair, David leaned his head

back to stare at the fan circling above him. He had been young, virile and successful then, a Spitfire pilot with hair like spun gold and the brand of good-looking charm girls could rarely resist. In company with other golden lads he had flown in the Battle of Britain and earned a DFC, living up to what had been expected of the nephew of Rex 'Sherry' Sheridan, RFC, ace of aces. Then his gun had jammed so that he accidentally shot down and killed a squadron colleague, an American who had been conducting a personal feud with him, resenting his success, believing it was due to nepotism. From that moment on David had been psychologically unable to take his aircraft off the ground.

After a period behind a desk he had asked for a posting to a squadron abroad, where he was not known, but his official record always travelled with him and they had all been aware of his humiliating hang-up when he arrived in Singapore. His answer to their pity had been to indulge in the good life still rife there in 1941. Tennis and bathing parties, balls, cocktails, sweet seduction and a fast car ... and all the time he had eaten his heart out for another chance to climb into a cockpit, switch on the engine, and discover if his gremlin had yet found a fresh victim. No one would give him that chance. Half-drunk, he had smashed up his car and returned to conscious-ness to see a face he had then thought the loveliest he had ever seen. Su Lim had been resistant to his 'line' but had swept him off his feet, offering him tranquillity in his fever of personal failure. He had married her without the RAF's permission and been ostracized, but gained inner peace. Not for long, he recalled, as the blades of the fan over his head became those of a Hurricane's propeller.

Those last days here had been hectic and doom laden. The unthinkable was about to happen. Because his wife was Chi-nese, David had found it almost impossible to get a permit for her to leave on one of the boats. When he did, at the last minute, she had refused to go unless he found places for her seven brothers and sisters. He then learned that she had married him only so that he would maintain her large family. Sitting in that stifling room four years on he could still see the contempt on her face as she told him love had made him so weak she had been able to persuade him to do anything.

43

When he returned to collect her for the dash to the docks she had vanished, taking everything from their home except the silver and expensive trappings of Western living.

Tipping up the whisky bottle, David drank in the hope of banishing the rage which had been revived when he stepped from the aircraft a week ago. All his enquiries had ended in failure. He had never known the name of her village and Lims were two a penny in Singapore. There was one more office he could try tomorrow, but if that approach proved fruitless his only hope of freedom seemed to be to wait for years and then claim desertion or presumed death. He could not ask Pat openly to live in sin with him, yet how could they wait now she had surrendered to him? Since he came here he had been unable even to enjoy thoughts of those two stolen hours wrapped in blankets before a log fire. They had been unbelievably wonderful, yet here in this tropical island with its humiliating memories they seemed like a guilty coupling. He should not have touched a lovely, fresh girl like Pat after sleeping with an Oriental. He had made her as tainted as himself.

The overhead fan appeared to be revolving faster now, and he could hear the roar of the Hurricane's propeller as Japanese Zeros zoomed down on their airfield with guns chattering, and enemy troops pushed through the trees at the end of the runway. *One Hurricane still on the ground, the pilot lying fatally wounded some yards from it.*

The nightmare was returning. The aircraft was rising and he was in the air again after more than a year. Singapore was overhung by a pall of smoke. The emerald island had become a black opal with a fiery heart. Sumatra. A collection of men and aircraft who had somehow escaped, but who knew time was running out. Java had fallen. The enemy was already landing on this island. They all took off to machine-gun the invaders and stayed up as long as their fuel lasted. Back to the makeshift landing-strip in the heart of poisonous jungle, refuel, then up again. And again. The unmistakable sound of bullets raking the fuselage; oil and glycol spattering on the windshield. Crashing into sea breaking on to white sand, so peaceful a scene. Intense pain in both legs; blood spilling into the surf. Men appearing through his haze of pain. Men with Australian accents, dressed in khaki, who tore his flesh further while

44

extricating him. Men who carried him deep into the jungle where they had a store of tinned food, ammunition and a radio transmitter. Six men commanded by a brutal sergeant named Kershaw, who had no time for fliers, officers, Englishmen or lame ducks. David was all of them.

Japanese troops coming in search of the pilot of the crashed aircraft. They must not know of the existence of the Australian group. Everything packed up ready to leave. Kershaw rules that the pilot must be left behind to be found, thus eliminating a further search. *When they get to you, use that revolver!* He mistakes the significance of this and uses all his bullets on the Japanese. They reach him and ask him questions he must not answer. They keep asking, their sadistic faces thrust close to his. They tear the bandages from his legs and take out knives. He prays they will kill him outright. They do not.

They drag him to a place near the beach and strip him. The questions come thick and fast. He must not answer, but he screams with agony. They break his fingers one by one. He will not answer. They slowly cut into his face and his body. He prays for death. It does not come. They stuff his mouth full of rancid rice time after time and force him to swallow. Then they pour fetid water down his throat until his stomach swells. They beat him with wet bamboos. He will not answer; *he cannot speak*. They tie him, naked and spreadeagled, on the sands which looked so beautiful from the air. The tide is coming in. He will drown, slowly and painfully, but he is beyond recognition of anything save a burning hell. He is blinded by the killing sun, deafened by the echo of his own screams and their chorus of sadistic demands. Life is fading, fading.

Fighting his way back from the nightmare, David stared at a *chit chat* on the cream-washed wall of the room. It suddenly represented the East and everything Oriental. He hurled the empty bottle at the lizard. It moved like lightning across the wall so the glass shattered without harming it. Dregs of whisky slowly dripped to the floor leaving ochre runnels against the pale wash. His door crashed open to admit a furious neighbour dressed in saggy cotton boxer shorts, who let forth a tirade concerning David's parentage and what would be done to him if he made one more sound that night.

The man's raised voice and the slamming of the door as he departed would almost certainly have disturbed everyone along that corridor.

Knowing peace was not to be had indoors, David pulled a pair of shorts on over his underpants, went on to the low balcony and vaulted down to the garden. He landed badly and fell over to lie winded, not caring whether or not he ever got up again. There was no peace out here, either. That hated Australian voice swore at him, told him he had no guts, that he was just a pretty-boy flier who had been to a bloody fancy English school and learned nothing but how to play the game. *Now you're playing my bloody game, mate, and it's one you'll never forget. Move!*

He scrambled to his knees, then to his feet, driven by hatred for Rod Kershaw who had abandoned him to torture, then rescued him as life was finally ebbing and led him to eventual safety seven months later. Staggering to the nearest palm, David clung to it as his fevered mind wandered amid recollections of those months. For the first of them Kershaw had carried him in his arms. Hour after hour the big Australian had borne his helpless burden as if doing penance. David remembered little of that time save for the fact that he was dependent on Kershaw for *everything*, as a child would be. The man fed him, washed him, settled him for sleep, soothed him when he cried out during nightmares, tended his wounds, *dominated him.*

Later, when David was able to walk in a curious, loping fashion resembling that of an ape, Kershaw was always there beside him to steady him when he stumbled and order him to keep going. When their food supply began to run out David was given double rations and forced to eat them. When it had all gone they ate anything from berries to raw snake and lizard, which Kershaw caught. When water ran out they drank their own urine. When they were sick with fever or dysentery Kershaw drove them all on with insults and oaths. Whenever a Japanese patrol passed nearby, the Australian sergeant refused to give David a rifle. Dominating him again, because David would have fired it until there were no bullets left.

Half in the present and half in that time, he thought he saw a Jap patrol weaving between the palms of that garden and

46

ran forward with a howl of revenge. He had his fingers around the throat of one, revelling in the fear on the man's flat Oriental face as he shouted for mercy. Then hands were dragging David away; English voices yelled at him to take it easy. They led him to a place that smelled of antiseptic. There was a room containing a bed with a white cover and mosquito net. He had been in places like it before so it held no fears for him, and he lay on the bed with a sense of relief. The men who had brought him went out, leaving him isolated. Before long he began to sob because of the acute sense of loss he felt. They had all been in hospital, at first, but the others recovered more quickly than he and were one day whisked away in a truck commanded by two military policemen. Kershaw had gone out of his life as swiftly as that – no farewell, no final binge, no sign that David had ever meant anything to him. He had hated the brutal sergeant, yet an inexplicable bond had been forged between them which, when abruptly severed, left David desolate. Kershaw had controlled him for so long he was lost and desperate without him. Loathing the Australian yet longing for him, it had seemed frighteningly possible to David that he would never break free of the other's dominance. That fear returned now.

A nurse peered in, saw him sobbing curled up in a ball, then went out again swiftly. A dark-haired man in pyjamas and dressing-gown came and bent over the bed with soothing words. David was unable to speak but he heard the man say, 'Yes, he's been drinking, but this is something more. Let's calm him down first.'

When he awoke David was uncertain whether or not he had seen the room before. A nurse was standing at the window, looking out. A golden oriole was singing nearby, and the scent of frangipani wafted to him. A sound and a perfume he had once thought magical. Now both turned his stomach over. The figure of the nurse in a crisp white dress did worse things to him. When she turned he drew in his breath sharply because she did not have a deceptively beautiful Oriental face with slanting black eyes that had been soft with something he had believed was love.

'How are you feeling now, sir?'

'Pretty good,' he lied. 'Was it that damned fever again?'

47

She was non-committal. 'Possibly. Wing Commander Braden is on his way to see you. He had very little sleep so make allowances if he's a bit abrupt. He sat with you until five-thirty, then went off for a shower and breakfast.' A half-hearted smile appeared. 'I'll bring you some after he has seen you.'

'I don't want anything.' He already felt sick. Bacon and eggs would finish him off.

'You must eat something.'

Hatred rushed through him. 'Don't *you* bloody well start ordering me about!'

The woman's mouth tightened. 'If that's the mood you're in, Squadron Leader Sheridan, I'll put some carbolic in your tea.' She opened the door on hearing footsteps approaching, and the smile she gave as the doctor entered suggested that an aphrodisiac would be added to *his* tea if she ever got the chance, because he treated her to no more than a professional nod before concentrating on David.

'Good morning. Feeling better?'

He recognized the dark-haired man now dressed in starched khaki shorts, and a shirt bearing a wing commander's bars of rank. 'I think I might throw up before long,' David confessed.

The doctor signalled to the nurse, who brought a kidney-shaped bowl to place on the bedcover. She was then told she could leave. David was glad. She unnerved him. The doctor did not, despite his brusque manner.

'My name's Braden, by the way,' he told David, drawing a chair up to the bedside. 'Spent most of the war in North Africa and France, with a spell at home between. I've seen a number of men in the state you were in last night. Drink never drives out the demon, you know. Care to tell me about it?'

'Not really.'

'Mmm, I thought that's what you'd say. I'm afraid I'm completely in the dark, because you're just passing through and your service record is with your squadron in England. All I know about you is that you hitched a lift here so that you could try and trace your wife. Had no luck?'

David struggled to sit up and was immediately sick. Recovering, he shook his head. 'Everything's in a bloody mess. The Japs leave everything like that.'

'Including their prisoners. ' After a pause, the man said, 'You were one, I take it. In Changi?'

David shook his head again. 'It was all a long time ago.'

'Last night it wasn't. Was that why you tried to choke to death one of our Chinese sweepers?'

He vaguely remembered having his hands around a man's throat. 'Is he all right?'

Braden smiled. 'There'd be a guard each side of your door if not.' He leaned back and crossed his legs. 'I can't understand why there's no information on the whereabouts of your wife. She would have been making enquiries about you since we reoccupied Singapore, surely.'

'No.'

'You're pretty certain she was killed?'

'That's what I'm trying to find out,' he said with annoyance.

'What about her relatives? They usually have very large families who stick together.' Seeing David's hostile expression, he added, 'I'm not just a nosey old bastard. I think I might be able to offer a source of help you won't have tried yet.'

'What?'

'Aha! You've got to tell me a few things first. Fair exchange?'

David sighed. 'You might not be a nosey old bastard, sir, but you're a crafty one.'

'I've got to be with chaps like you. Tell me how you and your wife were split up when the Japs got here.'

'We married for the wrong reasons. I thought she represented tranquillity; she wanted a provider for her seven brothers and sisters. Because I couldn't get them places on a ship with her, she left me four days before the island surrendered.'

'And?'

'I flew out at the eleventh hour in a Hurricane no one else was left alive to fly.'

'So you were captured on Sumatra or Java?'

He wished the golden oriole would stop singing. Its rich notes mocked him. 'I escaped to Australia,' he stated shortly.

'Mmm, I see.' The caustic comment told David he was not believed. 'Can't the people of your wife's village tell you anything about her?'

49

Leaning his head back on the pillow, David had to confess to never having known the name of Su's village. 'Her relatives didn't approve of the sacrifice she had made on their behalf,' he added bitterly, 'and I had no interest in her life before we met. She was a nurse.'

'Then her hospital would have a record of her address.'

'Their records were lost in a fire during the final bombardment – like so many. She's probably dead, but I've got to know for sure.'

'You want to make a fresh start?'

'Yes. Without *her*.'

'And if she's alive?'

'I'll get a divorce.'

'That's all?'

David frowned. 'What do you mean?'

The medical man got to his feet. 'You claim to have escaped to Australia when this island fell. You could have sustained those severe injuries in any number of ways, of course, but if you were never a prisoner of the Japs what has given you a psychological hatred of anyone Oriental? You damn near killed a bloke last night. If I help you, is there any guarantee you won't try to do the same with your wife?'

'Yes. My word.'

Braden pursed his lips while he studied David thoughtfully. 'What are your feelings for the girl?'

'I have none. I don't even remember what it was like to . . . the entire concept of intimacy with her fills me with repugnance.'

'Not anger, feelings of revenge?'

David grew furious. 'God Almighty, I just want to be free of her so that I can marry someone at home. We've waited all this time because of my stupid mistake. I'm not likely to muck it up now by facing a charge of murder, am I?'

'You were well on the way to it last night.'

There was no choice but to give the man facts he was determined to know. 'All right. I crashed on Sumatra. They found me and tried to make me talk, night and day, for three days. I didn't, so they left. And that's all I'm going to tell you.'

Braden smiled. 'It's enough. After I've done my rounds I'll

50

get in touch with a friend of mine who's Anglo-Chinese and runs a pharmaceutical business. His men go all over the island delivering supplies to apothecaries. One of them is certain to learn the name of a village housing someone who married an RAF officer just before the invasion. I suppose you've been enquiring for Mrs Sheridan. She's more than likely reverted to her Chinese name, which is?'

'Su Lim.'

'Right. I'll see what I can do.'

'That's very good of you.'

'Don't you believe it! The sooner you find her the sooner you'll go home and get out of my hair, because you're going to have to live *here* from now on. We managed to avoid a charge of assault with menace by some clever talking and greasing the bloke's palm, but I want you under my wing at night so it doesn't happen again.'

'It won't,' he said.

'Are you certain?' At David's silence, he added, 'You should never have come back here. It was asking for trouble.'

David was driven to the village in official transport. It had taken the Anglo-Chinese pharmacist just five days to come up with information official sources had failed to find in nine months. It was understandable. The British were more intent on discovering the fate of hundreds of missing servicemen than that of the Chinese wife of an officer who had married in defiance of regulations.

While waiting for the breakthrough David had moved his things to the sick bay. He had been free to move about during daytime, but was under curfew at night. It was no punishment. He had no wish to frequent bars and brothels that had risen from the ruins of the city, nor did he have an urge to go back to places like Raffles Hotel where he had once chased pleasure at breakneck speed. The peace of the sterile room was welcome, and so were the strong sedatives he was given at bedtime. He also appreciated the company of John Braden but, although the man encouraged David to talk about himself, he never spoke of the undercover Australian group who had engaged in activities even he had not understood around the islands of Indonesia. Kershaw had told him often enough to keep his bloody mouth shut, or else!

The lance-corporal who drove the jeep looked smart and alert but far too young to have played an active part in the war: a national serviceman whose parents had doubtless sighed with relief when hostilities ceased. Yet trouble was brewing all over the world in the wake of peace, so there was plenty of danger ahead for young men like him. I suppose I looked like that once, David thought, studying the driver's smooth, unblemished skin, and his strong brown hands on the wheel. Is that why they did it; because it gave them pleasure to destroy beauty and strength? It must have been obvious I was not going to tell them anything on that first day. Why did they continue for two more if it was not just because they enjoyed it?

The driver glanced round looking slightly nervous. 'Is there something wrong, sir?'

'No.' David realized he had been staring and looked away quickly. It was no secret that he had run amok and almost killed a sweeper. The lad was probably on his guard now they were driving through jungle on the wilder side of the island but, deprived of the ability to concentrate on him, David could no longer escape his growing dread. Braden's informant said only that Batu Hock was the village of Su Lim who had married an English officer before the Japanese came. Nothing about whether she was alive and still living there, nor if any members of her family – there was an aunt who looked after them all – could be found to give information. What if this was not the end of the line and Su had moved on?

The nausea which had plagued him so much since his arrival returned with a vengeance. What if she was there and would not accept a white-haired monster as the man she had married? Suppose she did and demanded that he take her and the seven brothers and sisters to Tarrant Hall as his legal dependants? What if the sight of her aroused such loathing he felt the urge to . . . Dear God, no! He had given Braden his word that he would do her no harm.

He was shaken from his fears by severe jolting. Gazing around he saw the encroaching jungle on each side of a rough track winding between the trees.

'The road to Batu Hock, sir,' said the driver grimly. 'You sure this is the place?'

52

David made no reply. He was back in another jungle, another life. When the vehicle stopped, he simply sat there staring at the footpath that led into the depths of growth so tall it almost blocked out the light.

'I can't go no further, sir. You'll have to take the rest on foot – that's if you're sure this is the place you want.'

'Yes . . . yes,' he murmured, climbing from his seat. 'The village will be in a clearing somewhere. They always are.' He could already see it in his mind's eye. They had all looked much the same. So had paths like these. Mosquitoes descended in a cloud, but he was hardly aware of them as he followed the narrow, muddy trail. Distant voices told him he was growing near. The trees thinned. He saw pigs grubbing in the under-growth, and chickens roaming free. There were small children in no more than tattered vests playing the usual games of beetle-baiting, cockroach-racing or a form of foot badminton with an old shuttlecock. They caught sight of him and fled to the group of attap huts in a clearing which allowed streaks of sunlight to brighten the green gloom. How many times had they come upon a village like this to find themselves driven away by people terrified of reprisals, or to find everyone dead and all the food gone?

The people were alive here. They appeared from their simple houses to watch his approach with expressionless faces and hostile black eyes. The familiar stench of rotting undergrowth and primitive sanitation entered his nostrils; the smoke from fires cooking rice, with fishheads or strips of fatty pork, completed an atmosphere he knew well. He was no longer a bearded, starving desperado in a loin-cloth, yet they seemed equally hostile to a clean-shaven Englishman dressed in starched khaki with a peaked cap. As he silently identified his present self David recalled why he was there and knew why he was unwelcome.

The attitude of the villagers was so intimidating, he halted by the first of the huts and greeted them in the words he had learned from Su. Even as he said them he could visualize her slender figure in the white nursing dress. How could she have lived in a place like this yet worked in the antiseptic cleanliness of a hospital? Small wonder she had seized her chance to escape when a lovesick fool offered her a large airy bungalow, running hot and cold water, servants, and money for her family. They were well worth the onslaughts upon her body which she had never enjoyed but endured with contemptuous passiveness.

Coming back to the present David grew aware of someone pushing through the crowd to walk up to him; a man around his own age, possibly, whose right arm ended at the elbow. David prayed his own eyes did not contain similar venom to that in these black ones. The man stopped a few feet away.

'You Sheridan?' he challenged in wary tones.

David had to clear his throat before he could speak. 'Yes, I'm looking for Su Lim.'

'You not want call her Sheridan?'

'She . . . she . . . yes, I married her in 1941.'

There was nothing inscrutable about this Chinese expression and David's skin began to crawl. Oriental aggression spelled only one thing to him.

'Man say you come soon. We wait.'

The villagers began crowding forward in a threatening manner. Perspiration ran down David's temples. He could also feel it on his back, and trickling down his legs as blood had once done. He would not let them see he was afraid. 'Where is Su?' he asked through a tight throat.

'She die. One year gone.'

It took a moment or two for him to accept that it was all over: the waiting, the letters and telephone calls, the apprehension, all at an end. He was free! 'What happened?' he asked, feeling it was expected.

'Devil come at night. Put fire here and here.' The man pointed to his mouth and stomach, which David took to mean Su had caught a fever. These people believed in devils and omens; they accepted what befell them on the understanding that it was because their gods were displeased or offended. With Western medicine Su would probably have recovered. David could not banish relief that she had not.

'Do you have any proof of her death? A paper?'

The man instantly became furious. He flung his whole arm out to encompass the village and the people now ranging along behind him. 'No paper, no house, no food. Japanee come take everything. White men go – *you* go – leave Chinee

54

here. Many die. *Many* die! Englee no good! Go way leave Chinee wife, Chinee fiend, Chinee servant. No care!'

'We had no choice,' David cried in defence. 'Many of us stayed – those poor devils in Changi. Do you know how many of *them* died? Do you? Don't tell me we didn't care.'

The man's face was thrust close to his, and shafts of remembered terror shot through David. 'You no care of Su Lim. No care of wife. You no good! Japanee man come take her, take others, go hotel Singapore. Take clothes, make stay. Give rice, no money. Come sick, send home; come better, take back Singapore. Su Lim much pretend sick. Come home, bring rice. Japanee no more wanchee, no more rice. Devil come Su Lim. She die.'

Still in the euphoria of freedom, David took in without reaction the news that his wife had been forced to serve in a brothel for Japanese soldiers. All he wanted was to leave and quietly celebrate the beginning of his new life. He would be home by the end of the week. However, as he turned to go, one of the women in the group of villagers came forward, holding by their hands two small children. They looked incongruous in Western-style gaudy cotton smocks, with clean hands and faces. They were thrust forward none too gently.

'These your child,' announced the spokesman. 'Su Lim give eight month you go. Japanee no take her come one year. You take, go!'

Before David could think straight the villagers turned away and hurried back into their huts. Within seconds the clearing was deserted save for chickens and black pigs searching for food. The two little girls stood gazing up at him with wide black eyes. He was dumbfounded. How dare these people try to foist two of their unwanted children on him? Did they think he would swallow their stupid tale and believe they were his? Girls had little value in Chinese eyes, so it was obvious the village people, knowing in advance that an English officer would be coming, had dressed the two in clean smocks with the intention of finding a wealthy benefactor for them. Well, they had chosen the wrong man.

He turned and walked back up the track, glad to be shaking the dust of this place from his feet. Escape was not so easy, however. He became aware that the children were following him. Rounding on them, he waved his arms and said savagely, 'Clear off!' They looked at each other, then back at him. One gave a tentative smile; the other obediently followed suit. Growing angry, he walked on. They followed. Unnerved, David spun round and shouted abuse at them which was meant for those who had told them to go with this white stranger. They seemed cowed by his ferocity, but again summoned up the smiles they clearly had been ordered to produce at regular intervals.

The nausea he had been fighting surfaced violently. Pushing his way between the trees David began retching in painful spasms, his mind full of visions he would not face. When he was able to turn back to the path he found the children watching and patiently waiting. As he stared back at two identical smooth faces framed by short black hair cut in fringes, at four black eyes shining with hope, he gave an inner cry of protest. He could not have spawned these Oriental dolls; *his* seed could surely never have developed into replicas of people he hated and feared. Yet, deep down beneath conscious protest, something told him it had. They were the right age, and he had been so crazy for Su he had often been careless. These two had a right to his name and protection. They were entitled to return with him to live at Tarrant Hall. In time, they would produce others who looked as they did; and *they* would produce even more. He would never, ever be free.

Those almond eyes and flat expressionless faces mocked him. When one child suddenly spoke in a high, sing-song, nasal voice something inside David broke and he knew he must rid himself of this unbearable burden.

The streets were gaudy with lights and colour. From bars tinny music and the voices of those well on the road to drunkenness spilled out to add to the noise of traffic and the clatter of clogs on broken pavements. Passers-by hawked and spat carelessly; whores in tight satin cheongsams chatted to each other in shrill voices, their painted faces almost weird in the harsh lights of the brothels. A raucous symphony of motor-horns split the evening atmosphere as Indian and Chinese drivers attempted to prove racial superiority along rough roads, with scant regard for their passengers.

David paid off the cruising taxi which had picked him up on the other side of the island, and made for the nearest bar. He ignored the prostitutes. There had always been girls ready enough to give him what he wanted in return for dinner or a bottle of perfume; European society girls only too eager to jump into bed with a Spitfire pilot. That was not what he wanted right now, anyway. The mere thought of sexual coupling repulsed him. The Golden Mountain Bar beckoned.

The nearest barmaid was fiftyish made up to look twenty. The bizarre result added to his sense of wandering in a grotesque labyrinth from which there was no exit. She leered at him from beneath a concoction of piled black hair fastened with cheap, sparkling combs, her mascaraed lashes fluttering, her fleshy bosom, almost certainly false like her lashes and fingernails, settling obscenely on the counter.

'Wha' you wan', dearie?'

The whisky was cheap and raw, but it was what he needed. He ordered two more to line up on the counter while he downed the first with his eyes closed. He thought it would be easier, that shutting out the scene would make a difference, but those two Oriental dolls would not stop smiling at him whether his eyes were open or shut. Time passed. Three more whiskies were in a row before him. The laughter and shouts had grown even louder. Voices, mostly speaking English, bombarded his ears making him want to cover them. Next minute, he knew why.

Reflected in the glass-covered wall behind the bar was a face he had not forgotten but thought never to see again. Rod Kershaw was staring back with the same brand of shock he himself was undergoing. The man was no longer the filthy, bearded creature half his normal weight David had last seen, but in that tanned, healthy face dark eyes contained haunted echoes of those seven months in the jungle. They watched each other in that mirror for some time, and David gradually sensed that the Australian somehow knew he was again weak and helpless. With his gaze on David's reflection, Kershaw spoke briefly to his companions; then came round the bar still betraying shock at the unexpected encounter.

'I thought I'd seen the last of you,' he greeted grimly. 'You were bloody near to death when we got you to Australia.'

'Not near enough,' he snapped, hating the man as much as ever. 'If you'd bothered to say cheerio when you left, you'd have known I was determined to stay alive even though you'd presented me on a plate for the Japs.'

Kershaw's face began to work. 'I had no bloody choice! It was you or us . . . and you hadn't the brains to shoot yourself when they got to you.' Fighting for control, he added, 'How in hell did you persuade the RAF to keep you in uniform? Your old school tie, I suppose, and that fancy bloody accent.'

David downed the two remaining whiskies, then said, 'It was my fancy bloody flying, *actually*. But you'd never understand that. You told me often enough your opinion of "pretty-boy fliers".'

'Yeah, well that's what you were when my blokes first brought you in. All clean and scrubbed, with great big blue eyes and a giant ego. Time soon changed that, *mate*. You ate raw snake with the rest of us and washed it down with piss.'

The heat in the bar was suffocating; the laughter was growing in volume and seemed to be directed at him. The glass wall gave an illusion of hundreds of people all around his high stool. His head was starting to spin, and every face was that of a smiling Chinese doll. The man was reminding him of humiliations which had reduced him to a creature totally dominated by and dependent on someone he despised.

'Why can't you leave me alone?' he demanded with drunken aggression. 'What are you doing in Singapore, anyway?'

'Giving evidence at the enquiry. Me and the blokes came here after we got back home with you. Up in the jungle, we were. They caught Jacko, Pete, Greg and Digger. Their heads were stuck on poles when I last saw them. No one does that and bloody gets away with it,' Kershaw said, pounding his fist on the counter. 'I'm here to nail as many of the mucking bastards as I can. Those I can't won't get far from the courtroom. I wasn't specially trained for nothing.'

David goggled at him, wondering if he could possibly be real or just an extension of his present nightmare. 'You mean you'll finish 'em off?'

Kershaw leaned closer. 'You keep your bloody mouth shut, or else! Understand?'

David turned from that face and pushed his empty glasses

towards the leering barmaid for refills. 'I'm here to finish 'em off, too.'

'Good on yer.' Kershaw signalled the woman to serve the drinks along the counter where his friends were, then manhandled David from the stool and marched him along there. They all gave alcoholic cheers and made a place for him.

'This is Dave,' Kershaw announced. 'He's a very special mate of mine. So be nice to him.'

Hands thumped David's back and he was urged to drink up because there was more of the same on the way. Hemmed in and unable to walk away, he did as he was told. These men from Australia had always told him what to do, and he had done it because Kershaw had insisted that he survive. There had been times then when he had not wanted to. He was not sure he wanted to now. He nevertheless drank whatever they set before him and, before long, he could not remember any place other than this, and no friends but these.

After some time they took him with them to another place, with red lights and numerous doors. It frightened him. All the people there had dolls' faces, with black hair and black, pitiful eyes. He stumbled from the building, feeling sick again. A little later someone pulled him from his slumped position beside a wall, and led him away. They glided along between so many flashing lights he was forced to close his eyes. Then he was being half carried up a number of steps to a dark room. The sudden silence in there unnerved him, because he knew he had done something terrible and could not remember what it was. All he could see were two dolls' heads on poles. He sank on to a bed and began to sob, a sense of terrible desolation sweeping over him.

Someone sat beside him. A voice he knew said with barely contained anger, 'Of all the bastards to turn up in Singapore, it has to be you. I couldn't believe my devil's luck when you walked into that bar. For four bloody years I've tried to forget you. I've seen just about every form of bestiality they could think of, but you were different. I remember how you looked when we walked away, and the terrible mess you were in when we went back for you. The sound of your screams is still in my ears. Because you didn't take the easy way out, you made *me* responsible for what you are now. Why d'you think I made such a mucking fool of myself carrying you about and giving you my rations?' Hands dragged him to a sitting position and shook him. 'You couldn't bloody leave it at that, could you? You had to turn up here and accuse me with those great big blue eyes. I've got to get you out of my system once and for all, and there's only one way left to do that.'

CHAPTER FOUR

BANKS bordering the lanes were yellow with daffodils, and
forsythia echoed that happy colour in cottage gardens as
David drove through Tarrant Royal. People waved to him but
received no acknowledgement. They were puzzled. He *always*
waved back.

Robson opened the door as David took his bag from the
car and crossed the drive. 'I was passing the window and saw
you arrive, sir. Her Ladyship failed to mention your visit.'

'She didn't know I was coming.' David walked past him to
the hall and kept on walking.

'Have you had luncheon, or would you like Cook to prepare
something for you?' called the bewildered man from the open
door.

'You can bring me up a whisky. That's all I need.'

Robson's disapproval followed David to the first landing.
'Very well, sir. Shall I inform Madam that you are here?'

'No need. Her sixth sense where I'm concerned will already
be working.' He slammed the door of his room and flung the
empty bag on to the bed. Then he stripped off the heavy polo-
necked sweater and crossed to the washbasin to splash his face
with cold water. As he combed his white hair his hands slowly
stilled. *Clean and scrubbed, with great big blue eyes and a giant
ego.* All that remained were the big blue eyes, and they were
now dark with terrible secrets.

Someone tapped on the door. It was not Robson with
whisky, but Marion with glowing face and outstretched hands.
'David, how naughty of you not to let me know you were
coming.'

He retreated from her. 'Will you *ever* realize I'm no longer a
small boy, Mother?'

She halted, her hands slowly lowering as she studied his
face with an expression of fear. 'It's bad news! Oh, darling,

whatever is going to happen now? You surely don't mean to bring her here?'

'No.'

'Thank heaven! You've arranged for a divorce, then?' When he said nothing, she assumed what she needed to. 'How long will it take?' When he still said nothing, she approached almost nervously. 'It'll soon be over. The whole wretched business will soon be over, my dear. Then we can go ahead with our plans.' She put out a tentative hand. 'We'll be happy here again. It'll be a new start for us all and we can forget all those unpleasant things.'

Something inside David exploded as he stepped away from her touch. 'It's happening again! You said the same thing last time I came back from there. You forced that bright smile and tried to pretend I was still the way you have always wanted me to be.' His voice grew harsher. 'For God's sake, look at me. We can *never* forget. You went through the war wearing a blindfold, worrying about nothing more than forms and restrictions. Didn't it ever occur to you that your son and daughter were being brutalized by things no civilized person could imagine?' He threw down the comb. 'You've always seen me as a replacement for Father, who didn't turn out the way you hoped. I had to be all you once believed him to be, and you've shut your eyes to the fact that I'm not and never will be. It's the same with Vee. She should be marrying "some nice boy" instead of a cynical divorced newsman who's done things you don't even know exist. We *all* have. Christ, Mother, you're unbelievable. A kiss from you won't ever make us better. We're no longer your *children*.'

Marion had paled dramatically. 'You're certainly no longer my son if that Chinese woman can change you so much. You left here a happy, laughing young man fond of us all. Now you back away from me and shout abuse.' She was clearly struggling for control. 'Don't use me as a whipping-boy because you married that creature in an obvious fit of madness and soon saw your folly. You've just demanded that I look at you, David. What you've never understood is that whenever I do I simply see *my son*. Whatever you do or become, it will always be the same. When you have children of your own you'll understand.'

David turned away to beat his clenched fists on the back of a chair, her last words unwittingly turning the blade in his stomach. A knock on the door heralded Robson with the whisky. He took it from the old man and had tossed it back before the door closed again. One drink was not enough. He needed more. He also needed to end this conversation. When he turned to her she was dabbing at her eyes with a handkerchief.

'I have to telephone Pat.'

Marion looked up sharply. 'Aren't you going across to the farm?'

'No.'

'I see.'

He bit back the comment that she did not see anything unless it was pleasant, and walked past her intending to go downstairs. She said in a toneless voice that he should use the telephone in her bedroom for greater privacy, so he turned along the corridor instead.

The tall room revealed his mother's flair for colour and style. The tall windows were curtained by cream drapes splashed with mint-green roses. On the toffee-coloured carpet stood chairs covered in mint-green velvet and twin beds with cream-and-amber-striped covers. The telephone was on a low table bearing a vase of daffodils by the window. David ignored the convenient chair. His call would not be long enough to demand getting comfortable. He dialled the familiar number.

'Hallo. Wattle Farm.'

Damn! It was her father. The Australian accent momentarily made his skin crawl. 'Is Pat there?'

'David?'

'Yes.'

'Where are you ringing from, lad?'

He fought the urge to shout that he was no lad. 'The Hall.'

'Christ, why didn't you let us know you were back?'

'Is Pat there?'

'Out in the yard, I think. Is everything all right, old son?'

'Can I speak to her?'

Bill Chandler paused a moment, then said less heartily, 'I'll get her. Hold on a moment.'

It was longer than a moment, and her father must have had a few words. He was a canny old devil. Pat sounded scared.

'Oh, darling, if it had been good news you'd have rung me the minute you set foot in England. Did you trace her?'

'Yes.'

'Well . . . well, that's good, isn't it? I mean, we know where we stand and you can go ahead with the divorce.' Her disappointment came over in her voice, despite the mock optimism. 'How long will it take? After your last visit' – a tactful reference to their lovemaking because she might be overheard – 'every day will seem like a year.'

God, how could he have forced her to surrender to him, and under such conditions? 'We can't get married, I'm afraid. I've decided to stay in the RAF.'

There was silence, then she demanded, 'What do you mean? *Why* can't we? What's happened, David?'

'It's impossible, that's all. You always knew she existed.'

'Are you . . . are you telling me you *can't* get a divorce?' Pat was extremely worked up and clearly fighting for command of herself. 'Surely you haven't brought her . . . David, I can't talk about this over the telephone. Come over here.'

'I can't. I'm going back to the station tonight.'

'Well, I'll damn well come over to you. You can't . . . you can't plan to marry someone and . . . and do what we did, then ring her up and say, "Sorry, you'll have to forget about it." What's got into you? What happened over there?'

'It's no use coming over, Pat. It won't alter anything.'

'Oh, yes it will, if it's only the shape of your nose. You can't break my heart and get away with it.' The line went dead.

David went downstairs to collect the whisky decanter, then returned to his room. Marion was still there, red-eyed. He walked past her and, after another stiff drink, began taking things from his wardrobe to pack in his carryall.

'What are you doing, David?'

'Taking back the things I brought home last time.'

'Why?' It was quiet and fearful.

'I've told them I'll be staying on after June.'

She moved forward between the wardrobe and the bed so that he could not pack the jacket he held. 'Please stop and give me a little time to understand what is happening. Whatever your opinion of me, you owe me an explanation of why you have changed your decision to resign your commission and run the estate. Your father had no interest in farming, so I have managed his affairs for twenty-six years. I believed you were finally going to relieve me of the responsibility.'

Standing with the tweed jacket on a hanger David heard all this as if from a distance. He was back in a jungle where the harsh cries of birds and monkeys sounded like human screams; he was in a garish bar where a woman with huge breasts leered at him: 'Wha' you wan', dearie?'; he was in a dark room with a man determined to get him out of his system.

'You've just told me you're staying in the RAF, but said nothing about your plans for the estate – *your* estate, David. Are you thinking of selling it? If not, and you expect me to continue to run it for you – an easy job, in your opinion – don't you think you should ask if I'm prepared to do so?'

He realized she had stopped speaking and was looking at him with concern.

'Darling, *whatever* is wrong?' she begged, on the verge of tears again. 'Please let me help you. You know I'd do anything for you. Tell me what happened in Singapore.'

'It brought back memories and I knew I couldn't give up flying,' he recited carefully. 'It's the only thing I've ever really wanted to do.'

'That's what you said to Pat?'

'More or less.'

'But *why*? Is it to do with that woman?'

'It's what I've decided to do,' he said savagely. 'It's *my* life, you know.'

'And a number of people who have shared it were promised things you now dismiss without even an apology or satisfactory explanation. Pat has her life, too.'

A discreet tap on the door caused David to swing round sharply. Robson still looked disapproving. 'Colonel Chandler and Miss Patricia are waiting downstairs, sir.'

'Tell them I'm out.'

Marion forced a smile and moved forward. 'We'll come down, Robson.'

'Very well, madam.'

David was now able to reach his bag on the bed, so he began folding the jacket into it. His mother stopped in the doorway to address him. 'Bill and I will wait in the small parlour while you speak to Pat.' After a moment or two, she added, 'David, you *must* see them.'

He looked up. 'It won't change anything.'

'I know . . . but you owe her some kind of explanation.'

They went down the wide staircase together but not speaking. As soon as he walked into the room David felt exposed, as though what he had done was written on a placard around his neck. He could not meet Pat's gaze and glared instead at her father. Bill looked somewhat strained and, for once, there was no cheerful smile. He opened the proceedings immediately. 'I'm here only as a chauffeur. Pat was a little upset. Your mother and I'll leave you two to sort this out.'

'There's no need to go,' David said swiftly, as Bill turned away. 'You'll want to know what I said, so you might as well stay and hear it. The whole thing is quite straightforward. Getting away for a while made me realize that what I really want is to carry on flying, not breed pigs at Tarrant Hall.'

'Did you trace your wife, David?'

He had to turn to Pat then. She was very pale and had been crying, but she still looked so fresh and clean his sense of shame made him hit out. 'She died of fever after serving a Jap brothel for three years.'

Shock turned Pat even paler, but she took it on the chin in typical fashion. 'Poor thing!' She approached him. 'I'm sorry you had to learn something so distressing, David . . . but you had to find out the truth, didn't you? That's why you went.'

'Shall we all have a glass of sherry?' said Marion into the resulting silence. No one answered her.

'If you really want to stay in the RAF then you must,' Pat told him with great control. 'You said on the phone that we couldn't get married, but if you're free what can stop us?' He simply continued to stare at her, overwhelmed with guilt, so she forced a smile. 'I'll adapt to being a service wife, given time. It'll be a lot different from pig farming, but we'll be together. That's all that matters.'

'No, it isn't,' he heard himself say. 'You all sit here in this cosy little village having no idea what's going on outside it. I have. Being reminded of it has changed my mind about getting married again. I'd rather be free. That's all there is to it.'

66

After a tense pause Pat stepped forward and smacked him hard across the face. 'I should have done that a long time ago,' she cried. 'A leopard never changes its spots. All right, you got what you wanted, but I at least made you wait a damn sight longer than the rest of your conquests.' She cast an anguished look at Bill before moving quickly to the door. 'I'll wait in the car, Daddy.'

Bill remained where he was regarding David with a frown. When Marion ran out after the distraught girl, leaving David alone with the man who had saved his father's sanity thirty years ago, David mentally girded on his armour. Bill opened his strategy by sitting down and lighting his pipe. David was thrown. Tempted to walk out, he decided against it. The other man would only follow him.

'Bit of a shock going back there, was it?' Bill asked, leaning back.

David felt vulnerable standing in the centre of the room, so he sat down as far away from his inquisitor as he could. 'In some ways, yes.'

'What did you feel when you heard the fate of your wife?'

'Christ, is this a professional consultation?' he demanded. He was trying hard to appear relaxed, but he was as taut as a drum.

'No, David, it's the offer of a helping hand from someone who has known and loved you all your life. Your father trusted me to the extent of placing his sanity in my hands when he was very seriously wounded and had no idea who he was. That trust continued until he was killed. The gratitude I owe him for that means I want to try to help his son when he is very obviously in a state of confusion. What *did* you feel when you heard about your wife?'

'Bloody relieved.'

Bill remained calm. 'It didn't bother you that she had been forced to prostitute herself?'

'They did far worse things to some women.'

'And men. You for instance.' He puffed at his pipe. 'When you said you were going back, I was afraid this might happen.'

David was immediately defensive. 'What do you mean by *this*?'

'The old demons have returned. It was only four years ago, old son, and the subconscious retains traumatic events in our lives for a very long time, ready to surface and grab us by the throat.'

He got to his feet in anger. 'This *is* a bloody medical examination. I've simply changed my mind about what I want to do. I'm not off my chump.'

Bill stood and crossed to him casually, enjoying his tobacco. When they stood side by side, he said with a smile, 'You used that same expression when you finally got around to telling me you had a psychological problem about getting airborne. I'm an experienced old bugger who can tell when a bloke is in trouble. When he's someone as near to being my son as you are, I can make a good guess at what it is.' His hand gripped David's shoulder. 'When you feel ready to spill the beans, I'll be here. Meanwhile, there are several things to tie up, you know. You've hurt Pat deeply; not so much by what you said but the manner you've used to do it.'

David moved away. Physical contact with this man who was trying too hard to make everything come right was unbearable. 'She should have kept on loving Father. He was a far better bet as a hero.'

'Pat doesn't want a hero, she wants you as you are. And she's waited a long time.'

'She's always known the score.'

'And you've just told her your wife is dead, which leaves you free to marry again. David, you *can't* simply tell her you've changed your mind. I've no doubt the silly girl will wait for you until this problem passes, but she deserves an apology and some kind of explanation of why you feel it's unfair to let her commit herself to you just now.'

David walked over to the cabinet, remembered that the whisky supply was in his room, then poured himself a double gin instead. With much of that inside him, he said tonelessly, 'I'll write to her.'

'There was a period when you wouldn't touch that stuff,' Bill said quietly.

David moved to gaze from the window. 'When you've been deprived of water and had to find any substitute, water is the most marvellous drink in the world. Now, I need this.'

Bill arrived beside him. 'Marion was looking forward to being relieved of responsibility for the estate. What are you going to do about that?'

'Nothing. She'd be lost without it. Now the war's over she won't even have to worry about forms and regulations. It'll be a piece of cake.'

'You think so?'

The remainder of the gin slid down his throat. When he poured more, Bill made no attempt to stop him. He drank it defiantly. 'Mother can do it blindfolded after so long. She has little else to occupy her time. Nothing much happens in this tiny world between the church fête and the Harvest Festival.' The mixture of whisky and gin was starting to affect him. 'She's totally out of touch. Christ, she didn't even suspect Father of doing something other than translations of documents.'

'Did you?'

David swung round aggressively. 'Don't drag up that old turkey.'

'I wasn't.' Bill was still calm. 'I know you two were reconciled some time before he was killed, and that you then loved him as a son should. I was making the point that Marion knew nothing of his real work because she was not meant to know. None of us were. He kept the secret from even those closest to him. Don't condemn your mother on that score.'

David hit out in a different direction. 'She expects me to compensate for the love she never had for him. I can't.'

'Of course you can't.' Bill came round and perched on the broad windowsill to face him. 'She loved him enough to seduce him and get pregnant with you. She loved him enough to marry him against his will and have his child. She loved him enough to pretend to be his nurse when he first returned from Gallipoli with all memory gone. That must have been a terrible thing for her to make herself do. Not only was he bandaged like a mummy, he spoke to her as you're now doing. Except that he had no idea who she was. She loved him enough to try to make the marriage work when he recovered, having herself learned to love my wife's brother, and knowing how Chris felt about Laura. She loved him enough to bear three more of his children, and stand the loss of the twins.

69

And all through these last twenty-six years she's looked after his home, his children and a vast estate.' He paused for effect. 'I'd say your mother is hardly out of touch with life, as you claim.'

David said nothing. He just wanted to collect what he came for, and leave. Bill had not finished, however. 'She's certainly unaware of what many people suffered, but that doesn't make her less of a person. She keeps going while people like you and your father fight your demons. Oh yes, I knew what you and Chris were doing during those latter years. Because of the trust we had shared since 1916, he came to me when he was desperate, as you are now, and told me everything. Yes, old son, including his love affair with a female agent working with the Free French. I saw you in confidential conversation with her at his memorial service, so you must know about it, too.' At his nod, Bill continued. 'Marion didn't suspect that, either, thank heaven. He respected her too much to be cruel. And that's what you must do, David. Whatever you might presently be feeling mustn't make you lose sight of the fact that, if you choose not to confide in those who love you, they can't be expected to make allowances and understand.'

Feeling trapped and transparent, David moved back to the gin bottle. 'You're saying I'm not worthy of him. That's what all this has been about, hasn't it?'

'It's been an offer of help when you feel you're ready for it, and also an attempt to prevent people being hurt by your sudden rejection. You've always been worthy of him. Chris knew that.'

'He was wrong. I'm not. *I'm not!*'

After a moment's silence, Bill said, 'I should go easy on that stuff if you mean to drive back today.'

He deliberately poured even more. 'Mind your own bloody business!'

To David's surprise the other man laughed. 'A chip off the old block. Chris fought me every inch of the way in those far-off days, you know. Cursed me up hill and down dale. We had some real old ding-dongs. He was craftier than you because that brilliant mind of his was always one step ahead of me. But I got there in the end.' He crossed to take David's arm in an encouraging grip. 'And you'll get there, too, I promise. It just takes time.'

David jerked away. 'I thought you were here only as a chauffeur. Your passenger is waiting.'

Bill nodded. 'So she is, poor little soul. I'll tell her you'll be writing. Take it easy, old son. You've been through worse and pulled out of it. You will again, and we'll all be here when you do.'

As soon as Vesta returned from her weekend with the Gaynors and heard the news she telephoned Pat to ask if they could have a talk, as she might be able to throw some light on what had happened. They arranged to meet after breakfast the next day. Vesta then had the difficult task of trying to calm her mother. They sat together in the room where Brad had told his life story – if, indeed, it was – while Marion tried to come to terms with the shocking change in her son.

'He spoke to me as if I were nothing more than a country bumpkin concerned with make do and mend. And the way he looked at us all! A wild expression that made me almost afraid of him. It was as if he suddenly hated us all.' She sat in her favourite chair, twisting her hands in agitation. 'He said I'd gone through the war blindfolded, with nothing but a few forms to worry about. Hasn't he – haven't *you* – any notion of what it was like to dread a telegram at any time to tell you your world has fallen apart? In the other war Roland, Rex and poor Laura were lost. I remember what it did to me to receive such news, and this time I feared for my own children. It was a nightmare. Doesn't David understand?'

Vesta was baffled. It did not sound in the least like her brother to say such things to those he loved, with no regard for how he was hurting them. All she could say was that returning to Singapore must have been so upsetting for David, they must all give him time to recover. She, herself, had received something of a shock during the weekend and still could hardly believe what she had been told. This was certainly no time to reveal the facts to her mother.

'Bill was wonderful,' Marion said. 'I don't know what we'd have done without him there. Poor Pat smacked David very hard across the face – and I didn't blame her – then ran out to the car. I went after her and Bill tried to reason with David for some while. I don't think he discovered any more than we'd already been told, but David was certainly a little quieter afterwards.' She glanced at Vesta in distress. 'He drank so much I'm certain he was unable to see straight when he left here in that car. I've been sick with worry since he went.'

'It isn't the first time he's been drunk, Mummy, and it certainly won't be the last. Don't be anxious. He's sensible enough to stop somewhere and sleep it off. He's done that before now.'

Marion sighed. 'What are we to do about this, dear?'

'Try to get some sleep so that we can think more clearly tomorrow.' She stood up. 'Come on, I'll get us both some hot milk to take up with us. Nothing ever seems as hopeless in the morning.'

'To think of him suggesting an under-manager to take my place! I've run all this with old George Caldwell since David was a little boy,' Marion pointed out as they went through to the hall.

'I expect he was trying to make things easier for you until he's got over what's upset him and comes home as planned. It sounds as though David needs some time to think it all out, and it can't have been easy to learn that kind of thing about his wife. He must have loved her very much at one time.'

'Not now. He doesn't love anyone right at the moment.'

Vesta lay awake for a long time reviewing all she had learned in the past forty-eight hours. She was more than a little upset, but the importance of *The Afterglow* had grown and made her thankful she had painted it before this had happened. It would have been too painful to work on it now. Her mind eventually tried to make sense of David's visit, but failed. He had made no secret of the fact that he wanted Su out of his life and hated any mention of his marriage, so he should not have been so badly affected by her fate that he would act as he had. He was definitely very much in love with Pat – he had told Vesta so, many times – so he certainly had not been playing his old games again. Anyway, the young man who had seduced girls wherever he went had vanished long ago. David was sincere and true these days. Why, then, had he treated Pat so heartlessly? It did not make any sense. Should she telephone his station and try to find out what had gone wrong? If Uncle

Bill had failed to get to the bottom of it she was unlikely to. Better to write a friendly letter and wait to see if he replied with any clues. Of one thing she was certain; her brother had had a rough time of it over the past six years, and she was not going to condemn him out of hand. He needed friends, not inquisitors.

It was well into the early hours before painful thoughts of Brad took over, keeping sleep at bay, reminding her that she, too, had had a rough time during the last years of the war. She needed friends, also, and the determination to pursue her career despite her nagging suspicion that she had thrown away something far more valuable than artistic success.

Everyone at Wattle Farm looked strained when she arrived. Pat was positively haggard. The two young women went to her room with cups of coffee after a few minutes with Tessa and Bill in the kitchen of their home built in the style of an Outback homestead. Since it lay at the edge of Tarrant Maundle, it did not spoil the pretty effect of the thatched cottages along the main street, and it blended well with the surrounding sheep country. Pat's room expressed her personality: bright yellows in stripes and squares, with honey-coloured wood and large framed landscapes of her parents' homeland that she had never visited. Ledges and shelves contained a conglomeration of mementoes from many of the officers stationed at Longbarrow Hill over the years who had been entertained by the Chandlers. There were glass cats, squadron badges, cigarette lighters made from bullets, books, china dogs, a stuffed toy horse and numerous group photographs. On the table beside her bed she kept a pottery lamp, a small radio and a picture of David as he was now. This was presently lying face downward.

They settled in their usual chairs beside a window overlooking the stables and a marvellous view of Wey Hill, sipping their coffee in silence for a while as they gazed at the familiar scene. Eventually, Vesta murmured, 'I'd like a pound for every time we've sat here for a heart-to-heart, wouldn't you?'

Pat nodded as tears slowly rolled down her cheeks. 'Daddy says David's gone back to how he was when he first came home from the East, but he hasn't, you know. That time he telephoned me and asked me to meet him at the station.' Her head turned and Vesta saw the full extent of Pat's distress. 'I'll never forget that day. It was terrible. I couldn't believe it was David. He looked . . . grotesque. I had to hide my shock and carry on normally. I don't know how I did it, Vee. To give Mummy time to get across to Aunt Marion I suggested tea at the Punch and Judy. We ordered sticky buns. Mine almost choked me. David sat looking at his as if . . . as if he had never seen anything so wonderful before. When I thought enough time had passed, we left. Oh, Vee, he took the sticky bun *and* the plate. You know those lovely ones they have with the partridge on? Poor Mrs Bates didn't know what to do when I said, "Two teas, two buns and a plate."' The tears were flowing freely now. 'He took it with him in the pony and trap as if it were the most natural thing to do. We set off, but as we drew near Tarrant Royal I realized he was starting to cry. Have you ever seen a man cry? It's the most upsetting thing. I pulled off the road into Lower Meadow, and he put his head on my lap and sobbed.' Her eyes appealed to Vesta for understanding. 'He turned to me for help; he *trusted* me, Vee. It was me he called to fetch him from the station. This time . . . this time he pushed me away. He wouldn't even come across and see me. He's turned against me completely. So it's not the same as last time. It's not.'

Vesta put her arms around her friend, near to tears herself. 'I thought because the war was over we'd all live happily ever after, but Brad's gone off to write about it, David's reliving it, and we're both exactly where we started with them.' She sat back, giving Pat a handkerchief. 'Can you bear to tell me your side of it all, and what Uncle Bill made of it? Mummy's in too much of a state to be rational.'

Pat glanced up from the handkerchief. 'You said you could throw some light on it.'

'I *might* be able to, but until you tell me what happened, I can't be sure.'

As Vesta listened to Pat's impassioned account she grew even more baffled. She had been in Egypt when David first returned from the East, but she still could not imagine her brother presently behaving as Pat described.

'He looked kind of wild, Vee. It was almost creepy. And he came out with the news of his wife's suffering and death in a

74

tone that suggested *I* was responsible for it. I thought it was that which had so upset him he couldn't face me, but Daddy said David told him he didn't give a damn about her.' She screwed the wet handkerchief into a ball. 'I smacked him hard on the face and told him he hadn't changed his spots. I wish I hadn't, but I didn't know how to handle him! I couldn't recognize him any more. When . . . when we all came over to view *The Afterglow*, he and I sneaked into the other part of the house with a couple of blankets, and I let him make love to me,' she confessed.'It seemed such a betrayal of that afternoon to hear him say, quite coldly, that he'd simply changed his mind about getting married.'

Vesta thought of Brad in her own bed last month, sending her to the heights then destroying *their* plans because he had changed his mind. 'Perhaps it's time we called their bluff, Pat.'

'Whose bluff?'

She shook her head. 'Sorry, I was away on another tack.'

'What did you come to tell me, Vee?'

'Oh, heavens, I'm not at all sure it's relevant to this problem, but it certainly *concerns* David. Listen to this. Right from the start of the war Daddy was working at Beaulieu Manor, where agents received their final training before being dropped into enemy-occupied territory. His knowledge of languages and so many cultures made him invaluable. So, when we all thought he was safe behind a desk at his dull old ministry, he was concocting false histories for people and unscrambling coded messages sent from those already in place all over Europe.' Seeing Pat's astonishment, she added, 'It seems incredible that none of us knew, doesn't it? It's upset me. We used to give him a hard time about forgetting our birthdays, and so on, little realizing he was working night and day on such vital business.'

'How did you find this out?'

'From the Gaynors. Paul made a comment about Daddy that I didn't understand, so I followed it up this weekend. His father used to work there, too. It was very hush-hush, of course – the Gaynors didn't know about it, either – but they thought I knew now the war is over. I daren't tell Mummy while she's in such a state about David. It'll have to wait until the time seems right.'

Pat blew her nose and made an effort to be her normal sensible self, saying, 'I still don't see how this news concerns David, although he jolly well ought to be told about it.'

Vesta took her friend's hand. 'He already knows, Pat, because he's also been keeping secrets from us all. After returning from the East, he said he was with a transport squadron ferrying goods around Britain. He wasn't. The agents Daddy helped to train were flown over to France by David's squadron, landed and picked up again in rough fields beneath the noses of the Germans on moonlit nights. The strain must have been terrible. Oh, Pat, he's been through so much, and going back to Singapore must have been the last straw, don't you think?'

Pat was so upset by these words her parents came in in some concern. Vesta repeated the facts she had been told by Colonel Gaynor, but Bill showed no surprise which led her to believe he had somehow been in on the secret all along. They all returned to the kitchen where Vesta made more coffee, feeling as she had often done in the past. She had been necessarily shut out from the lives of her father and brother, but her mother could think only of David, as she always had. No one seemed concerned about Vesta's dilemma. Marion was relieved that Brad had left the scene; the Chandlers were only worried about their daughter and the man she had hoped to marry. Perhaps they all thought a successful artistic career was enough for her but, as Brad had once told her, art would not keep her warm in bed.

Pat's distress subsided enough for her to say, 'If only we had known. Poor David, he must be feeling so wretched and lonely. I'll write him a lovely long letter telling him I understand and want to meet to sort things out.'

'You won't, girl,' her father told her in kindly fashion. 'He needs time to come to terms with his demons. He's done it before; he'll do it again. He's a Sheridan.'

Vesta sat apart from them, sipping her coffee. She was also a Sheridan who needed time to come to terms with demons. They might not be as terrible as David's, but they would not go away without a fight. It looked as if she would be fighting on her own.

CHAPTER FIVE

NINETEEN forty-six was not the marvellous year everyone expected after six wartime ones. Peace was an illusion. There was unrest all over the world. Nations which had banded together to fight a common enemy were now free to fight each other in the big push to seize territory or change boundaries. Riots in Cairo, terrorism in Jerusalem, mass killings in India, civil war in China, martial law in Vietnam, Communism spreading over Europe. Millions were homeless; as many were facing starvation.

Cities had been flattened and remained strewn with unexploded bombs. Rebuilding plans were drawn up, but where was the money to do it? The relentless hunt was on for those who had committed war crimes; their victims lay in overcrowded hospitals, victims still. Prisoners of war were slowly being repatriated; a legion of souls unable to forget incarceration and those who had been caged with them. Demobilization brought unemployment, a yearning for continuing excitement and danger, and divorces by the thousand. Women who had felt wonderfully emancipated in the three services, in factories, on the land or in hospitals mostly objected to resuming a subservient role at the kitchen sink.

Those who had brought up a number of children alone for six years resented interference from returning husbands. Fathers discovered additional offspring at home whose ages did not correspond with the dates they had been on leave. People who had kept hope alive after receiving telegrams stating *Missing, presumed killed* had to face the terrible truth. Life did not go on as before. It would never do that again.

Marion Sheridan had suffered the aftermath of what had been termed The Great War, so she should have known what to expect this second time. Perhaps because 1919 had been so very difficult, she *wanted* to believe the last six years could be

77

put behind them all in a drive to recapture the happiness of the early thirties. It was a vain hope, but one which had kept her going for six months until David returned from that brief visit to Singapore, and Vesta's American breezed in and left again to pursue a story. Happiness seemed an impossible commodity for the Sheridan family. Yet, when she thought of the tragedies all across the globe, Marion could not deny her own problems were small.

Her daily routine continued. Jack Marshall, son-in-law of George Caldwell, the elderly manager who had decided to retire, knew his job but had an extrovert personality. Used to the dignity of Robson and old Caldwell, Marion was ill at ease with the young ex-corporal who said 'Righty-ho' or 'Okie-dokie' instead of 'Yes' in agreement with her directions. He always called her 'Madam' and never took a major decision without consulting her, but Marion felt out of her depth with the large, energetic young man who seemed unable to do anything quietly. He was constantly clattering or whistling around the place so that she was glad when he was in the fields or supervising logging in the distant woods.

After one such noisy morning she watched from her office with relief as he started up his jeep and raced off down the driveway. In the old days everyone had ridden across the extensive estate. Life had been slower, more peaceful. Now, they bumped across meadows in jeeps with engines roaring. The village had lost its serenity. On impulse, she changed into jodhpurs and a sheepskin jacket, tied a scarf over her hair, and took her mare, Cleo, over Longbarrow Hill. On a November day when rain threatened, the long level stretch was deserted. Yet the gusting breeze seemed to carry the sound of masculine voices calling to each other as trucks rattled towards Dispersal; the distant rumbles of thunder could have been aircraft engines revving up.

Marion slowed her mare to a trot as she drew level with the wire perimeter fence of the deserted airfield. The aircraft had all gone. Those who had flown them were mostly trying to pick up the pieces of broken lives or marriages, and once more becoming bank clerks, insurance brokers or factory workers. A faint whiff of aviation fuel still hung in the air – or perhaps Marion imagined it – and the echo of hearty voices singing around a piano filled her ears. Huts stood empty. The door of one was unlatched and banged as it was blown back and forth. How long would it be before the huts and hangars were pulled down and removed? How much time would pass before the ghosts left? The runways and perimeter track would surely remain as a sign to future generations that the peace of this high range had once been broken by the deafening noise of warfare.

Marion's thoughts travelled back to her girlhood when Rex Sheridan had kept his old bi-plane up here in a large shed. How would he view today's machines? Lost during the final days of 1918, "Sherry" Sheridan's name lived on in aviation history. David had grown to maturity yearning to emulate Rex; women had flocked after the dashing hero; Laura had adored him. Yet, despite Rex's charm and élan, and the sterling worth of his elder brother, country-loving Roland, it had been the scholar, Christopher, set on an academic career and totally out of touch with lesser mortals, whose outstanding good looks had captured the emotions of the eighteen-year-old daughter of Tarrant Royal's doctor. Caught up in her infatuation, Marion had been unprepared for Chris's instinctive response to her sexual teasing. The heady excitement of domination by someone who had always been so far out of reach had cost them both their youth.

All these years later Marion still recalled the shame, and the condemnation of villagers. There had been little censure for the schoolboy known to have no interest in girls but so many brains he was a walking encyclopaedia. It was generally agreed that he had been trapped by a scheming creature out to marry well. The village had forgotten the scandal and now respected Marion as their first lady, but she, herself, had never forgotten those bad days when she had been scorned by everyone, especially her husband. Seeing David kiss and cuddle Pat reminded her of that passion she had been unable to control. Coming upon Vesta in the embrace of an extremely assured, blatantly attractive American had highlighted the lack of affection in her own life.

After the first war Chris had tried to make their marriage acceptable enough to tolerate, and they had slowly established a warm fondness for each other. Vesta and the twins had resulted from moments of rare passion from Chris. He was able to experience strong emotions – she had known him to cry over music and be immensely moved by visual beauty – but she had never again felt as she had during that brief seduction in her father's surgery. The subsequent shame and rejection had killed any hope of further ecstasy in his arms. She had been contented, however. David had compensated for lack of sexual fulfilment, and she and Chris had lived their separate lives with understanding and affection until David had been listed missing, presumed killed. She had said things to Chris in her grief which had brought to an end the tenderness they had worked to maintain. She had never been able to revive it; something she deeply regretted.

Urging Cleo to a canter Marion passed the silent airfield, ignoring spits of rain now in the wind. At fifty-one she should accept that love for her children was the only brand left to her, yet even that had once more imposed conditions. She had been looking forward to having David and Pat living at the Hall after so many lonely years. Since that dreadful day in March, he had stayed away and left her letters unanswered. It seemed improbable that he would come home for Christmas and she felt so helpless. How could the situation be resolved if he cut himself off like this?

Vesta had become deeply involved with her work and spent hours in her studio fulfilling the commissions she accepted. When she did emerge it was to meet professional engagements or to go out with Paul Gaynor. Her feelings for him appeared to be no more than friendly despite his obvious wish for a deeper bond. Marion liked him and sincerely hoped he would get his heart's desire, but it seemed unlikely, as yet. Brad was still in Japan. His initial article had led to a contract for an entire series on the country and people after defeat. His letter had made Vesta more bitter, but she had not yet reached the stage of seeking affection elsewhere. Marion supposed she should discuss it with her daughter, but Vesta avoided the subject. In any case, what could a woman with so little experience say to another who, as David had pointed out, had seen and done so many dramatic things?

As rain was starting in earnest Marion reluctantly turned homeward. The Hall was not a welcoming place these days.

Curious how she was nostalgic for the noise created by men whose departure she had longed for. She almost wished them back. Someone was coming tomorrow to discuss repairs and restoration, although the work would probably not be done for many months. Whatever would she do with all the rooms? Life would be even lonelier in a vast empty mansion.

Five hundred yards from home a deluge began. After drying off Cleo and settling the mare in her stall, Marion ran across to the house, entering by the side door where there was a lobby for boots and outdoor wear. Her jodhpurs and headscarf were saturated. She walked on stockinged feet, tugging the wet scarf from her head, anxious to change into dry clothes for lunch.

Robson, looking considerably put out, met her in the hall. 'We have a visitor, m'lady. Major Roberts from the War Department.'

Marion halted, drips from the scarf she held pattering on the polished parquet. 'He's not due to come until tomorrow.'

'That's as I thought, madam. Someone would seem to have informed us erroneously, because the gentleman insists that his appointment was for today.'

Conscious of her bedraggled appearance Marion turned into her small office to glance through papers on her desk. With dismay she saw the letter from Leo Roberts and her reply stapled to it. She had agreed to his visit today, but put the wrong date in her diary. She returned to Robson.

'Where is Major Roberts?'

'In the sitting room. I have served him with a whisky and soda, but have not enquired if he will be taking luncheon.' His expression lengthened. 'I was unaware that you had left the house, madam.'

Glancing at the clock at the foot of the stairs Marion saw that it was almost one. Cook would have everything ready. 'What is for lunch, Robson?'

'Rabbit pie with brussels sprouts and buttered carrots, to be followed by apricot fool.'

'The main course will be fine, but tell Cook to serve soup first. We'll have to have a more substantial alternative for dessert, and cheese to round off the meal. We shall need a good wine, Robson.'

'I have already taken the liberty of selecting one,' came the heavy response. Robson, like Cook, did not approve of his ordered life being upset by silly mistakes.

As Marion made to move off a voice said, 'Please don't go to a lot of trouble. Apricot fool will be fine.'

Marion swung round scattering drips from her sodden scarf. Standing in a relaxed manner in the doorway of the sitting room, glass in hand, was a stocky, dark-haired man in khaki who looked entertained rather than embarrassed by the sight of his hostess resembling an orphan of the storm. He came forward with a broad smile, hand out. 'I'm Leo Roberts, Lady Sheridan. There seems to have been a mix-up over dates somewhere along the line, I'm afraid. I apologize if my visit is inconvenient.'

Marion heard herself say, 'Not in the least. Please help yourself to another drink. I won't be a moment.' Then she fled from the amusement in his light brown eyes.

There was no time to fuss over how she looked. She towelled her hair until it was reasonably dry, deploring the unkempt image in her mirror, then snatched a blue wool dress from her wardrobe and tugged it on. After applying make-up in a slapdash fashion she ran a brush through her curls (which had more threads of grey than she cared to acknowledge) and finally slid her feet into black shoes. The heels were higher than she usually wore during the day, she realized, but they were the nearest to hand. On the point of leaving her room she sprayed herself with perfume – also not usual for daytime, but it would offset the smell of still-damp hair.

The clock chimed the quarter hour as she passed it. Robson was hovering so she told him to announce lunch in five minutes, then entered the sitting room, which was bright with vases of autumn leaves and honesty. Leo Roberts was standing before *The Afterglow*, studying it so intently he was not aware of her entry. With a physique ideally suited to the smart uniform bearing a crown on each shoulder, and a well-shaped head where a sprinkling of silver enhanced brown hair shining with health, he did not appear to fit Vesta's somewhat acid supposition that their visitor would most probably be a nitwit whose usefulness to the army stretched no further than inspecting houses. If nitwit he was, he was certainly very taken with her painting.

82

'Did you see the church as you drove through the village, Major?'

He turned quickly. 'I mean to stop and spend a little time in it on my way back. It was a beautiful example of seventeenth-century architecture, judging by your daughter's painting. She's extremely gifted.'

'She's presently in Cumbria working on a study of an ancient mill commissioned by the local squire. I'll tell her you admired *The Afterglow*.'

As she crossed to him he said, 'It's an emotive title for a very thought-provoking picture.'

'It's taken from a couplet on the headstone above the grave of Rex Sheridan's wife.'

'The grave with a candle at its foot?'

'Yes.'

'I'll make certain I see it while I am there.' He glanced back at the picture. 'The symbolism of the single set of footprints is very moving, isn't it?'

'Very,' agreed Marion, though uncomfortably, because she truly did not understand the meaning of the footprints. If someone had walked there to light the candle, he or she *must* have left prints in both directions. Yet this man apparently was moved by their absence – or was he merely being polite?

The visitor turned his full attention on her. 'It's very good of you to offer me lunch at short notice. I could have eaten at the George and Dragon down in the village.'

Marion thought his offer rather late in coming and knew he *was* simply being polite this time. 'It's the least I can do, although you would have had a better meal tomorrow.'

His smile was disarming. 'Shall I go away and come back in twenty-four hours?'

Relaxing beneath his friendly manner, she said, 'It was my mistake, I'm afraid.'

'And I've been very ungallant by staying, but it will be some time before I am again in Dorset and work on restoring this beautiful house would be greatly delayed if I didn't do what I came for today.'

Robson made his formal announcement, and Marion led the way to the dining room.

Over celery soup, which was one of Cook's standbys,

83

Marion thought she should explain the situation. 'My son will be living here when he leaves the RAF. The Hall and the surrounding estate are his, of course. I'm managing it, as I have done for a number of years, until he takes over. I hoped he would drive down for your visit, but getting leave was difficult.'

'He's very fortunate that someone so able is here to run the place in his absence. It could have been no easy task coping with the vagaries of the Min. of Ag. during the war. Forms, requisitions, demands – all in triplicate. You must be a genius at organization.'

'So much so I booked your visit for the wrong day.'

He chuckled. 'Shall we draw a discreet veil over that and pretend it never happened? This soup is delicious. Your cook must be one of those gems one is forever hearing about but can never find.'

They talked for a while about domestic staff, during which Marion deduced that this man of humour and charm lived alone in a Cambridgeshire cottage when he took leave. A widower? He did not have the mannerisms or attitudes of a middle-aged bachelor. She thought she detected some kind of foreign accent but it was too slight to identify. Attractive, though.

Over the rabbit pie Marion asked him about Cambridge, and they then spoke at some length about Dorset's many beauty spots. Eventually, he said thoughtfully, 'It's clear you love it all with the passion of a true countrywoman. How will you deal with the changes that are certain to come?'

'I don't understand,' she said with a frown.

There was a break in conversation while Robson asked in glum tones whether they would have Eve's pudding or apricot fool, and Leo Roberts said he probably should have the former as Cook had so splendidly produced it at the drop of a hat. When the old man departed Marion explained that he had been with the family for many years, and was thrown by anything he could not plan at least three days ahead.

Leo grinned. 'He's like a character from Wodehouse. I'll wager he was a tower of strength during the war.'

'Absolutely.' she laughed. 'But he was immensely patriotic and refused to buy anything on the black market or under the counter from the local grocer who managed to get his hands on "unobtainable" items the way everyone did, now and again.'

'I know the type.'

She sobered. 'You spoke of changes a moment ago.'

It seemed he regretted having said what he had because he shrugged non-committally. 'It's the same after every war. Nothing stays as it was. Look what happened after the last one. But that's too deep a topic for a pleasant lunchtime. May I say instead how much I admire your flower arrangements? I can't imagine the doughty Robson is responsible, so they must be your work.'

'I enjoy the task. A house without flowers is not truly alive,' Marion told him, pleased that he should have noticed them. 'My gardener ensures that there is something attractive to use all year round.'

'You'll be glad to have your home restored to its original glory, I'm sure. I trust your compulsory lodgers treated everything with respect? I can't guarantee when the work will actually be done, of course. My job is only to assess what's needed. Some houses which were completely commandeered for use as offices will have priority so that the owners can move back as soon as possible.'

'Naturally. As you can see, I live very comfortably in this small wing. My daughter is away a great deal, which means I am the only one here for most of the time, as I was during the war.'

He set down his spoon. 'You must have felt very lonely and anxious. Most people forget what war does to anyone left behind knowing they're helpless to protect their loved ones. Fighting is difficult and dangerous; waiting is soul destroying.'

Marion gazed at him in astonishment. 'You're very perceptive, Major. Your wife must surely have spoken to you of her own loneliness during your absence.'

'My fiancée. She decided instead to marry a factory owner who was there whenever she needed him.' He summoned a faint smile. 'There was no acrimony between us. Life then was too uncertain for such self-indulgence.'

As his earlier praise had pleased her, so these words touched a vulnerable spot. She recalled the times Chris had arrived unexpectedly for a few days' leave and she had spent most of them berating him for forgetting important dates. This man now reminded her that the anniversaries she had thought so vital mattered nothing against those days lost for ever. He was unwittingly reiterating what David had accused her of eight months ago. Her life *was* self-indulgent.

'Will you have some cheese?' she asked, indicating the board Robson had placed on the table after serving dessert.

'At the risk of further offending your retainers I must decline on the grounds that you have fed me too well, ma'am,' he said warmly. 'I also think it would be wise to see what needs to be done to the Hall while there's enough daylight, don't you?'

For some unaccountable reason she took this as a slight rebuff, although it was said in the same friendly manner. She had been enjoying his company to the extent of forgetting that he was there to do a job. She got to her feet. 'Yes, of course. You must want to make your assessment and be on your way.'

She walked from the room to be accosted by Robson waiting outside. 'Shall I serve coffee in the sitting room, madam?'

'No, we're going through to the main house. Major Roberts has a journey to make this afternoon.' Over her shoulder she asked, 'Do you need a measuring tape or a notepad?'

'I have all I need,' he said as he caught up with her. 'It wasn't my intention to deprive you of your coffee, Lady Sheridan.'

'Not at all,' she replied, finding the high-heeled shoes uncomfortable as she fetched the key from her office and recrossed the hall. 'Having inexcusably delayed you by being out when you arrived, the least I can do is ensure that you get away before darkness, which comes so early now.'

Unlocking the door she walked through the impressive main hall where, in past years, a huge fir tree had stood in decorated splendour each Christmas. From the hall rose an elegant polished wood staircase carpeted with a tea rose design against pale green. The RAF had cleaned up meticulously so the overriding smell was lavender polish. Yet there was also the undeniable odour of unoccupancy mixed with chill fustiness. With coal still in short supply it was impossible to warm all these empty rooms. There were logs in plenty for fires, but they needed constant watching. If winter proved hard this year some form of heating would be essential.

'This is quite *beautiful*,' breathed a voice at her side, and she turned to see brown eyes glowing with appreciation.

'I've always thought so. It was built by my husband's grandfather, but his descendants haven't used it much. Branwell Sheridan left his three sons here to be brought up by a governess while he lived in Madeira with the wife he adored. He committed suicide soon after her tragic death in 1914. The boys then all went off to war leaving the place in the hands of a manager. My husband was the only one to survive, and we took up residence at the end of that war. He was rarely here, however, because he was deeply engaged in work for world peace.' She sighed. 'Our son wanted to fly from an early age and took little interest in farming the land. During that other war this part of the house became a convalescent home for officers. In this one, it was invaded by air forces both British and American. Poor house. It hasn't yet known continuity of ownership.'

'Except from you,' he said quietly. 'You love it, don't you?'

Feeling her colour rise in embarrassing fashion, Marion nodded, then began climbing the stairs, saying, 'Do wander as you please. I'll follow and provide any information you might require.'

They moved from room to room and her companion wrote notes in an official notebook as he commented on features he found exciting, while Marion reminisced about the time it had been full of hospital beds and wounded men. Her restraint melted until she felt on such easy terms with him she slipped off her uncomfortable shoes and carried them dangling from her fingers as they descended the stairs to inspect the ground-floor rooms.

'Heavens, they seem so large now!' she exclaimed.

'When you put furniture back in them you won't think so,' he murmured, examining a heavy frieze.

Marion wandered in the past as she gazed from a great square bay across lawns sloping away to the row of chestnuts bordering the long upward drive only just visible in the approaching dusk. These views had been denied her for four years. Suddenly, the memories contained in these rooms filled her with pain. Those happy family days were gone for ever; those early days before Chris had become obsessed with ensuring there would never be another war like the one which had taken his two brothers and Laura, and which had changed him from a boy to a creature without a past who fought insanity; the days when Vesta had been a dreamy child finding pleasure in this house and its beautiful grounds, and David alone had loved her unconditionally.

The deepening late afternoon gloom settled on Marion as she wandered through the silent rooms. What would be the point of restoring them? The three Sheridan brothers had been lost in their prime, and David seemed unable to find peace here. The hope of grandchildren running through these rooms, growing up in a fine old house set in peaceful countryside, seemed a vain one now. This would not be a house; merely a large echoing mansion presided over by a widowed caretaker.

'Lady Sheridan?'

The tentative probe into her thoughts brought Marion from them with a sense of regret. Another long winter evening to be spent alone when love and happiness should be within these walls. She summoned a smile. 'I was dwelling in the past; a sure sign of ageing.'

Leo smiled back, closing his notebook and slipping it into his pocket. 'After six years during which the prospect of ageing was pretty slim, it's a welcome sign, don't you think? I shall recommend an early start on Tarrant Hall. It has been treated with respect, leaving very little to be done compared with some I've seen, so the work shouldn't take long to complete. With any luck you'll have men in here shortly after Christmas.'

'Oh.' She could not think what else to say.

After a visible hesitation, he added in less vigorous tones, 'As it happens, I have a personal reason for wanting to restore this lovely house as soon as possible. I worked with your husband at SOE during my training. He was a remarkable man. His linguistic ability, and his love for and intimate knowledge of so many countries and prominent foreigners made any agent's job much easier. Those of us he trained had greater confidence because they knew he would not have slipped up on even the smallest detail. When he went over himself to bring out Raoul du Vivier our respect for him deepened further.' He sighed. 'Although we were used to losing friends and colleagues there was still general sadness when we heard of his death in France. It seemed particularly cruel that your son should have been the pilot that night, who had to fly back leaving his father fatally wounded. I've not met David Sheridan but, if he's anything like Sir Christopher, you must be extremely proud of him.' He went on almost shyly. 'To be instrumental in returning the house of those two men to its original state is a privilege.'

Marion gazed speechlessly across the semi-darkness at him. Agents killed in France, David leaving his father fatally wounded? It made no sense. What was SOE? Chris had worked for Lord Moore at the Ministry all through the war. Whatever was this man talking about? Silence reigned as she stared at his features smudged by fading light.

As it continued, he said, 'Forgive me. I shouldn't have revived something which clearly is still very painful.'

'Painful?' she echoed through stiff lips. 'I have no idea ... no idea what you ... *Agents?* I don't understand.'

'*You didn't know?*' He sounded incredulous.

'You're mistaken. Chris was too ... He'd fought in the first war. He said ... he told me there was no question of active service this time.'

'Oh, lord, I thought you ... Forgive me. I'm so sorry.' He stood in helpless silence for a moment or two, then said unhappily, 'I would never have mentioned it if I ... I'm so very, very sorry.'

Although she knew in her heart he was sincere she would not allow herself to believe what he had said. It was beyond her acceptance. 'David would have told me,' she declared aggressively. 'Do you think my son could have done what you said and not told me? Do you think a man like David could have deserted his dying father? He was with a transport squadron, that's all. His hands were damaged. He could scarcely fly after coming back from the East. And Chris never reached France. The aircraft was shot down over the Channel.

Frank Moore came here to tell me the details. You're wrong. Quite wrong.'

Warm hands took her chilled ones in a steadying grip. 'I think we should go back to your sitting room where there's a fire. Please, Lady Sheridan, let me take you out of this cold room.'

Marion went in a dazed state and allowed him to settle her in a chair beside the hearth. While he summoned Robson and asked for tea to be brought, her brain was full of tumbled thoughts. This man must have confused Chris with another Sheridan. Yet he had mentioned linguistic skills and foreign friends. He had also known David's name. Chris had never been a secret agent; David would never have left his father to die. The notion was completely crazy. Was Leo Roberts? Her feet were frozen. She must have dropped her shoes somewhere. Robson brought tea and poured it before leaving again. Marion felt so weary she could hardly hold the cup, but the tea warmed her and drinking it gave her something to do.

Her unhappy guest drew forward a footstool to sit on, hands loosely linked between his knees, and said quietly, 'By rights, I should ask your son's permission before saying any more to you, but I can't drive away leaving things as they are. Will you allow me to explain?'

'You're mistaken.' It was her desperate defence against anything he might say.

'I'm afraid not. You see, Sir Christopher was recruited into SOE – the Special Operations Executive – because of his exceptional talents and specialist knowledge of many countries all over the world. He proved invaluable in concocting cover stories for agents, giving detailed descriptions of areas in which they were to operate. He also decoded messages in foreign languages from our agents already there, and those intercepted between enemy agents. I understand he worked as a decoder in the other conflict.'

Marion nodded. Her head was like a lead weight.

'After collecting Raoul du Vivier, your husband apparently vowed he would never take up cloak and dagger again. Nor did he until several years later.' He paused for a moment to take the cup and saucer from her hands and place it on the low table. 'A very experienced agent of the Free French – a

90

woman – was sent to bring out an Austrian engineer prepared to give us details of Hitler's new rocket. After the failed assassination plot, security was tightened so that established contacts and routes were highly dangerous. Delays and bad weather put the fear of God into the Austrian, making him volatile and unpredictable. When the go-ahead was finally given, your son was the duty pilot for that night and Sir Christopher went over with him to assist the agent with her high-risk passenger.' After a moment of uncertainty, he plunged right in. 'They were ambushed on the ground and your husband was shot. The pilot had no choice but to leave without him. We later heard that Colonel Sheridan had died almost immediately. There was no question of ill-treatment.'

The logs crackled and spat in the hearth as Marion considered the notion of her gentle, peace-loving, artistic husband engaging in preposterous activities such as one found in espionage thrillers. She studied this man's clean-cut face, the network of lines around his eyes. It wore an expression of grave sincerity. 'What authority do you have for the telling of this . . . fantasy?' she asked, at length.

'I was an SOE agent in Norway.'

'*You* were?'

He spread his hands apologetically. 'When hostilities cease so does the need for us. They've given me this job as a winddown towards demobilization. A "cushy number", it's known as.' After a moment he asked, 'Had you really absolutely no idea your husband was doing something hush-hush?'

'He was rarely here.' Even as she said it Marion knew that was no excuse. She should have sensed the strain he was under, should have seen the change in him. If she had taken more interest in him when he had come home, asked about his work, spent time devoted to him, surely she would have guessed he nursed a secret. All she had done was to chatter non-stop about the problems of ministerial dictates, about David or the men billeted in their house, then berate him for forgetting birthdays or failing to answer her letters.

'Of course, we were directed to tell no one, not even our families, what we were doing,' Leo said. 'My fiancée had no notion why I was never there when she needed me.'

That last sentence delivered a blow so severe Marion felt the pain of it in her throat and breast. Things she had said to Chris, words intended to wound, returned from the past to overwhelm her. She began to shake; her eyes burned with tears. The anguish of six years spent here dreading a telegram announcing the loss of her children, but never that of her husband, rose up to increase her sense of shock. When someone put strong arms around her in comfort she clung to him in desperation, because there was nothing else left for the young girl who had seduced a schoolboy and ruined his life.

CHAPTER SIX

MARION awoke to find a late autumn morning of the kind that usually delighted her. Today, the sunshine through pale mist sheening holly leaves and silvering cobwebs strewn like bunting along the shrubs made her inexpressibly melancholy. Bill and Tessa had come over last evening. Robson had telephoned them when Leo Roberts suggested that a friend be called. He had been upset over the distress he had unwittingly caused, but had talked freely to Bill about his revelation. They all agreed that David must now tell his mother about Chris's death, and Bill had called the squadron Mess there and then. The Chandlers had departed late, leaving Leo to stay overnight at Tarrant Hall.

David would be arriving by mid-afternoon. The prospect of going through another stressful encounter with her son made Marion view the lovely morning with sadness. She seemed as powerless to reach him in this present crisis as she had been to reach Chris in his. Robson brought a breakfast tray, but she drank some tea then put it aside and got up. Dressed in a tweed skirt and a pink sweater she went in search of her unexpected guest. She found his bag in the hall with a greatcoat and cap nearby. The man himself was standing by a window in the sitting room.

'Good morning, Major, have I detained you?' He turned and came towards her looking rather strained. 'I must apologize for keeping you here so late last night. I hope you were comfortable in the guest room.'

'Comfortable, yes. Relaxed, not at all. I feel responsible for causing a family crisis.'

'You didn't *cause* it, just uncovered it, I suppose. Please don't blame yourself further. I'm only sorry that your schedule was interrupted. Have you far to go today?'

He shook his head. 'An easy drive. I had planned to stay

93

overnight at the George and Dragon, so there's no question of having delayed me.'

'Have you had breakfast?'

'Thank you, yes.' He tried a faint smile. 'Robson served me very straight-faced.'

She attempted a smile too. 'Life at the Hall is very ordered and unexciting, you know. Robson and Cook are used to that. It was upsetting enough when Vesta's American friend came and ate his meal with a *fork*. Military surveyors who turn out to be secret agents are really beyond the pale, I'm afraid.'

He studied her with an intentness that was strangely disturbing, then said, 'You are a remarkable person. After receiving a shock like the one I delivered to you last night, most women, understandably, would have declined to face me this morning.'

'Coming from someone who spoke of female agents bringing men out of France that's a remarkably old-fashioned comment. Over the past six years women have endured shocks of every description and become far more resilient.'

'But you've not been exposed to the hideous reality of war first hand, thank God, and remain the gracious lady of the manor. You have no idea how refreshing that is.'

On impulse Marion asked, 'Do you have time to see the grounds? The view from them is quite spectacular on a day like this.'

'As it happens I was just wondering whether I dared wander out there when you came downstairs. I'd love to see the view.'

Marion slipped on a light coat and they stepped out into the still, chill morning and strolled along neat paths leading through a series of contrasting gardens that were eye-catching throughout the year. In summer there was a blaze of colour; now a universal impression of yellow and gold. Leaves crackled beneath their feet as they walked, and the clear, fresh air invigorated them after the dreariness of the previous day.

'You must employ an army of gardeners,' Leo commented, gazing around with pleasure.

'Heavens, no,' she said with a laugh. 'Just a retired postman, and his son who is slightly consumptive. They do all the heavy work, and I do the rest.'

He stopped. '*You* do? But there's an entire estate you're responsible for.'

'Only the administrative side. I've a manager who oversees the workers, does the actual buying and selling and supervises logging from the forest. I rarely get out into the fields, as the Chandlers do. Believe me, I'm no agricultural worker. I'd be lost without Jack Marshall. He knows all there is about crops, livestock and forestry, yet was made an officer's batman throughout the war.'

Leo chuckled. 'That's the army for you.'

They walked on and she said, 'I wasn't born a "lady of the manor", as you put it. My father was the local doctor. I acted as his receptionist before and after my marriage, taking six months off to help in a nearby hospital when there was a shortage of volunteer orderlies. Organizing ability is essential in medical circles.'

They reached the spot giving a view of the valley in which the village nestled, and of the gentle hills beyond, stopping to study it in silence for a while. Then Leo said, 'When I see a scene like this I know why we fought tooth and claw to preserve it. So many of our cities are no more than heaps of rubble it's difficult to recall what they were like before the Blitz, but here we have the true essence of England.'

'Apart from the damaged church. Chris was here on a rare visit and saw the blazing aircraft come down upon it.' She glanced up at her companion. 'I still remember how he looked when he came in after helping down in the village. The church meant a great deal to him and he was deeply shocked at the intrusion of war in the one place that should have been safe from it. The aircraft was jammed in the roof, and for weeks its tail with the black cross was there beside the other on the steeple. Chris found it obscene and arranged for its removal as soon as possible.' She glanced away again at the peaceful view. 'He made provision for the estate to finance much of the rebuilding. Vesta painted *The Afterglow* as a tribute to her father.' She glanced up at him again, slightly emotional. 'He was a lover of beauty in every form; a man who lived with ideals. That's why I found it so hard to believe he could have done what you described to me yesterday.'

'I know.' He frowned. 'Few of us were people whose personality revelled in doing what we did. Unfortunately for us, we possessed skills or knowledge that made us candidates for such work and we were asked to volunteer.'

95

'Were . . . were you ever tempted to reveal the truth to your fiancée, particularly when she perhaps grew angry because you failed to turn up when promised?'

'Yes, I was tempted.'

'But you never succumbed?'

He shook his head. 'When I was first recruited I kept quiet because I didn't want to put extra worry on her shoulders. As time passed, so many other lives depended upon my silence there was no question of telling anyone.'

She turned to him. 'How does a person settle to ordinary life after facing constant danger?'

'Haven't you asked your son?'

'No.' The question had not occurred to her until today. In her naïve manner she had willed everyone to live happily ever after when her second war ended.

'Some never settle and crave excitement from any possible source – even criminal. Others want peace at any cost.'

'And you?'

'That's easy. I would forgo all the excitement in the world to live in a place like this and watch the seasons pass.'

'David felt that way until eight months ago.'

His smile was warm and friendly. 'Perhaps he's not yet ready to surrender excitement. At forty-eight, I am.'

She thought for a moment before asking slightly reticently, 'Would you think me presumptuous for asking why SOE chose to recruit you as an agent?'

'Not in the least. Having revealed my knowledge of your family, I owe you a short potted history of mine in return. Sadly, we are not in the same league as the Sheridans. I spent some time on the Russian Front in the first war growing used to moving around in arctic conditions. When it was over I took a number of holidays in Norway, climbing and skiing, then married a local girl who excelled in those sports. We lived in her village on the edge of a fjord, teaching in the school. We were both members of the rescue team, and when she was killed during a rescue I stayed on, but the peace I had found there was gone. I returned to my old teaching job in Cambridge and gave private lessons in Norwegian. During that time I became interested in amateur radio and was soon contacting men in Norway who later became loyal friends at a time when

Britain needed such people.' He sighed. 'I hadn't your husband's unique qualifications, but I knew Norway, I spoke the
language and I had trusty contacts there. I responded to an
appeal for anyone who had knowledge of European countries
and could speak one of their languages, then found I had
become an agent for an organization in its infancy and pretty
well feeling its way as it went along. We made some terrible
mistakes, but people in occupied countries felt that they had
not been left to their fate. Many of our agents eventually
shared it. I was lucky.'

'Perhaps . . . but I'm sure there were other elements responsible for your survival. I'm sorry your marriage ended so
tragically.'

He gazed across the valley into the past, saying quietly, 'It
lasted a mere three years. For a long time I asked why her and
not me? She was by far the better mountaineer and knew
those peaks well. When my fiancée returned my ring because I
was never there when she needed me, I stopped questioning
fate. Until the world settles to peace none of us can order our
future.' He turned back to her with a smile. 'Which is why I
accepted the undemanding job handed out to old soldiers past
their prime. It'll give fate time to sort something out for me.'

'You have relatives?'

'A few cousins in Scotland and a sister in Australia.'

'So you have no plans; simply leaving the future to chance?
That seems surprising for a man who has been risking his life
to make events follow a certain pattern.'

'Maybe it's because of that.'

Marion fell silent, thinking of David. Was he abandoning
his plans because returning to Singapore had led him to
believe he was meant to do something else? She shivered.

'You're cold,' he said immediately. 'I shouldn't have kept
you standing here while I related my life story.'

'Hardly that,' she returned as they continued walking. 'You
have no wish to go back to Norway?'

'I'm ashamed to say I have no wish to make *any* decision, as
yet. Do you find that rather cowardly?'

'Gracious, no. A most inappropriate adjective for a man
who has done what you have over the past six years.'

He halted on the sun-washed flagstones. 'I hope you haven't

97

received the impression that we were impossible heroes. We merely did the job for which we were best suited, like everyone else. There were people of every kind in SOE and, believe me, none of us were saints. Far from it.'

They walked on in silence until they neared the house, then Leo said, 'I was wrong. Your husband was an exception.'

Marion gave a wry smile. 'Chris would be the first to refute that. He was a genius, certainly, but never a saint.'

They were back in the hall next minute, and there was no further reason to extend the visit. Marion regretted it. The hours until David arrived would be full of anxiety. She would have welcomed this man's company. He had an appointment to meet, however.

At the door he once more expressed his regret over what had happened, adding, 'I hope your son will put your mind at rest over the tragedy. I daresay it will be something of a relief for him to bring it into the open.' He held out his hand. 'Thank you for your hospitality at short notice ... and I still think you're a remarkable person.'

She put her hand in his in farewell. 'Nonsense! As I said before, I've done nothing to warrant that opinion.'

'Most certainly you have.' He smiled broadly. 'You changed from a drenched, dumbfounded equestrienne into an elegant, attractive hostess faster than any woman of my acquaintance would manage it.' Out on the driveway he threw his bag and greatcoat on the seat of his car, then turned back. 'If I happen to be this way again, may I call on you?'

'To see how work on the Hall is progressing?'

'Yes,' he agreed, after a moment's hesitation.

'Of course,' she said. 'That would be very nice.'

Marion watched him drive away then turned back into the house, wrapped in thought.

It was already dark when the lights of the blue MG swung round to the front door. Marion deliberately remained in the sitting room so that Robson met David in the hall to take his coat, cap and travelling bag. She heard a short subdued conversation between them before David came in. He looked thin and very tense, but the wildness of his last visit was no longer apparent. Having vowed to be as calm as possible,

Marion remained in her chair beside a huge log fire until he came across to her. She made no attempt to embrace him, merely stretched out both hands and thanked him for coming so promptly. For a moment she thought he would make no contact, but he eventually took her hands in his.

'I'm sorry you had to hear about this from a stranger,' he said quietly.

'No sorrier than Major Roberts. He was deeply upset and means to write to you.'

'There's no need for that.' He did not kiss her, just let go of her hands and put his own in his pockets.

'You've brought the smell of autumn in with you,' she said. 'I told Robson to bring tea when you arrived, but I expect you'd prefer whisky.'

'Tea will be fine, thanks.' He was gazing at *The Afterglow*. 'Vee painted that as a tribute to Father. I wish I could have done something worthy of him.'

'You did. You have. So many things, David.'

He shook his head, moving around the room moodily while Robson came in with a tray and filled two cups from the teapot. When the old man left, David came up to her. 'Father knew all along that I was with that squadron at Tangmere, but said nothing to me. I only found out he was with the SOE when one of the agents I picked up made a comment about keeping things in the family. You see, we didn't tell anyone at all what we were doing, so he and I had been lying to each other for months before the truth came out. I could hardly credit it. Those constant cracks about his dull old job at the Ministry! We *all* made them, never dreaming he was –'

As he broke off emotionally Marion said, 'You don't have to tell it all in the first five minutes, my dear. You're staying overnight, I hope.'

'Of course.'

'Then sit down and have some tea. We have the whole evening to talk, and everything always stops for tea in this wonderful country of ours.'

Marion was amazed at her own calmness in the face of her son's obvious distress. She sliced cake to put on two plates, and if her hand holding the knife was a little unsteady David was too wrought up to notice it, she felt certain. He swallowed tea as if time were running out, and it was soon apparent that he *had* to talk about the tragic events which had so unexpectedly come to light.

'We were alerted to bring out an Austrian willing to detail the design of a new German rocket, and Father had been assigned to translate his words for the benefit of one of our engineers.' He stared into his cup and spoke tensely. 'The operation was called off twice because the pick-up locations were swarming with Jerries on the rampage after the attempted assassination of Hitler. The female agent accompanying the Austrian signalled that he was getting so nervous she was afraid he'd do something risky. When she finally gave us the go-ahead, Father turned up unexpectedly at Tangmere to take the passenger in hand the minute he arrived. It was aborted. The Lysander was shot down going over. Jess Parker ditched in the sea and was picked up by fishermen.'

Marion was afraid to speak into the silence. She watched her beloved son who, it was clear, was mentally reliving that time. He stared back into the past, seeing nothing of the expensive china cup and saucer tightly gripped in his hands. Her heart went out to him, but she dared make no gesture of comfort. He no longer wanted such things from her.

'Fog set in for two nights, then we received a message that unless he was picked up pronto the Austrian swore he'd commit suicide.' David's large blue eyes met hers across that elegant room in the peaceful Dorset countryside, and they were dark with pain. 'I was duty pilot for that night. Conditions were right, and Father pulled rank to go along in case our passenger kicked up rough. He was . . . he was tickled pink to be flying with me.'

Unable to sit still, David crossed to *The Afterglow*, still gripping the Royal Albert china, and focused on Vesta's re-creation of the church which no longer looked that way. He spoke at the painting. 'I had to find a field we'd never used before, because the usual ones were too risky. It wasn't very good. The surface was bumpy and there were too many trees close by. I landed all right and turned into the wind ready for take-off. Before I knew it he had jumped out to help them aboard. It was unnecessary, but . . . I suppose he thought she needed help with the Austrian. They got him aboard, then she was on the ladder. I heard shots. Gunfire. We'd been ambushed. I *saw* them. They were coming from the trees, guns blazing, just as they did in Singapore. I . . . I saw him stagger and fall. There was no time to think. He shouted at me to go. He *ordered* me to go.'

David turned back to Marion, his face working. 'I'd have stayed with him if I'd been alone, you know I would. But I had two other lives in my hands, so I did what I had to do. I believe . . . I believe he was probably prouder of me as I took off than he had been at any time in my life.'

Although Marion had suffered the shock of revelation yesterday, hearing David repeat it as he relived the tragedy was almost too much to take. Even now she found it difficult to accept. She had known Chris as a husband, as the father of her children, and as a man of immense intellect. David was her firstborn, conceived in a moment of adolescent lust but at the centre of her life. How could two people she knew so intimately have been involved in this thing beyond her imagination? How could David have suffered this alone for more than two years without her sensing it? How could he have attended Chris's memorial service, knowing the official version of his father's death to be a lie, and not break down?

After a while she got to her feet and went to him. 'Why didn't you tell me this before? The need for secrecy ended over a year ago.' When he said nothing, she asked, 'Did you think I would blame you?'

'No, Mother, you love me too much to do that. I suppose I was unwilling to burden you with a sense of guilt.'

'*Guilt?*'

'For taking so little interest in him. We're all guilty of that.' He finally put the cup and saucer down on the mantelshelf. 'Because he was away so much we tended to treat him as an outsider when he *was* around, yet he financed me, and Vee, in our chosen careers and took us abroad to further our education. I suppose we looked on all that as mere fatherly duty and never thought of it as his way of showing us love. I used to think he didn't care a fig about any of us.' He put his head in his hands. 'Oh God, what a mess!'

Longing to reach out to him Marion curbed her need, sensing that he was still locked inside himself and unreceptive to her. Then he looked up and she was convinced of it. 'When I came home from . . . from the East, he was the only person who understood. He didn't fuss, didn't try to pretend nothing had happened, didn't keep telling me everything would be all right.'

'As I did?'

He began to move about the room restlessly. 'It *wasn't* bloody all right. He knew that. Knew it would never be bloody all right again.' He swung round to make another point. 'And when Vee was injured by the doodlebug on the London apartment, it was *he* who persuaded her to paint again. She wouldn't listen to anyone else. Too late in the day we both realized love didn't necessarily mean hugs, kisses and all our favourite meals.' He came back to the painting once more and stood gazing at it, head tilted back. 'This is Vee's acknowledgement of all he gave us. All I've done is to – I should have been the one left behind that night,' he finished savagely.

'He would never agree with that, David. He'd say his time had come. After defying death and insanity in the last war, his time had finally come.' She now dared to put out her hands and gently turn him to face her. As she studied the scars on his cheeks she saw him as he used to be; as Chris had looked all those years ago. Impossibly handsome and untouched by pain. 'He was a highly gifted man dedicated to the ideal of world brotherhood. I knew about his tremendous courage in overcoming what happened to him in Gallipoli. I was there to witness his fight against amnesia and the agony of his wounds. Now I've learned that he summoned up that same courage in this war, and you echoed it. When Major Roberts unwittingly let slip the fact that you had both kept secrets from me over a long period, I broke down. I felt I had failed you. I blamed myself for not sensing the truth or questioning your lies. Then he told me *he* had had to suffer a broken engagement because he couldn't tell the woman he loved why he was never there when she needed him, and I realized you and Chris had made certain I *couldn't* suspect the truth. My feeling of guilt faded. You had both lied too convincingly. Waiting for you to arrive today gave me time for reflection; time to put it all in perspective.'

David stepped away from her gentle clasp on his arms, and she said swiftly, 'Please hear me out. I think you owe me that.'

Although he said nothing, she had his attention. 'I'll admit I sometimes treated your father with impatience; showed little interest in his work when he attempted to tell me about it, which was rarely. I'm guilty of regarding him as an infrequent guest rather than the head of the family. We probably all did that. I'll confess my devotion to you was greater than that to him. I've now been forced to accept that I never fully appreciated him ... but neither did he fully appreciate me, David. While he was away gaining accolades and pursuing those things closest to him I was bringing up his children, looking after his home and supervising the estate which provided the wealth he needed to achieve his aims. We all play our part in life, however unremarkable. I'm not sure he ever recognized that because *his* world was peopled with the clever and gifted.'

Leaving time for that point to sink in, she continued. 'Chris was able to help you when you'd been disabled because he'd been through a similar experience and knew what you must overcome. He managed to coax Vesta to paint again because he understood artists. That ability to understand when you were both bruised and uncertain was invaluable ... but *I* was the parent who was always here for you, who kept your home going and who gave you the assurance of being wanted and loved from the day you were born.'

She put a tentative hand on his, to add gently, 'What I'm trying to say, my dear, is please don't turn him into a saint because of what happened that night, and think yourself unworthy by comparison. Have you forgotten that for fourteen years you found it impossible to forgive him for hating his child so much he abandoned all responsibility for it and ran away?'

The good weather held the following day, but David noticed little of the russet beauty of the copse cladding the western slope of Wey Hill as he rode the bridle path he knew so well. Some ageing fool had spoken out of turn two days ago and awoken more slumbering demons.

Bill Chandler's telephone call had suggested Marion was in a state of shock, and in desperate need of reassurance from the one person who could tell her exactly what had happened in France. David had been granted compassionate leave, but his mother appeared remarkably in control of herself. He knew Uncle Bill would not have called him unnecessarily. Something or someone must have wrought a significant change in the situation in the interim, leaving David a worse victim of circumstance than the woman he had rushed to console.

Tense and angry throughout the drive to Tarrant Royal, he had nevertheless vowed to keep an iron grip on himself, for his mother's sake. He knew he had been cruel on his last visit, subjecting everyone to a form of defensive attack born of his self-disgust. He had stayed away since then because he could not face them. Yesterday his hand had been forced, and he had come home determined not to drink too much or lose his temper with someone who had no capacity to understand anything outside her tiny country-life world. Then his mother had immediately offered him whisky – something she had never before done – and confounded him with simple wisdom and a reminder that had dealt him a crushing blow. Far from easing her sense of remorse he now found himself suffering further from it because, for fourteen years, he had held his father in contempt for something he, himself, had now done. The remorse was not for *what* he had done, but for not previously understanding that there could be justification for it.

What had happened on that night two years ago had been just one of so many terrible things he had had to do. Life had then been so full of shocks, fears, impossible effort, exhaustion, pain, death and a constant battle against despair, that they had all grown partially immune to those things. Friends died before one's eyes in flaming aircraft; enemies swooped from nowhere in the determination to make you die the same way. Orders demanded the unthinkable and it was carried out. Night and day were hardly distinguishable any more. Hours of waiting in smoke-filled rooms, with stomach churning and throat dry. Desperate living before life ran out. A sense of being alone and abandoned. That had been the pattern for six years of his life, and his father's death had been one tiny part of it. Thousands more had died after that night; he had killed some of them. The fear, pain and exhaustion had continued for another eighteen months and that single horror had been swallowed up in the immensity of it all.

Suddenly, it had ceased. They had slowly recovered and begun to feel human again. Hope was there on the horizon. It was possible to make plans, cement relationships. Living grew more leisurely because now there was time stretching ahead; a new certainty that tomorrow would come.

Sick at heart David took the gelding at a slow pace up the winding path. Sunshine was faintly warm on his face; a zephyr ruffled his hair. It was the kind of day to make a man feel glad to be alive, yet the sense of release, the hope on his horizon had vanished. Divorced from that pattern of unnatural acts and acceptances, the events of that one night in France now assumed a horror he found hard to bear. How could any man have left his wounded father to fall into the hands of a ruthless enemy? Something he had come to terms with long ago now became a burden too heavy to endure. Together with the shame that had been with him since his return from Singapore, he again felt alone and abandoned.

For the last eight months he had taken refuge in flying, solitude and whisky. He had volunteered for any extra duties. In the air he felt free and in control of himself. Back on the ground Kershaw threatened to take over. Although he had been helplessly drunk David remembered enough about that night in Singapore to flinch from a comradely arm across his shoulders, or any kind of physical contact with those he had once regarded as his friends. He avoided company. Men were dangerous. They did unspeakable things to each other.

Breasting a rise leading to the level stretch atop Wey Hill, he saw Pat waiting for him by the lone tree which had been a rendezvous since they had been children – handsome, laughing David, dreamy artistic Vesta, plump, practical Pat. Where were those children now? He had thought it the best plan to settle things with Pat away from their respective families. It would be easier to leave if the situation grew tricky. She never gave in without a fight and he was not up to full-scale combat. It was he who had committed all the sins and was therefore arriving without a single weapon. No one could battle for long on those terms.

Pat did not give her usual wave of greeting, merely waited

by the tree until he reached her and dismounted. She never looked pale and wan however much she suffered. Right now she presented a picture of wholesome attraction. A yellow jumper beneath her jacket emphasized the rich darkness of her hair tumbled by the wind, and the November temperature deepened the healthy bloom on her cheeks. She had been there all his life. He was now going to tell her to keep out of it.

'Thanks for coming,' he said after looping the reins over a branch.

'I always will, you know that.' She moved nearer, gazing up at him with unshed tears silvering her eyes. 'Why didn't you tell me? I would have understood what you were going through. Darling, you could have told *me*.'

'I was in no state to tell anyone.'

'How long were you going to bear it alone? Would you *ever* have told us? Did you think we'd all blame you for leaving him there?'

David was thrown. He had come to tell her to forget him, but she was caught up in something else and he had no choice but to answer her. 'I would have explained to Mother what had happened, when I believed the right time had come. I didn't imagine she'd ever hear about it from someone else. That was damned bad luck.'

'I couldn't *believe* it when Daddy broke the news. They should have sent another pilot. You'd already been through more than any man could be expected to endure. They *knew* that.'

This was not what he wanted. It had been enough to resurrect it last night. He must stop Pat before the main issue became lost. 'Knowing how fond you were of Father the truth must have come as a shock, but such things happen in war and you become hardened to them. Secrets have to be kept from those close to you, lies have to be told. You must accept that I was duty pilot that night and he *chose* to go with me. No one ordered him to, Pat. There was a job to be done. Sentimentality didn't come into it. My first duty was to bring back the man I'd gone over to pick up. He knew that.' As she made to go into his arms, he held her off. 'Don't turn me into a martyr. I was no different from thousands of others.'

'I'm not in love with thousands of others,' she told him emotionally.

It was the perfect opening. 'Perhaps you should consider that prospect,' he said carefully, moving away to the tree. 'That's what I came to discuss . . . in a more civilized fashion than last time.'

Pat was unprepared for the change in direction. She came round to confront him. 'But I understand. I *do*, David. I'd never hold you to blame.'

He angled his glance from her troubled face to the peaceful scene of the village below, and said what was now a lie. 'That's not it. I came to terms with the manner of his death long ago.'

'Then what is wrong?' She started the fight using her best weapon. 'Come on, lover, tell me what else you've been keeping to yourself for too long.' Turning his face towards hers with palms cradling his cheeks, she began kissing him tenderly.

He twisted away, panic overwhelming him at the sensation of her soft mouth against his. Such intimacy must not be allowed with this girl who had no notion of evil. With his back to her and grasping the trunk of the tree with his outstretched hand, he said, 'You've read too many romantic novels. Life doesn't get sorted out like that. This happens to a lot of chaps. The war's over. No more excitement. Time to settle in civvy street, marry and become a family man. Then, when it comes to it, they realize they can't do it. They need the thrill of taking off, diving and wheeling thousands of feet above the ground. They need to be *free*.'

Pat came round to stand in front of him. She gave him a long, silent look which unnerved him because he sensed she knew he was shooting a line. 'Rubbish!' she said forcefully. 'I've known you all my life, David, and I know damn well you were *longing* to leave all that and settle down with me. *Until you returned from Singapore.* Something happened there which, for some reason, has upset you so much you have retreated into your shell again.' She took hold of his other hand by his side, and gripped it tightly. 'I believe what you told me concerning your wife's death, but the part about that place reviving a need to be single and carry on flying is balderdash, darling. For a while I believed it, believed you were up to your old trick of getting what you wanted from a girl then saying cheerio. Then Paul Gaynor told Vee about your work for SOE and I knew you had become an expert liar. You're lying now, aren't you?'

To give himself time to think David walked the few yards to where the hill sloped away down to Tarrant Maundle. Pat loved the village, the farm, life in the peaceful beauty of this country. She always would. The girl's loyalties never changed. He knew she would continue to love him whatever he said now. That was the most difficult aspect of this meeting. When she came alongside a few moments later the scent of her perfume reminded him of those two hours wrapped in rugs in the empty section of his home, and he felt deeply ashamed.

'At least answer this truthfully,' she said. 'Have you stopped loving me?'

'I've always loved you.'

'All right, have you stopped being *in love* with me?'

He had to put an end to the interrogation. Turning to her, he said, 'Look, you're right about Singapore, to a certain extent. It . . . well, going back brought to the surface ghosts I thought well and truly laid. I wasn't up to my old tricks that afternoon, but I shouldn't have talked you into it because I've ruined things for you and some other chap.' He moved away again, finding her expression too daunting. 'You're twenty-six and you've waited far too long for me already. On the verge of marrying Dirk van Reerdon and going with him to South Africa, you decided to ditch him for a physical wreck married to a Chinese. In the three years since then you've passed up umpteen chances of a good life with someone else.'

'I don't want someone else,' she said softly, 'especially after your old tricks under the blankets. No wonder all the girls followed you around.'

Desperate to get his message through he confronted her. 'I've applied to join a squadron based in Scotland. The posting is for two years . . . and I won't be coming home during that period.'

Tendrils of hair fluttered on her temples as she gazed at him, stricken. 'Oh God, you're not lying now, are you?'

'No.'

Her courage began to fail as she said brokenly, 'Please tell me what happened in Singapore to make you do this. I love you enough to understand, whatever it is.'

Knowing he had to get away, he unhooked the reins and mounted swiftly. 'Find someone who'll give you all you deserve instead of waiting around for something that'll never happen. Do it for my sake if not for your own.'

He left at the gallop knowing he had hurt her once more. There was no kind way to tell someone all she had been led to expect was no longer on offer.

The start of 1947 was disastrous for the British nation. A strike by lorry drivers created worse food shortages than there had been during most of the war, and cessation of coal deliveries caused serious problems with power supplies. Troops were deployed to deliver essential goods to shops and factories, but this eased only a fraction of the problems and basic rations were reduced even further. People who had endured war united in their resilience found peace too much to handle. A mood of general depression settled throughout a country that had defied the worst their enemies could throw at them. Now their own government was doing it.

The news from abroad was little better. The situation in Palestine had deteriorated to the extent of necessitating the evacuation of all British women and children, and Lord Louis Mountbatten was appointed the last viceroy of India to oversee the transfer of power to the people of that country. The end of the British Raj was in sight. Malaya, South Africa, India, Egypt, Malta, Palestine, all were seeking to shake off British involvement. It seemed to those who had somehow muddled through six terrible years and survived that they had less than when they started and counted for little in the eyes of the world. Spirits were at a very low ebb and trust in the new Labour government faltered. Many who had voted the party in had regretted their decision and added their voices to those who claimed 'Winnie' would have done a better job after all. Churchill, viewed with reverence while hostilities lasted, had been rejected once they ended. The overwhelming desire for a new approach in peacetime Britain had changed the government, but the 'new' was proving worse than the old.

The general air of unrest, the seeking of any kind of change, the liberation of most women and wholesale reluctance to go back to being as they had been before 1939 brought an attitude of selfishness to life in Britain. As with the whole world, individuals looked to their own best interests in the shifting pattern of their lives. Understandably, people who had gone without, made do with very poor substitutes, shared with others in need and lived in blacked-out surroundings now wanted as big a share of what was available as they could seize. To hell with one's neighbour. It was each man for himself. One way or another, the dreams and plans they had had for when the last 'all clear' sounded had somehow been lost beneath the grim austerity of victory.

Two young women whose dreams and plans had certainly never come to fruition were dancing in the arms of the military on Salisbury Plain on an evening in early February. Resplendent in expensive ballgowns, neither of them paraded their sadness before their eager partners in scarlet Mess jackets and tight-fitting blue trousers, as they circled beneath chandeliers which had lit such occasions for many decades.

Paul Gaynor and Jeremy Stanstead had invited Vesta and Pat to this special ball to commemorate one of the regiment's past victories, and they had accepted in a mood of defiance. David was voluntarily hibernating in Scotland, and Brad was still in the Pacific fulfilling an extended contract to follow up his acclaimed articles on Japan with a study of how the Philippines and other war-torn islands were adjusting to peace. Spasmodic letters, which were more like offshoots of his articles than intimate messages to someone he apparently still expected to marry, were forwarded to Vesta from the news agency in London. This in itself seemed to rob them of the personal touch, although she knew that including them in his official dispatches meant that she received them far quicker than by mail. Brad always knew 'a guy who is flying out at dawn tomorrow', so the letters were short and written in haste. Each ended with the information that she was missing the chance of a lifetime, so how about it? Vesta was unsure whether he was referring to pictures she could paint, or nights she could spend with him. Not herself knowing any guys flying out at dawn, she had to send replies by air mail to the address on his last letter. Brad had invariably moved on by the time they arrived.

Since the day she heard from him that he had teamed up

with a Eurasian photographer named Minnie Wing, the replies had ceased. Vesta knew her man too well. Pat, on the other hand, appeared not to know hers at all. For these two bruised, uncertain women in the full flush of their youth, an evening of gaiety, wine and flattery was a partial antidote. Although they had set out in a 'we'll just show them' mood, it was not long before they were truly enjoying themselves. Paul and Jeremy were attentive partners offering the brand of sexual gratification that did not go beyond what they were prepared to accept, so they were able to relax and have fun.

By the time a buffet supper was served the dreariness of peacetime had been pushed to the back of everyone's minds. The Mess staff had produced a wonderful spread despite the severe rationing.

'Heavens!' exclaimed Pat as they approached a laden table. 'How on earth did you get hold of all this?'

Jeremy grinned as he handed her a plate. 'We're the army. We not only win wars, we drive supply lorries when unions call a strike.'

'And we're not mugs enough to deliver it to all and sundry without commandeering a little extra for ourselves,' added Paul. 'Have you noticed that you're a few sheep short, Pat? One of our lads diverted through Tarrant Maundle last week.'

They all laughed and helped themselves to what was on offer before seeking a cosy, intimate alcove away from the general hubbub. There, Pat continued the theme. 'Do you mind about having to deliver food because other men have gone on strike? I would.'

'We're not supposed to think that deeply,' Paul said in breezy tones. 'Theirs is not to reason why: theirs is just to do and die – or words to that effect.'

'But it's not fair, is it?' she insisted, munching a salmon patty. 'Why should you do their job for them? You don't ask them to do yours.'

'Yes, we did,' Jeremy pointed out quietly. 'We're the professionals, but we expected them to pick up guns and help us out with something too big for us over a period of six years.'

'That was different,' she persisted. 'We *all* did our bit because it was that or Hitler in charge. A strike is for their benefit only and others have to go short until they get what they want. And the army has to fill in for them. *You* can't go on strike.'

'We can,' said Paul, 'but it's called mutiny.'

'And you can be shot for it,' Vesta put in. 'As Pat says, it's not fair. The lorry drivers are causing a lot of misery and will end up getting rewarded for doing so while you do the job for them. If a regiment mutinied in the middle of a battle, transport men wouldn't step in and finish it off on their behalf. Not only would the battle be lost, the troops would be put against a wall and shot for causing it to be lost.'

The two men looked at each other and laughed. 'We have a pair of firebrands here,' Jeremy concluded, and Paul added, 'We also have two ladies who weaken at the knees at the sight of brave fellows in scarlet jackets.'

'No, we don't,' Vesta and Pat chorused together.

'Shame! There we were thinking we had you eating out of our hands,' said Jeremy.

Vesta sobered. 'Not us, Jerry. We've tried that and decided it's a fool's game.'

The sharpness of her tone banished the jovial mood of the moment and Paul changed the subject swiftly. 'Have you finished painting *The Old Mill* yet?'

Knowing she had spoken without thought, Vesta answered with a little more warmth. 'Finally. It took longer than I expected for a reasonably easy subject.'

'How does it look?'

'Like an old mill.'

'Good. That means the wealthy old lunatic will pay you.'

Vesta was forced to smile. Paul was adept at countering her bad humour. 'Please don't repeat every word I say. I only called him a lunatic because he rhapsodized over the mill as if it were the eighth wonder of the world. He's a very distinguished silk.'

'Then he *is* a lunatic,' avowed Jeremy through a mouthful of pigeon pie. 'One of my great-uncles was a silk, and a madder fellow I've never come across.'

'He probably says the same of you,' put in Pat slyly.

'Guard, arrest this woman!' cried the victim of her jibe. 'Not only is she a dyed-in-the-wool Tory, she's rude, to boot.'

A lighter mood restored, the four finished their refreshments in the comparative solitude of the alcove, then Vesta and Pat went to the room set aside for ladies and applied fresh lipstick.

'You were a bit rough on the boys, weren't you?' said Pat to Vesta's image in the mirror.

She turned to her friend. 'What do you mean?'

'All that about a fool's game. They were only having fun.'

Vesta resumed tidying her hair. 'So was I.'

'Oh no, you weren't! If Brad's getting to you so much why don't you go out there to him?'

'Why don't you go to Scotland?' she flashed back.

Pat took a moment to reply. 'I've been told to look elsewhere because I'm no longer wanted. Each time Brad writes he asks you to join him. That's the difference.'

Vesta put down her comb and gazed at their reflections: a brunette with gorgeous eyes and a curvaceous figure, wearing a strapless red shot-taffeta dress with a matching stole; and a slender girl with a cap of shining light-brown hair, in a chiffon gown of misty-green which added to her air of dreaminess. They were in their mid-twenties, wealthy and vital. Why were they wasting their youth on a tortured pilot and a news-hungry war correspondent? Life was too short. They were of a generation which knew that all too well.

'Jerry's invited me to his people's place for the weekend.'

Vesta came from her thoughts. 'Then go.'

'They're awfully posh.' Pat sounded doubtful.

'So are you.' On impulse Vesta hugged her. 'Love's so damned painful, let's have fun for a change, shall we?'

'What about the boys?' asked Pat, still doubtful.

'What about them?'

'Jerry's getting a bit serious, and Paul's in love with you.'

'That's their lookout,' she declared vigorously. 'Makes a change to turn the tables, doesn't it? Come on, let's give 'em what for.'

They emerged to find organized uproar. Paul came up to them looking rather concerned, and spoke above the babble. 'While we've been dancing the night away, it's been snowing outside. And I *mean* snowing. There's a blizzard in progress.' He reached out and lifted a curtain from a window. 'Look.'

'Heavens!' said Pat in dismay. 'We can't drive in that.'

'Jerry's making arrangements to put you up here for the

night. Everyone's doing it. If you don't object to sharing, we'll put his bed in my room, which is the better of our quarters, and I'll bunk down with him.' He grinned. 'You'll both be perfectly chaperoned. A dozen or more ladies are having to accept our hospitality. Some who have only a short distance to go are braving it, but we'll have tanks standing by to pull them out if they get stuck in a drift.'

'These are the only clothes we have,' Vesta pointed out. 'Everything else is in the hotel room in Salisbury.'

At that point they were momentarily separated from him by several people dressed for departure, who pushed past in eagerness to be on their way. Then Paul reached them again to say that pairs of pyjamas would be put at their disposal by himself and Jeremy, and toilet articles would be supplied from Mess stocks. By the time Jeremy returned having organized the shifting and making up of the beds, everyone remaining in the Mess had begun to relax and regard the situation in a more adventurous light. The orchestra resumed its programme of dance music, and Jeremy persuaded Pat to carry on where they had left off.

By unspoken consent Vesta and Paul found two chairs in a corner of the less crowded room, and he asked a steward to bring them coffee at her request. While they were waiting for it, Paul smiled at her. 'Just my luck! When I finally get you to spend a night in my room, I'm sleeping with Jerry.'

She smiled back. 'You've done worse in the desert.'

'And elsewhere.' He leaned back in his chair. 'As I remember it, you slept in a truck guarded by two stalwarts on the sand beneath it.'

Her mind travelled there immediately. The elegant surroundings faded to be replaced by visions of herself huddled in blankets, staring from the back of her wheeled bedroom at the unforgettable vision of a tank battle by night. Flashes of light as guns fired, great flares of it as tanks exploded and burned, rumbles and thuds that suggested the splitting of the earth. She had cried as she watched, her bravado melting away. Then Brad had climbed into the truck and . . .

'A penny for them?'

A cup of coffee was on the table beside her, and Paul was studying her intently. She gazed at him, still under the spell of that memory.

'I should know better than to dwell on that subject. It always takes you away from me,' he said. 'He still affects you, doesn't he?'

She drank her coffee. Paul then asked, 'Now the old mill is finished, what's the next project?'

'I don't know,' she admitted. 'After the first rush of commissions everything appears to have quietened down. I suppose life has continued to be rather more earnest than we all thought it would be, and art is considered too frivolous for these dreary times.'

'All the more reason for something beautiful to cheer us up.'

'Like the old mill?'

He grinned. 'Well, perhaps not that.'

The orchestra was playing a dreamy waltz tune, and a few couples were still dancing slowly beneath low lights. The atmosphere was conducive to giving confidences, and this man with her was full of understanding. Vesta spoke impulsively. 'My work isn't inspired any more. It's good but lacking emotion.'

'How emotional can you get over an old mill?' he suggested gently.

'The person who commissioned it can.'

'He's not an artist, just a sentimental old buffer.' After watching her expression for a moment or two, he asked, 'Did inspiration vanish with Brad Holland?'

Now they had gone this far in the conversation Vesta was committed to finishing what she had begun. 'I don't know, Paul. I honestly don't know. I had it before he came on the scene. I had it until a month or so ago. I think . . . Perhaps all these revelations about Daddy and David that seem to have affected everyone I love have killed it. While I'm being so emotional about that I've none left for art. Who knows?'

'I'm sorry. I was responsible for starting it all off.'

'We'd have heard it from that wretched man Leo Roberts anyway. Don't blame yourself.'

He took her hand and began to play with her fingers. 'Would you rather not have known about it?'

'Of course not,' she said swiftly. 'Apart from awful guilt over the way we took what they said at face value, it has made us appreciate them even more ... except that Daddy's no longer here for us to show it, and David's wrestling with a problem which has driven him away from everyone who wants to help him.' She looked at Paul with something akin to confusion. 'The happy ever after isn't what we all imagined it would be, is it?'

'It never is.' After a moment he said, 'You know I'm in love with you.'

Vesta nodded. 'I guessed, but hoped you weren't.'

He took in the import of that comment, gazing at her with frank disappointment. 'Am I to take it that I don't stand the slightest chance?'

'I don't know, Paul. During the war we were caught up in a tumult which made decisions for us, took over our whole lives. Now it's ended I seem to be uncertain of *everything*. It's not like me to sway like a grass in the wind. I've always been so determined.'

'I had the impression you still were.'

'You're wrong.' It all came out in a flood then. 'I've no idea what direction to take with my career, which probably accounts for my lack of satisfaction with all I've done recently. I feel I should do something to help David, but what? He's taken himself off to Scotland for two years. I can't very well chase him up there when he went to get away from us all, can I? My best and dearest friend is heartbroken because of him, which is another reason why I should try to get to the bottom of it all. Yet I do nothing. I'm ... I'm not even sure of my feelings for Brad. Our plans all went wrong ... and he's been away for so long. I don't know when he intends to return. Or how I'll react when he does. See what I meant about the happy ever after not being what we imagined?'

'I know only too well what you meant,' was his gentle comment. 'My peaceful spell as a lecturer on Salisbury Plain is coming to an end. I've been posted to Germany as head of a bomb-disposal team. The industrial cities are slowly being cleared for rebuilding, but it's a mammoth and unenviable task. Bodies lie unrecovered even now beneath the devastation, and rescuers are being killed when they disturb bombs beneath the debris. It'll be our job to defuse them.'

Vesta was filled with alarm. 'But it's so dangerous! Isn't

there some other way? If the cities are no more than ruins anyway, it won't matter if the bombs are detonated from a distance.'

'It will, I'm afraid. People are living in the ruins – thousands of them. They've nowhere else to go.' As she continued to regard him with dismay, he added, 'Maybe it's as well the posting has come up now. Another six months and I might have managed to persuade you to ditch Brad and marry me. What a disaster that would have been! Adoring bride terrified her husband might come home to her in several pieces.'

'Don't joke about it, Paul,' she begged, surprisingly near to tears.

'Sorry. That was in terribly bad taste.'

She swallowed some coffee hastily before saying, 'I'll miss you dreadfully.'

'Will you? That's an encouraging sign.'

'I've enjoyed our friendship.'

'Took the edge off missing you-know-who?' After a pause he asked, 'May I write to you?'

'Yes, please.'

He got to his feet and pulled her up beside him. 'As my hopes have been thwarted and I have to sleep with Jerry instead, I can at least have a good cuddle before bedtime. Let's snuggle up and dance.'

Vesta went into his arms, finding unexpected comfort from his nearness. His news completed the uncertainties she was facing and she wanted to enjoy him while he was still there. His grim joke about returning in pieces had affected her deeply. The fighting was supposed to be over, yet his life would be at risk once more. So much for peace.

CHAPTER SEVEN

THE snow continued. Britain was gripped by severe temperatures. Roads became impassable; whole areas were completely cut off. The transport strike had left business and houses short of coal, which now led to widespread power cuts. Those marooned beyond impenetrable frozen drifts suffered long evenings by candlelight in addition to lack of warmth and sufficient food. Some of the worst-hit villages spread messages for help on the snow in the hope of their being seen by aircraft. Troops who had been driving lorries to deliver vital supplies now lent their efforts to clearing roads under blizzard conditions in attempts to reach isolated communities. As fast as contact was made fresh falls of snow covered the narrow access once more. The freeze of February 1947 was one of the worst on meteorological record.

The villages of Tarrant Maundle and Tarrant Royal lay beneath deep snow, cut off from Greater Tarrant, which was served by the railway although only a limited service was maintained. Farmers and their employees toiled to open a route to the little market town but the drifts were frozen hard and successive snowfalls hampered their efforts. Food supplies ran dangerously low, animals perished from sub-zero temperatures or from being buried in great mounds piled up by high winds, and power cuts added to farmers' problems.

Tessa Chandler was having a hard time alone in her 'Outback' farmhouse. Bill was attending an international conference in Paris, and Pat was still stranded with Vesta. Even telephone contact had been broken when lines came down in a heavy snowstorm. Until then Marion had kept in daily touch with Tessa, and with the girls in Salisbury. Once the telephone went dead Marion felt a renewed sensation of loneliness in her mansion on a hill overlooking a scene more nearly resembling Siberia than Dorset.

Jack Marshall had struggled up from the village at the start of the freeze, but soon gave up trying to negotiate a path cleared one day then obliterated overnight. His main concerns were the cattle and poultry. The rest of the estate had to be left until the thaw brought waterlogged fields and mud, mud, mud. Marion had little work to do in her office but, as Mrs Parfitt could not get up from the village to clean, she took on the polishing and dusting. Even so, time hung heavily, especially during evenings when reading by candlelight soon made her eyes ache. With telephone contact denied her it was easy to resume brooding on her future. Running the Sheridan estate was no longer her contribution to the war effort. Although still under regulations from the Ministry in the bid to grow enough food to bolster the nation's supplies, the sense of doing a vital job had faded. Jack was forever urging her to consider new machinery and up-to-date methods, both of which meant greater financial investment.

Marion was worried about costs. Although the estate had prospered throughout the war there had been some heavy demands on profits recently. Chris had set aside a very large sum to help restore the church, and it was practically all gone. Work on the ancient building had cost more than expected at the outset. The Rector had been apologetic, but had nevertheless taken full advantage of Chris's generosity. Annual donations to the cottage hospital, the farm workers' benevolent fund, the cricket club (in memory of Rex, one-time stalwart of the team), and the local British Legion branch had had to be increased to cover rising prices, and this was echoed in minor things like prizes for the gymkhana, swings and roundabouts for the summer fête and the Christmas party for all village children, which the Sheridans had always paid for.

Wages had risen, too, but Marion had hesitated over increasing rent on employees' cottages. Jack declared it to be a necessity, but she argued that the men would demand another pay rise to cover it and they would be no better off. It would have to come, of course, but not while the general situation was so grim. Chris had earned a large salary as an international interpreter before the war; rather less during it for doing much, much more. That was no longer swelling the bank balance. Marion could only hope this present severe weather would soon end and be compensated for by a perfect summer which would ripen crops and produce a record yield.

On yet another evening of candlelight and basic fare from dwindling stocks Marion felt pessimistic as she sat close to a fire that was smaller than usual to make the pile of logs last. What if David had abandoned home and family for ever? Would she still be burdened by responsibilities when she was old and tired? Sighing, she reflected that if she had seduced *anyone* rather than Chris Sheridan she would probably now be surrounded by children and grandchildren like other women in the village. They would all look after her in later life.

Into her melancholy mood came an astonishing sound. The doorbell rang. Startled and curiously alarmed, Marion left the fireside to go into the hall. The house was inaccessible – had been for days. How *could* there be someone outside demanding entry? The bell rang again, making her heartbeat quicken. There was something sinister about a visitor at nine p.m. on the doorstep of a place which had been cut off from the village for ten days. Marion shivered as she stared at the front door just visible by the light of a single candle, remembering ghost stories Bill Chandler used to tell on long-ago Christmas Eves. It was not possible for anyone to be there, yet something was making that bell ring once again.

Robson appeared at last. He had certainly expected no further duties that night and seemed as startled as she, but his professional manner remained unshaken. 'It would appear that a way has been forced through from the village, m'lady, although it is snowing hard still. Cook will be glad. The larder is almost empty.'

With his presence to help stifle her dread fancies Marion followed him to the door and watched him draw back the bolts. Her heart leapt with alarm at the sight of a large figure in white with huge eyes just discernible in the driving snow. Then a white-gloved hand pushed up snow-goggles to reveal a face she recognized.

'*Major Roberts!*'

Leo smiled. 'I shall make something of a mess of your polished parquet, I'm afraid, but there's no help for it in weather like this. When you see what I have with me you'll think it a small price to pay, I hope.'

In a state of disbelief Marion watched her visitor stamp snow from his ski-boots before stepping inside and shrugging off a huge, heavy haversack. She was slow to accept what she saw, but Robson closed the door on the squall of snowflakes and waited, visibly unmoved, for Leo to take off his fur-lined, hooded white suit.

Trying to adopt a similar manner Marion asked, in the tradition of good hostesses, 'Have you eaten? Cook can do soup and sandwiches.'

Busy with zip-fasteners and toggles, Leo shook his head. 'I dined at the Plough and Wheatsheaf in Greater Tarrant. A stiff whisky would be welcome.' He glanced up at her. 'And a bed for the night, if possible.' He indicated the haversack gleaming wetly as its covering of snow melted in the comparative warmth. 'What's in there should keep you going for a while.'

Beneath the padded suit he was wearing grey flannels and a polo-necked Norwegian pullover. In these, and thick cream socks, he shouldered the weighty haversack to follow Robson, who was bearing the wet clothes to the kitchen. Leo flashed a smile at Marion, who was still standing in flickering candlelight unable to believe this was happening. 'As soon as I've handed all this to Cook I'll be back for my whisky.'

Robson held the suit and ski-boots as if they were offensive, the gift of food in no way alleviating his deep disapproval of this unconventional visit. They vanished behind the baize door leaving only a puddle on the floor to prove that this man had caught them unawares a second time. Marion returned to the sitting room and piled logs on the fire from the neat pile beside the hearth, no longer caring how many she used, and lit more candles to stand around the room.

Melancholy thoughts had fled on recognition of that face. Leo Roberts had a habit of bursting on to the mundane scene of her life and turning it upside down. Her earlier fancy of being surrounded by children and grandchildren had been kicked aside by his arriving, having apparently achieved the impossible to reach her. There was nothing she could do about her appearance. He had already seen her so a swift change of clothes would look too obvious, but she wished she was wearing something more attractive than her old black wool skirt and a moss-green jumper. In the morning she would choose carefully from her wardrobe.

He came in offering an apology for his own appearance. 'I weighed up the merits of smart clothes against those of a leg of lamb and tinned vegetables. The food tipped the scales.'

As he stood before her, solid and rosy-cheeked, Marion was more than glad to see him again. He had sent a card at Christmas with a message concerning the probable commencement of work on the Hall. She had then thought no more of his request to call in when he was in the area, dismissing it as one of those polite things people say, not to be taken seriously.

'I can't believe you just happened to be passing,' she said now, still finding it difficult to accept that he was really there.

He grinned. 'I told you I was very experienced in moving around in arctic conditions. We have something approaching those at present.' He indicated the crystal decanters. 'May I?' She nodded, and he poured himself a generous whisky before turning back to her. 'I guessed you might be cut off and short of supplies so I tried to call you to find out the situation. When I was told the telephone lines were down I knew it must be pretty bad. As it proved impossible for me to get around to the houses on my list I took French leave, got out my Norwegian gear, collected some things together and came along with a peace offering.'

'A peace offering? You surely didn't imagine I would be put out by your visit?'

'My last was pretty catastrophic.' He sipped his whisky. 'I rang your son to apologize. He was very decent about it. Said he'd been home to put the record straight. I hope it didn't worsen relations between you both.'

Marion did not want to dwell on that subject. She reoccupied her chair beside a fire now blazing merrily and looked up at him to ask, 'Just how did you manage to get here?'

He accepted her rules and sat in a matching chair in relaxed fashion with his whisky, the flames playing on his flushed face as he explained. 'I hung around Waterloo Station until a train coming in this direction was announced. I hoped to get a branch connection to Greater Tarrant from Bournemouth, but the track is apparently blocked west of Wimborne. I detrained there, put on skis and followed my compass.' He gave a faint smile. 'I'm used to carrying my own supplies, but it seemed senseless to eat what I'd carted across country, when food was available in the Plough and Wheatsheaf. It was for you, anyway. After a reasonably decent meal I headed for Tarrant Royal and was soon thankful that I'd brought one or two other useful items with me. Where clearing has been attempted solid walls of ice have formed. They'll be a long time melting even when the thaw sets in.' He sipped more of his whisky. 'Norwegians accept the power of snow by donning skis or snowshoes and leaving it alone, but weather like we're presently seeing happens so rarely in this country we attack it with everything we have and often make the situation worse. They learn as children in Norway that the elements can't be defeated; they must adjust to them. I suppose that maxim has stayed with me and I used it to get here.'

Marion was deeply touched. 'Why all that effort?'

He leaned forward with his arms along his knees and spoke surprisingly diffidently, although he still held her gaze. 'I wanted very much to come here again. I started several letters then tore them up. Although you had agreed that I could call if I was passing through, I wasn't entirely sure you'd welcome another visit from someone who had caused you such distress. When telephoning proved impossible I found the perfect excuse to come and test the water.'

'Test the water! How foolish of you,' she said softly.

'You didn't acknowledge my Christmas card.'

'There was no address in it. How could I?'

He sighed with comprehension. 'Thank heaven for arctic weather! I might never otherwise have plucked up the necessary courage to come.'

'I think you would have,' she countered. 'You strike me as a person prepared to tackle any obstacles in his path.'

Marion was awoken, as usual, by Robson entering with her morning tea. He switched on the twin bedside lights after placing the tray on the swivel table, which he wheeled within her reach. 'Good morning, m'lady. Snow has stopped falling and the sky is clear, but it is very cold. Will you take breakfast here or downstairs with the . . . um . . . gentleman who arrived last night?'

Marion's spirits rose dramatically on being reminded of Leo's presence. She replied swiftly. 'You may serve breakfast for Major Roberts and myself in the dining room at eight-thirty. If you've not already lit a fire then please do so now so that it will be reasonably warm by the time we come down. Have you taken our guest some tea?'

'Yes, madam. The gentleman was very soundly asleep so I left the tray and retired.'

'He is probably exhausted after skiing from Greater Tarrant with that heavy pack. Tell Cook to make breakfast rather more substantial than usual.' Marion smiled from her pillow. 'About the same quantity she prepares when David is here.'

'I believe Cook has already taken into account the size of the gentleman's appetite. Are there any other instructions, madam?'

'Not for the moment, thank you, Robson.'

The minute Robson left the room Marion sat up, poured herself some tea and mapped out every minute of the next three-quarters of an hour. She meant to go down for breakfast looking as good as she could within that time. Leo had not indicated how much French leave he could risk taking, so she wanted to make the most of his unexpected visit. His arrival had had a profound effect on her. It was a heady feeling; one she had not known for a very long time. During the first war of her lifetime Tessa's brother, Mike, had offered fleeting devotion while Chris wandered in the realms of total amnesia. But she had been rearing Chris's son, and Mike was flying alongside Rex with a life expectancy numbered in days. Youth had called to desperate youth for a short while, until Mike joined those daredevils who had gone before him. When Marion now saw pictures of him and Rex together, laughing and handsome, hiding their fear behind hi-jinks, she found it difficult to believe the young Australian had ever touched her heart.

Leo had certainly done so with his extravagant gesture. It was still a source of wonder that he could have made it for her; that he should be so concerned for her welfare he would embark on a quixotic journey to Tarrant Hall after just one meeting. Perhaps she should regard it with cynicism. What, after all, could be his true purpose in coming? Maybe she should keep him at arm's length, be suspicious of his motives? Yet, although she lacked the worldliness of Chris and his two children, she sensed that this man's interest in her was sincere, astonishing though it seemed. They had talked until almost midnight, discovering a mutual interest in detective novels, rose cultivation, and Viennese operetta. What had seemed plebeian against Chris's passion for fine art, the great masters of music, and literature by the world's revered writers and philosophers, now became perfectly acceptable when shared by a man who had worked with her intellectual husband. It had been so enjoyable to talk of Lehár, Dorothy Sayers and rose fertilizers without feeling gauche or boring.

Shortly before eight-thirty Marion flung back her curtains on to a scene of frozen beauty. Dawn had broken clear and bright with a silver-blue sky promising sunshine. She was pleased with her efforts. Newly washed hair fluffed around her face, which looked surprisingly youthful today, enhanced, no doubt, by the dress of strawberry-pink wool woven with angora to soften both colour and line. It had been new at Christmas, worn only then. Marion had not before realized how well it suited her.

On her way to breakfast she halted, then turned back to knock on the door of the guest room. Robson had said Leo was soundly asleep forty-five minutes ago. She should check that he was up and ready to eat. Cook would have to be halted, if not. She knocked a second time. No response. After a slight hesitation she turned the handle and went in. The bed was empty. Across it were strewn pyjamas and a dressing-gown provided for impromptu guests. The tea tray had been used. There were two spoons in the saucer. Marion smiled. She had told David off numerous times, but all to no avail. He invariably read in bed and found it easier to add sugar and stir with the same spoon. A magazine beside the dressing-gown told her Leo had done the same.

'Am I keeping you from your breakfast?' Marion turned almost guiltily to find Leo in the doorway leading from the bathroom. He was holding a folded tissue against his cheek. 'I've cut myself, I'm afraid, and nothing will stop the bleeding.'

He was dressed as last night and looked just as full of

vigour. The faint whiff of shaving-soap and hair-cream reminded Marion how long it had been since there had been a
man in the house. She moved forward instinctively. 'There
should be some plasters in the cabinet.'

The borrowed razor lay in the washbasin half-filled with
reddened soapy water. Towels were draped over the side of
the bath; the tiled floor was remarkably wet. A typical man,
she thought as she found a tin of adhesive plasters and took
one out.

'Sorry about the mess,' he said, offering his cheek for her
ministrations. 'Haven't had time to clean it up yet.'

Dabbing the tiny cut with a dry tissue, then touching the
spot with an iodine stick, Marion covered it with the plaster,
saying in a teasing manner, 'My visions of the courageous
secret agent facing every danger and hardship imaginable
haven't allowed for scenes like this.'

He looked down at her, the plaster firmly placed, and shook
his head. 'I told you once before we were not impossible
heroes, just people doing a job our qualifications made us
more suitable for than others. We caught colds, cut ourselves
shaving, and got chilblains on toes and fingers like anyone
else.' He took a breath. 'You come in looking, as Americans
say, like a million dollars and calmly ignore the blood-stained
shambles in here to sort me out. How do you do it?'

She laughed, conscious of his nearness. 'Don't be foolish.
I've had a husband and a son. Razor cuts were part of my life
when they were here . . . and so were bathrooms in this state.
The girl who came in to clean had to clear up the mess, of
course.'

'She can't get here because of the snow, so who does the
cleaning now?'

'Robson and I do it between us.'

'You'll not do this room,' he said firmly. 'It's my
responsibility.'

'Nonsense! You're my guest.'

'I've had a wife,' he echoed her. 'Helping out was a part of
my life in Norway. I know how to clean up a room.' He gave
his attractive smile. 'You might as well make me work for my
keep while I'm here.'

Sudden awkwardness made her say, 'There's a spot of blood

on your pullover. I'll lend you one of David's.' She made her escape past him, adding, 'Breakfast will be ready. We'd better go down as soon as I've fetched one from his room.'

They sat at the table to eat porridge while Cook prepared scrambled eggs, bacon and tinned tomatoes brought by Leo. Recovered from the moment of uncertainty in the guest bathroom, Marion enjoyed his company for a meal usually eaten alone and sparingly. Today she was hungry and ready for a plate of eggs and bacon.

'However did you manage to bring eggs in that haversack without crushing them?' she asked.

'It's filled with pouches to take containers,' he told her, helping himself to more porridge from the chafing dish. 'We carried thermos packs more often than not. It was essential to have hot food to keep us going in low temperatures. When we went on mountain rescues we carried supplies for people suffering from hypothermia and starvation – special medical preparations which fitted exactly into the pouches. It's surprising how much it's possible to cram into one of those haversacks.'

'What about the weight?'

He shrugged. 'We got used to it.'

Marion watched him thoughtfully for a moment or two. In David's fawn cable-patterned sweater he looked a familiar stranger; one about whom she wanted to know more. 'Are you still waiting for fate to decide your future for you?'

When he glanced up she was struck by the intensity of his gaze. 'No, I know what I want it to be, but someone other than fate will have to make the decision.' She waited for him to elaborate but, instead, he touched on something quite different. 'How do things stand between you and your son at the moment? On my first visit you hinted at some change of mind on his part concerning leaving the RAF. Not enough excitement here after the dangers he faced during the war years, possibly. Has he discussed it with you since then?'

'He's only been here once, and that was on the day you left.'

'Because of my unforgivable foot-putting-in?'

Marion shrugged. 'The truth would have come out eventually.'

'Better to have come from him than a stranger. Did he give any indication why he hadn't said anything about it before?'

She did not resent his questioning. He was entitled to know the outcome of his unwitting revelation. 'He was unwilling to burden me with guilt.'

'Why guilt?' came the sharp question.

'Because I never suspected Chris of doing more than his normal job at the Ministry; because I had so little understanding of what my husband and children were going through while I was safely here concerning myself with nothing of comparable complexity and danger. He feels I failed them all . . . and continues to do so each time I suggest that war memories should be set aside to concentrate on the future.'

Leo frowned. 'A somewhat ruthless judgement.'

Robson brought bacon, eggs and tomatoes along with toasted slices of Cook's delicious home baked bread and another pot of coffee. As he left, Marion was driven to defend her son to the man who had brought these supplies on his back across the snow.

'David has always been ruthless on *himself*. From boyhood he tried to live up to the legend of "Sherry" Sheridan and made himself work harder than anyone else because of it. During the Battle of Britain his gun jammed one day so that it continued to fire until the ammunition was exhausted. He shot down one of his own squadron who crossed his path, and was then psychologically unable to take an aircraft off the ground for a long time because he felt he had failed his famous uncle. He blamed himself for a tragic accident not uncommon in aerial dog-fights. Then he was sent to Singapore.'

Now she had begun Marion found herself telling Leo everything: David's marriage to a Chinese, his escape in the last aircraft when its pilot was killed several feet from it, the months during which he was posted missing, presumed killed, his return, maimed and white-haired, his determination to fly again, his reunion with the father he had formerly scorned, his love for the girl he had known all his life, his plan to leave the RAF and start a new marriage with her at Tarrant Hall.

'He went back to Singapore last year to trace his wife, and returned bitter, aggressive and alienated from us all. Poor Pat was told to find someone else to marry, I was ridiculed as a country bumpkin with little understanding of life, and Bill Chandler was more or less advised to go to the devil when he tried to help. None of us heard another word from him until your visit obliged him to come and tell me about Chris's death.'

'How did he behave on that occasion?'

'Less aggressive but equally censorious. He'd asked for a two-year posting to Scotland and informed us all he was bowing out of our lives for that period at least. His assessment of me was right. I have no idea how to approach him . . . no understanding of how to help.'

Leo paused in the midst of helping himself to breakfast, servers poised over silver dishes. 'Has the girl who loves him?' At the shake of her head, he added, 'If neither Pat Chandler nor her eminent neurologist father can get through to him, why are you giving yourself such a rough time?'

Taken aback by his forceful tone, Marion said, 'As his mother I should understand him better than anyone.'

'Not true,' came his retort as he replaced lids on the serving dishes. 'A mother understands the boy, a lover understands the man, a specialist understands the patient. All you can be expected to do is continue to love and stand by him. Pat must decide whether or not she is willing to do the same, even if it takes several years. I suspect David feels once more that he has failed in some way. Failed *somebody*. If he rejects medical advice he'll have to find release from it another way.'

Still surprised by his reaction, but not unpleasantly so, Marion sighed. 'Poor boy.'

'He's *not* a boy,' Leo said with gentle firmness. 'He's a man who has suffered more than the human body can cope with, like millions of others. We're none of us the same as we were in 1939. Thank God for people like you who remind us of peace and sanity.'

His smile washed over her to ease the ache brought about whenever thinking of David. 'The lady of the manor who merely fills in forms and attends village functions?'

'The person who has wrongly been made to feel of little consequence beside her talented family,' he corrected with warmth. 'Hasn't it ever occurred to you that your children have aspects of you in them, too? If they hadn't Vesta would now be occupying a garret in London or Paris, not painting here in a place she loves because of what *you* have made it, and David would never have contemplated abandoning flying to take over an estate you have maintained so magnificently all those years.' He studied her shrewdly. 'Sir Christopher might well have given them talent and tenacity, but you've provided the security everyone needs to be confident enough to tackle life. They owe you a great deal.'

Covered with curious embarrassment Marion laughed it off. 'What a serious conversation for breakfast time . . . and yours is growing cold on the plate.'

He turned his attention to it but silence only reigned a short time. 'Did David trace his wife in Singapore?'

'She died after ill-treatment by Japanese soldiers.'

'Were there any children?'

'No, thank God. They hadn't been married long when Singapore fell.'

'And he didn't manage to get her on one of the boats?'

'He said she wouldn't go without her family.' She hesitated before adding, 'He arrived here seven months later hating her.'

'Maimed and white-haired, you said.'

She nodded. 'He refused to tell us what he had done during that period except that he had been lost in the jungle. I suppose he was attacked by animals of some kind.'

'Yes.' He cast her a strange look as he agreed. 'Perhaps I can find out.'

'How could you?'

'I've kept in touch with my SOE colleagues. We had people in the Far East, you know.'

'It all happened so long ago there seems little point now, especially as David prefers not to remember it.'

'He remembers it all right!' Leo said forcefully. 'Which is why he has never spoken about it. I've a hunch it has something to do with his present trouble. He was happy, in love and planning his future until he went back to Singapore. If the Chinese wife he hated is dead, it's something else connected with that terrible period in his life which is now haunting him. I'll do my utmost to find out what I can. Then we'll tell Colonel Chandler who might be able to help him.'

Marion gazed at him in a state of inexplicable confusion. 'Why should you bother to do all that for someone you have never met?'

'Because you've been grappling with life on your own for too long. It's time somebody gave you a helping hand.'

Vesta and Pat travelled home by rail as soon as the road from Greater Tarrant became passable. They had gone away for a weekend and stayed almost three weeks. What had started as something of an adventure had turned into a difficult situation for them both. After the first night in Paul's room they had been accommodated in the quarters of a married officer, as had others stranded there. When the army bulldozed its way through to Salisbury the girls were pressed to stay with their hosts until the thaw came. Not averse to this scheme because long days in a hotel room promised boredom, they soon found themselves regarded as the steady girlfriends of Paul and Jeremy who were invited to call whenever they were off duty. The two lieutenants had been delighted. Vesta and Pat found their host's assumption placed them in a role they did not occupy.

They could have stayed longer on the military camp, but it took only basic intelligence to work out that a complete thaw would bring floods to produce further difficult travelling conditions. Pat was anxious to return to the farm to help her mother, and Vesta had other reasons for getting away. So they set out at the first opportunity, prepared to trudge the last few miles, if necessary. A corporal drove them to Salisbury station through roads bordered by banks of snow and running with thaw water. Jeremy was on duty; Paul was packing for his delayed flight to Germany where, it appeared, the severe weather was killing thousands of under-nourished people living in the ruins of their cities: a grim prospect awaiting the young engineer being sent to defuse unstable bombs.

In their thick coats and borrowed boots, the two friends sat watching the wintry scene from their carriage, lost in thought. Vesta was leaden-hearted. Saying goodbye to Paul last night had been a shock. Having spent so much time in his company over the past two weeks, the prospect of not seeing him at all from then on had affected her badly. She believed it was due more to the knowledge of what he would be doing in the weeks to come than to anything else. But that was before he had taken her into his arms. He had kissed her before, of course, and quite comprehensively, but he had last night embarked on an overture to full-blooded passion with every intention of reaching the finale. Vesta had been caught unprepared. He had always before accepted her limits. This time he overcame her protests with physical insistence, betraying a tougher aspect of himself than she had encountered before and, heaven help her, she had responded with instinctive delight. Only at the last minute had she struggled free and straightened her clothes, leaving him breathless and painfully aroused.

'Someone could have come in,' she explained, equally breathless, from the centre of the room.

'For God's sake, why d'you imagine they left us alone in here,' he panted, buttoning his trousers with difficulty. 'They think we want a lovers' farewell.'

'*On a settee in their spare room?*'

'You wouldn't have cared where it was if you'd closed your eyes and pretended it was *him*,' he responded savagely.

The following minutes had been difficult and upsetting, while Paul tried to wind down and Vesta grew miserably aware that she had encouraged him to reach that state. They could not join the family for the rest of the evening, neither could Paul leave without looking just as much a fool and creating speculation. So they had pretended to read books from the shelves in the room, and emerged an hour later for coffee with their tactful, understanding hosts. Paul had departed looking strained and angry; Vesta had spent a miserable night. All she could think of as the wheels clicked over the tracks leading homeward was Paul being blown apart by a bomb possibly dropped several years ago by one of her brother's friends.

When they had changed to the little train bound for Greater Tarrant there was immediate evidence of more severe conditions even than around Salisbury. 'I'm glad we borrowed these boots, aren't you?' murmured Pat, surveying it after wiping from the window the cloud created by her warm breath on the cold glass.

'Mmm.' Vesta gazed moodily at the white countryside where sheep gathered in clearings strewn with hay, lambs seeking warmth from ewes' bodies. It looked so desolate all around them. Yet it could be so beautiful.

'Last night we went into Jerry's room after dinner and a few drinks. Very much forbidden under normal circumstances, of course,' Pat mused. 'We sneaked there when the others weren't looking. He *said* he wanted to show me something his grandfather, the earl, had sent him recently. Well, he did, but he must have had it some time because no one in his right mind would send something valuable through the post in these disrupted conditions, would they?'

Vesta turned her head towards Pat on the seat facing hers. They were alone in a compartment reeking of stale tobacco, dust and wet boots. It was unheated and the seats were lumpy. Pat was a sight to behold in the midst of dreariness. Her cheeks, rosy as ever, were enhanced by her red wool coat and soft cream scarf. No one would guess she was pining for a man who had promised to marry her then told her to forget it.

'What was it?'

'An ancient map of Salisbury Plain. Jerry likes things like that.'

'Did you ooh and ah appropriately?' asked Vesta without much interest.

'Didn't have much chance. He tried it on.'

'What, there in his room in the Mess?' she commented indignantly.

'There was nowhere else. It's too cold in a car, and you were occupying the spare room at the Thompsons' with Paul.'

'What did you do?'

'Smacked him round the chops. He took it very goodnaturedly. Said he guessed I would.' The train began to slow. 'Oh, we're coming in to Blandford. Still looks pretty grim, doesn't it?' She turned back to Vesta. 'It wasn't that I didn't want him to, I just didn't want it to happen *there*. When I go to his home for the weekend he'll try again. I'll probably let him then.'

Vesta was astonished. 'I thought you were in love with David!'

'I am. I suppose I always will be,' Pat replied calmly, 'but I'm tired of waiting around until he gets whatever's bothering him out of his system. He was in love with me, wanted to get married. But how many girls do you reckon *he's* done it with? Too many to count, I'd guess. He expected me to accept that, so why shouldn't he accept that he's not the only one for me, if he ever conquers his gremlins and comes home?' She leaned forward with a pleading expression as the train squealed to a halt at Blandford's empty platform. 'Vee, I'm twenty-seven. I was very fond of Dirk – thought I loved him – but I never gave him what he wanted. When David came back from the dead I realized why. I wouldn't give in to *him* because of that Chinese girl. Eventually I did, because he was so worked up about what he'd find when he got back to Singapore. Just once, Vee, that's all. Then he told me to find someone else. Well, I have. I don't love Jerry, but he's fun to be with and I'm not going to die an old maid with just the memory of two hours beneath a blanket in the empty wing of a house to look back on. I'm going to enjoy myself.'

'How do you know you will?' Vesta asked as several doors slammed behind departing passengers, and the train jerked forward. 'All that experience with girls has probably made David an expert. Like Brad,' she added hollowly. 'Other men might not be half as good.'

'Of course they will. They're all at it whenever they get a chance. You've no idea how many I had to fight off when they were stationed in the Hall.'

'You must have encouraged them,' was her tart observation. 'They never got as far as being fought off by me.'

'That's because you're so brisk and exude that touch-me-not air. I like men's company. It's simply that I was saving myself for David. There's no point now.'

Vesta was angry. 'Of course there is! Just because he's gone off into a world of his own, you don't have to turn into a *floosie*.'

'It's better than turning into a *nun*,' Pat declared equally heatedly. 'How long are you going to keep yourself for a man who has gone off into *his* private world? You don't think Brad's behaving himself, do you?'

'I'm not planning on giving myself to all and sundry under the guise of enjoying myself.'

'Jerry's not all and sundry. Neither is Paul. It wouldn't have cost you much to send him on his way with something to remember while he's risking his life.'

Vesta turned away to gaze from the window once more,

mouth tight, eyes stinging. Pat softened her tone. 'Things have changed, Vee. Traditionally men have played the field and been indulgently regarded as lads who *will* have their fun. The girls who provided that "fun" were dubbed outcasts of society, or fallen women. You and I were brought up to remain chaste until we were married. Heavens, look how poor Aunt Marion was treated when everyone realized Uncle Chris was being forced into a shotgun wedding. No one blamed *him* – apart from Roland, apparently, and old Dr Deacon. It was your mama who was condemned for what had happened. This war has changed everyone's outlook on the subject; and neither of us waited for marriage, did we? The big snag is that most women still want total dedication from their particular man, whereas men see their girls as just one part of their lives. That's the attitude I'm going to take from now on. Love shouldn't be so intense; it should be fun. You don't have to become a floosie to get some pleasure out of life. We're getting damn little waiting around for our lovers to return.' Her hand rested on Vesta's knee. 'Sheep, haymaking and darned hard work are all I have at the moment, and for the foreseeable future. The only way I can deal with the pain of loving David is to allow someone else to be fond of me. Jerry soothes my wounds, Vee.'

Vesta turned back to her friend, close to tears. 'I'm no longer certain I want Brad to return, yet I still couldn't give Paul what he wanted. I wish I had your commonsense attitude to life.'

Pat smiled, saying as she got to her feet, 'You wouldn't be a renowned artist if you had. You've always been a dreamer, Vee, but perhaps you should let a few of them go until you really know what you want. Come on, up you get and prepare to walk six miles if the bus isn't running.'

It was mid-afternoon before Vesta began the slippery climb to her house. The village bus was giving limited service, so she and Pat had bribed Bob Sandalwood to get out his taxi and attempt to take them as far as he could. Vesta had walked from the far side of Tarrant Royal because the going had been slow and he wanted to get back before darkness fell. Pat was taken on a little further towards Wattle Farm, but she would have to walk the last mile home. Although the thaw was a slow one the packed ice underfoot had water on its surface making it dangerous to negotiate, especially once she attacked the driveway to the Hall. So intent was she on keeping her feet it was a little while before she noticed curious tracks in the softening snow, which reminded her of tobogganing with David in their youth. She paused a moment as it struck her that she really meant pre-war. Why did she feel her youth was over? She was only twenty-seven.

Resuming the climb with her heavy overnight bag on her shoulder, Vesta thought of Pat's declaration in the train. Sheep, haymaking and darned hard work. Nothing more until David came to his senses. As for herself, there was the prospect of further commissions like *The Old Mill* which brought artistic frustration, accompanying her mother to village functions, and lying alone at night remembering how it had been in Italy during that final campaign. Stopping for breath again between the stark bare-branched chestnut trees, she wondered if she had been wrong not to go with Brad, but she truly had not wanted to visit Hiroshima with its horrific evidence of the ultimate weapon. Perhaps Brad had been entitled to change their plans and pursue that special commission, but he need not have taken others and moved on to the Philippines. Even if she chose to join him now, she had no idea where he was. His infrequent letters had ceased soon after she stopped replying to them. She trudged on.

Robson was delighted to see her and marvelled that she had managed to reach them just yet. 'We've been completely cut off for nigh on a fortnight, although Mr Marshall reached us by tractor for the first few days. The road's open again, is it, miss?'

'Only partially,' she said, pulling off the boots loaned to her by Jeremy who had wangled them from stores with a few smooth lies. 'I had to walk from Littleton Farm. It's still pretty bad through the village, although there are definite signs of a thaw.' Taking off her coat and scarf to give him, she said she could do with some tea and a sandwich because she had gone without lunch. 'I'll have it in my room, please.'

The old man was flustered. 'There's no fire in there, miss. I'm afraid we had no notice of your arrival and fuel has been

136

very short. I'll set to and start one immediately. Perhaps you'll take tea in the sitting room.'

Marion appeared at that point from the room in question. She looked amazingly smart, Vesta thought, almost as if she were on her way to attend the parish council annual tea which David always termed the village bun fight. There was a wide smile on her mother's face as she approached. 'I could scarcely believe it when I heard your voice, dear.' She embraced Vesta warmly. 'You must be tired and frozen after that dreadful journey. Come in by the fire.'

'I'd rather get out of these things first, Mummy,' she said. 'My feet are wet in spite of the boots, and I've worn this skirt with one or other of my jumpers for the past eighteen days. What I need more than anything are some tea and sandwiches, a hot bath and a complete change of clothes. Then I'll feel human again.'

Her mother took her arm and began walking to the stairs. 'I'm afraid there's no fire in your room, but you can use mine. Cook will provide tea and sandwiches, but the hot bath won't be possible, I'm afraid. You'll have to make do with a wash in my bathroom.' They started up the stairs. 'We've had to make the most stringent economies, but I expect you've had to do the same.'

'Not really,' she said, surprised by her mother's cheerfulness after incarceration alone for so long in difficult conditions. 'The army is a law unto itself. Soldiers are extremely resourceful. We were kept beautifully warm and fed. Oh lord, I suppose you're on starvation rations here,' she added in dismay. 'I brought some chocolate and biscuits from the NAAFI, but they won't go far.'

They reached the landing and headed for Marion's room. 'As a matter of fact we're doing rather well for food, dear. I had the most amazing visit one evening from Major Roberts.'

Vesta stopped, uncomprehending. 'Roberts? Not that idiot who spilled the beans about Daddy and David! How on earth did he get here?'

'He's an expert on moving around in arctic conditions. He came on skis.'

'Whatever for? Surely not to look at the house again?'

'To bring food. Having tried to telephone he guessed we were in dire straits.'

Vesta moved on, conscious of her cold, wet feet. 'What an odd thing to do. Still, I suppose he felt bad about his other visit. Are there any left?'

'Any what?' asked Marion as they entered her warm bedroom.

'Any of the goodies he brought?'

'You sound like a character in a detective story. "Spilt the beans" and "goodies".' Marion laughed. 'Your father would have forty fits.'

'No, he wouldn't. He'd be amused. Daddy was always more liberal minded than you.' Vesta dropped her bag and went to enjoy the warmth of the fire. 'The trains were unheated and took *ages*. If we hadn't used our combined charms on Bob Sandalwood we'd still be waiting for the bus. The poor sheep looked sorry for themselves. Has Aunt Tessa lost many lambs?'

'Quite a few. Fortunately, she and the shepherds took steps to get them down as soon as the snow began, but once the telephone lines went down I had no means of contact with her until Leo arrived.'

'Leo?'

'Major Roberts. He very kindly went across to see how things were at Wattle Farm.'

'On his skis?' she asked caustically.

'Yes, on his skis. I thought it very good of him.'

'He *has* been trying to compensate for his gaffe. It might have been better to leave you in peace instead of materializing out of the snow and overdoing the gallantry. He must think he's still with SOE. I'm surprised about the skis, though. I pictured him more as Colonel Blimp than Trevor Howard doing his hero stuff.'

Robson came with tea and sandwiches, then went to start a fire in Vesta's room. She stripped off her clothes and donned her mother's woollen dressing-gown to sit beside the fire and eat, while regaling Marion with details of the family she and Pat had lodged with. 'They couldn't do enough for us. Poor things found themselves entertaining *four* most of the time because the boys came over whenever they were off duty.'

'How is Paul, dear?'

'Fine. Just fine.' She bit into another ham sandwich and

munched for a moment or two. 'Actually, he's flying to Germany tomorrow to help defuse unexploded bombs. Most of their cities are still little more than ruins.'

'So are many of ours, even now.'

Vesta nodded. 'I know, isn't it awful?'

'You won't be seeing him again, then?'

'I promised to reply if he writes.'

They were quiet as the logs in the hearth crackled. Then Marion said, 'I believe the poor boy thinks a great deal of you.'

'He'd marry me if I let him.'

'Did he ask you?'

'Not in so many words. He knows better than to do that.'

'Because of your American?'

Vesta looked up aggressively. 'His name is Brad.'

'Are you still intending to marry *him*?' her mother asked gently.

'At the moment, I'm not intending to marry anyone,' she replied, getting to her feet. 'A girl is far better off fancy free.'

Marion rose, too. 'You're probably right. After all, one is chasing about the Pacific pursuing his demanding career, and the other is about to embark on a very dangerous duty. You have a lovely home and plenty of commissions to fulfil. Better to remain single than to marry the wrong man.' She began walking away. 'I'll see Cook and tell her to allow for one more at dinner.'

Vesta was left staring at the closed door in surprise. Her mother had never discussed the subject so frankly before, preferring to drop hints or avoid any mention of Vesta's future. There was also an unusual calmness about her, despite the months of worry over David. Perhaps it was simply that she looked younger in a yellow dress she wore rarely. Or maybe she was comforting herself with the thought that David would have written, except that he knew the letter could not be delivered in the present severe weather. Vesta shrugged and walked to the bathroom for a wash before fetching fresh clothes from her room where Robson was holding a newspaper against the fireplace to coax infant flames into a blaze.

As it was so late she dressed for dinner in amber-coloured wool, then thought what a foolish gesture it was just to eat with her mother. For the past two weeks or so she had dined in her tweed skirt and a jumper, because she had had no other clothes with her. Neither had Pat. Their hosts had also dressed casually in deference to them. So had Paul and Jeremy. In Italy she had . . . Her thoughts switched from the memories. Her father had always upheld the rituals of gracious living, so that was why she now went downstairs holding the long skirt free of her high-heeled shoes.

Entering the sitting room she pulled up with a start. A man was standing beside the fireplace with a glass in his hand. A man of medium height, stockily built, with dark hair silvering at the temples and very noticeable brown eyes. He wore grey flannels and one of David's pullovers with a cream shirt. Walking forward with a broad smile, he said, 'It's a great pleasure to meet you, Miss Sheridan. I'm Leo Roberts, a fervent admirer of your work and the idiot who spilled the beans about your father and brother.'

Vesta had the grace to blush because he had overheard her words, but the unexpectedness of finding him still at the Hall and so at home in it, as well as the impact of a personality so different from the one she had imagined, kept her silent.

Leo continued in an assured manner. 'You travelled from Salisbury without too much difficulty? That means conditions are improving. I'll have to get back to work, more's the pity. I've been playing hookey.'

With her composure back in place, Vesta asked, 'How long have you been here with my mother?'

'Four days.' He was unperturbed by her cool tone. 'I planned to leave in the morning, anyway. The supplies I brought have pretty well run out and I intended to fetch more, but if trains are running normally and roads are becoming negotiable there'll be supplies coming through again. And I shall be expected to get on with what they are paying me for.'

'Restoring lovely homes to their former glory. Did you ski-lift supplies to owners of *all* the places you've visited?'

He regarded her shrewdly. 'I apologized to your mother – on several occasions – and over the telephone to David. I expressed my deep regrets to Colonel Chandler and his wife. If I now say to *you* that I'm sorry I mistakenly revealed facts about something which was strictly a family tragedy, may I finally take off my sackcloth?'

Once again Vesta was thrown by his unexpected approach. Wondering why her mother had not yet joined them, she still could not reconcile herself enough with this man's apparent ease in her home – to the extent of wearing David's clothes – to surrender to his challenge. She moved to the side table and poured two glasses of sherry in expectation of Marion's imminent arrival, then sipped from one before turning back to Leo Roberts.

'I painted *The Afterglow* in memory of my father.'

'I know. It's a very moving piece of work, made all the more emotive by the single set of footprints leading to the candle at the foot of the grave. From the little I knew of him I'd say he'd appreciate that symbolized homecoming.'

Curiously, Vesta resented his perceiving what others had failed to; resented this assured stranger reading her mind and heart so effortlessly. She hit out in the only direction open to her. 'You must have known Daddy even better than the person married to him for thirty years, because she hasn't worked that out. She still thinks there should be another set leaving the grave.'

Leo finished his whisky and put the glass on the mantelshelf. 'Have you explained it to her?'

'How can you explain something like that to a person who hasn't immediately seen its message? David did, but our mother has never been in the least artistic or imaginative, so there'd be no point.'

'Then don't go on nursing your wound.' As Vesta opened her mouth to protest, he continued calmly. 'I think she's very gifted in the art of arranging flowers and choosing interior decoration. It can't be compared with the considerable creative talent you have but, in its own way, it's artistic and imaginative, wouldn't you say? The rooms you presently occupy in this house are most attractive and colourful. I suspect no one but your mother is responsible for making them so.' He smiled at her stony expression. 'It takes unusual understanding and flair to paint something like *The Afterglow* . . . but it wouldn't look as impressive as it does in a room whose charm didn't do it justice. You are indisputably the diamond, but your mother provides the perfect setting.'

Stirred to unexpected anger by this man who appeared to be

one step ahead of her all the time, Vesta finally took up his challenge. 'You arrived here to do the sort of measuring-up job any fool could do, then proceeded to upset the whole family by telling Mummy her husband was shot by Germans in a French field in front of her son who flew away and left him there dying. You told her they'd both been doing highly dangerous work as some kind of secret agents all the while she had believed they were safe, and consequently forced my brother to dredge up the details of that terrible experience when he's already going through some other kind of hell. As if that weren't enough, you arrived uninvited on skis with an offer of food, and appear to have settled in remarkably well to the extent of helping yourself to David's clothes and his whisky. Just what sort of game are you playing with my family?'

He looked her straight in the eye. 'No game, believe me. As soon as your mother knows me well enough, I'm going to ask her to marry me. Contrary to what I suspect has been the general opinion in this household, I happen to think Marion Sheridan is someone rather special.'

CHAPTER EIGHT

DINNER that evening was a strained affair. Reduced to candlelight halfway through it Vesta was relieved when they could
leave the table and settle in the sitting room by the fire. She
was tired and would normally have turned in early, but she
had no intention of leaving Marion alone with a man who
already acted as if he was master of Tarrant Hall. His
announcement regarding the hope of becoming her stepfather
had knocked Vesta off course. The entire situation seemed
unreal.

This man, supposedly engaged in nothing more demanding
than estimating damage caused to commandeered premises,
claimed to have been an undercover agent in Norway throughout the war. Having now met him Vesta was inclined to
believe that possible. His calm, enigmatic manner and obvious
intelligence came as a surprise to her but, at the same time,
made her deeply suspicious. Why had he been given the job he
presently did? Were there really other houses on his list, or
was he actually doing some kind of follow-up on the activities
of Sir Christopher Sheridan? Or David, come to that. Her
brother had been involved with transporting these agents,
after all. The nonsense about planning to marry her mother
was most worrying, because it was evident Marion was willing
to be manipulated by Leo Roberts. The extent of that willing-
ness dismayed Vesta.

Distrust of the man was deepened by a treacherous sense of
attraction to him. He exuded the same kind of underlying
ruthlessness as Brad; a similar brand of suspicious honesty
which she hesitated to believe. He was complex. That made
him dangerous in Vesta's view . . . and exciting. For several
reasons, then, she re-erected all those old defences she had
built against men after Felix Makoski seduced her. Brad had
knocked them down one by one, but his absence left the

143

barriers available for use, if needed. Along with all those feelings was a heartfelt cry against the notion of anyone attempting to replace her father. Knowing how he had actually died made the prospect even more unacceptable, particularly when it concerned the very person who had betrayed the truth. All in all, Leo Roberts was so blatantly acting a part, Vesta was furious with her mother for not seeing it, or *wanting* to see it.

Marion looked younger and happier, admittedly, but she was playing right into Leo's hands by allowing him to stay for as long as he wished and by lending him David's clothes. Surely she had not been swayed by that ridiculous move of skiing in with supplies; she could not have thought it *romantic*! She was over fifty, and had never been less than practical in her life. Vesta conveniently silenced the voice that reminded her David would not be here but for a youthful unbridled passion. The eighteen-year-old Chris Sheridan had been so incredibly handsome any girl would have felt that way about him.

As Marion poured coffee, her face glowing with an unusual near-beauty in the firelight, Vesta brooded further. What was the man after? Had the end of the war brought hard times for him, as it had for many? Was he intending to woo her mother into parting with a large sum of money before vanishing? Would he get as far as becoming master of the Hall and estate by marrying? David had washed his hands of all responsibility, so Marion would continue as before if she took another husband. Was that what Leo was after, so that he could milk the estate dry whilst living in high style? Or was there an even more sinister object behind the plan to worm his way in to the Sheridan family – one Vesta could not yet see?

She thought David ought to be told, then put aside any hope of his doing anything about it. Bill Chandler was like a second father, of course, but he had seemed impressed with Leo at their meeting. Few people deceived Uncle Bill. Was Leo that clever? The only person who might be able to help was Paul. His father had worked with SOE in a static capacity and could at least verify Leo's story of being one of their agents. Unfortunately, Paul was flying to Germany to risk being blown to pieces.

'A penny for them, Vesta,' offered Leo quietly.

She looked up at him. 'They're worth more than that, Major Roberts. I was thinking about my father.'

'An exceptional man.' He sipped his coffee with assurance Vesta found annoying. 'You could always have his body brought over to be buried at the church, you know.'

'He wouldn't want that,' she replied without hesitation. 'Both his brothers are buried in France.'

Leo smiled. 'That's exactly what your mother said.'

'You've already discussed it?'

'He was her husband as well as your father.'

Marion put down her coffee cup, saying, 'I told Leo that I'd see what you and David think about it before making a final decision.'

'But David's in no state to reach rational conclusions,' Leo added, 'and the vote is now two out of three.'

Vesta's anger could no longer be held in check. Turning on her mother, she cried, 'Is there *anything* you haven't told this man about strictly family matters? Good God, he's only been here four days but he seems to have slipped into a position of trust and authority that entitles him to make declarations on your behalf. None of us has once considered bringing Daddy home. Just because he's mentioned the possibility, it's suddenly become an issue to vote on.' She swung to face Leo again. 'Were you really intending to leave tomorrow, or has my sudden return made your position untenable?'

'*Vesta!*' cried Marion.

'Mummy, can't you see that he's up to no good? I haven't worked out what it is yet, but I've no intention of letting him get away with it. I can hardly believe you were so taken in by his act that you invited him in, gave him the guest room and the run of David's wardrobe, then proceeded to talk about us all with complete frankness. Poor David wouldn't want all and sundry knowing how he is at the moment, and God knows what you've revealed about me!' She moved to the edge of her chair to make her point more forcibly. 'Hasn't it struck you as suspicious that, after one visit during which he let slip information so secret even *we* didn't know, he should appear at your door late one night, knowing no one else was able to get here in the terrible conditions, to bribe his way in with food? Why? That whole business of checking on damage to the Hall is a front for his real purpose. He told you workmen would be here soon after Christmas. They weren't. There *are* no workmen. He's either still acting as an undercover agent, or he's a fortune-hunter. You've fallen for his charm hook, line and sinker. He's clever . . . and very smooth. I've met the type before. You haven't, which is why he has succeeded this far, but that's as far as it goes.' She got to her feet in agitation, saying to Leo, 'You have skis, with the correct clothing and equipment to enable you to get here over difficult terrain in darkness, so I suggest we forget about a morning departure and you leave as soon as you can get ready, Major Roberts – if that's your real name.'

He remained unperturbed. 'I think it's up to your mother to order me off the premises if I've outstayed my welcome. She's the mistress of the house.'

'And David's master of it – as well as the whole estate. He wouldn't approve of what's going on here.'

'I don't approve of what *he's* doing, but I'm expected to accept it,' Marion cried, looking tense. 'I'm also expected to continue being the Sheridans' custodian as I have been for almost thirty years.' She stood up to confront Vesta. 'You've been extremely rude to my guest and, therefore, to me. You've spoken a lot of nonsense more suited to a melodramatic film. I can't imagine what you mean by "what's going on here", but Leo is welcome to stay for as long as he wishes. I suggest you apologize.'

Leo got to his feet. 'Please, don't make me the subject of family discord. There seems to be enough of that as it is.'

'There he goes again,' flared Vesta. 'What right has he to comment on what's happening in our family?'

'The right of a friend. He's going to see if he can find out what happened to David in Singapore,' said Marion.

'David won't want strangers probing into his private life. Leave him alone! He'll sort it out eventually.'

'And maybe he won't. If Leo's enquiries meant we then understood and could help him, it wouldn't matter what David felt about what we had done.'

'Yes, it would. It's invasion into his privacy,' Vesta declared, still on the defensive.

'What about his invasion into mine?' replied Marion. 'No one ever thinks of that. I've been the only permanent resident here this century, which gives me the right to treat this house as my home. David has only ever used it as a lodging place. The same can be said of you. Neither of you ever asked before bringing friends to stay. You simply told me they were coming. Sometimes not even that. You just turned up with them and took it for granted that I would feed and accommodate them in welcoming fashion. Wasn't that invasion?

'A year ago I was looking forward to your brother and Pat settling here to run the estate. An end to loneliness and responsibility. I thought *you* were going to be married, with a house nearby. An end to worry over your safety and wellbeing. Instead, David arrived to tell me he had changed his mind, hinting that I was so small-minded I didn't rate an explanation. Brad Holland left this house before I was up the morning after he arrived, and you also deny me the courtesy of explaining the situation between you now.' She drew in her breath. '*My* future is apparently of little concern to my children, who have always regarded me as one of the fittings and fixtures of Tarrant Hall. The long, lonely candlelit evenings before Leo arrived made me realize that. Until David comes home permanently, and you stop using this house as a resting-place while you sort out your feelings, I shall behave as I wish and invite here whomever I choose. You must accept my friends as I've accepted yours over the years. If you find you can't, maybe you should find somewhere else to set up your studio.' She indicated Leo. 'Perhaps you'll now apologize to someone who went out of his way to bring me food and an offer of help during a crisis.'

The muscles of her face were so stiff Vesta had a job to retaliate further. 'I think congratulations are more in order. He's achieved his object, but you'll find he brought a fresh crisis with him. When the moment's right, he'll produce it. I hope one of your children will be around when he does, Mummy. Goodnight.'

Sleepiness appeared to have vanished when Vesta reached her room, which was still chilly despite the fire Robson had lit. Physical weariness remained, but she made no attempt to lie in bed once she had undressed. Wrapped in her fluffy dressing-gown, she sat before the fire and tried to come to terms with a difficult day which had left her quite shattered. She had started it by saying goodbye to Paul, and ended it with an unexpected quarrel over a man whose impact on her had aroused old sensations of insecurity.

Brad had walked from a desert oasis to affect her the same way. Ultimate surrender had been glorious, but where had it got her? Yet if he walked in right now she knew he would make her tingle with life, and the old magic would be irresistible. She would give in to it to her eventual cost, however, because he would soon reveal news that would turn her life upside down again.

Leo Roberts was doing that to her mother, she was certain. Within four short days he had her eating out of his hand. All that business about being the Sheridans' custodian had been put into her head by that man. It was totally out of character for her mother to claim she was a fixture and fitting, much less say what she had about her children. David had been adored from birth. He could do no wrong in Marion's eyes. When he did, and it could not be glossed over, she made excuses and declared it to be so unlike him. In truth, until he returned from the dead early in 1943 David had been no end of a lad living life as selfishly as a handsome daredevil could.

Right up to the day Vesta had gone with Pat to the military ball, Marion had still been speaking of David with fond sadness and concern. In the space of four days she had been charmed into seeing her beloved son in a vastly different light. Certainly, she wanted to help him over his problem, but the golden boy she had doted on for thirty-two years had suddenly been acknowledged as uncaring. To say nothing of the daughter who had been an also-ran throughout her life. Vesta had accepted her place in the shadow of her splendid brother because her relationship with her father had more than compensated.

The war had changed everything around. The shocked and disabled David had been reconciled to a father who understood from personal experience what he was going through. Marion's inability to accept a white-haired wreck in place of her beautiful boy had made her try too hard to pretend nothing had changed, and she had lost David's respect. Only then had she remembered she also had a daughter. It had been too late. Grieving for the loss of her father, Vesta had succumbed to Brad's promise of happy ever after and gone off to Italy with him.

After peace was declared a new era of family unity seemed inevitable. What a false hope! All three members were now unsettled and unhappy, unable to meet without wounding each other. What had happened to those wonderful times when peace lay just ahead, and it promised to be wonderful?

Hugging her knees and shivering slightly from a mixture of cold and agitation, Vesta conceded that she had spoken wildly this evening. It had been due partly to the unwelcome prospect of another man proposing to fill her beloved father's shoes, and partly to her own reaction to those same qualities she could not resist in Brad. Leo had none of the teasing audacity of the man she loved, but she knew it would take no time at all to be won over by that dangerously fascinating latent domination.

What could she do about this unexpected development? It was futile to count on David, yet he should rightly be the one to handle it. His inheritance was at stake. Once that man married their mother he would surely persuade her to do anything he wanted. Vesta was certain Leo was playing a hand close to his chest. Neither she nor David could stop Marion from marrying him if she set her heart on it, but she felt they should at least ensure that the skiing Lothario could not get his hands on Sheridan money or land. On deciding to telephone their solicitor in the morning she was further frustrated by remembering that the lines were still down. Her remaining hope was Bill Chandler, but he was attending a conference in Paris. Maybe Aunt Tessa could intervene. A woman-to-woman talk between long-standing friends might go some way towards foiling the plans of the pseudo-renovator. Vesta finally slept to dream of a faceless skier racing downhill with the deeds for Tarrant Hall, only to be blown sky-high by an unexploded bomb.

When Robson brought her morning tea and switched on the bedside light, he indicated an envelope on the tray. 'Major Roberts asked me to give you this letter as soon as you awoke, miss. He left very early in the morning rain.' He walked back to the open door. 'Rain means there will be a thaw. Routine will return to normal, thank goodness. It's been one thing after another lately. Breakfast will be served at the usual time.'

Vesta sat up swiftly, pulling on a bedjacket. The contents of the envelope were brief.

I'm not the villain you would have me be. Here's the name and telephone number of my CO. Check my bona fides with him. Perhaps next time we meet we'll get off to a better start. I'll wear my own pullover. I still admire the artist despite her temperament.

Leo

Screwing the page into a ball Vesta flung it across the room. Damn Leo Roberts! Brad could have written those lines. She had no intention of doing what he suggested. Whoever answered that number would almost certainly be in on whatever Leo was up to – and the lines were down, anyway.

As she sipped her tea Vesta suddenly felt weary of it all – weary of David's inexplicable behaviour, of her mother's ridiculous response to the plausible stranger and of her own inertia. The Sheridans were letting circumstances rule them. She herself had allowed Brad to put an end to her personal happiness and artistic inspiration. She should either join him or show him two could play the same game. What she needed was fresh impetus; the kind of challenge her war paintings had posed. Her father had always maintained that whether an artist painted a halved apple or a great cathedral, if he approached it as a masterpiece it would become one. That had been her trouble lately. She had approached each canvas as no more than a job to be done.

Getting out of bed she walked to the window and pushed aside a curtain. Sleety rain was falling on the stark whiteness. The barren scene all at once highlighted her sense of loneliness, the cold sensation around her heart. She could not even turn to the tranquil affection of Paul in the coming months; and if that man Roberts was to be a frequent visitor here it might be as well to do as her mother suggested and find another location for her studio. Another location which would provide fresh energy and enthusiasm. Somewhere right away from old mills and nurseries of blue-blooded children. Somewhere completely different.

Marion was already at the breakfast table when Vesta walked in. They exchanged polite greetings as Robson brought fresh coffee, then Vesta began on her porridge. When they were alone, she said, 'I'm sorry if I upset you last evening, Mummy. It was a bit of a shock finding a man in the sitting room wearing David's clothes and making free with his whisky. You might have told me he was still here.'

Her mother looked flushed but calm. 'You were so derisive about him when I introduced the subject, I thought it best to leave it until you met him and realized how wrong you were. I didn't mean you to walk in on him as you did – Robson delayed me when I came down for dinner. He's been very petulant lately. But there's no excuse for the way you behaved towards Leo. Whatever came over you? All that nonsense about a false name and undercover checking on your father! I could scarcely believe my ears. It was so unlike you. Almost as if you were intoxicated or ... I don't know ... under hypnosis.'

'Oh Mummy, really!'

'Well, it certainly wasn't the daughter I know. You're normally so sociable. Chris and David invariably vanished when certain people visited, but you've always been tolerant of even the most tiresome callers and behaved charmingly towards them. What you did last night was unforgivable.'

Vesta sighed. 'I *have* apologized.'

'To me, but not to poor Leo.'

'Leo is to be neither pitied nor consoled. He's a man well able to hold his own in any situation. Mummy, you know nothing about him. The whole affair strikes me as bizarre, yet you seem to have accepted it as perfectly normal for someone you met just once to turn up on your doorstep in a snowstorm with a haversack filled with food. Haven't you *once* asked yourself why?'

Marion set her cup in its saucer as her colour deepened further. 'If you hadn't been so aggressive and rude you would have discovered that Leo is sensitive and a lover of beautiful things. His wife was tragically killed during a mountain rescue; the second woman he loved threw him over because he was never there when she wanted him. Talking to me has helped him understand her side of the problem. We can't imagine what he went through as an agent in Norway. You will more easily than I understand the fear, the constant anxiety, the pain of seeing one's friends die, but neither of us has any conception of the dangerous work he did. He's not had much happiness in his life, and he's lonely. He sensed that I am, too. That's why he came.'

Longing to ridicule the hearts-and-flowers picture her mother had painted, Vesta merely said, 'You appreciate what the war must have been like for *him*. Why haven't you ever been as understanding towards David and me?'

'Probably because you've never confided your experiences to me. You've both adopted the belief that someone who spent her days safely at home wouldn't understand. Being the only ordinary person in a family of talented ones is an unenviable plight. While providing stability and the basics of life for them, you are regarded as being incapable of anything more.'

Stung by this accusation of which she was guilty Vesta cried, 'You could have changed that by being Daddy's constant companion.'

'No, Vesta, he moved in such highly intellectual circles I would have been a constant embarrassment to him instead. We both knew and accepted that. Besides, who would have looked after the estate that provided the ample funds he needed to do all he wanted?'

Vesta was nonplussed, not knowing how to deal with this person who seemed to have emerged overnight. Marion took advantage of her silence. 'You, David and Chris have all pursued your individual talents with great success. In the course of doing so you met interesting people and had enough excitement to satisfy anybody. In my own way, I've been doing something *I* have a talent for – with great success – but I've had no excitement to offset the stress and worries in my life. I'm only fifty-two, Vesta. *I* also have a future to think about. Like you, I'm suddenly bored with a job I normally love doing, and I'm lonely.' She poured more coffee for herself. 'You and your brother are impatient when I offer advice, and you make your own decisions mostly without ever discussing them with me. Please keep *your* advice to yourself and never insult my friends again.'

Stung by these candid truths, Vesta said heatedly, 'He's aiming to become more than a friend. He told me that as soon as he thinks you're ready, he's going to pop the question. It's marriage he's after . . . and I don't think he's going to wait all that long before he bamboozles you into it. *Now* do you understand my attitude towards him?'

'No,' came the calm response. Marion was clearly not in the least thrown by the news. Certainly, her colour deepened even further, but she betrayed no sign of being disconcerted by Leo's plans. She sipped her coffee (which Leo had brought, of course) before saying, 'David broke my heart when he sent a letter from Singapore saying he had married a Chinese girl. No engagement, no consultation with me and his father; the deed was irrevocably done. No sooner had Chris been killed than you went off to Italy with a married American and returned announcing that you were going to be his wife as soon as he was divorced. No engagement, no discussion with me; the decision was made. In view of that, do you really feel you have any right to interfere in my friendship with a man who is widowed, like me, is English and is unlikely to give me the terrible problems my children are now facing?'

'But you hardly know him, Mummy!'

Marion took up the cup again, saying over its rim, 'I already know him better than I knew Chris Sheridan when I was forced to marry him. Bear that in mind.'

Silenced by dismay, Vesta tried to get her thoughts in some kind of order. Robson brought boiled eggs and toast, which she ate automatically simply because they were there. In the midst of her own restlessness and confusion the one aspect of her life which had remained constant now looked set to change. Her mother had produced an unarguable case, so it would be pointless to contact solicitors, David, or either of the Chandlers. Leo Roberts looked set to become a member of the family. It was no worse than the Chinese Su Lim marrying David for a slice of Sheridan wealth.

A sense of futility washed over her again. Why not cease trying to sort out everyone else and get her own life going again? As she buttered more toast a solution suddenly presented itself. A solution far off course from any other she had had, and yet it now seemed the obvious answer to her present stalemate. She looked across the table at her mother. 'I'm sorry we've quarrelled at a time when we both really need each other's support. I just couldn't bear to think of anyone taking Daddy's place.'

'No one ever will, Vesta. No one could. He was unique. Leo's very different. We have a lot in common.'

Vesta forced a smile. 'I'll try to be glad for you. Put my aggression down to the fact that, as you said, I'm bored and lonely.'

'You're going to join Brad?'

She shook her head. 'You suggested I should move my studio elsewhere, so I plan to set it up in Germany.'

Marion looked aghast. '*Germany!* You can't, Vesta.'

'Why not?'

'Because it's enemy country. I mean ... I know you went there for holidays with your father, but we've been at *war* with them. How *can* you go over there? What will you do? Where will you stay?'

'I *know* we've been at war with them, Mummy,' she said as gently as she could. 'Of course it won't be like our schoolday holidays ... but I'm not a schoolgirl, am I? *How* I can go over there depends on the outcome of approaches to some of Daddy's influential friends, and to some of mine still in the army. *What* I shall do will be to paint something more exciting than *The Old Mill*. *Where* I shall stay will depend on Paul Gaynor.'

Marion was taken aback. 'You mean you're going over there to marry him?'

'Of course not. I'm going in pursuit of the means to revive my flagging career and he's the ideal person to help me with ... various problems.'

Getting to Hanover took longer than Vesta imagined. The thaw brought massive flooding which very soon produced equally hazardous travelling conditions and again isolated those places near rivers or set between hills. Tarrant Hall was not invaded by melt water as were many of the cottages in the village, but the supply of goods was this time made even more difficult because Greater Tarrant itself was under water, with trains running along an embankment resembling a track through the sea. Passengers and goods were taken off by boats, and many a house and store had people living upstairs amid boxes of food and household supplies. The farmers were the worst hit. Following the big freeze of February which had killed livestock beneath deep snowdrifts, there now came flood water to drown them, invade pastures, barns and stables, to say nothing of the homesteads themselves. Spring crops were awash; cows gathered in forlorn groups on muddy high ground. Sheep fared better, more used to hillsides, but even these were drenched and dirty and hungry. Owners worked alongside their farmhands, with very little sleep. Unusually high spring tides added to the problems, and day after day it rained.

Jack Marshall had his work cut out trying to save livestock on the Sheridan estate. The young crops in the fields would have to be written off. That meant not only financial disaster for the estate, but there would be less food for the people of Britain who were on short rations already. By the third day, Marion had a splendid idea and told Jack to take their animals up Longbarrow Hill where the old airfield buildings would provide excellent byres and barns. It was not long before those huts and hangars haunted by the shades of British and American fliers were filled with cattle, fodder and poultry. Other farmers of Tarrant Royal who had latched on to Marion's brainwave muttered darkly that if anyone in uniform came there and dared order them to leave and mend the wire fence they had cut, they would not be responsible for his safety.

Prevented from departure by a sense of obligation, Vesta did her bit by 'sailing' to Greater Tarrant for supplies. In villages some distance from the sea or any vast stretch of water there was not a glut of boats. Several wealthy residents owned beautiful craft, but they were berthed in coastal harbours which could not be reached. These people were secretly glad, because they did not relish the thought of their expensive yachts being used to ferry vegetables, sacks of flour, milk, fodder and coal along the streets of thatched villages. Country dwellers were great improvisers, however, and it was not long before a veritable fleet of curious floats and boats began gliding back and forth with supplies from Greater Tarrant.

Jack Marshall hammered together *The Saucy Sal* which Vesta took to the market town along with a sturdy hand to lift the heavy stuff.

She took the boat to the Chandlers' farm one morning. Pat's visit to Jeremy's home had had to be postponed and she appeared to be having second thoughts about 'having fun'. She and Tessa were horrified on hearing of Vesta's plan to go to Germany. 'Where will you live, how will you survive, what is the point?' they asked. Her reply had been that as she had been through three battle campaigns and managed, there should be no problem. When they were alone Pat asked, 'Does this signify the end of Brad?' 'It signifies the end of confusion, that's all,' had been her firm answer. She made no mention of Leo Roberts to them. That problem had ceased to concern her. She noted, caustically, that he had not turned up late one night in a canoe. Presumably, he was not an expert at survival in floods. Or maybe he had sensed the game was up and was looking for another susceptible wealthy widow.

It was not until mid April that Vesta was able to complete her arrangements to join Paul. When the flood receded a batch of letters written one each week reached her through the Army Post Office. The contents were not encouraging. Paul's descriptions of life in Hanover were grim, but as the letters had been written during freeze and thaw conditions similar to those in England Vesta told herself summer was on the way and everything would have improved by the time she arrived. Unlike Brad, she did not know a guy who was flying there, so she had to follow complicated overland arrangements to reach her destination. She *did* know a number of influential friends of her father, however, so the permits, papers and vouchers she needed were produced faster than if she had not been Sir Christopher Sheridan's daughter.

Three days before Vesta's departure her mother received a telephone call from Leo asking if he could call in on his way to a house in Sidmouth that weekend. Telling herself she should have known a man of his type would not give up easily, Vesta decided to leave on Friday and stay overnight in London before catching the boat train. She had no desire to meet Leo again, although he was certain to believe he had driven her away leaving him victor on the field.

Marion was upset on saying goodbye. 'The second of my children going off with no definite plan to return.'

'Of course I'll return,' she said, hugging her mother. 'So will David.'

'Everything seemed so certain. David marrying Pat and living here; you and Brad in a nice house nearby. What spoilt it all?'

Vesta produced an encouraging smile. 'Human nature. I guess none of us was ready to settle down. Give us time, Mummy.' She picked up her overnight bag while Bob Sandalwood loaded her larger ones in the taxi. 'Take care of yourself, I'll write.'

'Don't go near Paul's unexploded bombs.'

She laughed. 'As if I would!' Yet that was exactly what she planned to do.

In the race to reach Berlin in 1945 the Russian army had been the nearest to it and had fought a particularly bloody battle to capture the German capital. With lack of foresight, and because they were heavily engaged during their own advance from the west, the British and Americans did not rush to Berlin once it had fallen, They were therefore unaware that the occupying Russian troops were plundering and raping on a horrific scale in an orgy of revenge on a merciless enemy. Their political counterparts were equally busy stripping the area of all industrial and commercial machinery, its stocks and assets, its raw materials and most of its food before their allies could lay hands on it. An agreement as early as 1943 had allowed for substantial reparations for what Russia had suffered at German hands, but no firm details had been approved. The British and Americans had arrived to find a *fait accompli*, but registered only mild protest when so much else had to be decided and organized.

With the French graciously included in the apportioning of Germany, a four-power ruling body was set up in the one natural headquarters of a large multi-faceted country. Yet Berlin was smack in the middle of the eastern zone allocated to Soviet occupation, so the capital itself was divided into sectors in which all four allies set up their individual military and political staffs. Each sector had its own airfield and railway stations, but passage across the Russian zone from the western ones was restricted to narrow air corridors, and roads and railways managed and guarded by armed Russian soldiers.

At first, the arrangement had worked well enough, but it was not long before the four-power ruling body split into a three to one situation. The Russians wanted their pound of flesh despite the fact that the flesh was not there to take. Thousands of Germans were dying of starvation and disease. The cities were devastated, leaving millions homeless. Industry was at a standstill. The victors were faced with a choice of letting Germany become a barren wasteland in the heart of a Europe dependent upon its industries and rich coal sources, or of splitting it into permanent satellite states of the occupying countries. The British and French were on the verge of bankruptcy and national collapse at home, so they could not sustain a large area of Germany. The Americans, who could have afforded the proposition, felt that Europe was not their real concern and planned to remain as an occupying force for only two years, anyway. They wanted to go home and get on with living.

For the Russians either course was attractive. A broken power robbed of its means of wealth, and with a starving, demoralized population, was ripe for domination and conversion to Communism. Such a place, right in the middle of Europe, would make easy the gathering in of all those impoverished countries surrounding it. The whole of Europe under the red flag! It was a mouthwatering prospect. The other alternative, that of a permanent satellite state containing Berlin, was also attractive and would serve as a start for the grand plan. It *was* a long-term vision, after all, because Russia was also impoverished.

A bone of contention swiftly materialized when the three Western allies decided that the only solution to putting the whole of Europe back on its feet was to get the German people to work as soon as possible. This meant giving them enough food, and houses to live in. Of course it would be expensive, but they would gain a huge workforce of trained men and women to produce essential commodities that would earn back their initial outlay. Although this way forward was

158

grudgingly accepted by the Russians it was not followed. The Soviet zone continued to be robbed of its assets, and skilled workers were transported to Russia as slave labour.

The plan was not completely successful. The cost was greater than expected. The British and French had too little food for their own people, who had to have their rations cut to feed their late enemies. The Americans had enormous quantities of it and, soon, an Anglo-American bizone was formed so that all resources could be pooled. The French, in a huff because they were not always invited to policy meetings, stayed aloof from this merger and pursued their own system within their zone. Despite American largesse the terrible winter of 1946–47, which had put further strain on the British people trying to find the golden life they expected when the war was won, set back the plans to revitalize Germany. Hundreds died of cold and starvation because root crops were frozen in the ground below snow banks, and transport came to a standstill on impassable roads.

By the beginning of summer 1947, work on rebuilding and regenerating industry had slowed almost to a standstill. Coal production was negligible because miners were on starvation rations, and the clearing of cities had been reduced to lethargic shifting of bricks and rubble by the hands of those barely able to stand, much less lift. Action had to be taken fast when a series of hunger strikes, and a fresh outbreak of epidemics, threatened complete collapse throughout the country. Rations had to be increased, and this meant less for those at home. Yet an end to Germany's vital production would lead to even harder times in Britain in the future, so it was better to pull belts in a little tighter now than wait until tightening them would be much more painful.

It was to this situation that Vesta arrived at the end of April, armed with the passes and authorities needed to get her from Hamburg to Hanover on trains run by the army, who checked and scrutinized in triplicate. She had been very seasick crossing to Hamburg, and it had taken two days to secure a place on a train. Had she still been in the ATS everything would have been fine, but soldiers were suspicious of civilians possessing papers signed by very high-ranking officials, and especially of young women travelling alone with such documents. It had been galling to discover that no one she crossed swords with knew of her reputation, but they were mostly military policemen with more brawn than brains who were very definitely acting the part of an occupying army. The war in Europe might have been over for two years, but Germans were still the enemy to them and they did not let up on their grim aggression for one moment while on duty.

The train journey had revived memories of the Italian campaign. Although Vesta was hardened to the sight of ruined cities and villages, of countryside laid waste, of people living in any conditions which provided some degree of shelter, she was appalled by the extent of devastation viewed from the carriage window. British towns and cities had also been reduced to streets of ruins, of course, but they had not then been fought over with tanks and heavy artillery by armies ferociously deciding the outcome of a six-year war.

By the time she arrived at her destination Vesta was tired, aching and doubting the wisdom of her decision. Paul was unaware that she was coming to Hanover, or he would have certainly arranged some accommodation for her. Evening was not far off and she first had to find him. All the guidance she had was an Army Post Office box number on the back of his letters. Hanover station was busy with people, mostly in uniform, so Vesta stood for a while beside her two cases until the other passengers had passed through the military checkpoint. She had no idea how far from the station Paul's unit was but she would have to find some kind of transport that would take her there. In addition to her heavy cases, she carried over her shoulder the hessian bag containing paints and some canvases – a wise precaution since evidence suggested she was unlikely to get hold of any here.

When she eventually approached the armed lance-corporal with a red cover on his cap, he looked from her papers to her face several times before saying, in a caustic voice, 'Shouldn't there be someone here to meet you, miss? You can't go wherever it is you're going on your own.'

Bridling at the familiar military approach, she said, 'I didn't have time to let anyone know. I've been sent out here at short notice. Are there any taxis at all?'

His caustic expression became a leer as he mimicked her

cultured accent. 'Hoe, aym afraid there are noe texis.' Then, in his natural voice: 'Where've you been for the past six years? There's been a war on.'

That did it. With her best ATS officer's approach, she said, 'I know. For the first two years of it I was an army radio operator, and for the next four I covered the last push against Rommel in the North African desert and the Italian campaign as a war artist. When I drove into Rome as soon as it was liberated, I saw battered old vehicles being driven by battered old men eager to earn a few lire by taking simpletons like you to see the sights. Now can we start again? Are there any taxis?'

Red-faced with affront and anger, the lance-corporal said, tight-lipped, 'Fuel's restricted to those with permits.'

Spotting another man with three stripes on his sleeve inside the cubicle serving as a control post, Vesta said, 'Perhaps your sergeant would be more helpful.'

'He doesn't know any more than me. Besides, he's busy right now.'

'Keep an eye on my luggage while I have a word with him, will you?' She pushed open the door and walked into an atmosphere of smoke and sweat, overlaid with the perfume of Brylcreem to make it bearable.

The carrot-haired sergeant was sitting with his feet on the table, reading a crime magazine with a lurid cover. 'Is our bleedin' relief here yet?' he growled without looking up.

'I'm afraid not,' Vesta said sweetly. 'You'll probably have time to find out who dunnit before they arrive.'

Grey eyes lifted from the book and widened in surprise. Heavy black boots scraped veneer from the table as he drew his feet from it and struggled upright. Tall and toughly built, he nevertheless blushed deeply as he self-consciously tugged his battledress jacket straight. 'Sorry, miss ... ma'am. We don't get many ... I mean, the girls ... ladies ... well, they're with the army, or secretaries with the Control Commission, or Foreign Office. You *are* English, aren't you?'

'I know it's a bit unusual for a woman to arrive here out of the blue – I was made aware of that all the way from Hamburg – but mine are unusual circumstances, Sergeant ...?'

'Grogan, ma'am.'

She held out her papers. 'I'm Vesta Sheridan, the artist,

commissioned to paint a series of pictures depicting the work of an occupation army. My contact in Hanover, Lieutenant Paul Gaynor of the Royal Engineers, is unaware of my arrival because I hadn't time to let him know. Your colleague outside was averse to giving me any help, so I'm appealing to you.' That was always a successful approach with men like Grogan who were probably as bold as brass with passing girls, but who were nonplussed when faced with someone they would regard as a 'lady'. She pulled out one of Paul's letters and showed him the wording on the back of the envelope. 'Do you know where this is and how best I can get there?'

Taking the envelope Grogan stepped across to a map on the wall. 'It's around here.' He jabbed with his finger. 'REs, you said. Ah, your friend must be attached to a bigger unit for accommodation and feeding because there's only an infantry barracks in Kugelstrasse. Well, it ain't so much a barracks as a collection of huts. Mr Gaynor was probably in charge of putting them up.'

'No, he's in Bomb Disposal.'

Grogan swung round. 'Poor so –' He turned red again. 'Beg pardon, ma'am. It's just that it seems a bit hard to have to do that when the war's over.'

'It's his job,' she said calmly, not knowing then how she would later view the whole business of what Paul did.

Having collected himself, Sergeant Grogan rose to the occasion as Vesta had known he would. 'There's two things I can do, Miss Sheridan. First is I can ring through and get Mr Gaynor to come for you, but he might be on duty. Or, if you'd be happy to wait till our relief arrives – won't be more'n ten minutes – me and Jenks could drive you there. Yes, that'd probably be best. 'T'isn't far out of our way, and I'd know you was all right.'

She smiled. 'You mean you'd satisfy yourself that I really was going to the barracks?'

Caught on the hop he said, 'We're supposed to check everyone in and . . . well, I've never seen no one come through here with papers like yours, miss. General Clarkson, General Hislop and Lord Moore. You sure you're just here to paint pictures?'

'Just to paint pictures,' she assured him, her smile broadening. 'I'm not some kind of spy checking that you're doing your job properly. These letters and permits are signed by friends of my family, that's all.'

That news led him to a thought. 'We'll be in an open jeep, I'm afraid. Will that be all right?'

'Heavens, yes.' She sat on a chair alongside the wall. 'I drove one throughout the Italian campaign. At Monte Cassino a blazing aircraft came down on us as we sat watching the battle. It was quite an experience. Yes, I'm *perfectly* at home in a jeep.'

And so she was when they set off from the station five minutes later, Grogan driving and the aggressive Jenks in the back seat. As they progressed through pitted streets the sergeant gave Vesta an insight into life in Hanover.

'Ladies don't go out unescorted. Not anywhere! It's not safe. The people are hungry and desperate. They'll do anything that'll get them food – especially for their children. There's nothing in their shops – or very little – and their money's worthless. Only way they can get anything is by barter – fags and coffee are the prize commodities. We're not allowed to fraternize, although some of our younger lads give way to temptation and hand over to girls their cigarette ration, or some NAAFI coffee. If we catch 'em at it, they're for it. We buy all we need at the NAAFI. It's got better stuff than at home. Of course, if you have a chance to cross into the Yankee zone and go in their PX stores you'll think you're dreaming. They got stuff in there we ain't never seen, even before the war.'

While he rambled on, Vesta was studying the devastation around her. They had reached a district which appeared to be nothing but acre after acre of rubble, and it suddenly struck her that it was in such places that Paul might be working. Dusk was now falling to add a further sense of gloom and desolation. She could not paint *this*. Had she been mad to imagine she would find inspiration in this defeated country, when she had refused to travel with Brad to another on the excuse of being unable to use it as a subject for her art? In coming here she had been going to show everyone, including those clever lads Brad Holland and Leo Roberts, that she knew where she was going. Right now, even her two police escorts did not seem to know. They had stopped to look at a map.

'Ah!' cried Grogan, making Vesta jump. 'There's the turning. Right at the other end of this street.'

The 'street' was no more than a swathe cut through wasteland. Surely Paul did not live here. In the deepening darkness the headlamps threw beams of light which soon picked out signs of more substantial buildings. Although these were little more than shells, the pale flicker of candlelight was evident within them and, now and again, Vesta could make out figures shuffling along the broken road to disappear through doorways invisible to those who were unaware of their existence.

The so-called barracks was set within a wired compound with a guard on the gate. This man looked at Vesta with amused interest as Sergeant Grogan announced that he was taking the lady to Lieutenant Gaynor, and it occurred to her that the guard believed an RE officer was about to have an unwelcome confrontation with a girl from his past. As they drove in past other interested soldiers she then wondered if they believed she was some kind of prisoner. Worst of all, she began to worry about Paul's reaction to her unannounced arrival.

Sergeant Grogan pulled up before a set of four huts standing apart from the others, with a board proclaiming that they housed Paul's unit. Lance-Corporal Jenks vaulted over the side of the vehicle, and went in through the door of the offices where a light was burning.

'Just checking that Mr Gaynor's here,' the sergeant explained. 'Then Jenks'll take in your luggage and we'll be off, miss, if you don't mind.'

She gave him a smile, pretending assurance she no longer felt. 'You've been extremely kind and helpful. I'm most grateful. Of course you must go. I've taken you out of your way and you'll be anxious to relax after your hours of duty.' As Jenks came out nodding, she climbed to the ground. 'And you've satisfied yourself that I've gone to the place I said I was heading for.'

Grogan flushed slightly. 'I didn't really think . . .'

'I know. Only teasing,' she said as Jenks took her cases up the three steps into the office.

'Well, good luck, miss. Pity it isn't more romantic, but I guess you and Mr Gaynor are used to places like this after all that time in Italy together.'

'*He* wasn't with me in Italy,' she said without thinking.

'Oh . . . I see.' There was that in his tone which seemed to support the knowing wink Jenks gave her as he passed to climb back into the jeep. They now *both* thought she had chased out here after a man who had ditched her in England. As she walked into the lighted office she felt too weary and uncertain to care.

The face of the soldier sitting at a desk inside the door was covered in a broad grin, and there was a knot of other soldiers in a corridor leading from it. None of them appeared to be very busy, because they were more intent on her than their discussion. The stocky, brown-haired man who had got to his feet beside his desk was still grinning as he told her Mr Gaynor was giving a lecture and would be out any minute.

'We're just packing up, miss. Another fifteen minutes and you'd've missed him.'

'You all live on the camp, though, don't you?' she asked.

The grin broadened even further. 'Oh yes . . . but the Red-caps would've had to take you to the Officers' Mess, and that could've been more awkward.'

Resenting his attitude, she said coolly, 'I've been in Officers' Messes before. In fact, I lived in one in North Africa when I followed a tank assault.'

'Is that so, miss. Well, well!'

While struggling with the desire to throw the contents of his ink-pot over his pimply face, Vesta heard the sound of boots approaching along plank flooring and grew aware that the knot of soldiers had become a gleeful audience. Instinct told her she had handled this all wrong.

Paul looked bleary eyed and drawn, despite his smart turn-out. He pulled up short and stared at her with evident shock for so long, Vesta began to think he did not recognize her. He seemed incapable of speech.

'Hallo, Paul,' she said, conscious of the many watching eyes. 'I'm sorry I didn't have time to let you know I was coming.'

He seemed almost mesmerized. 'I was interrupted in the middle of a lecture and told there were two MPs here to see me on an urgent matter.'

She now understood the grinning audience. 'They drove me here from the station. I thought it was very good of them. There were no taxis.' She knew her words were inane, but this meeting was not turning out as she expected. Brad would have grinned, said, 'Hallo, Vic,' as if the months between meetings had never happened, and they would have taken up where they left off. Not so this man. He looked furious as he came across and grabbed her arm.

'Come into my office while you tell me what this is all about ... and my feeble-minded staff can get on with their work. No one has said they can pack up early, and Sapper Beresford is liable to be on charge tomorrow for giving false information about the military police.'

Vesta was virtually dragged along the corridor and thrust into an office containing two desks and some filing cabinets. Paul kicked the door shut and turned on her. 'What the hell is going on? I'm summoned from a lecture on clearing mine-fields to meet two MPs and come out to find you, of all people, standing there complete with matching luggage as if you're on a luxury holiday, complaining about the lack of taxis.' His voice was raised enough to reach his staff, who almost certainly were gleefully noting every word. *This is a city under military occupation!* There's been a war raging over Hanover, for God's sake, and there are still bloody live bombs out there. Have you gone out of your mind?'

After a few seconds of mixed emotions, Vesta turned and headed for the door. She was stopped before she reached it. Paul's eyes were now blazing with something other than anger. 'Just where do you think you are going?'

'Get back to your lecture! I can look after myself. I've done it in places quite as bad as this. Don't keep telling me there's been a war. I know. I've been *in* it, the same as you and those grinning louts out there, and I can manage without the help of *any* of you.'

She was pulled into Paul's arms and kissed very hard. 'Don't ever do anything like this to me again,' he ordered unsteadily, still holding her close. 'When you didn't answer my letters, I thought it was over. How *dare* you turn up without any warning?'

'I came here to paint, not to be with you.'

'Oh yeah?' he murmured. 'We'll see about that.'

CHAPTER NINE

A DISCREET tap at the door was followed by a voice informing Paul of the time and asking if there was anything he wanted, or could they all go home. The tramping of boots, a slammed door and voices outside the window indicated that the men had obeyed his dismissal with alacrity. As a precaution Paul checked that no one was eavesdropping at the door or the windows. Then he came back to where Vesta was sitting beside his desk.

'They've had no end of a treat today,' he said with a rueful smile. 'The tale will be all over the barracks by midnight, highly exaggerated, no doubt. It'll be ages before I live this down.'

'You'll survive,' she responded calmly. 'Soldiers are nothing but full-size little boys with guns, I've discovered.'

He perched on the edge of the desk to study her hungrily. 'You'll have to pinch me to prove I'm not dreaming. I thought I'd lost you when you didn't reply to my letters.'

'I only received them a few days before I left. You know what the weather was like last winter. With the thaw came the floods.'

'Same here. Can you imagine this place flooded? It looked like a scene from the Bible. I expected the Ark to come floating past.'

Seeing his bubbling happiness Vesta thought she should put the record straight for his sake. 'Paul, you couldn't have lost what you never had.'

His smile faded. 'Then why are you here?'

'I told you. To paint.'

'Acres of ruins?'

'An army of occupation. The differences between its wartime role and that of the conqueror. All aspects, including one that has barely changed.'

168

'And what's that?'

'You and your team defusing bombs.'

Several seconds passed before her words sank in, then he stood up with a thud of boots on brown lino. 'Is that supposed to be a joke?'

'Why should it be?'

Anger had returned with a vengeance. 'You're out of your mind! Have you any idea . . . You seriously thought I'd allow it?'

'It's not simply a case of *your* permission, Paul,' she informed him as gently as she could. 'The only way I could get out here was to flutter my eyelashes at some of Daddy's influential friends. Because of the success of my war pictures, and the subsequent portrait of Jerry Stanstead and his tank now hung in the Cavalry Club, I've been given a firm commission by my former masters, and a free hand to go wherever I like.'

'Not near my bombs, you won't.'

She sighed. 'If you're going to be difficult I'll show you the official pass requesting cooperation from all military personnel in the British Sector.'

'And if that doesn't do the trick you'll show me something more persuasive, I suppose,' he snapped. 'My God, you had me totally fooled. After your near-surrender on that last night in Salisbury, I thought you'd come here to . . .' He was deeply upset. 'So that farcical business of covering your breasts in mock modesty in case someone walked in on us, then pretending to read a book for an hour to save my face was really the softening-up strategy for *this*?'

'You know it wasn't. That's ridiculous!'

'I should have realized I'd only got that far with you *after* I told you about my posting to Germany.'

'That had nothing to do with what happened that evening,' she protested. 'I got carried away because I discovered I was going to miss you more than I had expected.'

He rounded on her bitterly. 'You mean you discovered the perfect opportunity to recapture public interest in your work. *The Old Mill* was standard stuff anyone could do, and you wanted something spectacular. Aha, you thought, Gaynor's going off to Germany to blow himself sky high. Just the ticket! Capture that on canvas and I'll go down in art history.'

She got to her feet. 'Please, Paul . . .'

'Please, *nothing*.' He shook her hand from his arm. 'I don't give a toss how many bloody passes from Daddy's influential friends you've brought with you, I refuse to let you make a *picture* of my lads risking their lives. And to save you the bother of working me up to fever pitch then going all maidenly on me again, I'm leaving. You're so certain you can look after yourself. Go ahead!'

Paul strode from the room and the outer door slammed behind him. Vesta was dumbfounded. She knew him as a considerate man with a quiet sense of humour, but he had turned into a firebrand within three months. She sank back on to the chair while her tired brain tried to sort out what next to do, and all the time an inner voice told her there was an element of truth in Paul's translation of her behaviour.

Someone appeared in the doorway; a tow-haired second-lieutenant wearing an expression of undisguised anticipation on a face designed for merriment. He minced towards her in a comical fashion. '*Guten Abend, Fräulein, ich bin* . . . er . . . Oh, hell, I've forgotten how to say it. Ah, yes. *Mein Name is Shannon. Wie geht es Ihnen? Wie heissen Sie?*'

'How do you do, Mr Shannon. I'm Vesta Sheridan.'

'Good Lord, you're English!' he exclaimed. 'Those blighters told me two MPs had brought a Fräulein who gave Paul no end of a shock. When I passed him a moment ago resembling a tornado, I thought . . .'

'Yes, *what* did you think?' she demanded coldly.

He grinned, pulled up a chair, and straddled it to look over its back. 'Well, you know how it is. A fellow meets a girl and gets a bit friendly, then she turns up on his doorstep making out there's more to it than there is.'

'That is indeed what all your men thought, and the MPs who drove me from the station. Nothing could be further from the truth, Mr Shannon.'

'The name's Jim,' he said. 'What *is* the truth, then?'

'I don't think it's your business.'

'No, it isn't . . . but tell me anyway. Life's so uncertain in my game we all need something to take our minds off the danger and tragedy of what we're doing.'

His overdone pathos brought a reluctant smile from her. 'Is

170

that the line you use to get friendly with girls? It's lost on me, I'm afraid. I went through the war alongside fighting men so I'm used to their atrocious gambits ... including the kind you've just trotted out.'

He laughed in acknowledgement. 'It was worth a try. Where did you serve during the war?'

'The desert and Italy.'

'With Paul?'

'In North Africa, although he was always ahead clearing mines so I don't really remember him being there.'

Jim Shannon frowned. 'You mean you were actually out in the open desert? Are you a nurse?'

She shook her head. 'I was there through a mistaken message. They were expecting a *Victor* Sheridan. Colonel Villiers was furious when I turned up, but he was in the throes of a tank battle and could do nothing about it.'

'You're the artist,' claimed Jim, putting two and two together triumphantly. 'The woman Paul's crazy about. Vesta Sheridan. Took over the transceiver during the battle, didn't you? I've seen your pictures. They're good.' His eyes narrowed speculatively. 'What's going on then? Paul's been in a real state. Thought you'd thrown him over. So why's he stormed off now you've turned up on his doorstep?'

Vesta looked across at a young man who could easily become her friend, if she encouraged him. In that strange room in the midst of devastation, with night advancing fast and Paul alienated by her own mishandling of their reunion, she really needed one. 'I think I made a mistake in coming here.'

'That's a swift decision after only an hour in Hanover. Are we all so awful?'

She gave a faint smile. 'Look, although I put you down just now, I do know what you're doing out here. The strain on Paul is very apparent, and I'm afraid I said all the wrong things.'

'Yes, we're in a risky business, but we're trained to handle it. The strain on Paul is because of you. When a chap has personal problems it means his mind's not entirely on the job, and he can get careless. Paul knows that and it worries him. He had a couple of narrow shaves during the war, but they weren't through his mistakes.' He was now completely serious. 'He talks about you all the time. I was beginning to get fed up with it, but now I've met you I understand how he feels.'

'That's a swift decision after only an hour in Hanover.'

'Ah, I know far more about you than I should, but when there are only two officers in a small unit they become chums of necessity. Paul's pretty heavily in love with you, you know.'

'That's why I shouldn't have come.'

'I see. Why did you?'

She sighed. 'Because everything at home had gone wrong. Throughout the war I'd set my sights on the day it would be over and everything would be roses. How foolish of me!'

'How foolish of most of us.'

'My work no longer satisfied me, everyone I knew had gone off along unexpected tangents ... and I missed Paul more than I expected to.'

'So you do care about him?'

'Of course, but don't get any wrong ideas,' she warned.

'He's the one with those, Vesta. How are you going to convince him there's nothing doing without adding to the strain he's already under?'

'That's only one of my worries. I've no idea where to find accommodation, or what I shall find to paint in this flattened city. I should never have come.'

Jim got to his feet with a sense of purpose. 'That's the third time you've said that, but you have and *I'm* glad of it if no one else is. I can't help you with your artistic dilemma, but the question of accommodation can easily be solved. There are only two or three places British women can stay at in Hanover, and I ought to be able to bully one or other of them to take you in.'

'You make me sound like a foundling,' she protested, standing up.

'So you are. Orphan of the storm. Night's closing in; snow lies thick on the ground. The poor young girl stands shivering on the doorstep,' he quoted dramatically.

'Shouldn't I have a baby in a shawl?' she asked, cheered by this man's uncomplicated company.

'Not if you want to get into any of these places, and especially if *I'm* going to be with you.'

'You're not,' said Paul from the doorway. 'I've already arranged for Vesta to have a room at the club, and I've booked a table for dinner . . . for *two*,' he added with heavy emphasis. 'We'd better get going if you want to settle in before we eat. I've got a jeep outside . . . and, by the way, it's pointless getting to work on Jim. I give the orders and he does as he's told. Being nice to him won't get you anywhere.'

'It already has,' she told him wearily. 'After days of travelling, the snide attitude of men who thought I was some kind of floosie, and your flash of temper, Jim's pleasant company was a godsend. You may give your orders with my blessing and he can do as he's told or not, as he sees fit, but I hope he'll be my friend. Goodnight, Jim.'

'Welcome to Hanover,' he said, 'and remember what I said.'

'I will.'

He called after her as she walked the corridor with Paul, 'You understood my German very well. Do you speak it too?'

She called back, 'My father insisted. If you'd like lessons I'll gladly give them to you.'

'You'll be too busy painting,' said Paul. 'And what was it he told you that you must remember?'

'I've forgotten,' she countered serenely.

Her room at the club was a familiar sight to an ex-army girl. Basic furniture, standard pattern curtains and rugs, small washbasin, and the toilet was along the corridor. Her preparations for dinner were perfunctory, but she was taken aback to find the other women present at the dinner tables in elaborate dresses. Paul was waiting for her at the bar, where he had evidently been liberally fortifying himself.

'Heavens,' she said under her breath. 'I didn't expect to see everyone all dressed up. It's so colonial. Mustn't let the side down in front of the natives.'

'That's right. *We* won,' he said bluntly as he guided her to their table.

The meal was nowhere near as lavish as old-style colonial ones, however. It was plain and filling. Solid NAAFI fare, Vesta thought. But it was good to be eating in a room that was not on the move, at last. Bed was also just along the corridor. A very attractive proposition. Conversation was strained, at first, and she was disturbed by Paul's tenseness.

He wasn't the same man she had known in England, and Jim Shannon had suggested she was the cause of the change. If that were true she had assumed an unwelcome responsibility by coming here.

Halfway through the main course, Paul said, 'Look, I'm sorry about the things I said, only . . . well, when I came out expecting fresh problems with the military police and saw you standing there with all your worldly goods I . . . I jumped to the conclusion that you'd finally decided between him and me. I thought . . . silly, really, because you've always made it clear that he's the one. My anger was with myself, but you were on the receiving end, I'm afraid.'

'I was less than tactful,' she admitted. 'Let's make a fresh start tomorrow.'

He would not drop the subject, however. Pushing meat about his plate with a fork but unaware of doing it, he said, 'When I stormed over to my room I started to get my thoughts straight, and what I don't understand is why, if you want to paint the aftermath of war, you chose to come here instead of Japan. Isn't that where he is?'

'I don't know where he is at the moment.' Knowing she owed him an explanation, she told him about her restlessness, her sense of letting life slip past with no sense of direction, the loss of artistic inspiration, and the feeling that she was trying to sort out a family who resented her efforts, culminating in the disturbing influence on her mother of the mysterious Leo Roberts.

'Pat was up to her eyes helping her mother with the disastrous effect of snow on their livestock, and trying to decide whether or not to sleep with Jerry, so I couldn't talk to her about it at all. Uncle Bill was in Paris. When Mummy suggested I move my studio if I wasn't happy at home, it suddenly occurred to me that I'd have gone to Salisbury if you had been there. That's when I decided to try and get out here. I thought it the ideal opportunity to do some work which will not only satisfy me but will put me back where I was. Thank heavens for 'Daddy's Connections', as we used to call them. I'm sort of on attachment here. I'm awfully lucky to have been given this commission.'

'No, you're not. It's due to talent, not luck,' he said with a

174

smile. 'You're a damn good artist, but you'll be a miraculous one if you find anything worth painting here, Vesta. The whole set-up is dreadfully depressing.'

'So was war, but I managed to find the human side of it.' She pushed away her plate and looked at him frankly. 'I must admit I missed you more keenly than I'd expected, but I don't want you to read too much into why I've chosen Hanover as my base.'

Covering her hand with his, he murmured, 'Let *me* worry about what I read. Thanks for overlooking my foolish outburst, and for explaining everything. You know I'll give you all the help I can . . . but there's no way I'll let you near my bombs.'

Glad they were back to their old relationship, she smiled rather sleepily. 'Oh, yeah? We'll see about that.'

Vesta reluctantly admitted she had not bargained for what she found in Hanover. Desperate people lived in the rubble, in cellars and beneath bridges. Stealing was rife. Some did it to survive, others to cling on to a sense of importance in the humiliation of defeat. There was a dark element of this society which traded on hunger and poverty to prosper; perverts gained all they needed in exchange for a few potatoes or some coffee in a twist of paper.

For the first few days Vesta came to terms with her impulsive decision to make Hanover a temporary base. She soon realized there were two drawbacks at the moment. The more pressing of these was lack of transport; the other was a need to find different accommodation. The club was too expensive and too noisy. She could not possibly paint there. The answer to that problem came from Jim Shannon.

Paul's second-in-command was easy to get on with. At twenty-three he was widely experienced in life. After narrow escapes from German invaders of several Mediterranean strongholds, he had gone on to India and the Burmese border. At the tail-end of the war he had been a prisoner for a month before being released by advancing Allied forces. He was an inveterate flirt, which meant a foursome could be arranged for any evening. When Vesta mentioned her wish to find a room which was more private, he produced the ideal solution. One of his former girlfriends who worked in the NAAFI as a secretary was about to marry a sergeant and move into married quarters, leaving a vacancy in her apartment block. A combined application from Paul and Jim, plus the impressive credentials Vesta produced, gained her the large bed-sitting room which had a basic stove and a large cupboard in an alcove to serve as a kitchen. It suited Vesta's needs, however far a cry from her studio at Tarrant Hall. She had worked in tents, on mountainsides, in tavernas. All she needed was inspiration, the raw materials and peace. The last two she already had. The first still had to materialize.

By the end of the second week, all she had done was to sketch cameos she would later consider as possible subjects for a full canvas. One was that of a woman dragging through the street a wooden crate on runners, containing a baby and firewood gathered from the rubble. On the crate in heavy black lettering was: 'DANGER. HIGHLY EXPLOSIVE'. The second featured the shell of a building, surrounded by emaciated workmen under the direction of an army detachment who were slowly demolishing it. Balanced on a high wall that stood without support had been two cats, backs arched in aggression, ready to fly at each other. Beneath them swung a board announcing in English and German: 'UNSAFE. KEEP WELL CLEAR'.

The question of transport remained unsolved. Nothing, not even her letters from 'Daddy's Connections', would move anyone to allocate a jeep for her private use. Knowing full well that if Brad were with her one would be immediately forthcoming, Vesta simmered with anger and pondered how she could get around her problem. Paul had kept his promise to help her all he could, but he was unable to drive her around each day. Yet the only way she would ever get started on her work was to find a military escort with a vehicle. After giving it a great deal of thought, she believed she had hit upon the perfect answer and told Paul. He then offered her the use of his telephone which connected with all the military establishments.

Picking her up after breakfast, he drove her back to his office. Vesta then had the first insight into the routine of this special unit as he showed her around the group of huts. In the outer office where she had waited with her suitcases was the sapper who had treated her as a floosie. He was meticulously polite and poker-faced this morning. In the next office were several clerks sitting at desks covered with forms and indents. Beyond that was another room where a sergeant was making notes from a manual. On the wall were several maps of Hanover and its environs, with coloured markers dotted quite thickly in several areas. The NCO was friendly, and clearly on good terms with his commander.

'Sergeant Gates is my right-hand man,' Paul explained after introducing Vesta. 'It's essential in our game to have someone you can trust beside you, and he's one of the best.'

Gates smiled at Vesta. 'He's being modest, miss. Without Mr Gaynor's quick action I'd have been playing a harp up top by now.'

After this exchange of compliments, Paul indicated the map. 'Those markers show where bombs or landmines have been discovered and put out of action. If there looks to be rather a lot it's because that map went up when the unit first arrived here. As the city is cleared so our job grows lighter.'

Although this exchange had been in casual tones Vesta was suddenly invaded by a chill of apprehension. At each of those locations either Paul or Jim had been in acute danger from live weapons which had lain undisturbed for many, many months.

The men of this Royal Engineers unit were typical of those she had encountered throughout her career as a war artist, and she very quickly banished the impression that she was their officer's bedwarmer by telling them what she intended to do in Germany and what she had done in Italy during the struggle to take that country. Their expressions showed her they were confounded, bringing an inner smile.

Paul's smile was very evident, however, as he showed her the room used for training. Charts, diagrams and photographs adorned the walls, and several tables bore unarmed samples of weapons of every size and variety. 'You've now made my men more in awe of you than of any of these. You certainly know how to cut a man down to size. Including me,' he added on a sudden quiet note.

'What nonsense!' she returned uneasily. 'I simply like to get things straight with people who find it hard to think of women as anything but someone to cuddle at every opportunity. You're not like that.'

'I am where you're concerned.'

She changed the subject. 'What do you do with all these?'

'Show the men how the weapons work, then how to prevent them from doing so when they happen to be nearby. The routine's a bit different here. It's Jim or me, accompanied by a sergeant, who takes a close look to decide how best to deal with each one uncovered, then we send the NCO away and get on with it. In wartime men can find themselves suddenly minus their officers in a highly dangerous situation, so they need to know what to do with these blighters.' He indicated some mines like ones Vesta had seen in the desert. 'Remember these? Thousands of them all over North Africa, buried by every force that passed by. What d'you bet camel caravans for years to come will be wandering across forgotten mine-fields and wondering what hit them?'

The chill touched her again at this reminder of what he was engaged in here. 'Can I make some sketches of this room, at least?'

'I shouldn't think it would make a very exciting picture,' he said. 'Come on, let's go back to the office so that you can ring Major Palmer.'

After a fruitless ten-minute conversation which told Vesta Tim Palmer very definitely needed cutting down to size, she rang off and appealed to Paul. 'How do I get to Zirkusstrasse?'

He raised his eyebrows. 'I got the impression friend Palmer was not being cooperative. Are you planning to beard him in his den?'

'Of course. I'm not letting him get away with a total refusal to allow me to study what he does out here.'

'I did.'

She made a face at him. 'I'll go to work on you, in time.'

'Do so, and all you'll get is a fate worse than death.'

'How do I get from here to Zirkusstrasse?' she asked again to get on to safer ground.

He stood up. 'You ask me very nicely if I'll send you there in one of my jeeps.' After she kissed him, he added, 'That wasn't nearly nice enough, but I'll have to make do with it until this evening. Good thing you're dressed in workmanlike fashion. Not only will it make you look less obvious in an RE vehicle, it won't give Palmer ideas I won't approve of.'

It was good to be out in pursuit of her work, and Vesta had a fresh sight of the city as the driver crossed it almost diagonally to reach Major Palmer's office in a reasonably undamaged area. On arrival, the Vesta Sheridan formula for getting what she wanted from bumptious military males did not have to be used. The first man she clapped eyes on had been a senior subaltern at headquarters in Cairo when she was there.

'Billy!' she cried with pleasure. 'What on earth are you doing here?'

William Dodd swung round in surprise, then gave a broad smile. 'Good God, Vesta Sheridan! Still as lovely as ever. You're the only woman I know who looks equally edible in khaki serge or powder-blue chiffon.'

She laughed. 'You haven't changed a bit, you old flatterer. Oh, it's *good* to see you.'

He took her hands. 'Are you working again?' When she nodded, he asked, 'With Brad Holland?'

'On my own,' she told him, her jollity fading.

'I read his articles on Hiroshima. Brilliant.'

'Yes, he's very good at what he calls heart and soul stuff.'

'So are you, as I recall.' He put a hand on her back and indicated a hut across an open clearing. 'Let's go to my office and I'll rustle up some coffee.' They began walking. 'I've several chums in the American sector who give me good coffee whenever we liaise.'

'In exchange for what?' she asked, trying not to dwell on Brad's brilliance.

'My uninhibited cooperation of course.' Billy opened the door for her. 'What do we have on offer that Americans don't already have in ten times the quantity and at least twice the size?'

'Culture,' she suggested quietly.

Billy's corporal went off to make coffee for them, and they exchanged reminiscences of Cairo and others who had served with them. Then Billy asked, 'How long have you been here and where have you been living?'

Vesta told him, giving no hint of a relationship with Paul. 'I

179

was hoping to do something based on the work of the bomb-disposal unit, but Lieutenant Gaynor – his father was a colleague of Daddy's which is how I know about his presence here – flatly refuses to let me anywhere near one of his jobs.'

'Hmmm. Can't say I blame him, I suppose. Have you explained what you did in Italy?'

'Oh yes, he knows all that, but he's one of the old-fashioned gentlemanly kind who need to protect women.'

Billy made a face. 'Does that mean you think I'm not?'

She laughed. 'I hope you're not, because I'm after your help to enable me to go where no one in pale-blue chiffon would dare to tread.'

'Still the relentless pursuer of the gritty side of life?'

'That's me.'

Over American coffee they discussed possibilities, and Vesta was delighted with the scope of the work undertaken by the Military Police in Hanover. 'Can I sit in on some of these activities?' she asked. 'I have a letter from General Noble and another from Lord Moore requesting that I be given every assistance. Do you think they'll be enough to soften up Major Palmer? He was dreadfully stodgy when I rang him earlier this morning.'

'His wife is giving him a hard time, that's why. The Yanks have discovered she has plenty to exchange for their coffee.'

'How's your wife, Billy? Is she here with you?'

He shook his head. 'She got her supply of coffee while I was in a POW camp. The Yanks may not have our culture, but they have our women.'

Vesta expressed sympathy but swiftly returned to business. 'Do I have any chance of winning Major Palmer over, d'you think?'

Billy got to his feet, and Vesta thought his wife a fool to leave a nice, reliable man who, beneath his outer flippancy, was really quite intense. Yet she knew too well how fatal it was to fall for easy American charm and persuasion.

'I'll introduce you to a few people, then give you lunch in our Mess, such as it is. Once he sets eyes on you, Tim will agree to anything. If he doesn't, we'll do it without him. I'm his two-i-c and, in his present state of misery, he takes little interest in what I'm doing.'

Billy was right. Major Palmer was tense and unresponsive over lunch in the basement of an office block, which was furnished with a large dining table of army pattern and a scattering of armchairs to suggest an ante-room. 'We don't miss windows, Miss Sheridan,' he told her. 'The view is hardly worth seeing from here in any direction.'

He glanced at her letters then told Billy to see what he could do about giving their guest access to the dog compounds and the vehicle yard. Vesta thanked providence for that friendship in Cairo, without which she would have got no further than she had with Paul. Billy seemed as pleased as she over the reunion, and they spent a large part of the afternoon discussing the possibilities and how to carry them out. That evening she was full of enthusiasm and, over dinner at the club, regaled Paul and Jim with details of the day, of the happy chance of Billy Dodd being in exactly the right place at the right time, and of her time in Cairo.

'It was there I received a telephone message at some ungodly hour telling me David had turned up alive in Australia. The caller claimed to be a Major Ronson from Headquarters, but I knew the names of all the staff there and his wasn't amongst them.' She looked at Paul. 'I suppose he was something to do with SOE.'

'Or some other secret group. There were a number of them operating.'

'Yes, and most of them didn't know of the others' existence,' put in Jim, always ready with an anecdote. 'When I was on Crete, one bloody stupid gang with blackened faces took prisoner another lot there on a different mission. There was a hell of a stink about it when it was discovered they'd mucked up two secret operations.'

They all laughed, and were then accosted by a former girlfriend of the irrepressible Jim (who was presently looking for a new conquest, which was why he was odd one out at their table). While this cheerful conversation took place – Jim's 'exes', as he called them, always appeared to retain affection for him – Vesta studied Paul, who had fallen quiet. He was revealing a new facet of his character which she found unexpectedly appealing. As a lecturer in Salisbury, he had been calm, amusing and attentive. Here, he was alert and vitally positive. It was as though he had come alive with a vengeance. Yet he now sat taking little part in the laughter radiated by Jim, the girl and her latest escort. When the pair had departed and a steward served their pudding, Vesta asked Paul what he had been doing that day.

'Had to attend a staff meeting after lunch which went on until gone five,' he told her. 'Everyone's getting edgy about the Russians. They've never been happy about splitting Berlin into sectors and it's growing more and more obvious they want us out. They're taking all manner of liberties – crossing the sector boundaries, prohibiting the transit of people in their sector into others to visit friends and relatives, and needlessly rubber-stamping everything within sight.'

'What has that to do with you and the military units in Hanover?' Vesta asked curiously.

'Quite a lot, indirectly. Several canny scaremongers are urging us, the French and the Yanks to speed up our rebuilding programmes so that we don't rely so much on Russian cooperation. They have control of all the manufacturing and supply centres. If they ever got stroppy and laid out impossible demands for full control of Berlin, they could make life damn difficult for us. We've been told to expedite progress.' He ran his hand through his hair in a nervous gesture. 'I don't see how we can. The chaps in charge of demolition and clearance have a workforce of skinny, undernourished, demoralized Jerries who just aren't up to the job. Without a massive injection of food – it would have to be from the Yanks; neither we nor the French have enough for our own people – or a massive influx of brawny labourers, it can't be done.'

'Did you tell 'em that, Bulldog?' asked Jim with interest.

'I joined a concerted chorus. They're right, of course. The whole business of dividing a conquered country between the victors has caused trouble throughout history. It's often led to further wars.'

'I wouldn't put *that* past the Russkies,' said Jim thoughtfully. 'Stalin has his sights on expansion of borders and Communist indoctrination of as much of Europe as he can control.'

Vesta grew concerned. 'You're not really serious, are you?'

'Yes,' they said together, Paul adding, 'The alliance with our vodka-quaffing neighbours is an uneasy one.'

'Very po-faced, their officials,' Jim commented.

'And their troops are trigger happy. I shouldn't like to be in Berlin with them all around me, should you?'

That conversation, and Paul's subdued mood, put a slight damper on their evening so it broke up early. As they walked to the jeep, Paul complained of a heavy day on the morrow. 'I've got to write a full report on today's meeting, and give two lectures on explosive devices at opposite ends of Hanover. It would be on a day I'm also on call.'

'On call for what?' asked Vesta, climbing into the front seat and thinking that dresses were not designed for riding in jeeps.

Paul flashed her a curious glance as he settled behind the wheel, but it was Jim who answered her question. 'Emergencies, like the discovery of a whacking great landmine sitting in rubble next door to the sewage works. Can you imagine the disaster if it went off bang?' he finished jovially from the rear seat. As they drove from the car park, he said to Paul, 'I'm not going to offer to swap duties. I did my stint today. After defusing the bloody thing we were held up bringing it away by a mob of Jerries on hunger strike, who chanted abuse at us and called us murderers. Talk about the pot and the kettle! I'd just been risking my life to make their city safe and that's all I got for my pains.'

Vesta twisted in her seat to study his face. 'You dismantled a bomb this afternoon? Oh, Jim, why didn't you say so before?'

'What difference would it have made to the evening?' demanded Paul. 'It's our job. It's what we do.'

'Don't worry, girl,' Jim reassured her with a smile. 'It was a piece of cake.'

Vesta did worry. While she had been enjoying Billy Dodd's company, Jim had been in mortal danger. She was quiet until she reached her room.

Then, as the two men prepared to leave, Vesta gave Jim an impulsive kiss on the cheek. 'Take care, won't you?'

'Hey, what's this?' asked Paul. 'I thought that kind of concern was reserved for me.'

In a fey mood brought on by their conversation she kissed *him* more lingeringly on the lips. 'Don't do anything rash, will you? I'm rather fond of you . . . *both*,' she added swiftly.

'Aha!' crowed Jim. 'I've made a conquest at last.'

Vesta pushed them towards the jeep. 'Go home. I've a busy day tomorrow.'

Paul returned to kiss her again, in possessive fashion. 'You take care, too.'

'Oh, I'll be in the best possible company,' she responded lightly. 'No one will dare to challenge MPs . . . and Billy will be with me.'

'Yes,' he agreed hollowly, 'I suppose he will.'

CHAPTER TEN

FOR the next few weeks Vesta was tremendously busy. Billy arranged opportunities for her to see and draw many aspects in the life of an occupation force. She spent an hour or so at the station checkpoint where she had sought help on arrival. She had a fascinating day at the centre for tracing missing persons, and another with a team which tracked down the sources of black-market goods. Their percentage of success was low. The racketeers were wily and knew every cellar and sewer better than the British army policemen. Many of the activities involved working closely with some members of the German civil police, which was gradually being revived as a law-keeping force in accordance with the plan to get nationals back to work on restoring their country. Vesta learnt something about these men by speaking to them in German, and occasionally helped out by translating when the MPs had difficulty explaining what they wanted.

After initial resistance from some of the British troops, she was very soon regarded as one of the boys and became popular with them all. All save Major Palmer, who nodded coolly whenever they happened to pass, and eventually asked Billy, 'How long will that woman take to finish painting the dog compounds?' His second-in-command gave a non-committal reply and hoped Mrs Palmer would continue her antics and thus prevent her husband from seeing what Vesta was really doing.

When Billy himself had to go to a small outlying village to check on the reported sighting of a Nazi wanted for war crimes, he took Vesta along. It proved to be a false alarm, but she enjoyed being an observer while he and two soldiers questioned the residents and the cobbler who had made the report. She enjoyed even more the chance to quit the devastated city and see fields and animals for a few hours. It was a typical pretty Germanic village with an ancient church at its centre. As the weather had been good for a day or two, Billy had told the Mess sergeant to pack a picnic for two, and they sat beside the river to eat it while the other pair found a dilapidated beer-garden.

Gazing around at the distant low hills and spread of open countryside, Vesta sighed with pleasure. 'In Hanover it's difficult to believe this kind of thing exists, isn't it, and I've only been there for five weeks.' She leaned back on her outstretched arms. 'This reminds me of home, in a way, although the last time I saw it it was under flood water.'

'So was this,' he said, also surveying the scene. 'On a day like today we shouldn't be sitting beside a jeep, me in full fig khaki and you dressed like a mercenary in some nabob's private army. I should be in a comfortable sports shirt and grey flannels, and you should be wearing a pretty low-necked cotton dress so that I could now turn around and lie with my head in your lap.'

She smiled, lost in the pleasure of the scene. 'Sorry about the no-nonsense shirt and slacks, but you're welcome to my lap.'

He touched her arm lightly. 'Thanks, but starched collar, rather tight webbing belt and gun in holster tend to hamper such delightful pastimes.' After a momentary silence he asked, 'What's the situation between you and Gaynor? From all you've let slip over the past weeks I suspect there's more than friendship between fathers behind it.'

'Do you?'

He studied her face. 'Keeping mum on the subject? All right, but if he's not in the running I wouldn't mind taking my chances.'

The pleasure of the moment was fading. Turning to look at him, she said, 'You'll hate me for saying any girl would be flattered to be told that, but I'm more concerned with getting my career back on course than with romance.'

'Unless it was Brad Holland beside you. I heard you two were a pair for life. What happened?'

'He went after an exclusive. Shall we pack up and go for a walk?'

When they were strolling along the towpath Billy said, 'Can

I make amends for my *faux pas* by offering you something which would give Tim Palmer forty fits?' He had her immediate attention. 'We're making a big effort to crack down on all the subterranean dives selling false papers, hooch, desperate girls and anything under the sun that people want. It's on for tomorrow night and it's a maximum effort job. Would you like to come in my jeep and see what my lads dredge up?'

'*Would I?*' she cried, filled with excitement. 'Billy, you're a lamb!'

'Just be glad I'm not a wolf,' he riposted. 'We're very, very alone along this path.'

She decided not to mention to Paul what she planned to do the following evening. He would be certain to object; possibly try to stop her from going. Their date for the evening was cancelled, however, by an apologetic note from him explaining that he had been summoned to a promotions board and had to leave early in the morning. As he would be away four days there was some paperwork he would need to catch up on before he left. He bade her not to take any risks in his absence, and hoped her study of the dog compounds was progressing. It was a private joke between them and Jim. The note ended with a message of love which made her feel guilty. She had not seen much of Paul recently, and when she had all she had done was to prattle about how well her ideas were progressing. Yet she had been aware of lines of strain reappearing on his face, and Jim had let slip the fact that they had both tackled a landmine lodged in the piled debris of a gutted textile factory on a day when she had been sitting in the sunshine, sketching food supplies being unloaded from goods waggons ringed by armed guards. While she had been perfectly safe from aggression by starving Germans watching boxes of food passing before their eyes, two men she had been very fond of had been grappling with danger. She vowed to make amends when Paul returned, and she was glad he would be away from danger for four days.

The operation was due to commence at eleven p.m. Vesta dressed in trousers and shirt, then pulled a black jumper over it. Billy had a sergeant with him and Vesta recognized the man who had driven her from the station on her arrival. She greeted him gaily as an old friend and climbed into the truck, amused at the NCO's astonishment at her presence with them.

Billy turned to her. 'On no account are you to leave the vehicle. You do understand that, don't you? Officially, you're not here.'

'Don't worry,' she told him. 'I won't do anything silly.'

Once they set off, Vesta was ignored. While Sergeant Grogan drove, Billy kept in touch with the occupants of other trucks by walkie-talkie. It was a fine night with a heaven full of stars. The looming ruins took on an almost romantic guise as dark, uneven outlines against a moonlit sky. She was mentally back in Italy, driving through the night to reach a bridgehead or bottleneck where the action was happening. Brad had always wanted the latest news. She had observed and memorized to add reality to her pictures. Racing along uneven streets in a military truck tonight set her pulse thudding. Small wonder *The Old Mill* had represented nothing more than a job to be done. *This* was art in the flesh; creation from stark reality. Inspiration had returned with a vengeance.

Sergeant Grogan pulled up and switched off the engine. Billy spoke into his walkie-talkie, checking that everyone was in place. All over the city traps were being set. From where they sat it seemed impossible that any kind of seedy nightlife could be underway, but the Military Police knew their locations well enough. From the back of the truck jumped four armed soldiers. They were then joined by Grogan, and Billy Dodd. Vesta had been forgotten in the urgency of the moment.

'Are you certain the entrance is down there?' asked Billy of one of his men.

'Yessir. It's cleverly hid, but it's there all right.'

'It had better be,' came the grim response. 'Right, let's go.'

From her seat in the truck Vesta could see dark figures moving forward to melt into the larger mass of broken building. Next minute, a pale wedge of light appeared below ground level and the place came alive with shouts and screams. Like a sudden doorway opening to hell, thought Vesta, watching rapt. The shouted commands of the policemen gradually silenced other voices, and Vesta could soon see figures outlined against that wedge of light as people were marshalled ready to leave.

The organized scene then broke up as a shot rang out. More screams. Panic. A silhouetted figure scrambled from the depths of the building too intent on escaping to stop and fire again. Two Redcaps came up after him, cursing and firing blindly while ordering him to stop. Ruins are easy to hide in. The figure vanished as the other MPs came up to street level, leaving one of their number guarding the doorway. The soldiers shouted to each other. Billy told them to fan out and search.

'He's the one we really want. The rest are chicken-feed,' he said savagely.

Flashlights pinpointed the way the troops were moving, which told their quarry how to evade them. Yet it was impossible to search without illumination. It was too dangerous in shifting rubble. Vesta watched with a matching sense of frustration and disappointment. The whole affair had been going well before that shot was fired. She felt there was little hope of catching the one who apparently was a top man in this curious post-war underworld. Then, as she sat viewing the fruitless action from her seat in the truck, she spotted a figure stealthily climbing a mound of rubble to the rear of the search area.

She leaned from the window. 'Over here. About fifteen feet up!'

Flashlights swung round to converge on the mound, as soldiers ran forward firing. Intermittently illuminated by the swaying beams, the figure fired back at them before scrambling higher. Hoarse voices yelled at him to stop, but a slither of masonry betrayed his further progress. Caught up in the drama, Vesta instinctively did what Brad would have yelled at her to do. Sliding along the seat she switched on the engine and headlights at full beam. The angle was wrong, however. Slipping back into her role as a driver for a war correspondent, she put the vehicle into reverse gear and brought it around until the powerful double lamps picked out the black-coated figure clinging to a crossbeam about ten feet from the summit. Shots were fired from almost beside her, and all around, as the Redcaps covered their quarry from each direction. He no longer had a hope and sagged against the broken masonry while his captors climbed up to get him.

Vesta was elated. She had her prime picture. That pathetic

but vile creature caught in strong white beams and circled by brawny MPs was as evocative an image of the work of an occupation force as she had yet seen. It was exactly what she had been seeking. When she turned in excitement, Brad was not, after all, beside her. The pang of disappointment lasted no more than a few seconds, but she there and then understood why he had gone to Japan instead of settling at Tarrant Royal to write a book.

The night Paul returned to Hanover Vesta was having a celebration dinner with Billy Dodd, and the following evening there was a compulsory Mess night to greet high-ranking guests, so it was not until six days after the police raid that Vesta entertained both Paul and Jim to dinner in her apartment, in order to tell them of her success. Paul seemed disinclined to elaborate on details of the selection board, so she did not press him, believing that he was apprehensive about his chances. In any case, she was bursting to relate her own story.

As she was not exactly a magical cook, one of the other women in the block had helped her with the preparation of a meal she assured Vesta was perfectly light enough for a hot summer evening yet sufficiently substantial for hungry men. Jim ate heartily, but Paul appeared unusually uninterested in what she placed before him. Waiting until she had served up creamed chicken with mushrooms, potatoes and green beans, Vesta embarked on the tale she had been saving for the right moment.

When she had finished, she added, 'The part I played couldn't be included in the official report, of course – Tim Palmer would be *livid* if he knew about it – but Billy has promised me a big favour as a reward. And guess what! The boys today presented me with one of their official armbands.' She took it from a pocket to dangle it from her fingers. 'Wasn't it sweet of them? I was ridiculously touched.'

There was a moment's silence, then Paul exploded. 'What a bloody damn fool thing to do! He should be court-martialled for allowing you to go on an armed raid. And you're just as stupid. Christ, if I'd been here there's no way you'd have been exposed to such danger. I'll bloody well tell Palmer his two-i-c is risking the life of a girl who seems able to make him do anything she wants.'

Vesta should have expected this reaction, but the incident

was over, she was all right, and she was exultant about it. 'Don't be melodramatic,' she said dismissively. 'What I did with Brad was infinitely more dangerous.'

'Then he's another stupid bastard,' came the savage response. 'That seems to be the type you go for.'

Jim intervened with an attempt to lighten the atmosphere. 'I thought it was your ambition to *paint* the Military Police, not *join* them.'

Ignoring the inexplicable facial gestures Jim was making, Vesta continued as if Paul were not acting up. 'They took me back to the spot in daylight so that I could make sketches. All I now need is a volunteer to spreadeagle himself on the rubble so that I can check the angle of arms and legs.' Flashing Jim a smile, she said, 'How about you?'

'Ask dear *Billy*,' sneered Paul. 'He'll do it like a shot.'

Vesta's patience ran out. 'Stop being childish! I've a commission to paint what's going on in Hanover. Billy Dodd is an old friend offering me every assistance to do my job by giving me access to his. Which is more than can be said of *you*.'

With a sudden movement Paul stood up, sending his chair on to its back. 'Perhaps you'd like to have come with me yesterday. What appeared to be a straightforward job went wrong. The bloody thing exploded and I blew up an entire family. Wouldn't *that* have made a fine subject for a painting!' He walked away to the window, one white-knuckled hand gripping the back of his neck.

'I tried to signal you to ease off,' said Jim in an undertone.

Greatly shaken, Vesta whispered back, 'You should have tried harder. What do I do now?'

Jim's expression said it all as he got to his feet. 'I thought you knew how to handle truculent men, dearie. I'll nip upstairs and thank your fellow chef for a delicious meal.'

Vesta stayed where she was after Jim left to give herself time to think. Brad had been brutal with words but perfectly controlled when angered. This man was the type who might lose his control and do something he would later regret. She would hate that to happen after the tragedy of yesterday. Jim was wrong. Although she frequently boasted of being able to handle men, especially self-important military ones, it was purely on a professional level. Vesta Sheridan was fine as one of the boys. It was when they treated her as a girl that the barriers came up and she backed away.

'There were three children,' Paul said suddenly, in stark tones. 'Terribly skinny. One was a girl. About three, I suppose. Born during the last desperate months of the war. As I looked at her I thought, she probably never had a doll.' A pause. 'Every little girl should have a doll, however short and violent their lives. I can't stop thinking about it.'

From her place at the table Vesta said softly, 'She had one, Paul, I promise you. It might have been only a broken piece of brick wrapped around with a piece of cloth, but she would have seen it through the magical eyes of childhood. I remember many children in Italy cuddling 'dolls' of every description, from shrivelled turnips to scraps of wood. They don't have to be made of porcelain, with long hair and satin dresses. Make-believe turns even a scrubbing-brush into a beloved toy when there's no other.'

He swung to face her. 'What kind of picture would your artistic make-believe turn that tragedy into?'

'I don't paint make-believe. That's why I'm a war artist.' She knew how to handle the situation now, and approached him with confidence. 'I've seen people die, too, don't forget. Friends, strangers, foreigners. I know how you must be feeling. My pictures are intended to make others know, too. Just because the war's over, the danger and dying hasn't stopped. At home they're all grumbling about bread rationing. They should know what's going on elsewhere. Yes, I'm human enough to want artistic recognition and go all out to get it, but don't condemn me as totally heartless.'

Coming back fast from the place he had been in, he asked, 'When have I ever said you are?'

'You implied it just now.'

He reached out to touch her cheek lightly with his fingers. 'Sorry. You going on and on about your Redcaps got me on the raw.'

'I didn't then know what had happened,' she protested.

Taking her hand he played with her fingers for a moment or two before glancing up. 'I'm bloody jealous, that's the problem. It's getting worse. I'm even jealous of Jim, and I know *he* hasn't designs on you.'

'Neither has anyone else. All the men who've driven me around or explained the ins and outs of their jobs have been no more than friendly and helpful.'

'Then they must be blind.'

'It's a *working* relationship,' she explained as patiently as she could. 'I've had a lot of practice at establishing them. Most men read signals from women very swiftly and adjust their behaviour accordingly. The few who don't read mine very soon regret it, believe me.'

Paul took hold of her other hand and placed it so that it rested on the one he already clasped. 'I'm in the Engineers, not Signals, so *I'm* not very good at reading yours. All I know is that I long to tell every chap who comes near you to clear off, and I want the right to do it. A captain's pay isn't bad, and I have an allowance from my father each month. I'm sure to get a posting when my promotion comes through – there's no vacancy here for a captain and we're bringing in more and more German explosives personnel to take over this job from us. When the move comes I can apply to transfer to another branch of the corps. I've been in explosives quite long enough to be reasonably certain of getting what I want. My record's good enough to take me a long way up the ladder before I retire, so you'd have a comfortable life. I wouldn't interfere with your work, although you'd have to be prepared to go anywhere in the world at quite short notice. That might be an advantage to a war artist.' He gave a nervous smile. 'I can't swear I'll never be jealous of other men, but I'll have the right to knock for six any who overstep the mark with you.'

Filled with dismay, Vesta drew her hands free. 'Oh Paul, I told you not to read too much into my coming here.'

'I know, but I've just explained that your signals are confusing. I'm trying to find out where I stand with you.'

She did not herself know the answer. 'I thought we had the perfect arrangement here.'

'It's a bloody awful arrangement . Jim's always around, and I want you so much I can't concentrate on anything else. If you won't let me take you to bed legally, I'll end up doing it the other way one night. I mean it. If I have another day like yesterday, you'll be for it, whether you agree or not.'

Vesta sighed, looking up into his drawn face. 'You could do that with any number of girls who'd gladly give you what you wanted. If you ever take me to bed I know it'll be because we're both happy about it, not simply to get something out of your system.'

He gave a bitter laugh. 'The officer and gentleman? I'm just as basic as Brad Holland, and I'm bloody certain *he* didn't wait for your permission.'

'He had to wait two years,' she said flatly. 'In the interval he found solace elsewhere. Perhaps you should do the same.'

At that he flared up again. 'Perhaps I should, but bear in mind I made you an honourable proposal first. *He* was cheating on his wife with every girl around, but I won't be cheating on anyone, because you don't care a damn.'

After the door slammed behind Paul, Jim came through it to ask tentatively, 'Is that the end of the first round or the whole boxing match?'

Vesta sat again to stare at the remains of their meal. 'He asked me to marry him.'

'I gather you didn't accept.' Jim occupied his former place at the table and poured two glasses of wine from the bottle he had brought with him. 'You'll be sorry when he grabs someone else on the rebound. I speak from experience, dearie.'

'Jim, he's a wonderful person who I know would give me a good life, but I'm not ready to marry *anyone*. I'm here to work, and inspiration is growing daily. In any case, no girl likes to receive a proposal of marriage immediately after being told the man has just inadvertently killed five people. He's shocked and vulnerable at the moment. He's seeking comfort, that's all.'

'Then why not let the poor chap into your bed tonight?'

'Don't you start,' she warned aggressively.

'Oh, already suggested it, has he? Is that why he went off with a flea in his ear?'

'There'll be one in yours if you stay on that subject.' She drank some wine to fortify herself. 'Tell me what happened.'

'He blew up five people living in the rubble. It's not wartime. They weren't enemy troops. We got used to blowing *them* sky high. He was bloody badly shaken when he got back.'

194

'How is it no one knew they were there?' she asked in deep concern.

'God knows. Your police friends scouted the area to check that no one was hiding there or had set up a temporary home. It's the usual procedure. When they've done that they rope off the spot and inform us. We then toddle along and decide whether we can disarm it by fixing a clever device which will withdraw the fuse when slowly turned by a length of cord we wind in from a safe distance, or whether the fuse will have to be taken out manually. Those are the tricky ones, because we have to sit alongside the damn bombs throughout.' He frowned. 'I've no idea what went wrong yesterday. Paul's very experienced and judged it to be a straightforward job. Something must have jammed when he began winding in the cord, and the bomb could have shifted enough to set it off. He's blaming himself. Thinks he muffed it. But you never know with bombs. They're so bloody volatile. You do all the right things, but nothing's certain until the fuse is safely in your hands.'

He frowned again. 'It's bad enough when one goes off on site but if people get killed it really bothers you. There've been other cases, of course. The chap Paul replaced here blew up two drunks just before Christmas in much the same way. The coppers had no idea they were there, and I suppose the old sots never knew what hit them, but John Dell did and went on a bender for several days.'

'Oh lord, Paul won't do that, will he?' She was deeply worried. 'I thought I was handling it just right, then he went off at a tangent and started blaming his state on jealousy of every man around – even you. Before I could get him back to the subject of the tragedy he asked me to marry him. I couldn't just . . .' She appealed for his understanding. 'It was all wrong, Jim. Accepting his proposal wouldn't make things right, would it? It wouldn't have wiped out the sense of blame he's suffering. He needs to have that put into perspective, surely, or he'll go on feeling guilty.' She gave a heavy sigh. 'He did mention a possible transfer to another branch if he gets promotion. It would be the best thing to happen right now. I suppose that's what his predecessor did.'

'Er . . . no.'

Vesta knew the dread answer before she asked, but was compelled to do so. 'Where did he go from here?'

Jim threw the truth at her. 'A bomb went off while he was manually defusing it. Lost concentration momentarily, I suppose. It happens.'

CHAPTER ELEVEN

AFTER the terrible winter came hot rainless months which ruined crops that would have fed the population during the coming winter. The situation was grim. An influx of food, to end hunger and boost production in the coal mines, would not be enough to avert further wholesale deaths from cold and malnutrition in the icy grip of a European winter. The target rate for rebuilding had not been met; coal was being mined well below the level needed to provide heating for the German nation. The British, American and French authorities were deeply worried about this land they had defeated which was turning into a gargantuan responsibility they would give anything to shed. Yet they dare not let up one iota with the Russians gloating over their dilemma and daily complicating it with their inflexible rules and demands. Life for the average German seemed not to have improved much since their surrender, and the work of the occupying army was just as difficult. A number of people in that large core of Europe were holding their breath in apprehension of what would happen when days grew short and bitterly cold.

During those hot late autumn days Vesta sat in the little courtyard of her apartment block to start on her first set of canvases. Inspiration was there in force and she worked well, yet she was subconsciously worrying. After carefully considering whether it would be best to accept Billy Dodd's offer of alternative accommodation on his side of Hanover, she had decided that that course would put greater strain on Paul than staying where she was. In any case, she had settled very happily and enjoyed brief conversations with the other women, who plainly regarded her as quite eccentric. Paul appeared – outwardly at least – to have recovered from his tragic accidental killings, and from Vesta's attitude towards his proposal. She concluded that men were hopeless at timing. Brad had offered her a job in Japan when she wanted marriage and a settled life. Paul offered her just that when she wanted freedom to work. Perhaps it was her perversity as well as their ill-timing.

Using her many sketches she gradually produced a set of pictures which more than satisfied her. One showed ragged, stateless refugees queuing for interrogation on their identity which might gain them official recognition. Another was a starkly observed scene of a seedy cellar club where the riff-raff of Hanover gathered to deal in any commodity that would earn money, cigarettes or food. It was easy to identify the pimp, the forger, the entrepreneur engaged in their business but looking around in alarm at the military policeman who had clearly just entered. The faces were good: not deeply detailed but sharp enough to betray greed, slyness or down-right evil; drawn from sketches Vesta had made of any interesting face she had seen.

On a lighter note there was a canvas of a jeep. On its bonnet perched a small boy wearing an over-large red-covered cap, left there by its owner who was talking to a comrade oblivious to the scene behind him. The boy wore an exaggerated frown, much to the amusement of his urchin pals before him.

The best was undoubtedly her main subject: the nocturnal capture of a leading member of the post-war underworld. She had paid one of the sweepers working for Billy to put on a black coat and trilby before climbing up the mound of rubble to pose for her. He had thought it easy money. So inspired by the memory of that vision was she, the picture recreated it in awesome fashion. Uncertain of Paul's reaction she showed it first to Billy, who wanted to buy it there and then.

'I'll do a special one for you of the dogs' compounds,' she teased. 'You'd be able to own that without awkward questions from Tim Palmer.'

He pulled a face. 'I'm in temporary command. The poor chap's been granted compassionate leave because his wife's taken up permanent residence in the American sector and sent their children home to her mother. He's trying to sort it all out.'

Although Vesta was basically sympathetic, she said, 'If he wasn't such a mirthless stick-in-the-mud, she might have stayed with him.'

He studied her shrewdly. 'In Cairo everyone knew you had a chip on your shoulder over some man. Is it still the same one, or manhood in general?'

'Don't forget you promised me a favour in return for my swift action which got *your* man for you that night,' she said crisply. '*Anything*, you said. I've decided what it's to be.'

'Not to pose for a nude study. I'd be recognized by too many females.'

'Be serious! I want to make pictures of the bomb-disposal unit. Paul flatly refuses to let me even go out with him, and Jim does as he's told. Now, *you* hear about the discoveries even before they do, so you could take me to one of their sites. Or Sergeant Grogan could, or Corporal Josephs, or –'

'All right, don't go through the entire strength,' he interrupted. 'I think Gaynor's got a point, but as he blasted my ear down the telephone line about that business you've just painted so vividly, I've a score to settle with him.'

Vesta was astonished. 'He didn't, did he?'

'Not half. Bloody nerve! I'm waiting for him to put a foot wrong sometime. It'll give me enormous pleasure to pick him up under guard one day and drive him through the streets with an armed escort.'

'Oh, for heaven's sake!' she cried. 'He'd accidentally blown up a couple with three children. You knew about it; must have done. He had to let off steam at someone. You're being childish.'

Billy's telephone rang. While he dealt with the caller Vesta crossed to look from the window at the Alsatian dogs pacing their enclosures restlessly. Had her colleagues in the ATS been equally petty? Yes. Girls had made a big issue of a lipstick loaned but not returned, over a missing card of darning wool, over a bath plug which had been filched so that no one but the culprit could have first bath that evening. *Was* she inexcusably hard on men?

Billy ended his conversation and crossed to her. 'About these unexploded bombs. Even if I arranged for you to be taken to the site of one, there'd be nothing there that you don't see every day. These things are often buried in the bowels of the earth. Certainly deep in the rubble. A wide area is roped off and no one, not even my men, go in there once

Gaynor or young Jim Shannon gets on the job. They disappear from view until it's all over.'

'I want to catch the atmosphere, sense the tension, get an idea of the urgency of the moment. It can't be created without personal experience of it. At least, *I* can't create it. Only because I was there when it happened is *this* painting so effective you wanted to buy it.'

'But you wouldn't see them defusing the bally thing,' he protested, 'and that's surely the essence of the whole business.'

'Of course it is, but I'm almost certain I could talk Jim into simulating what they do by using one of the disarmed bombs they have for instruction courses. I'd put the two images together with a little imagination.'

Billy shook his head in exasperation. 'You could talk him into posing with a live one, I shouldn't wonder.'

'What do you say, Billy?'

'I say that if Paul Gaynor blasted my ear over that night operation, he'd blast me sky high if I did as you ask.'

'But *will* you?'

'I'll see,' came his grudging reply, making Vesta smile because that usually meant yes.

When she got back to her room she made a cup of tea, then received a surprise visit from Paul. 'Hallo, what are you doing here?' she asked cautiously as she let him in. 'Would you like some tea? I've just made it.'

'You haven't got a cold beer instead, have you? It's even hotter today than yesterday.' As she poured the tea and his beer, he added, 'I was passing this way and took a chance on finding you in. I've some news for you.'

'I hope it's good.' She sat facing him. 'Gosh, you *do* look hot. Take off your tunic.'

His attractive blue-green eyes challenged her. 'I'll take the lot off if you will, too.'

It would be all too easy to do so, she realized. He was an extremely vital man who beckoned her sexually whenever she allowed herself to recognize the fact. On the heels of Billy's remarks concerning her implacable attitude towards men, the urge to take up Paul's challenge was strong. Eighteen months had passed since that night with Brad at Tarrant Hall, and she was a young healthy woman with the usual longings. Would it be a great mistake to start something so dangerous? Once they became lovers Paul would want to legalize their relationship, and she was not prepared for that. On the other hand . . .

Because she had taken so long to reply, Paul accepted what he thought was her aloof disregard of his suggestion and spoke about the news he had brought. 'I had two letters today which I thought would interest you. One was an invitation to Jerry Stanstead's wedding.'

Vesta knew a sense of shock. 'Wedding! That's a bit sudden, isn't it?'

'Not really. The girl who threw him over decided she'd made a mistake and asked to be taken back. He's going to make sure of her before she changes her mind again.' He frowned. 'You didn't think he was marrying Pat, did you?'

'I suppose I did . . . just for a moment,' she admitted, wondering if her friend had ever given Jerry what he wanted.

'No. They were both pining for someone else, and using each other for consolation, that's all. You're doing the same with me.'

Unsettled by the conflict between physical desire and mental commonsense, she rose to that. 'If I was after consolation I'd get it from someone who wasn't in love with me. I'm not completely heartless, Paul. That's the second time you've suggested I am.'

'Prove me wrong. My offer's still open.'

She got to her feet in anger. 'You men think the whole business is simple, don't you? See someone you fancy, go to bed, everything in the garden's lovely. Well, it isn't. When I was nineteen David brought home a Polish pilot for Christmas. I fancied *him* like mad. He told us all a heartbreaking story about the rape of his mother and two sisters after he'd flown to England to continue fighting for the freedom of his beloved country. I fell for it hook, line and sinker. When I eventually gave him what he wanted I thought I was somehow easing his pain and sense of national humiliation. Can you *believe* I was so naïve?' she cried with self-contempt. 'He was brutal, selfish and full of derision for my reaction afterwards. We never met again, and Daddy discovered that he had a wife and baby in Poland. There had been no rapes or burning down of his village. Who would you say had been heartless in *that* instance?'

Paul put down his beer and stood up. 'Darling, please . . .'

'No, Paul, you just listen to what I have to say,' she stormed. 'I could have been left with a half-Polish bastard that evening as payment for his ten-minute satisfaction of a basic need.' She moved away to stand gazing from the window into the little sun-washed courtyard. 'In the desert I encountered an American who took me by storm, but I'd learned a hard lesson. As the only girl in that little desert group I could have made them *all* happy for ten minutes. When Brad contrived to get me flown over to partner him in Italy, there's no doubt he blithely thought the partnership would be total. He was married, so it wasn't. I was in love with him, but determined not to be used again when there was no chance of a happy ending. It was hard, believe me, but I stuck to my guns.' She took a deep breath. 'Then he turned up at Daddy's memorial service when I was very emotional and told me his wife wanted a divorce. I went back to Italy as his unpaid mistress.'

'Vesta, don't –'

She swung round to face Paul. '*That's* what I was, because he was still married. He got divorced, spent one night with me at home, then went off again after offering me a trip to Japan on the same terms as before. Sure, he said he'd get some US army chaplain to marry us, if I insisted, but the chance of a journalistic lifetime was the really important thing. Do you brand me heartless for refusing to go?'

Very obviously upset, Paul moved forward and took her hands. 'I'm sorry. I'm *sorry*. You're a wonderful girl who's achieved more than any other I know. It's taken enormous courage to survive right in the heart of conflict, as you did for so long, and to survive as a woman in that man's world without losing your pride and femininity.' He drew her against his chest and wrapped his arms around her. 'You know I'm a jealous chap where you're concerned, and I hate anyone who has hurt you, but please don't rate me with them. I want you. I'd take you if you let me. It's only human, darling, because you're very desirable. But I also love you very much, which means I respect you enough to hold back when you say no but male enough to salve my silly pride by making snide remarks. Forgive me, sweetheart. I had no idea you'd been so hurt by other men. You should have told me before, then I'd have understood. I'd also have asked you to marry me before I left Salisbury for Germany.' His kisses were gentle and consoling. 'I still want you to. Just keep it in mind.'

The sizzle of challenge had been dampened by their change of mood, so Vesta made more tea and poured him another beer before attempting to get back on an even keel. Paul managed it first.

'I had another letter today which will be of particular interest to you. At my request, Father has done some research into the bona fides of your mysterious Leo Roberts.'

Vesta was taken by surprise. 'You didn't tell me you had written to your father.'

'I told you he could probably find out about Roberts. You were upset about the chap, so I wrote to him right away.'

'That was very sweet of you,' she said with warmth.

'I have other sweet ways I'll demonstrate to you when you're ready.' He smiled to soften the sexual hint. 'For now, I'll tell you about your prospective stepfather. Roberts was recruited as soon as Churchill set up SOE in 1940. He was a natural for their operations in Scandinavia. He spoke the language fluently, knew Norway and had friends as well as in-laws there – he had married a Norwegian woman and lived in her village for some years until she was killed during a mountain rescue – and he was also a radio ham with contacts up there.'

Seeing in her mind's eye the man she had insulted, Vesta found she could better equate him with espionage work than her gentle, aesthetic father. 'Is there any more?' she asked Paul.

'I'll say. He worked well for three years, then disaster struck. The cell began to collapse. One by one the agents were captured, their missions aborted by German troops. All the clues pointed to Roberts, and he was denounced by the only other agent still free in that area. He was brought home on a false excuse and allowed leave so that he could be watched. They did all the usual things – tapped his phone, doctored his radio receiver, followed him wherever he went. Then, when his fiancée upped and married a factory owner, they sent one of the prostitutes who worked for them to discover what he muttered in his sleep. Don't look so wide-eyed, darling, my

203

father had the full treatment at one stage and, presumably, so did yours.'

'That's *terrible*,' she said, abandoning her tea. 'It's taking someone over so totally he has no persona left. It turns him into a . . . a . . .'

'A member of SOE. Vesta, a large number of lives depended on those agents.'

'And a large number depended on you when you had to clear a mine-field. *You* didn't have to go through such humiliating treatment, nor did all the other service personnel who held responsibility for other lives.'

Paul kissed her lightly, and smiled into her eyes. 'So sparky! That's what I love about you. No pink-cheeked little English rose, *my* girl. Thanks for your description of me as a semi-hero, but *I* wasn't the possessor of very secret information. Those of us in the services would have been prisoners of war if we were captured. SOE agents were tortured to death if *they* got caught.'

Not liking what Paul was revealing, Vesta said shortly, 'You'd better get on with the story. I suppose you know what happened after that.'

'Friend Leo acted with such remarkable circumspection his masters decided it was a cover, so he was called in for questioning.' He frowned. 'Your father conducted the interrogation. It went on for most of a day, then Roberts was dragged from his bed, thrown into a cell-like room and bullied for hours with bright lights on his face. It was standard procedure, Father said.'

'I thought it was the Gestapo who did things like that,' Vesta said through stiff lips.

'The Gestapo *started* with that. For SOE it was the final step. Although Roberts acquitted himself well enough, he did know rather a lot about top Germans in Norway. The people at Beaulieu Manor decided on discretion. Roberts was sent to one of their isolated centres for suspected traitors and virtually imprisoned there for a year.'

Vesta was deeply shaken. 'I can't believe Daddy would be involved in anything of that nature. He hated violence.'

'So do we, darling, but the war left us with no choice. Your father did as he was ordered to do, as everyone did.'

'You said Leo was imprisoned for a year. Why was he released?'

Paul gave her a thoughtful look. 'You're not going to like this bit very much.'

'I haven't liked the other bits. The rest can't be worse.'

'It is, I'm afraid. When D-Day was planned, the most elaborate steps were taken to dupe the Jerries into believing the landings would be made elsewhere on different dates. SOE sent him back to Norway carrying coded messages giving false information, which they believed he would hand straight over to his German chums. He didn't, but the twelve months he spent at that detention centre had been so demoralizing he had lost his touch. Carelessness led to his capture in a mountain hut. He was ruthlessly tortured and left for dead by his captors. His brother-in-law, who had hidden nearby when he saw enemy troopers at the hut, nursed him back to life. It was then that Roberts revealed the hiding place of his documents so that they could be safely delivered to the Norwegian Resistance, who contacted SOE and asked what they were playing at because they'd just heard news of the successful landings in Normandy.' He paused to take Vesta's hands in his once more. 'I said you wouldn't like it.'

It was an understatement. She had treated Leo as a liar and a fraud, much the way SOE had treated him. How had he felt to have a second Sheridan putting him through the third degree?

'Father said they brought him home as soon as he was fit enough to travel, but he was of no further use to them. They gave him a medal, but I suspect it was little compensation for a man who had gone through hell. The experience changed him dramatically. No one doubted that he had added up the score and realized how he had been used. He became a loner; a man with no roots, no thought of tomorrow. He was given a desk job at Beaulieu Manor. Then, when the war ended, he was offered the sop of what he does now. An undemanding routine he carries out on his own, which gives him mobility and the opportunity to work in peaceful, attractive surroundings.' He gave a heavy sigh. 'I should think Tarrant Hall must represent the ideal retreat to a man who has sacrificed most of his life to two wars, wouldn't you?'

Overcome by this shocking revelation and trying not to show it, Vesta said, 'But it belongs to David. What will Leo do when *he* comes to his senses and returns to settle there?'

'That'll be Leo's dilemma, not yours,' Paul said tenderly. 'By then I hope you'll be sharing an officer's quarters with me somewhere in the world, and painting images more gentle than those connected with war. Like *The Afterglow*. It might not be adorning the walls of a military Mess or club, but I think it's by far the best thing you've ever produced, because it came from the heart. I know you've got one, darling. I was just unaware of how bruised it was. You should have told me long ago.' He got up, drawing her with him. 'I must get back. There's another staff meeting straight after lunch to discuss the latest party tricks of our Red neighbours. We're all pretending like mad that the situation isn't serious, but it damn well is. They haven't the cash and resources, as yet, to start a fight, but the way they're transporting machinery and slave labour east into Russia means it won't be long before they're in a position to challenge us over Berlin. God knows what'll happen then.'

Vesta frowned. 'It's really as serious as that?'

'Not half. You should hear the tales of what's going on at border checkpoints. Our Russkie chums insist on rubber-stamping everything in sight, reading every single word of every document, examining at length every rail passenger's identity documents, and often shunting trains on to sidings with no real explanation offered. As for river traffic, the whole business has slowed almost to a standstill.'

'What about the roads?'

He shrugged. 'Trucks are getting through, but the route lies through forests and drivers always have the feeling that an army will suddenly materialize from the trees. The Russians are happy to encourage that suspicion. Trucks can only take so much through to Berlin. It's rolling stock which moves the most in the shortest time. The way things are going our people in the capital might find life rather hard as winter advances.'

'It won't be long,' she said. 'I can hardly believe I've been here almost six months.'

'I can. I've put a red circle around each day on the calendar.'

Vesta followed him to the door. 'Thanks for coming to tell me about Leo Roberts. In *his* case I really was heartless.'

'You made a judgement based on the facts you knew.' He turned on the doorstep to add, 'Can we put my idiocy behind us now? My judgement of you was based on facts *I* knew. You've now enlightened me.'

'Of course,' she said apologetically, then reached up to kiss him briefly on the mouth. 'I haven't said "no", just "not yet".'

'I'll be patient and won't press you.' His endearing smile appeared. 'When you say the word I'll press you like mad. Be warned!'

In that autumn of 1947 the first fears of a split between west and east Germany began to grow. The Russians steadfastly refused to participate in plans to resolve the terrible dilemma of this giant ruptured country. The British and Americans could see the only solution as being the partial restoration of national control; to set up German authorities and ruling bodies to run, under the eyes of occupying forces, the country's economic and industrial affairs. The Allies did not believe in shouldering the weighty responsibilities when capable and experienced Germans sat idly by. The plan worked, but the Russians meant to crush their former enemies totally, and renewed their demands for reparations in cash and goods due to them as conquerors. Relations between the Russians and other Allies deteriorated dramatically, so that there were two vastly different regimes operating in the one country. Along with this accelerating breakdown of cooperation, Germans living in the Russian zone found they were more and more often being prevented from travelling to the other zones to visit friends and relations. The German people themselves began to fear the possibility of their country being irreparably divided.

Inspired by Paul's descriptions of the growing difficulties of sending supplies across the Russian zone to troops and administrators, to say nothing of Berliners in the British sector of the city, Vesta turned her attention to that area. Billy Dodd put her in touch with his counterparts elsewhere, who were responsible for providing guards on the trains which had to pass through Marienborn on the British–Russian border. After the usual initial resistance to someone seen as an outsider, and a female one to boot, she was then given every assistance by men growing aggressive and determined not to let 'Ivan' throw his weight about. Even the Vesta Sheridan formula for getting what she wanted failed to gain her a place on a train going right through to Berlin, however. She was turned off it at the British border post of Helmstedt, and no amount of pleading moved the guards to let her back on board.

'It's not safe, miss,' said one. 'There's a storm brewing in Berlin, mark my words, and there's no knowing when it's going to break.'

'But surely they wouldn't *attack* anyone? It'd start another war,' she protested.

'Egg-zactly,' came his significant reply.

'Come on, corporal,' she wheedled. 'You're exaggerating. Besides, I've been under attack so many times I've lost count.'

'Well, this is one time you won't have to count,' he said firmly, 'because you're plain not going any further on that train.'

Although she failed to get to Berlin, Vesta moved around the British zone studying the work of those whose difficult job it was to supply and feed both occupiers and defeated nationals, while working to a tight budget knowing the well into which they were dipping was almost dry. She thought it would be a relief to do something different, meet new people, but she encountered two men she had known during her spell in Italy, and an ATS driver who had been at the camp where Vesta had served as a teleprinter operator on first joining up. Life in military circles was like that; always bumping into people one knew.

The varying locations made a change from the grimness of Hanover, although much of what she saw bore the marks of intensive warfare. In the deepening autumn chill there was little to counter the general uneasiness over the tense situation, yet Vesta was glad of what she thought of as a breathing space. Her relationship with Paul had advanced another stage following her outburst detailing why she was not prepared to jump into bed willy-nilly. It had become more personal and, curiously, more committed, so a short absence was probably a good idea.

Throughout this time the truth concerning Leo Roberts hung over her and would not be banished. She had gathered some very evocative material for her next set of canvases, yet a single intrusive vision kept inspiration at bay. In her heart, the artist knew she would have to give it expression or it would never leave her in peace. This was brought home to her with a vengeance when mail which had been chasing her around for several weeks caught up with her in Finkenwerde, where she was sketching activity at the flying-boat base which had been established there, and fending off the flirtatious attentions of a pilot after the style of Jim Shannon. She knew quite well how to handle *them*. It was the men with greater depth who gave her the trouble. She first read a long letter from Paul in which he carefully omitted any mention of missing her or hoping she was saving herself for him. It was, in fact, an account of what he and Jim had been doing in her absence, in particular the tricky removal from the river bed beneath an important bridge of a cluster of mines, which had clearly been put there ready to blow it if need be and then forgotten. The summer drought had so lowered the level of the river they had been spotted by some children. Paul's description of how he and Jim had been smothered in foul-smelling mud afterwards some-how failed to raise the smile it was meant to. A letter from Pat gave news from home in her familiar chatty style, but there was no hint of what was contained in the other from Tarrant Hall. Vesta read, with a mild sense of shock, her mother's announcement of her marriage to Leo.

I think you won't be surprised to learn that I agreed to become Leo's wife, and we were married in Tarrant Royal church yesterday. It was intended to be a quiet affair with just the Chandlers to celebrate with us, but half the village turned up for the service. I should have expected it, knowing what they are like. This time they were there because they are glad for me, not because they sensed a scandal and wanted to study the outline of my wedding gown. I wore pale amethyst, by the way. Bill took photographs. If you'd care to see one, I'll send it next time. I would have liked my two children to be there to wish us well. I hope you will, dear, eventually. I wrote the news to David. He sent a formal card of congratulation and a cheque for fifty pounds. I'd much rather have had a telephone call from him. I've deposited the money back in his bank account. There's really nothing we need, and David can't be all that well off.

It's been a difficult year after the snow and floods caused such havoc. All the farmers have suffered and . . .

The letter ended with a report on estate matters which had never interested Vesta, so she left it unread. Her emotions shocked her. Now she knew what she did about Leo, now she was haunted by his terrible experience, she felt almost *jealous* of her mother. Ashamed to admit it, she nevertheless caught herself wondering how Marion Sheridan could have captured the devotion of someone as complex as Leo Roberts. Perhaps it was her very simplicity after his world of espionage.

Only as Vesta refolded her mother's letter did she see another single sheet at the conclusion. It had no more than a few words on it.

Dear Vesta,
    Please be assured I can never replace your father, but I hope to be your friend when you are ready.
                                                                Leo

Quite unexpectedly, she burst into tears, although she was uncertain why. It was then she decided to go back to Hanover as soon as she could make the arrangements.

As luck would have it, one of her contacts in Supplies was driving south that weekend and offered to take her. She jumped at the chance, and worked hard on some sketches of local scenes for possible future use apart from her present commissioned work, until she left Finkenwerde. Wangling access to the military telephone network, she rang Paul's office to tell him she was returning that day. Jim answered, and sounded delighted at her news.

'Thank God! I've been keeping company with a man acting like a dog whose bone has been carried off by a cat.'

She laughed. 'Thanks for the comparison.'

'Juiciest bone I've ever seen, dearie, I swear.'

'Look, I can't stop. My carriage is without. Book a table for dinner at the club for three of us tonight. My treat.' On the spur of the moment, she added, 'My mother's just married again. I want to celebrate.' In truth she thought it would be wiser for Jim to be there when the dog got his bone back.

'Will do. This'll perk the lad up no end.'

'Where is he?' she asked.

'On a job. Should be back soon. He's been out since just after breakfast. Must be a tricky one.'

Vesta rang off, suddenly feeling cold. She had been away too long. Just suppose . . .

It was lovely to be back. The other residents of her block welcomed her as an old friend; the small apartment seemed like home. Even Hanover's piles of debris were strangely comforting. Best of all was a note from Paul pushed through her letter box, telling her he would pick her up at seven. That meant he had dealt with the 'tricky one' and survived.

He brought an absurdly extravagant bouquet and kissed her with equal extravagance to demonstrate his delight that she was back. He did not appear to resent Jim's inclusion in her plan, and she soon discovered why, because waiting in the jeep beside him was a blonde with innocent blue eyes and a wicked smile. Vesta thought the name Marjoriana a bit much, but Jim's latest was great fun and seemed very taken with him. Nothing much was said about the marriage of Vesta's mother, although Jim proposed a toast to the happy couple at the end of the meal. From Paul's glower Vesta deduced that he had instructed his friend to play down the supposed celebration, but she smiled and raised her glass to show that she approved.

Paul dropped off the other two at Marjoriana's parents' house – she was a major's daughter – arranging to collect Jim after he had taken Vesta home. She made coffee for them both in her alcove kitchen and sat beside Paul on the sofa to drink it.

'Funny how one gets used to things, isn't it?' she said with a smile. 'By pre-war standards this coffee's pretty ersatz, yet we're happy to drink it. Daddy would shudder and tip it away.'

'How will you feel about having a stepfather from now on? Will you get used to *that*?' he asked quietly. 'I was sure you didn't really mean this evening to be a celebration of the fact.'

She put down her cup and saucer, relieved that she felt happy to talk about it with him. 'The news shouldn't have come as a shock because he'd warned me, yet it did. It's crazy, but while I believed he was up to no good I could accept his attentions to my mother. Now I know the truth about him, I find it difficult to believe they could become marriage partners.'

'Mmm, perhaps you don't know the truth about your mother,' he suggested. 'We're all the same. We see mothers as merely that, never as people in their own right. Doesn't each child feel shocked when it discovers how babies are created and realizes Mummy and Daddy must have done it? If there are brothers and sisters it's even worse, because they must have done it a lot.'

She nodded and took his hand. 'After Felix treated me so brutally I could hardly bear to speak to Daddy for months. You didn't know my parents had what is now known as a shotgun wedding. Daddy had just left school and was set to go to Cambridge. Mummy was the local doctor's daughter. After the baby was born Daddy couldn't take any more. He ran away, joined the army and was blown up at Gallipoli. Then, as he was being taken in a small boat to a hospital ship lying off-shore, further bombardment resulted in him being thrown into the burning sea. He fought a tremendous battle to survive and won, but total amnesia remained for two more years. My mother helped to nurse him but he had no idea who she was, or that the little boy with her was his own son.'

'Good God!'

'When his memory returned he had lost both brothers in the war, and so inherited Tarrant Hall. He determined to make the marriage work, but he had such talents, together with intelligence of the highest order, that running a country estate couldn't satisfy him. The rest you probably know.' She sighed. 'I suppose Mummy was so totally outshone by her brilliant husband nobody really noticed her.'

'Leo Roberts has, apparently.'

'Yes, but why?'

'You'll have to ask *him* that.'

She played with his fingers for a moment or two, then glanced up at him. 'You know what I said to you once about

212

men thinking it was all so simple, but it wasn't?' He nodded. 'I was really referring to myself in that context. No one else. Then Mummy's letter made me see something I'd missed all these years, because I so loved and admired my father. She wrote that this time the villagers came to her wedding because they were glad for her, not to study the outline of her wedding gown. Everyone's so used to Daddy having been the victim overcoming pain and adversity to win through, that *her* pain and humiliation have been completely overlooked. I raved at you recently that I might have been left with a half-Polish bastard after those ten minutes with Felix – I've been feeling martyred for years over it – but she *was* left with a bastard. The whole village must have known why a schoolboy was marrying a local girl in such a hurry.' Suddenly, Vesta was crying. 'It's never simple, Paul. Not for us, it isn't.'

He drew her close and stroked her hair tenderly. 'It wasn't me who said it was, darling. You put the words into my mouth.'

Tilting her face up to his, she said what she had to. 'I need to be alone for a week or two, have no distractions. There's something I must get out of my system, and I'll have to shut myself away until it is. Can you be very understanding for a while?'

His expression exactly mirrored his disappointment. 'You've only just come back. Couldn't you have sorted out whatever it is while you were away?'

'No. That's why I returned so suddenly. It's given me no peace. Please, Paul.'

His face grew set; his vivid eyes gradually lost their sparkle. 'If that's what you want . . .'

'Bless you.' She kissed him lightly. 'Promise me something.'

'What's that?'

'Don't go near any bombs meanwhile.'

Knowing that it was time he went, he got abruptly to his feet. He was very evidently upset at her sudden rebuff after what had seemed a growing intimacy. 'You'll be too busy emulating a nun to have time to worry about things like that.'

He left straight away, and Vesta knew she had hurt him. Yet she was so caught up with what she had to do, that she had to leave the situation as it was until she could explain herself to him.

*

213

In a fever to start work, Vesta scoured the NAAFI library for guide or travel books. Armed with these she bought a stock of food and retreated to her apartment. The sketches she had done during her recent tour lay forgotten as she gave birth to the vision that was overriding all others. Inspiration *burned* within her; governed by creative energy she worked without pause each day while the light lasted. At the end of a week, one dark, dreary day of non-stop torrential rain had her prowling around the confines of her small room unable to advance the picture because the light was so bad. She had not been so beset by the need to express herself, so fired by her subject, since *The Afterglow*. It showed. The painting was good. She knew it was *very* good.

When the canvas was completed Vesta 'lived' with it for several days, just contemplating what she had produced. It was a very emotional time because she was still experiencing all that the vision depicted. On the fourth day after completion she awoke at her normal time, made coffee and boiled an egg, took her tray through to where the painting stood on its easel and, after eating breakfast, crossed the room to add her signature to her work. There was nothing more to do to it.

The picture showed a mountain range covered in deep snow and washed by brilliant moonlight from a cold northern sky. A hut occupied the foreground – a hut typical of those provided for climbers in summer and skiers in winter – except that it had been used for a more terrible purpose. The interior, illuminated by sepulchral whiteness, showed a smashed radio standing on a table and survival supplies spilling from a rifled cupboard. There was no glow of embers in the stove, yet the tongs and a scattering of dead cinders lay on the floor. The room looked stark and cold. A wide band of moonlight through the window fell on a naked man sprawled on a bench bed where he had dropped or been thrown. Although there was little more than an impression of blood and bruising on his flesh, the attitude of his one outflung hand and the gauntness of his features told of his agony. Yet a near-transparent vapour coming from his mouth showed that he clung to life in that chill interior. A door in the far wall stood open to the bitter night. To the left of the picture half a dozen armed Alpine troops were skiing away down an incline. The title of the painting was *Betrayal*.

214

Now that it was over Vesta felt tremendous relief; felt free to do whatever she chose. *Betrayal* was not part of the work she had been commissioned to produce, it was a private painting she would exhibit but never sell. She might one day give it as a gesture of contrition, but not yet. It was far too soon for a decision of that magnitude.

Having emerged from her self-imposed isolation, Vesta set about returning to life amongst other people. There was no response from Paul's office when she rang, so, rather than leave a message to be chewed over by his staff, she contacted the Mess and requested that he should be asked to ring her number when he arrived there for lunch. She began a long overdue beauty treatment, before it was time to prepare a tasty meal after days of irregular quick snacks.

She was in the bath having washed her hair when the doorbell rang. Believing Paul must have already been given her message and had come in person, impatient to see her, she wrapped herself in a large towel and ran to the door. Billy Dodd, looking very businesslike, stood outside. The gleam that appeared in his eyes told Vesta he was not nearly as nonplussed as she.

'I was in the bath.'

He grinned. 'Don't let me stop you.'

'Is it important?' she asked in irritation.

'Very.'

'Oh. Will it wait until I dry myself?'

'Do you require any help?' He stepped inside.

'Billy, stop being childish!' She hurried back to the tiny bathroom. 'Help yourself to a beer from the cooler. I'll be no more than five minutes.'

'No time for a beer . . . and make it three. This won't wait.'

Very curious, she stopped in the doorway to glance back at him. '*What* won't wait?'

'Your pal Gaynor's bomb.'

Her heart jumped. 'What bomb?'

'I'll tell you while you're drying yourself. Go on!' urged Billy, sitting on her settee. 'I'm supposed to be out there already and you're holding me up.'

Vesta towelled her body vigorously, feeling suddenly sick with apprehensive excitement. So that was why Paul had not been in his office when she rang.

'You twisted my arm over this, and I'm not sure I'm doing the right thing to take you along. When Gaynor finds out there'll be hell to pay. I've experienced his reaction when his dander's up,' grumbled Billy.

Busy scrambling into the old clothes she had worn for breakfast, Vesta tugged a comb through her wet hair then hurried out hopping on alternate feet as she fastened each shoe. 'I'll get you off the hook with Paul,' she promised breathlessly. Then a dreadful thought occurred to her. 'There's no chance he'll blow up anyone sheltering in the rubble, is there?'

He shook his head. 'The only one liable to be blown up is Gaynor himself. This thing's stuck in a factory chimney and he's got to climb up there to defuse it.' As Vesta practically froze, Billy added, 'That's why I came for you. You should be able to see everything that's going on. Right . . . ready?'

Without a word Vesta collected her sketchpad, put on a thick jacket, then went out to the jeep. She shivered in the chill wind as they set out over streets still pockmarked and uneven, her scalp icy beneath her damp hair. The muscles of her face were stiff when she spoke, and the sick apprehension had increased.

'If it's stuck in a chimney, why can't it simply be blown up from a distance?'

'He and young Shannon have been chewing it over for some time, which is why I was able to come for you. The big snag is that this old factory is slap bang next to a power station. If the beast goes off it'll rob the city of the only limited power available in an industrial area. Our gallant RAF lads were presumably targeting the power station when they neatly inserted one of their weapons into the stack several years ago. It jammed so tightly it hasn't moved since then.' He swerved to avoid a very deep hole but only missed the worst of it. 'Sorry about that,' he muttered as they were both jolted violently.

Vesta clutched the collar of her jacket close to her neck. 'Surely it would have exploded on first hitting that chimney. It must be a dud.'

'Not necessarily. We dropped a number of delayed action bombs. Could be one of those.'

'Not delayed for two or three years, surely!'

216

Billy glanced at her swiftly. 'Not getting cold feet, are you?'

'Only in the literal sense.' She could not now tell him that perhaps this was not such a good idea. The emotional intensity of the last ten days was probably responsible for how she presently felt, because this was one of the reasons for her coming to Germany. She had pestered Paul, Jim *and* Billy for this chance to see a bomb being made safe. Once they reached the site she would be so busy sketching and getting atmosphere her nerves would surely quieten down. She had been taken by surprise, that was all.

The jeep was nearing a more congested area now. Billy pointed. 'There's the chimney.'

It reared above the buildings ahead. Vesta's heartbeat practically doubled. It was a monster. 'If the factory is a ruin how is it the chimney's still standing?'

'It's only *just* standing. There are gaps in it here and there. The army have been supervising the clearing of rubble for several weeks. It was pure chance that some particularly conscientious soldier decided to risk a gander up the chimney before authorizing a ball and chain attack on it. He was looking decidedly pale when we met him this morning, and there wasn't a navvy in sight. If that thing had slipped at any time during the past twenty-one days . . .'

None of this was music to Vesta's ears, and she snapped, 'Oh, shut up!'

His swift glance was shrewd. 'So *that's* how it is with the short-tempered lieutenant, is it?'

'If *you* were going to deal with it, I'd be just the same.'

'That's nice.' He smiled. 'Not as tough as you pretend, eh?'

'*Whoever* dealt with it, I'd be the same,' she said with heavy emphasis. 'Please keep quiet now. I want to absorb the atmosphere.'

It was a lie. She was simply plain terrified of what she was going to witness. How could she ever have thought this life-or-death activity a suitable subject to sketch on site . . . especially when the life in question was that of someone she was fond of? She knew well enough that, as the senior officer, Paul would be the man to carry out whatever he and Jim decided to do.

The road was cordoned off by MPs. A small crowd had

gathered by the barrier to watch what was happening. Something already was. Vesta gave a gasp as she saw a khaki-clad figure mounting an iron ladder fastened to the side of the giant brick chimney. Paul was ascending slowly because he was gingerly testing each yard of the ladder for safety, before reaching for the next rung and hauling himself up by it. There were some gaping holes in the side of the chimney and, consequently, gaps in the ladder to make the ascent even more difficult.

Vesta clutched Billy's arm. 'What's he going to *do*?'

'I'll go and find out for you.' He climbed from the driver's seat. 'Get busy with paper and pencil, and pray the lad doesn't glance down and spot you when he's halfway up.'

The sketchpad stayed in Vesta's bag as she watched the distant figure climb up a chimney containing a slumbering bomb, and she inwardly protested that a man's life was far more precious than a disruption of electricity for people who had been his enemies for six terrible years. As she watched, Paul reached a hole and paused, looking for the best way to pass it. Vesta prayed it would defeat him and he would come down, but she should have known the man better. He lifted the coiled rope he was carrying over his head and flung one end of it upwards several times until the grappling hook on it caught and held in the ladder. After testing the stability of the iron rungs, he went up the rope hand over hand until he reached an unbroken stretch of ladder again. By then he was about 150 feet up from an iron platform which was about an equal distance from the ground at the end of what remained of the factory roof. Vesta then realized Jim was on that platform with a bag at his feet. Her heart was in her mouth as she watched Paul go even higher, so she jumped nervously when Billy spoke. She had not seen him return.

'The sergeant says the idea is for Gaynor to lower himself down inside the chimney to get at the thing. When he reaches the top, young Shannon will send the stuff he'll need up on the rope. From then on they'll play it by ear. If it can't be done they'll have another discussion. Gaynor's team seem to think it'll be all right, so long as he's got enough room to manoeuvre when he reaches it. If it's lying the wrong way, he'll have to try and get past it and work from underneath. That'll be somewhat tricky.'

Vesta turned on him. 'That's the kind of understatement only someone not involved in danger could make.'

'I'm not in the Sappers, love.' He squeezed her hand. 'They're trained to cope with things like this. He'll be all right. He knows exactly what he can do and what he can't. He's no fool.'

'That's got nothing to do with it,' she murmured, watching the figure growing smaller as it drew further away. 'Suppose the bomb slips when he starts working on it?'

Billy climbed up beside her and sat heavily. 'I shouldn't have brought you.'

They both fell silent and watched. Vesta tortured herself by imagining all the things that could happen, the least terrible being the ladder tearing free of the bricks to dash Paul to the ground. Reaching another gap in the iron rungs, he stopped where he was for so long it was clear something had gone wrong. Vesta faintly heard Jim calling up to his friend, then Paul's voice answering as he made gestures indicating the gap in the brickwork just above his head. In an agony of suspense Vesta watched as the men held a conversation which suggested that they could not agree on something. After a while, Jim started up the ladder with the bag hung across one shoulder. Paul remained motionless staring into the chimney.

Billy spoke softly. 'I'd say Gaynor can see the bloody thing just inside the gap, and is going to have a crack at it from there.'

'It'll be safer than going down from the top, won't it? Less chance of the bomb slipping?'

Billy put a comforting arm around her shoulders. 'How safe it is will depend on the type of weapon and what he must do to defuse it. How it's lying will make a difference, too.'

Jim had reached the first gap in the ladder and took up his position there. Clipping his belt to a rung so that he had both hands free, he then took the end of the rope Paul lowered and tied it to the bag of tools. The pair then held another conversation during which Paul made gestures to suggest that Jim should retreat to the safety point. The junior man nodded agreement, and the bag began its upward journey while he made a rapid descent. Then, to Vesta's horror, Paul secured the bag before very gingerly starting to climb through the hole in the chimney to sit with his legs dangling inside. He remained motionless for what seemed an age, waiting for Jim to join the rest of their team behind the shelter of a wall above a shallow crater some distance away. It then became obvious Paul was taking something from the bag and concentrating on the bomb lodged a few feet from him.

'What's he doing now?' Vesta asked in desperation.

'Whatever they do to defuse a bomb manually. Don't ask me. It's not my line,' Billy said, his own tension betrayed by the sharpness of his tone. 'I told you all along this wasn't a good subject for you, didn't I?'

She was too tense to rise to that. 'How long does it take? You surely must know that.'

Removing his arm from her shoulders, he asked, 'Would you like one of my men to take you home? I'll let you know when it's all over.'

'*How long does it take?*' she repeated.

'There's no set time. It depends on how the bomb's situated, what type of fuse it has, how steady the man's nerves are.'

Wishing she had not shut Paul from her life over the past two weeks when he so clearly had wanted to make up for the time she had been away, Vesta huddled into her jacket and watched without another word. She was so overwhelmed by her fear for Paul that she was unaware of how her artist's eye registered everything. The cold, grey noon sky against which the dark tower of bricks stood like a sinister giant finger. The tall power station beyond, from which there came the rumble of machinery. The grouped Sappers, heads tilted back, standing motionless with Jim in the crater as they watched the man trying to perform a miracle three hundred feet up. The ring of red-capped MPs beside their cordon, also with necks craned. The knot of German labourers, augmented by passing onlookers, who wore expressions of sullen interest. The great mound of tumbling rubble at one end of a factory mostly gutted and blackened, with broken propaganda slogans painted on the walls. Military vehicles parked at a safe distance. Every person, save that khaki-clad man, well away from danger. Tension, fear, admiration, grimness – all these emotions could be seen somewhere amid the mass of faces watching the drama being played out as if through the wrong end of a telescope.

Time became nothing as Vesta stared with aching eyes at that far-off figure on his precarious perch, who appeared not to be doing anything. The autumn chill had settled inside her so that her body shivered from her own inactivity.

'God, he's taking his time,' murmured Billy, studying his watch. 'He's been on the job fifteen minutes already. It must be a real bastard.'

Vesta hastily clambered from her seat and ran for the nearest area of rubble. She reached it just in time to bring up her breakfast. 'You fool,' she told herself shakily, 'you got through a tank battle and the Italian campaign as cool as a cucumber. Well, almost. Now you're going all feminine over a bomb stuck in a chimney.' Putting it into words reminded her how terrified she was, and she walked for several minutes hugging herself closely against the cold and her fear, recalling Jim telling her that if a man had problems he could lose concentration at the vital time. She should have told Paul why she wanted to be alone; told him about the painting she had *had* to get out of her system.

When she returned to the jeep, Billy told her cheerfully, 'You missed the best bit. He gave a thumbs up; now he's on his way down with the fuse in his bag. At least, that's what it looks like. It's all over bar the shouting. Removing the blighter will be relatively easy, now it's been disarmed.'

Vesta saw Paul climbing down to the platform previously occupied by Jim. 'How do you know it's over? He might have failed and they're going to discuss what to do next.'

Billy shook his head. 'His men wouldn't be going forward in such a casual way if the thing was still armed. He's done it all right.'

Weak with relief, she asked, 'Shouldn't we give him a cheer or something?'

'Why? It's all in a day's work for him,' came Billy's cool reply. 'Now, Miss Sheridan, I'm going to get you away from here before anyone recognizes you and tells him. He'll have my guts for garters if he finds out. Corporal Green can drive you home, then come back for me.' He helped her back into the jeep, then gave her a straight look. 'Don't ask me for any more favours. If I'd known you were so stuck on the chap, I'd never have done this one.'

Corporal Green knew Vesta from the night they had caught the black marketeer, and he greeted her cheerfully as he climbed into the driving seat. 'Nice bit of excitement, miss.' He started the engine and put the jeep into gear. 'Blimey, just think what would've happened if they'd hit that chimney with a ball and chain early this morning.'

Vesta still had her gaze fastened on Paul as the vehicle swung round ready to leave, and gasped as she saw his foot slip and his body fall away from the ladder and drop.

'Dear God, he's fallen!' she cried.

The soldier glanced over his shoulder but did not brake. 'Lucky for him he wasn't further up it.'

'Stop! I've got to go back,' Vesta told him frantically.

'Sorry, miss, I've orders to get you home straightaway, then return for Captain Dodd.'

Short of leaping from the jeep, which she seriously considered, there was nothing else Vesta could do as the corporal drove with the carelessness of a maniac along the bumpy streets away from that accident. The cold had penetrated to her bones so that she ached all over, and numbness now affected her limbs and emotions. How had she imagined she could watch something so hazardous and make sketches for a painting? Paul had been right to dub her heartless. When they reached her apartment she discovered her emotions were not completely numbed, because she begged her companion to make Captain Dodd telephone news of how serious the fall had been.

'Tell him to ring the minute he knows,' she added, on the verge of tears.

'Okie-doke, Miss Sheridan. I shouldn't worry too much. REs is like rubber. They bounce. I knew a Sapper once who fell off a high bridge he was mining. Swept away by the river, he was, and his pals thought him a goner. Turned up a few days later with nothing worse than a cold.'

In no mood for soldiers' tall stories, Vesta repeated her instruction then went inside, exhausted. Once there, she poured herself a stiff whisky and curled up in a chair in an attempt to get warm. Ten minutes later, she got up and opened her front door so that she would hear the telephone in the corridor when Billy rang. She drank more whisky and fetched a blanket to wrap around herself because she was still no warmer. The telephone remained silent. Now she was away from the scene it came into her mind as clearly as a photograph. Had Paul lost his concentration on that ladder? Had he grown careless once the difficult bit was over? Had she been in any way responsible for what had happened? Why had Billy not rung?

After a third whisky she must have fallen asleep, because a woman was standing by her chair saying there was a telephone call, and the time was two-thirty. Casting aside the blanket she rushed along the corridor to snatch up the receiver. 'Hallo, what's the news?' she demanded.

'I've just been given your message,' said Paul's voice in her ear. 'Have you come out of purdah?'

'You're all right!' she declared in wobbly tones. 'You're . . . you're *really* all right?'

'Why shouldn't I be?' He sounded wary.

'I . . . I . . . When I rang the Mess they said you were . . . were out on a job,' she invented wildly. 'As you took so long to ring back I . . . well, I was beginning to worry, I suppose.'

'I can look after myself.'

'Yes. Of course. Of course you can!'

'How are you?'

How could he sound so normal? 'Would you like to come here this evening?' Did *she* sound normal? 'I'll cook something . . . and we can have a long talk. About seven?'

After a short pause, he asked very quietly, 'Did you sort out your problem all right?'

'Oh . . . yes. Seven, then?'

'Should I bring wine, or not?'

'Mmm. Lovely! Bye.'

Returning to her room shivering violently, Vesta suddenly sat on the floor and burst into tears. Feeling washed out but calmer, she then looked in her tiny larder for something to cook which was worthy of a bottle of wine. It still seemed incredible that Paul had spoken to her as if this morning had never happened. Perhaps Sappers really were made of rubber. Is that why Billy had not bothered to telephone? Oh God, why did she still feel terribly sick?

When Paul arrived, dead on seven o'clock, his left arm was encased in plaster and he looked incredibly tired. Vesta was shaken anew. 'What have you done?' she cried, as he stood at the door.

His smile was forced. 'I thought I was a fly and tried to climb a wall. Jim's not too happy. I fell on him and broke a couple of his ribs.' He held up the bottle of wine. 'May I come in?'

Having planned skilfully to coax from him details of what he had been doing that day, carefully guarding against any slip of the tongue which would reveal that she had seen it all as it happened, this development threw Vesta off her stride. Having no idea how to follow his throwaway explanation, she dropped the subject completely and led him inside, apologizing for the smell of cooking.

'It's the penalty for having a kitchen in an alcove so that you can cook breakfast while you're still in bed,' she added brightly.

She was glad Paul made no attempt to kiss her, although it was surprising. She usually had to fight for breath during the first few minutes of his visits. Because of the curious constraint between them, she served her unexciting dinner immediately. It turned out not to be worthy of the wine he opened and poured for them both in preoccupied silence. Sitting at an army-pattern basic table set with NAAFI china, which robbed the occasion of any glamour or romance despite the single candle she had lit, their conversation was dismayingly stilted.

'Have you been busy lately?'

'There've been too many damned meetings about expediting clearance of cities so they can start functioning again. It can't be done. We keep telling them.'

'Are the Russians playing up still?'

'They're certainly not growing any chummier.'

'Oh dear, what a problem it must be.'

'Paperwork on the subject has doubled.'

'That can't make the situation any easier.'

'It doesn't.'

'Would you like more vegetables?'

'No, thanks.'

'I'm afraid I'm not a very good cook.'

'I'm not very hungry.'

Nothing appeared to ease the tension between them, even

her having to cut up his meal for him, and it continued because she could not think of a way to end it.

'Is Marjoriana still on Jim's agenda?'

'Yes.'

'Perhaps it's serious this time.'

'Yes. Perhaps.'

Vesta ran out of questions, so they ate for a moment or two in silence. Surely Paul had not found out about her presence this morning. No, he would have burst into a rage. Perhaps his subdued mood was due to reaction after danger. Maybe he had been heavily dosed with painkillers. Should he be drinking wine quite so liberally? All at once it dawned on Vesta she was seeing him with new eyes. The man who had been comfortingly available and endearing, who loved her and obediently accepted her limits without becoming a nuisance, had suddenly become someone quite different. A man of immense strength and courage; someone whose proximity was exciting. A person whose withdrawn mood challenged her to probe it, discover his thoughts and emotions. This new Paul made her nervous. Shy, almost. That was why everything was going wrong. He was unconsciously calling the tune. She longed to dance to it but was unsure of the steps.

He glanced up and caught her studying him. His clear turquoise eyes darkened with emotion; a muscle in his tight jaw jumped. He looked almost ill as he threw down his fork. 'Look, I don't think I can take any more. I've had one hell of a day, so let's cut out the frills and get it over with quickly, shall we?'

'What?' she asked faintly.

He struggled to his feet, wincing as he did so, then stood looking down at her. 'As soon as you told me you had to be alone to sort something out, I sensed it was the end of us. Or, rather, of me. I'm here tonight to be given the brush-off, aren't I?'

'No!' she cried, getting up so fast she knocked over her chair. 'Good God, no!'

He seemed bemused. 'You *weren't* making a final decision between Brad Holland and me?'

'No.'

'He hasn't contacted you and asked you to hitch up again as a team?'

'*No!*'

He took in breath slowly as if easing pain. 'Then I don't understand what's going on tonight. Why did you ask me here? Why are you all brittle sociability and so bloody polite I'm frightened of putting a foot wrong? What's come over you, Vesta?'

She gazed at him helplessly for a moment or two, then said, 'I'd like your advice on how a woman should seduce a man. I've never done it before. It's always been done to me.'

Looking even more bemused, he asked, 'What sort of chap is he?'

'The kind who keeps suggesting we take off all our clothes whenever it's a hot day.'

As the truth slowly dawned on him his eyes grew bright again, and he gave a delighted groan. 'Oh hell, what a bloody awful time to choose.'

'It chose itself, I'm afraid.' She moved to him and began to loosen his tie. 'Is that how I should begin?'

Circling her with his free arm he pulled her close, then gave an involuntary cry of pain. 'This is no way to treat a man who is battered and bruised,' he protested half-heartedly. 'I'm *hors de combat.*'

Busy with his trouser buttons, she murmured, 'I told you I've never seduced anyone before. I'll learn as I go along.'

He then began to laugh, head tipped back and free hand help up in a sign of surrender. 'Christ, what a woman I've got myself! Do your damnedest, then. I'm all yours.'

CHAPTER TWELVE

By the first few months of 1948 it was no longer possible to doubt Soviet expansionist intentions. In the third week of February Czechoslovakia was seized and placed under total Communist control. This was swiftly followed by Russian overtures to Finland and Norway to form an alliance, which was certain to be the start of Communist dominance. To counter this threat to Europe, Britain, France and the Benelux countries signed an agreement to defend each other against armed aggression. The greatest threat of all, however, came in Berlin, where small irritations and petty bureaucracy grew into undisguised confrontation by the Russians in whose zone the city sat.

Supply trucks started being turned back because their loads, or drivers' papers, did not conform to new rules introduced only that day. Each time they were changed, traffic along the autobahn dwindled alarmingly. Barges laden with supplies for the three western sectors of Berlin were stopped and held indefinitely while supposed formalities were sorted out. Irate captains were told officials were too busy to deal with their problem. Goods trains were halted at Marienborn and either sent back or shunted on to a siding for days at a time. New Soviet regulations demanded that Russian troops search each train, and any box or package they deemed suspicious must be opened for examination. As the Anglo-American authorities refused point blank to recognize this latest demand, most supplies by rail were returned to base.

By May, the situation was so grave a last-ditch meeting was called. The Russians walked out with nothing resolved because they would not countenance the introduction of new currency to save the German economy. The Western allies knew this was a certain means of improving a situation grown so desperate that the fragile structure painstakingly created by the occupying countries would collapse within a few months, to leave an impossible burden on nations themselves struggling to recover. The British, French and Americans went ahead with the Deutschmark in June. On the twenty-fourth of the month the Soviets stopped all Western road, rail and water traffic from entering their zone, and cut off electricity supplies to the three other sectors of Berlin. Their former allies were told that severe transport difficulties would prevent through traffic 'for some time', and that a fuel crisis made power-cuts necessary. The gauntlet had been flung down.

To back this challenge soldiers crossed into the Western sectors of Berlin to seize prominent German adversaries in surprise swoops, and whisk them away to be indoctrinated in the depths of Russia, and Germans living in the Soviet sector were prevented from leaving it, no matter what their reason for wanting to do so might be. East German radio stations began transmitting propaganda programmes designed to persuade all Berliners to turn to Communism. They also broadcast 'scare' news claiming to have evidence that the Americans were already planning to withdraw all their administrators and troops, starting with women and children. The British, more arrogant and foolhardy, were set to stay with the intention of supplying their own personnel but leaving Germans in their sector to starve.

There was a grain of truth in all this. Foreseeing such a crisis as far back as early 1947, the Western allies had discussed airlifting supplies to their own considerable staff and dependants then judged it to be highly impractical. To feed and provide heating for a combined number of around two and a half million Germans as well would be impossible. There were not enough transport aircraft available; the flight to Berlin took between two and three hours; where would the huge amounts of food come from and who would pay for such an operation? Even if aircraft and foodstuffs were available in sufficient quantities, loading, flying there, unloading and flying back meant that only a fraction of the daily requirement could be taken in every twenty-four hours. No, it was completely out of the question to contemplate an airlift.

On June 24, after heated arguments, the British and Americans decided to mount one. The stockpile of food in Berlin was low and liable to run out within a matter of weeks. The Russians' bluff had to be called and an airlift was the only safe option – safe from entering into actual armed aggression. No one asked what would be done if the Soviet authorities declared their air corridors closed, too.

David Sheridan led his small group into Fassberg airfield in the British zone of Germany on July 22. Although the Berlin airlift would not exactly be operational flying, it carried a great enough element of risk to come very near it, which was why he had volunteered. Everyone had wanted to go, of course. There was a dash of schoolboy adventure about the concept of flying a narrow corridor across hostile territory to take food to those isolated in it. It was a siege, in effect, and there had always been a brand of romanticism about sieges. The British had been involved in many throughout their history: Delhi, Kabul, Khartoum, Ladysmith, Mafeking – names to send a surge of pride through British breasts, though why they should was a mystery. Most had been terrible disasters. Yet the very notion of defying starvation and surrender was stirring. To be part of an operation to help the besieged was even more stirring. Besides, it would be a jolly good lark, and nearly every young British male loved one of those.

It was only the element of risk that appealed to David. He had grown very bored in Scotland, despite the isolation he had sought. Peacetime flying was tame after enemy combat. Most pilots agreed. Some resigned and took up more dangerous occupations; some tried to recreate the old excitement by indulging in silly aerial pranks after which they were either grounded, court-martialled, or dead; some transferred to civil aviation and sedately flew passengers from here to there or, mostly, they went back to civilian jobs and flew with small clubs for weekend enjoyment. David would have done the latter. Now, like the Flying Dutchman, he felt compelled to keep going until he dropped. Fortunately, he possessed the right qualifications for what many others regarded as a quixotic adventure, despite obvious evidence that it was mainly a political move to hold on to territory too valuable to lose. David saw it as a lifeline. The lochs and silent hills of Scotland had provided escape from people, but not from demons. They were never far from him.

He was bringing into Fassberg his own and six more Dakotas gathered from several squadrons able to spare them. They were thin on the ground in Britain because trouble spots all over the empire had to be serviced by air transport. In addition, strikes and industrial unrest at home made it imperative to keep adequate aircraft available for domestic use. Dakotas had done invaluable service during the war years, and were past their best, so David's group were flying in with engineers and fitters aboard ready to deal with the problems certain to arise.

Fassberg, a former German airfield, had been extended, modernized and prepared for its emergency purpose in less than three weeks, so most of it was spanking new but very basic. The runway had been lengthened and strengthened to take constant traffic. Accommodation stood ready to house the influx of extra crews but, because this was regarded as a short-term emergency, the men would have to put up with severe overcrowding while it lasted. Rail track had been laid to supply new marshalling yards, roads now ran direct to stores with large loading bays. Under normal conditions Fassberg would have been an ideal transport station. On the day David flew in it resembled bedlam.

Coming in over trees, his distant view from the cockpit revealed aircraft standing higgledy-piggledy on the field where armies of worker ants swarmed around filling them from all manner of vehicles. Dakotas were taking off in elephantine fashion; others were landing in a manner which had him holding his breath.

'Christ, what kind of flying circus are we joining?' he muttered, but had no chance to receive an answer from anyone because directions for landing came from the Control Tower at that moment and he concentrated on doing it in somewhat better style than those he had just witnessed. Satisfied though he might have been with his performance, he was then baffled as to where they were meant to park. There was no marshaller waiting to wave them in, no indication whatever of recognition that seven Dakotas had just arrived from Britain. Taxiing along the runway searching for any welcoming sign, he asked the Control Tower where the hell the marshaller was.

'We're too busy for that,' came the calm response. 'Just find a clear space. You won't be there long.'

Passing this unbelievable information to his accompanying pilots, he added, 'Don't worry, I'll sort everything out with the first unlucky bastard I meet up with.'

This person was a cheerful, monkey-faced loader who arrived with two others on a laden truck almost before David cut the engines. 'Welcome to Fassberg, sir,' he greeted. 'We was told you'd be coming in about now. Time you've had a bit of lunch we'll have you refuelled, loaded and ready to go. It's sugar, flour, coffee and dried egg. Nothing smelly, sir. Not this time, anyway.'

David stared at this chirpy NCO as if he could not believe his eyes and ears, but he was so angry he did not waste words on him. Someone was going to get it in the neck and it would be an idiot of much higher rank than this. There was worse to come, however. With all his crews on the ground, as well as the cluster of ground staff, complete with an array of baggage, there appeared to be no transport waiting to take them to the other side of the airfield where administration blocks and quarters were sited.

'I don't believe this,' David said to the captains of the other crews.

'It looks a bit chaotic,' agreed one with a kind of bewitched amusement. 'It seems to be every man for himself judging by the take-offs and landings.'

David was already accosting monkey-face. It was none too warm for July, fine rain was falling, and the wind was strong. He was livid. 'You were bloody quick off the mark with your dried egg. How is it they're not so sharp about sending out transport?'

The man paused unwillingly, clearly more intent on filling the Dakota with provisions. 'They're a bit pushed, sir, Someone'll be along shortly.' He continued his loading, leaving the new arrivals to stand in the rain.

After ten minutes David had had enough of waiting. Seeing a man in dark overalls coming his way on a bicycle, he strode out in his path to bring him to a wobbly halt. 'I'm commandeering this,' he snapped. 'Off you get!' When the man said in German that he did not understand, David roared, '*Steigen Sie ab!*' and supported his rusty knowledge of the language by manhandling his victim from the saddle. Once in possession of this basic vehicle, David jumped on and pedalled furiously. Even with the wind behind him it took twenty-three minutes to reach the Admin. blocks, and he was uncomfortably wet. This added to his ire so that he was ready to throttle everyone in sight.

There was only one available for choking, but David was destined not to lay a hand on him because the name board on the desk shocked him into immobility. He had last seen Alan Winterbottom when Singapore was ablaze and being overrun by Japanese, facing the certainty of capture and fearing for the life of his Malayan mistress. Yet this grey-haired wing commander with lifeless eyes, and hands that shook slightly, was undoubtedly, unbelievably, David's former commanding officer.

He glanced up from his paperwork. 'Yes?'

Men who had been through the war betrayed no sense of unease on meeting David. They were used to disfigurement. It was the young ones who could not hide their reactions. David prayed he could hide his now for it was a sickening blow to find this particular man here. There was no escape anywhere, it seemed.

'I'm David Sheridan,' he said, the fight gone out of him.

'And?' Winterbottom's expression slowly changed as that name got through to him. *Now* the reaction came. It was easy to accept a crippled stranger. When he suggests he is someone you might have known, personal feelings creep in. 'Did you say David Sheridan? Any relation to Rex "Sherry" Sheridan?' He was feeling his way slowly.

'I thought you had surely died in Singapore.' David wanted to be spared the tortuous investigation. 'How's Rita?'

Alan Winterbottom paled dramatically as he clumsily got to his feet and held out his hand. 'Good God, I heard you were lost in Sumatra.'

It was just as David feared. This man would want to reminisce, chew over those months he, himself, was fighting to block from his mind for ever. 'I was found again,' he said brusquely, 'and now I've volunteered for this stunt. I've just cycled across to find out what the hell's going on. Control told us to fill any empty space, and a gang of emaciated foreigners under control of a maniac wearing a stripe on his sleeve is loading dried egg into our machines. My crews and some spare ground staff are standing around in the rain with their luggage, and no one is showing the slightest interest in getting them across here. I want some action, and quickly!'

Winterbottom gave a faint smile, showing that he had not yet accepted what he saw. 'You always did, David, as I recall. I really am glad that we've bumped into each other again.'

In the face of such sincerity, and because of those last doomed days they had shared, David's attitude collapsed. Sinking on to a chair, he said, 'I'm sorry I can't say the same. Look, can you get some vehicles out there to bring my people in? We had a bumpy ride over, and *they* need feeding as well as the Jerries. As far as I'm concerned they come first. Let the buggers wait for their dried egg.'

Alan sat down again and conducted a short, sharp telephone conversation before nodding at David. 'It's fixed . . . I think.'

'Thanks.'

'So you're not here on humanitarian grounds?' Alan asked shrewdly.

'Yes, mine. I want to do some flying that has a kick in it. I was bored and needed stimulus. *That's* why I volunteered. I don't give a hoot about starving Germans. They killed a lot of good chaps I knew. They also murdered my father. I don't want anyone thinking I'm here as a good samaritan.'

'I see.'

'I also don't want to talk about Singapore.'

'Neither do I, brother.'

David faced him frankly. 'Then we understand each other?'

'Oh, I think so. I'm still glad we've met up.'

He chose to ignore that. 'Tell me what's going on here.'

The other man offered cigarettes which David refused. Having known too well the demon of thirst, he could not bear the taste of smoke in his throat. 'We're not supplying Germans alone, David. There's our entire military garrison, hundreds of civil servants, diplomats and the supporting groups like NAAFI and the church fellowships. Then there are wives and children. We can't let *them* starve.'

'Cut out the hearts and flowers stuff. Give me the operational details.'

'Ha! That's a joke. We make them up as we go along. Our

job is to keep going twenty-four hours a day, but it's well nigh impossible. The weather has been appalling. Mid-summer? Don't you believe it. We've had torrential rain, fog, thunderstorms, constant low cloud – even snow. Timing is impossible. Our lords and masters have worked out on paper, while sitting at their desks, that take-offs should be at ten-minute intervals. You know as well as I that it will never work as smoothly as that. Even if all the aircraft were new and serviced up to the hilt, the ground work can become a shambles through any number of things. A loader gets his hand crushed, a tyre on a truck blows, a box spills its contents all over the place. Here, listen to this,' he urged, well into his stride. 'Some poor devils carted honey a few days ago, and one of the barrels leaked the flaming stuff all over the hold. When they reached Gatow half the other boxes were stuck to the floor. I tell you, David, the fellows who make plans on paper are often old men who did their flying along with your famous uncle. They've no notion what they're asking us to do.'

'Hasn't anyone the guts to tell 'em?' David asked.

'They've got the guts but not the time, lad,' Alan said with an echo of his old self. 'Pilots are flying in conditions which would normally ground aircraft, they're taking off with excess loads crammed in because some of their safety equipment has been removed, they're landing willy-nilly with no marshallers and parking where they can, they're hanging around Gatow in shocking weather while untrained men scramble to unload and service them, then they're taking off again in a mad panic to get airborne before some punch-drunk youngster decides to land right in their path. Everyone's overtired. Experienced pilots are coming in like pregnant ducks, they're forgetting basics like putting down flaps or reducing engine speed, and they're irritable on the intercom. The ground staff are the same; overtired, overworked and overbearing.'

All this sounded very familiar to David. As a Spitfire pilot during the Battle of Britain he had experienced much the same. But that unforgettable period had been aimed at keeping the Germans from invading Britain: now he would be doing it to keep them from starving. It made little sense to him.

'Instead of flying ourselves into the ground, why don't we take just enough for our own people and let the rest go to hell?'

Alan leaned back in his chair and frowned. 'Why don't we pull out and do away with the necessity of this Fred Karno set-up? In both cases we'd be handing Europe to Stalin on a plate. Would you be happy with that; happy for your children to grow up under the shadow of Communism?'

David got to his feet with a jerk. 'I'm here to fly, that's all. Just so long as I'm given a good maintenance team and somewhere to sleep, I'll do the job. The rest I'll leave to those who have a conscience, like you.'

'Not me, lad. I'm only saying what I'm meant to say. Three and a half years in Changi drove away any quixotic notions I ever had.'

David then knew this man really *did* have no desire to talk about Singapore. Anyone who had suffered in that infamous place would never want to reminisce. He shook Alan's hand again, this time with a sense of comradeship known only to those who understood another's demons. 'I'm glad we bumped into each other, too.' Hearing trucks pulling up outside he saw from the window his men arriving. 'When that idiot with a stripe said we'd be loaded and serviced ready for take-off after lunch, he wasn't being an idiot, was he?'

Alan merely shook his head. 'I'll try to fix up accommodation, if you ever have time to use it . . . and, David, I'm glad you got around to flying again.'

He managed a half-smile. 'After a day or two here I may live to regret it.'

Chaos reigned everywhere, yet it had a semblance of order about it. In the so-called Officers' Mess, which was clearly inadequate given the number of aircraft David had actually seen operating, to say nothing of those presently mid-air between here and Gatow or those on the ground in Berlin, meals were being served at all times of the day and night, David was swiftly informed. He and his pilots were hungry, but they had barely started on biscuits and cheese at the close of their meal before David received a message stating that his aircraft would be ready and scheduled for take-off ten minutes apart beginning at 16.40. When he relayed this news to the pilots, whom he hardly knew, their reaction was typical.

'Get used to it,' he advised. 'This is the start of the big fun adventure you came here to enjoy.'

They soon discovered it was no fun. The air corridor from the British zone to Gatow, in their sector of Berlin, was only twenty miles wide. Through this space flew a continuous procession of aircraft of several types, at different heights, varying speeds, and with sometimes doubtful skill, and in both directions. Aircraft from both Fassberg and Wunstorf used this space so exact timing, navigation and height control were essential to avoid accidents. Once in Berlin airspace, which was shared by seven Russian airfields, very particular care had to be taken, and when landing at Gatow, which was relatively easy because of the lack of obstacles, only a minor deviation in navigation could lead an unwary pilot to land at a nearby Soviet airfield instead.

David's first flight to Berlin was something of a disaster. The Operations Room gave him scanty information because they were inundated with demands, and the fine rain that had greeted him on arrival had turned to a steady downpour when he took off. There was no formation flying. Each of his aircraft was to travel at the same height going out, and at a lower common height on the return; each was to keep a steady distance from the one in front. It was not that simple, however. Owing to the varying makes of aircraft one kind needed greater height, another maintained higher speed, yet another lumbered slowly through the sky. As if that were not enough, a number of civil freight companies had been asked to join the airlift and the crews of these were a law unto themselves, knowing they were not under military discipline. These civil aircraft had been known to career along the corridor like yo-yos, going under or over their RAF counterparts in their eagerness to reach Berlin or home.

One of these crazy aviators zoomed up from beneath David three miles out of Gatow to throw schedules awry. As it is impossible to put brakes on a machine when it is in the air, the actual landing David made was practically on the tail of a bright blue Viking. He had made hair-raising landings before, but never on a strange airfield in the heart of hostile territory, with visibility poor and on a runway in the course of being extended. On the ground there was chaos similar to that at Fassberg, with aircraft parked all over the place amidst trucks, lorries, fuel waggons and mobile conveyor belts. He taxied into a spot just vacated by another Dakota, and the team of loaders went to work with a will until a second truck backed up to the hold and failed to stop in time. This left enough damage to prevent the doors from closing fast, and David had to wait around on the ground for more than an hour for someone to deal with it. When he eventually gained a place in the stream of departing aircraft, it was almost dark.

A storm broke on the return flight, making it difficult to keep track of those machines in front and behind him. When he spotted the lights of Fassberg ahead he sighed with relief. He was very tired and hoped his accommodation had now been sorted out. He had been obliged, with the rest of his men, to leave his baggage in a store room until sleeping places had been found for them all.

The runway was covered in standing water which, because it had only recently been laid, made landing more precarious than usual in wet conditions. A marshal materialized from the darkness and gestured him to a vacant area beside other Dakotas being loaded by floodlight. David felt sorry for the pilots about to go out in these conditions. He could not get to bed fast enough. It had been a very long day, and meeting Alan Winterbottom had deeply unsettled him, he now realized. He had flown in worse conditions, and with the threat of enemy gunfire, yet not felt the way he presently did. A good night's sleep would put him on target for tomorrow.

When he reported to an elderly wing commander with a huge moustache, he was told to 'cut along and get some cocoa and a sandwich or two' before his next sortie. 'Met. says the rain should stop soon after midnight so you'll have a decent trip this time,' he finished carelessly.

David was stunned. 'I only flew in this morning.'

'And we're very glad to have you.'

'My Dak's got a dodgy door.'

The man grinned. 'Don't worry about that. It's not *your* Dak any longer. Pilots take up any kite that's loaded and ready to go. Wish they'd let me go aloft again. I'd give anything to do my bit.'

'I'll be happy to let you take my place,' David told him.

He did not seem to appreciate that David was serious, just laughed and said, 'That's the spirit. Can't beat it. *That's* what won us the war, son . . . that, and men like you.'

David finally went to bed at five a.m. with the knowledge that he would be woken at nine ready for take-off at around ten. He discovered that he was sharing a small room with four others, but the happy-go-lucky Mess steward assured him they would never be all there at the same time so not to worry. There was one other occupant who turned over, opened a bleary eye, asked if he would be getting breakfast or dinner in a minute, then fell soundly asleep again. David stripped to his underwear and dropped on to the nearest bed to wrap himself around with the bedclothes like a cocoon. His baggage had gone astray somewhere so, even if he wanted to, he could not have shaved or put on pyjamas.

He lay rolled in blankets, dog-tired yet unable to sleep. The period in Scotland had partially soothed his raw, savage emotions. As he had become a loner after his first return from Singapore, so he had this time. Knowing from experience that the only way to stay sane was to face one day at a time and think of himself as nothing more than a machine, slowly he had created a limbo which provided an element of peace. There was no future, just one tomorrow, and if it never came what the hell did it matter?

Alan Winterbottom had destroyed that limbo. That familiar face, that voice, the shocked recognition, his words: *I heard you were lost in Sumatra* resurrected all the demons. When someone came for David at nine he had not slept and was once more possessed by guilt, degradation and a sense of overwhelming dread.

He ate breakfast with men who were unaware and uncaring of which meal it was, but who all talked with enthusiasm about potential disasters as if they were part of some schoolboy lark. Snatches of conversation about ripping out essential equipment to fit in ten more sacks of flour, of barely clearing the runway because some idiotic loaders had stacked inside a Dakota a consignment meant for a York's greater freight capacity, of a tail wheel which had folded on landing, or of packets of POM, the handy dried potato, which had split after being dropped by an exhausted loader, all sounded like Billy Bunter humour as it grated on David's ears.

Finally, one of his neighbours, red-eyed from too many hours in the cockpit, turned to him. 'Haven't seen you before. Did you bring in one of those Daks yesterday?'

'That's right.' He had no desire to be drawn into the ludicrous jollity.

The young, ginger-haired flight lieutenant grinned. 'Welcome to Operation Carter Paterson – although we're not allowed to call it that now, because the Ivans have sneered on their radio station that we've named it after a removal firm because we're leaving Berlin.'

'The Yanks initially called theirs Operation Knicker. Can't get their train of thought there,' said another cheerily.

'That's easy,' retorted Ginger. 'It refers to "harvest festival bloomers".'

'Eh?'

'"All is safely gathered in",' he quoted with gusto.

There was a shout of laughter from all except David, and Ginger studied him for a moment or two. 'Don't you get the joke?'

David stood up, pushing away his plate. 'The biggest joke is all of you ... and it's a pathetic one, at that. Some of you don't look old enough to have fought the Jerries, but those of you who did appear to have forgotten it very quickly.'

Another squadron leader spoke from the end of the table. 'There are hundreds of British people in Berlin too. If you feel that way about it why are you here?'

'To fly; to do a job. But I'm not going to do it at risk to the lives of my crew. Nor am I going to fly a machine which is faulty, overloaded or stripped of any essential equipment.'

As he walked away he heard a youngster say, 'He must have pranged his MG and spent the rest of the war behind a desk.'

'I saw him when he arrived,' said the squadron leader. 'He was wearing enough ribbons on his chest to tie a big bow on your rattle, Sonny Jim. Trouble is, he knows it.'

'His crew'll be the safest men on the airlift with his attitude,' said Ginger.

David's attitude did not change, but he could not assert it because he was caught up in something beyond his control. Weekly figures showed that the Anglo-American combined operation was supplying only a quarter of even the basic requirements to keep their sectors of Berlin fed and supplied. Everyone taking part in the plan to call the Soviet bluff saw the figures as a challenge to be met at all costs. Everyone save David.

More aircraft flew in. The British had exhausted their military capability and called upon yet more civilian firms to send machines. They responded in the same prevailing cavalier spirit, so that aircraft of differing design, capacity and power arrived in twos and threes flown by pilots who were as much a menace as a help.

More thought and care went into planning consignments after learning hard lessons. Barrels meant wasted space, so fresh fish was replaced by tinned in flat-sided boxes. Butter deliveries were scaled down dramatically because there were no cold storage facilities at either end of the flights and much of it had melted or gone rancid before it reached Berliners. The RASC staff in charge of provisioning soon learned to mix lightweight goods with heavier so that holds were filled to capacity, but not so overloaded the pilots had to fight to get off the ground. Many still did, nevertheless. There was also much delicate balancing of priorities after a pilot refused to carry six boxes of new tennis racquets for the British garrison when medical supplies were awaiting transport.

Recruiting aircraft from any source available made only minimal difference in the figures, because those machines which had been in service from the start began to fail in increasing numbers. They had been old war horses at the beginning, and could not stand up to such treatment. Even so, they were flown well beyond the regulation periods between servicing and it was a miracle that there were not accidents galore. Much of this was due to the fact that the men flying them were very skilful, and those who were not made up for lack of experience with enthusiasm.

Not all the enthusiasm in the world can keep men flying continuously, however, and the biggest threat to the operation was fatigue. Crews were getting an average six or seven hours sleep every one and a half days; loaders worked long shifts, although their numbers had been swollen by the addition of Germans and Displaced Persons who were given extra rations to enable them to handle heavy work. But those who suffered most from lack of sleep were the pilots. Their responses slowed, they grew careless, they suffered from oxygen deprivation, and they quickly lost their tempers. In order to ease this problem a little, every desk-bound man who had ever flown was called into service. Which was why David kept coming face to face with Alan Winterbottom when he could otherwise have easily avoided him.

Fatigue did not dim the determination of those taking part in the greatest airlift ever known, and men went through that narrow corridor time after time after time. David was snatched up by the treadmill and had no further trouble getting to sleep whenever he saw that rare object, a bed. Like the rest, he welcomed forty winks during unloading at Gatow and loading at Fassberg. Then this waiting time was extended when a decision was made to backload export goods and mail from Berlin to aid the city's economy. This practice slowed down the target of a take-off every ten minutes, but the British and Berliners alike believed it was for the common good.

David still did not share the bravado spirit of those around him. The weekly figures posted up to boost morale did nothing for his because he did not study them. When Berlin children stood on piles of rubble to wave as the aircraft flew over, the sight left him unmoved. He was merely doing a job which was exactly answering his purpose; that of so fully occupying him he had no time to think. Yet even he found it too much after going thirty-five hours without sleep, then being called from his bed after only six because a pilot had walked slap into a brick wall and concussed himself. Grabbing 'breakfast' at two in the afternoon, he let fly at whoever was sitting next to him at the table.

'It's bloody ridiculous, this whole business. There'll be a few more walking into walls before long. It's the only way to get a rest, if you ask me.'

'I didn't,' came the tense reply. 'Anyway, I don't know what you're complaining about. You said you'd come here to fly. Well, that's what you're bloody well doing, aren't you? Some people are never bloody happy.'

As the man was little more than a blur to his tired eyes, David only recognized his ginger hair when he left the table. He was too weary to call abuse after him. Yet there was worse to come. When he next prepared to land in Fassberg the airfield was covered in machines wearing US markings, and gum-chewing, drawling, too-chummy fliers were everywhere. David had never liked Americans since he had accidentally shot one down and been psychologically unable to fly for eighteen months. Someone told David it had been decided that the Americans should share Fassberg in order to boost the supply rate, because the airfields in their own zone were much further from Berlin.

If RAF personnel were unhappy about this deluge of transatlantic cousins, the Yanks were more so. They hated the impossible overcrowding, the spartan accommodation, the unappetizing, small meals (all served with boiled sprouts, it seemed), the RAF discipline and, most of all, the lack of everyday things the British regarded as luxuries. Some went so far as to call it Stalag Fassberg, which hardly improved relations between the two allies.

Despite all those difficulties the airlift continued, and what had been launched as a temporary thumb of the nose to Soviet authorities snowballed into a massive operation. Supplies actually in Germany began to run out, so that there was almost an additional airlift from the USA to Britain and hence to the Western zones. The trouble was, no one knew how long it would, or could, last. The Russians waited with uneasy confidence for the operation to break down; the Western Allies grew suicidally determined that it would not. Meanwhile, more and more commodities in Berlin grew dangerously scarce.

David had grown numb, as had most of his fellows. He was past caring about regulations, flight safety, and what was in the crates and boxes they stowed in the space behind his cockpit. Then, one day four weeks after his arrival in Germany, he staggered to the Mess to have whichever meal of the day was being served and was told someone had been waiting four hours to see him.

'Let him bloody well wait until I've eaten and slept,' he grunted, pushing past the steward.

'She says she's your sister, sir,' said the man, from seemingly a long way off. At least, that was what David *thought* he said. 'It's been a long wait for her, and there's no knowing when you'll get another chance to have a chat. Will you come through to the office? The only place where you'll be private, sir.'

David was more or less led by the arm to the tiny room at

the rear of the Mess, where he was physically encouraged to enter before the door closed behind him. A girl stood up and moved forward: a girl in khaki trousers and shirt, with a black jumper slung around her shoulders. She looked tanned and happy, despite the suggestion of shock in her green eyes as she studied him.

'I found out quite by accident that you were here,' Vesta said. 'An American we'd known in Italy saw me in the NAAFI and mentioned that he'd read the name Sheridan on a flying roster and wondered if it could be my brother. I came over to find out and ... here I am.' She suddenly flung her arms around him and burst into tears. 'Oh David, so much has happened since we last met, and I've heard about it all from other people.'

Already punch drunk from too many hours in the air, David found the greeting difficult to cope with. What the hell was his sister doing at Fassberg, anyway? The last he had heard of her she was making giant waves in the art world and up to her eyes in lucrative commissions.

Putting her away from him with a weary gesture, he said, 'Can we sit down? The room is starting to sway.'

The steward came in with a pot of tea and a big pile of bacon and tomato sandwiches. 'Thought you'd like something to be getting on with, sir. I can get you a couple of pieces of fruit cake, if you'd like them, miss.'

'No, thanks ... but the tea will be welcome,' Vesta told him. After the steward left, she poured it into two cups, saying, 'You look absolutely drained, David.'

'*You* look in disgustingly rude health,' he riposted bluntly. 'Have you married him yet?'

'Who?'

'*Who*? That Yank you're so crazy about.'

She took a long deep breath. 'A lot has happened since we last met, as I said before. David, it's *so* good to see you again.'

He began on the bacon sandwiches. 'What are you doing in Fassberg, of all places?'

'Oh ... I suppose I caught a dose of the same bug that attacked you. Tarrant Royal no longer seemed the idyll I thought it would be when the war ended, and painting to order didn't suit me. I met someone I liked, who got a posting

243

to Germany. I went home after saying goodbye to him, and found a man there wearing one of your pullovers and drinking your whisky. It ... well, everything had changed from the rosy future I'd expected. So I looked up some of Daddy's Connections and persuaded them to commission a set of paintings showing the aftermath of war.'

'Hmm,' he grunted through a mouthful of sandwich. '*The Aftermath*. A far cry from *The After*glow. Are you here with this chap you fancy?'

'We were in Hanover until Christmas. Then he was sent here to join the REs helping to expand the aerodrome facilities. I think someone pretty well knew this airlift would be launched before long.'

'Why aren't you married? He's not another one of your flames who's already got a wife, is he?'

She took exception to that. 'You make it sound as though I make a habit of breaking up happy homes.'

'Sorry,' he said, fighting to keep his eyes open.

'I want to finish what I came here to do,' Vesta said, 'then start a series of pictures dealing with the airlift. Paul's up to his eyes in work. We're engaged, and that's the best arrangement for now.'

'Who's this man Mother has married? I mean, what's he like ... apart from being the kind who puts his bloody great foot in it?'

Vesta seemed surprisingly vague about a person she had met. 'Just someone looking for a future – like we all are. David, you've been asking all the questions. How about some answers now?'

'I'm too tired, Vee.'

She would not let him get away with that. 'You can't go to bed until you've eaten that pile you're working through, so at least talk to me while you're doing so. As I said before, I've heard all about you through other people. I wanted to discuss so many things with you but couldn't, because you took yourself to Scotland and refused to answer letters.' She grew tearful again. 'Can't you guess how I felt when I heard how Daddy really died? Surely you could have told *me*. It was a shock hearing it secondhand.'

He took another sandwich while holding out his cup to be refilled. 'It would have been a shock hearing it *first*hand.'

'But you would have explained; made it easier to accept.'

'There's no easy way to accept news of that sort.'

His sister tried again. 'It bothered me to think of you keeping it to yourself all those years. How did you *bear* it?'

It was no lie that he was too tired to talk. He was too tired to eat, but food was necessary in order to keep going. This conversation was not. 'You get to the stage when you can bear anything. If you're going to marry this chap you're with, what happened to the Yank?'

'What happened in Singapore?' The question was quietly put, but it carried a note of determination. 'Whatever it was has driven Mummy to adopt a most uncharacteristic mode of behaviour, and it's ruined Pat's life. From the look of you, I'd say it's also ruined yours.' She put a hand over his misshapen one. 'We all love you very much. When are you going home?'

Sheer weariness made him suddenly vulnerable. He laid a half-eaten sandwich on the desk and sighed. 'I don't know, Vee. Perhaps I never will.'

'What about Pat?'

'Hasn't she married someone else yet?'

'She's still in love with you. Always will be. David, what happened in Singapore?'

He was not *that* vulnerable. 'It was a long time ago, and I'm doing this now. God knows how long they intend to keep it up. Until we all kill ourselves, I suppose.'

Vesta broke manual contact. 'All right, I won't ask any more about Singapore, but you do realize that our new step-father is running your property in your absence. How long are you prepared to let *that* situation go on?'

He abandoned the idea of eating and concentrated on getting to bed as soon as possible. '*I don't know, Vee.* I just don't know.' He stood up. 'Look, remember how you mooned around after you were injured by that flying bomb on the London apartment? You kept wondering why Sandy had died, but not you. Then you extended that question to cover every-one you'd ever known who had been killed, *but not you.* You vowed you'd never paint again, and generally gave up on living. I suppose the same kind of thing has happened to me. Father talked sense into you then. I'm not sure whether anyone can do that with me, but until they do I've got to carry

245

it around.' He bent and kissed the top of her head. 'Bless you, Vee. Take care of yourself.'

She was still holding her cup of tea when he left the office and walked like a zombie in what he *thought* was the direction of his room.

Relations between the RAF and the USAF worsened to such a degree that even the respective commanders could not work together. To ease this problem, the RAF Dakotas were moved to Lübeck during August so that Fassberg, then predominantly American, was given an overall US commander. The airfield at Lübeck was a pre-war Luftwaffe station which had been used as an RAF fighter base since the end of the war. With great speed extra huts had been erected, a rail extension right to the station was laid and additional parking space created for the transport aircraft.

David's first sight of Lübeck was on a glorious sunny day, the first in a long time. The airfield, a bare two miles from the border of the Russian zone, was set amongst wooded hills and looked very welcoming after the clutter of Fassberg. It was a relief to find a routine approaching normality but, of course, the madness of the airlift had not yet hit this attractive station. He supposed it soon would. For now he was blessed with a room of his own, from the window of which he could watch red squirrels cavorting in the trees and hear birds heralding the dusk. The demons retreated a little. Alan Winterbottom remained at Fassberg, thank goodness. So, presumably, did Vesta. In retrospect he wished he had been more loving to her – they had always been close – but she had appeared at the wrong time. A dread voice within asked if there would ever come a *right* time to face his family again.

The best part about removing to Lübeck was the granting of three days' leave in a requisitioned hotel within the city, which David took after just a week in his new surroundings. The muted noise of a city was infinitely less than that of the constant roar of aircraft, and he settled in a room of dilapidated luxury intending to sleep for at least two of the days. In fact, he stayed in bed for twenty-seven hours, waking just once to consume beer and sandwiches before drifting away again. On the second afternoon he decided to take a walk. He had spent so much time sitting in the cockpit or lying on a bed, he had almost forgotten how to do anything else.

It was a fine day with a hint of autumn in the air. The local population was enjoying the good weather after a disappointing summer by strolling through the streets, and especially beside the water. David felt relaxed and calm, although his legs did not take kindly to prolonged walking. It was good to be away from aircraft and other fliers; a relief to know he would return to a hotel room and sleep without interruption tonight. Aching thighs and feet eventually drove him to stop for a beer at a little bistro. The tables outside on the pavement needed a coat of paint, but there was a view of small boats on water sparkling in the sunlight – a sight most customers were enjoying. The lure of cold beer and a chance to rest were too strong to make him move on, yet he turned his back to the scene. His calmness began to evaporate as he relived that other time he had seen small boats on a sun-dazzled sea.

'*David* . . . David Sheridan?'

He came from a distant nightmare to find standing beside him a woman in her mid forties with questioning green eyes and dark red hair drawn back from her fine features into a chignon. She contrived to look extremely elegant despite her dress of poor quality beige linen, and high-heeled shoes which had seen a great deal of wear. There was a compelling quality about the way she studied him and, if he had not just been through six mind-numbing weeks, David might have experienced a spark of recognition. As it was, he stared at her in near hostility whilst wondering how she knew his name.

'I saw you arrive and *could not* believe it. I watched for a while feeling certain I was not mistaken, and yet marvelling at the slender chance that should bring us together. In that uniform, and looking the way you do . . . David, I cannot tell you how I feel to stand here looking into eyes that are so exactly like his.'

He struggled to his feet in disbelief, because he now remembered her. Sonja Koltay, the artist known to him by her codename Mirjana; the Free French agent his father had loved enough to go to France and die for. Only when they arrived back in England on that terrible night had David guessed why his father had been so anxious to accompany an unknown

Austrian engineer. Sonja had attended his memorial service, and had disclosed to David her real name and the fact that she and Sir Christopher Sheridan had been lovers for two years. She had asked that they become friends for his sake, and David had readily agreed. He had kept their secret from his family, but Bill Chandler had apparently known of the affair all along.

Sonja now took David's outstretched hands and lightly kissed his scarred cheek, accepting his inability to speak. 'I know. It is incredible, is it not?' she asked in her attractive European accent. 'In a poor little bistro in defeated Germany, I look up and there is the son of a man I loved so much I caused him to die unnecessarily.'

Starting to recover, David coaxed her on to a chair at his table, and sat again facing her, absorbing the classical beauty of this woman his father had loved too well; the perfect partner for a man of his intellect. 'Forgive me,' he begged, 'I've been flying until my brain has burned out, and this is something of a shock. Your last letter gave details of your success in Paris. Whatever are you doing here . . . and in such a cheap little café?'

'The coffee here is remarkably good.'

'Would you like some more?'

She shook her head. 'You have been flying the airlift to Berlin?'

'Out of Fassberg for six weeks. We've just moved here, and I've been given three days in a hotel to catch up on my sleep. I saw nothing but bedclothes for the first day and a half. I've just come up for air.'

'You also have his smile,' she said with a touch of sadness. 'We were fated to meet. Five more minutes and I should be gone.' Her eyes studied his face with concern. 'You still look so badly tired, my dear, but what you are doing for the people of Berlin would make him so proud.'

Guilt over her mistaken conception of his motives led David to guide the conversation back to her. 'Are you now living in Lübeck?'

'Nearby. I share a house with a young Estonian girl. It's small but very peaceful, and one of us is always there to look after Mirjana.'

It was a sign of his brain's exhaustion that he did not at first understand. Then he remembered. 'Yes, of course. How is she?'

'Your half-sister? As beautiful as Chris would want her to be. She is three already.'

David struggled to recall all he knew about this woman who had had his father's child six months after that fateful pick-up in France. 'Your work – the glass engraving. Is there adequate demand for beautiful luxuries in today's Germany?'

'No, no. Such pieces that I do I export. There are still markets for art. Even war does not stop people from desiring objects of beauty. Always has it been that way. So much the Germans took from galleries, museums and cathedrals, and some of it is not yet recovered.'

'That was avarice, not appreciation of art,' he said. 'Surely you'd do better back in Paris. What made you leave?'

She spoke as if he had not asked the question. 'You are married now to the girl next door with the lovely silver eyes?'

The pleasure of the moment began to dim with recollection. 'No.'

'The Chinese wife is still with you?'

He stiffened. 'You know a damned sight more about me than I know about you.'

'Chris spoke so often of his children. He loved you both very much, you and your sister who became the artist he dearly wished he had been. He confided so much to me of your lives.'

'And of my mother's?'

She was not thrown by the question. 'Oh, yes, also of what he had done when you were born, of how much he must have hurt her, and of how they had continued their marriage for *your* sake. It was sad that she never knew him as I did.'

'She's just married again. A man who came to put the house back in order. I had never told her about what happened that night, but *he* knew because he worked for SOE. It came as a terrible shock to her, of course. She still doesn't know about you, however.'

'There is no need for her to know now. Mirjana Sheridan is happy enough with her two mothers.' She frowned. 'I am sorry we lost touch two years ago, but these things happen.

We had all pinned so much on ending the war, we lost sight of what was certain to follow. It is not the paradise so many hoped for, is it?' When he made no comment, she said gently, 'The last letter I received from you told of your plan to give up flying and settle in that beautiful village married to the girl you loved. We agreed to be friends in honour of your father. Won't you tell me why the plan failed?'

He countered that with a question of his own. 'Why did you leave Paris?'

After regarding him for a moment or two, as if deciding her next step, Sonja got to her feet. 'Come with me and you will learn why. You will also meet your little sister.'

Although he stood, David made no move to join her. The invitation had thrown him. Speaking of his father's love-child was one thing. Greeting her as his close relative was another.

'Please, David, come with me,' she said, seeing his resistance. 'She is innocent of anything her parents did. Don't reject *this* child of his as he once did you.'

Those words banished what little remained of his pleasure in the meeting. She could not possibly know, and yet it was as if she could see into his guilt-ridden soul. Her arm linked through his to persuade him forward. 'I have a small car and promise to return you to your hotel whenever you wish.' To lighten the atmosphere, she added, 'And now everyone will think I am a woman of the night luring you away.'

'No one in his right mind would ever make that mistake about you,' he murmured through stiff lips, unable to walk away from her now.

The car was *very* small. David had to fold himself into the passenger seat. He was surprised that she owned one, and could get fuel for it. Maybe her international reputation as an artist gave her special privileges. In any case, she would not be listed as a defeated enemy. She was Hungarian by birth, and had once been married to a Frenchman, which was why she had worked for a Free French organization similar to SOE. He knew little of present regulations here concerning foreigners. He had been sitting in a cockpit at Fassberg or Gatow, or flying between the two, from the moment he arrived in Germany.

To his surprise Sonja left the city in the direction of the

airfield. His reservations returned. Sleep was what he needed, not an introduction to the three-year-old result of his father's secret passion. The child was unlikely to take to a creature with a scarred face and claw-like hands. Children were usually frightened by anything out of the ordinary. This was a great mistake, he told himself. Yet he had considerable respect for this woman beside him, who had risked her life countless times to bring from beneath enemy noses people who were willing to help in the war against this country they were now in. The last train of thought led him to wonder again why she should have come to live here when Paris had initially been the obvious choice for such a cultured, talented woman. In New York, of course, she would be highly acclaimed and successful, but he could not imagine her there. She was European through and through. However, she could not be selling or producing much of her work or she would not be wearing clothes that had seen better days.

The car pulled up, bringing him from his thoughts. They had reached a village of typical German style which looked mainly untouched by bombing. The houses had murals painted on them, and their little wooden verandahs were smothered with geraniums. The gardens boasted row upon row of vegetables, and poultry ran freely around the neat barns whose lofts were filled with logs for the winter. Charming though it seemed to David, the constant roar of aircraft shuttling to and from the nearby airfield intruded into the atmosphere of rural contentment. He also found this setting greatly at odds with the woman beside him. His sense of reluctance was now replaced by one of intrigue. If this was some kind of country retreat, what was she hiding from? Her only possible enemies would be living in this very country, surely.

Sonja took his arm again and led him to a small house lying behind and between two others, along a grassy pathway.

'Do you like it?' Sonja asked him. 'Better for a child than ruins and rubble, and people who have forgotten who they are.' She pressed the latch on the door and led him into a large room furnished with a hand-carved dresser, a table and four chairs, a long padded settle and two rocking chairs. In the far corner was a tiled stove with a shelf around it for sitting or lying on. The sills of two small windows were brightened by vases of wild flowers, and the wooden floor was covered by handmade rugs in a dazzle of colours. It was charming in a *Volk* fashion, but David expected to find a rosy-cheeked couple in lederhosen and dirndl, not the daughter of Sir Christopher Sheridan and her sophisticated, artistic mother.

Sonja put a finger to her lips and smiled at David. 'Miri, Miri,' she called in high tones. '*Kommst du her, Schätzchen!*'

There was the sound of feet running down wooden stairs, and the laughter of two girlish voices. Then the door burst open to admit a child of astonishing beauty. Mirjana Sheridan had her mother's glorious red hair, and her father's eyes, so deep a blue they were almost violet. These opened wide with surprise as her headlong progress halted with a skid on one of the rugs. As she studied David from head to foot, there was no sign of revulsion or distress on her delicate features, nor did her hands screw up her blue dirndl in an agony of shyness. She simply stood quietly assessing this white-haired stranger in a blue uniform with wings over the breast pocket.

Sonja squatted to encourage her daughter to come to her. Then, when Mirjana was within the circle of her arm, she said to the child in English, 'This is your brother, David, from England. He has come to meet you, Miri.'

But David had lost interest in the child. The young woman who had come in behind her was gazing at him from the doorway, with such intensity in her dark eyes he felt as breathless as if he had exceeded safe altitude and starved himself of oxygen.

CHAPTER THIRTEEN

THE girl was slender and dressed in a dark-green dirndl with a white puff-sleeved blouse beneath, but her face beneath coiled brunette plaits was sensitive, full of intelligence and extremely Slavic. No simple German peasant this. The fervour in her eyes continued to mesmerize David as she came forward.

'I cannot believe this should be happening,' she said in heavily accented English. 'David Sheridan should be *here*, in this tiny village house.'

Overwhelmed in more ways than one, David could think of nothing to say. Nor could he comprehend why this girl should greet him like some kind of childhood hero.

'You are here for the *Luftbrücke* – the bridge over the sky? Yes, of course you must be. *Still* you are fighting!'

Her words were interrupted by a voice saying, 'Mirjana is ready to greet you, David.'

He turned to the woman and child he had forgotten. The little girl curtsied and said in careful English, 'How do you do, my brother. I am pleased to meet with you.'

David had no idea how to respond to his father's daughter, and this curtseying doll reminded him of two others who had refused to stop smiling at him.

Sonja seemed unperturbed by his silence and encouraged his attention to return to the young woman beside him. 'My dear friend has for a long time been inspired by your story. She could not have known I would return this afternoon with someone she never dreamed she would meet.'

'My *story*?' he repeated, mystified.

'Shall we sit and have coffee? Monika shall make it while I explain.'

Shunning the rocking chairs David perched on the settee, already conscious of Monika's absence from that room and more intent on the sounds of her coffee-making in the kitchen than on what Sonja was saying. However, he heard enough to learn that when the two women first became friends, Sonja revealed the identity of Mirjana's father and the circumstances of his death. Over the months they had been together, more and more had been revealed about the son who had had to leave his dying father and fly home.

'I was with Chris when he received the telephone call telling him you had been shot down over the jungle, and there was little hope that you had survived,' Sonja continued, holding her daughter on her lap in the rocking-chair. 'David, I know that you were tortured at some time during your ordeal before reaching Australia and, of course, I know of your courage in overcoming your injuries in order to fly again.' She stroked Mirjana's bright hair with a caressing hand, as she added, 'We both of us know how you used your reduced skills to ferry agents back and forth. Chris once showed me a photograph of you taken when you were awarded a DFC. The girl with the silver eyes continued to love that man even when he was no longer so handsome, and so the person himself must be very special.' She smiled. 'We have met only twice before today, and yet I know you so well . . . and so now does Monika. You have often been her inspiration.'

'For what?' he asked with a frown, unhappy about being known so intimately by strangers.

'Her work as an agent for your government.'

'*What?*' He almost shouted it. 'The war's over!'

'That one is,' she responded calmly. 'The fight against Communism has replaced it.'

Monika came in with coffee and the kind of cake David remembered from boyhood holidays in Germany. He could not equate this rural domestic scene with exploits he had believed were long over. Monika gave him coffee, then sat on the floor with Mirjana to eat cake.

'I am teaching Mirjana a little English,' Sonja explained, 'but she will not understand what we are saying. It is quite safe. When she is older we shall have to be more careful.'

Light dawned, and David asked, '*You* are in on this work?'

'Only as a contact; a messenger. I have Miri to consider.'

'But *why*? Surely you did more than enough before. Why risk your life again?'

'It is Monika who does that. She goes into Russian territory. I stay here in safety.'

Still slow-witted from deprivation of sleep, David felt as if he had wandered into the realms of unreality. Perhaps he was still in bed at his hotel room dreaming all this. 'Shouldn't you tell me everything now you've begun? How on earth did you get involved in such work again?'

Monika sat with her arms linked around her knees studying him intently. The story she told added to his sense of unreality. 'I had nine years when the war began. In Estonia it was not good. We hear the Russians are coming so we pack our beautiful objects, our clothes, food and some animals, and leave in the night. We are overtaken. My father and brothers are marched away to fight, and I never see them again. The soldiers have taken our clothes, food and animals. The other . . .' She looked at Sonja, who provided the right word. 'The other *valuables* they take to sell for to have money to send home. My mother and my sister they smile and . . . and . . .' She turned again to Sonja.

'They fraternized with the Russians,' Sonja explained. 'Rape was inevitable. For women to offer themselves willingly often guaranteed violation by only two or three who were comrades, and protection by them from the rest. They also sometimes received a little extra food from their "protectors". Monika's mother needed it for her child who was put to work in the fields with them. They were ostracized by others who defied the Russians and suffered in consequence.' She shrugged. 'Sometimes it is wiser to conceal pride, but it burns all the hotter inside.'

Mirjana climbed back to her mother's lap and settled there sleepily while Monika continued her story. 'We must always speak Russian. For children it was soon learnt, so I speak it well. When the war is almost at an end my mother is too old, and my sister is ill, but I determine to leave and go to America where all is good. I hide away, hide away. Oh, many days. Then I came to France, and had to stay while I make enough money for the ship to America. My papers will not allow me to work there, and I have no place to live. Then, in the park one day, I see this beautiful child and start to play with her. God is soon rewarding me with meeting Sonja, who likes me to play with Miri.'

She moved from the floor to sit beside David. Her nearness disturbed him more than her words because she used her body to emphasize her emotions, and she was *very* emotional at this point. 'Without Sonja I think I would have died. I now have somewhere to live, I eat and have work to look after Miri. I know that I do not want to go to America, but to stay with this lady who makes beautiful glass and to be nursemaid to Miri. Then *everything* changed.'

Sonja took over once more. 'When you have worked for secret organizations you are never forgotten, David. I was one day contacted by a former colleague and invited out to lunch. I should have guessed why, but two years had passed since Chris was killed and I left their ranks to have Mirjana. I was also building a new life in the peace we had all fought for. I looked forward to meeting with an old acquaintance.' She shook her head. 'How soon innocence returns after years of guile. I actually *looked forward* to what I thought would be a pleasant reunion. This charming man flattered me, bought me the best lunch available in Paris, then revealed that he knew I employed an Estonian nursemaid who spoke fluent Russian and had every reason to hate the race. I was asked to find out from her if she would work for a new branch of the old organization.'

'That wasn't fair,' David protested. 'You had served them unstintingly during the war, and you have a daughter as well as a distinguished career.'

'My dear, they were never fair; never considered a person's private life. They worked your father until he was on the verge of mental collapse.'

'So you agreed to talk your nursemaid into taking up espionage?' It was almost an accusation.

'I agreed to give her his message. It was not for me to say what she must do.'

He turned to Monika. '*Why*, for heaven's sake?'

'David, please let us finish before you question our actions,' Sonja said. 'So that I could pass on his request I had first to explain my connection with this man. It was inevitable that the parts played by people like you and Chris featured strongly. Monika was deeply impressed by the fact that, although your father was temperamentally unsuited for the job, he used his talents to help those who were, and that you took up such dangerous work after all you had been through and suffered.'

'What about the part you played, which was far more dangerous? Didn't *that* impress her?' David interjected.

'Do not speak that I am not here,' flashed Monika. 'Yes, I think Sonja very, very brave. But you, you fly so many times against the enemy with courage. You have been tortured and made broken. Yet you fly again and fight back. I have known only men who hurt and steal and behave to disgust. When I hear of this David Sheridan I know what I must do,' she added with fresh passion. 'I must fight these bad men for what they do to my people.'

'But . . .'

Sonja silenced him. 'You must see it through her eyes, my dear. After a childhood of oppression and cruelty a young girl is ready for a hero. Monika agreed, and they found us this house less than two miles from the Russian zone border. I am the artist in glass who needs a quiet atmosphere to work, and Monika is my nursemaid. We speak all the time in German and dress modestly. I say the car is necessary for driving to the city for business. We have shared it to take an old man to hospital, and a woman to visit her dying mother. No one suspects we are not who we say.'

'And she's going into the Soviet zone whenever they ask her?' David demanded angrily.

'Speak to *me*,' cried Monika, tugging his arm so that he had to turn her way. 'Yes, I go. Did not you fly to France when they ask?'

'They need to know what's happening, now more than ever,' Sonja said quietly, causing David to look at her again. 'We have people in Berlin, but they are no longer able to move around freely.'

Deeply uneasy at the thought of this young girl putting her life at risk because of admiration for things that happened during a time of world war, David asked, 'How do you explain Monika's long absences? No nursemaid takes herself off for more than a day or two at a time.'

'We both go on a supposed business trip. I have a permit from the British allowing me to travel where I wish. Miri and I go to the mountains far from here. They let me know when

257

Monika is returning. I pick her up and translate into code what she tells me.' She smiled. 'The same code we used before. They never cracked it, you know. I passed the latest news to my contact in the bistro this afternoon, just fifteen minutes before you appeared.'

David stood up, partially to relieve the curious brand of anger this revelation had generated. 'My God, I thought we won the war to end this kind of thing. I'll accept that *she's* doing it in the headstrong belief that she's avenging her family, but why are you involved? Not to avenge *his* death, surely? I did that several times over after D-Day. It wasn't the Russians who killed him, anyway.'

'I know, David,' she said quietly. 'I'm playing my very small part for the sake of my daughter. The wonderful future I planned for her is being threatened. *Europe* is being threatened. The peace we so desired is flawed. Unless we fight Russian greed now it will flourish and swallow us all up. This is no time to sit back, as we thought to do. The war is not yet over. You know that, or you would not be here to help save Berlin.'

Monika got to her feet beside him. '*You* will not give in; so must not we.'

It was all too much. These women were bestowing on him virtues he did not possess. He was filled with a deep sense of guilt, and an inexplicable ache in his breast because he did not live up to Monika's ideal. Her hero had feet of very murky clay, and it was time he left before she discovered the fact.

'I really should get back,' he began. 'I'm supposed to be sleeping during this leave. We get little enough when we're on the circuit. It's more or less non-stop for hours at a stretch.'

Without thinking, he had painted the very image he sought to avoid, and Monika was full of understanding. 'I will drive you to the airfield. You *must* sleep!'

Sonja suddenly reverted to German to tell her maid that their visitor was not at the airfield but attending a conference in the city. Monika replied in the same language, without any sign of surprise, that she would be happy to return the officer to his hotel for madam. A moment later a man in lederhosen with a brown, weatherbeaten face arrived at the door with a dead chicken. It was a gift, he said, in return for taking him to the hospital in Lübeck. Monika accepted it while Sonja thanked the visitor graciously.

'The little girl has fallen asleep,' he pointed out with a smile. 'So bright and full of fun; the next moment they are sleeping. They are all the same, the little ones. Well, goodbye, and cook the chicken soon. It will not keep in this hot weather.'

David gave no sign of having understood what had been said, and resented having to do so. He had played the secret game for too long during the war. By telling him what they were involved in these two courageous women had dragged him back into it again. Mirjana had, indeed, gone to sleep on her mother's lap. She looked so defenceless and innocent David mentally acknowledged that his father would be delighted with his love-child.

'I'm sorry I didn't get to know her better,' he told Sonja, preparing to make his getaway. 'I find it difficult to believe she's a blood relation.'

'You resent her?'

'Oh no, not at all. Of course not,' he said hastily. 'It's tragic that he can't see her.'

'He sees her,' she told him with quiet confidence. 'And you will come to know her.' She glanced at Monika and then back to him. 'It will not be far to come from the airfield.'

'We have no time off. It's hard enough to snatch a few hours' sleep between batches of sorties.'

She nodded in a manner that dismissed his swift excuse. 'I cannot tell you how happy I am at our meeting. There is so much of him in you. Go and sleep, David. We shall have coffee and cake again together, and you shall grow to love your little sister.'

Absurdly, because it was quite out of character, he took one of her hands from around the sleeping child and kissed it. It was what his father would have done, and it seemed right to end an isolated meeting with that kind of gesture. 'Goodbye. Take great care.'

Monika was an atrocious driver. She threw the small car at the lanes as if it were made of india-rubber. To make it easier on his nervous system, David studied her instead of the road ahead. Her profile was exciting, especially when his gaze travelled as far as her waist and back up again. Her small breasts were emphasized by the dirndl bodice which thrust them upwards in the soft white blouse. Her nose was straight, her lips full and sensual, her ears beneath the coiled braids of hair neat and flat.

'You are quiet, David,' she said suddenly. 'What is it you are thinking?'

'I was wondering if you'd fly a Dakota better than you handle this car.'

She turned her head and smiled. It hit him smack between the eyes, and he realized it was the first time she had done it. 'You do not approve of my driving?'

'No,' he said, grabbing the wheel with one hand to guide the car around a bend coming up. 'Not when you smile at me instead of watching where you're going. I'd prefer to sleep in my hotel room tonight, not Lübeck hospital.'

She turned her gaze ahead again as they flashed past woodland, her smile fading. 'Be careful what you do, David.'

'That's rich coming from you!'

'They mean to have Berlin, you know. They believe you cannot hold it. When winter comes it will be impossible to supply coal as well as food, they say. People will then see it is best to accept Communist ways, and will turn their backs on you. When that happens all Germans in Western zones do the same. There will be strikes, riots, much upset.'

'Not if *we* can help it.'

Her hand fell on his knee, which created double jeopardy as she shot another fiery glance at him. 'I knew that is what you would say. So much a fighter!'

David snatched up her hand to put it on the wheel beneath his as a thick hedge loomed closer. That danger averted, he broke contact to minimize the other. 'What do you do over there?'

'Please?'

'How do you get across the border? They've stopped two-way traffic.'

'There is a place near here. It is possible.'

'But terribly risky.' She merely shrugged, so he said, 'All right, once you're in their zone how do you manage to move around without being questioned? I heard they change the format of their permits almost daily.'

'How is this "format", please?' she asked, racing over a narrow bridge about to be crossed from the opposite direction by a horse-drawn cart laden with cabbages. The farmer shook his fist. Every inch of David shook. He was a pretty wild driver himself, but it was vastly different being in the passenger seat with one, especially when she looked as Monika did. He did not attempt to explain 'format' in case it distracted her. She did not pursue the matter, either, but he was determined to know how dangerous was this work she was doing for his country.

'How do you get your information?'

'I have plenty contacts. They are taking back to Russia all machinery, all clever people, all things that are of value. This my contacts tell me. They mean to destroy Germany. They hate this enemy so much.'

'As you hate *them*?'

'You understand hate, David. You understand it very well. Nothing will stand in the way. I have no love of Germany. You even more have not. But we must not let it fall to this greedy, cruel people. It will not stop there. This is why I tell your people all this, and go again when they say.' She kept her eyes on the road because they had reached the outskirts of the city. 'The Russians are taking everything back to their country so there will be nothing here for the people. Then they think to rule them with Communism. You and the Americans are stopping this for them, so they will have no trains, boats or lorries coming in.' Her hand touched his knee again, accelerating a pulse-rate already fast due to the hair-raising way she was weaving through traffic. 'I think soon they will stop aeroplanes.'

'No, they won't,' he said firmly. 'We've got the bit between our teeth now. The only way to stop us would be to shoot us down, and they wouldn't dare do that.'

'They will do *anything*. That is why I tell you be careful.'

Any reply David might have made was prevented when the car pulled up so sharply he was jerked forward and hit his head on the windscreen. It was not a serious bump, but Monika made a great fuss and took his face between her hands to study the spot for damage. The damage being done was not to his head. The sudden feminine concern and gentleness after her account of cool-headed espionage was more than he could handle. *Monika* was more than he could handle. A swift farewell was essential.

'I'm fine,' he assured her, opening the car door and extricating himself from the cramped space. Once on the pavement outside the hotel he bent to say goodbye and leave, but was disarmed by the glow of admiration in her eyes for the man she thought he was. Regret flooded him. If only he looked as he once had. If only they had met in a more innocent age. If only he deserved the pedestal she had put him on.

'You will come again.' It was a statement rather than a question.

'While this airlift lasts, there'll be no time.'

'And when it ends – one way or the other?'

'We shall all go straight back to England.'

'What of Miri, your little sister?'

'Today was just a chance meeting, not a family get-together. She's too young to understand who I am, or to care if I never return.'

'I care, David,' she said softly.

It was time they parted. 'Look, you know only very little about me, and what you've been told by Sonja was told to *her* by my father, who was biased. You shouldn't have . . . You shouldn't read too much into it.'

'It is too late for you to say that . . . and you *will* come again. I know this.'

She shot away almost before he could jump clear of the car. As he watched it weaving madly along the street he regretted the drastic loss of his youth. She was eighteen and full of fire; he was thirty-three and riddled with guilt. Her inspiration was completely misplaced.

September heralded the coldest weather for that month in Berlin for three decades, and the men commanding the airlift were almost at their wits' end. What to do? Coal was now as vital as food. Without coal there would be no electricity, and Berliners would freeze to death in pitch darkness. The alternative was for them to die of starvation in warm, well-lit houses. Somehow, more flights had to get into Berlin per day, yet no one could work out how. They were marginally *less* because aircraft had been overworked, flown without regular overhauls, and loaded with substances which had actually damaged the equipment and controls. Much the same could be said of the crews. Medical staff at the Western zones' airfields were themselves exhausted from treating men with blocked sinuses, defective vision, migraines and oxygen deficiency.

Accidents grew more frequent on the ground. Loaders often collapsed. They grew careless and spilled what they were handling, or they ignored payload limits and filled holds willy-nilly just to get rid of a consignment. Some failed to lash crates and barrels securely so that they broke loose and shifted in mid-air. The operational side was equally disastrous. Pilots' concentration deteriorated, they grew extremely bad-tempered at the controls and, on the last run of their long, long stints, they often ignored instructions from the Control Tower by landing wherever they fancied and as fast as possible so that they could get to bed. Navigators began to make errors from sheer exhaustion. One aircraft landed at the wrong airfield, several wandered beyond the limits of the air corridor and were buzzed by Soviet fighters, another missed Berlin alto-gether and was on its way to Russia proper before the mistake was discovered.

It was inevitable that some men cracked under the strain after three months of impossible pressure, but most had by then acquired an attitude of bloody-mindedness which drove them on beyond the normal limits of endurance. Their opinion of Russians was unprintable. Even so, their superhuman effort was not enough, and the Eastern sector newspaper stepped up its sneer campaign along with East Berlin radio broadcasts concerning the feebleness of Anglo-American efforts to look after the Germans in their sectors. A group of punch-drunk pilots put forward a proposal to drop a bomb on the Russian sector radio station, but their bomb bays were all loaded with dried fruit, cereals or cod liver oil for babies so no one had room for it.

In September the Americans brought over to Europe a large consignment of their big military transport aircraft. The British had no more to spare, so a fresh requisition of civil Dakotas was undertaken. It swelled the number of machines and crews, but increased the stress on regular pilots who had to cope with aircraft zipping about all over the place and ignoring the rules.

On one pilot the demands of that September had a surprising

effect. Squadron Leader David Sheridan had become the most bloody-minded of all airlift personnel in his determination to defy the Russians. He willingly accepted any machine so long as it would take off, and any cargo that could be crammed into his Dakota so long as there was enough room in the cockpit for him. The first time he transported coal, one of the unpopular commodities, he and his crew returned to Lübeck resembling chimney-sweeps. Coal dust got everywhere, turning the inside of the aircraft into a dark, gritty tube, and penetrating instruments and controls. When the load was flour they came back resembling ghosts. After three consecutive coal runs towards the end of September, David had his first accident.

With twenty-four hours on duty behind him, he flew his Dakota towards Gatow at two a.m. in sleeting rain knowing he would be rewarded with sleep when he next returned to Lübeck. Although he had washed his face during the turn around each time, he could already feel coal dust settling on his skin and pricking his eyes. His flying-suit was thick with it, and the taste of coal was at the back of his throat. He had developed a cough – they all had – through transporting too many powdered substances. But each load had its own hazards. Fish left you smelling high for days, petrol was volatile and dangerous, meat bled all over the floor, salt corroded everything, fertilizers for encouraging home-grown vegetables had the aircraft stinking of horse-stables, and pilots who found some idiots loading into their holds gigantic emergency generators far exceeding the safe load limits would never be the same again.

It was cold at five thousand feet. David suggested to his crew that they cut open one of the sacks and light a fire. They both thought it a splendid idea except that no one had brought chestnuts to roast in it so there seemed little point. As a crew they worked well – when they could remember what they were supposed to be doing. It grew colder still as they drew near Gatow. Ice began to form a thin coat on the wings, and the Dakota started to lose height. David increased power, but not as swiftly as he would have done three months ago. Something told him he must keep his altitude, but he could not exactly recall why. Ah yes, two thousand feet below in the sleet-filled night was a long line of aircraft going in the opposite direction. Must keep above them. Was there a de-icing system somewhere? Yes, of course there was. Well, no use sitting there looking at it, you dozy bastard, he told himself. Turn the bloody thing on!

He did so, then rubbed at his sore eyes once more. It simply aggravated the pricking of the coal dust. When he looked at the altimeter he saw they were still slowly losing height. The de-icer could not be functioning fully. He turned the system off, then on again. Still the altimeter moved back. Hell, the thing must have packed up! His brain was not so fuddled that he did not realize they were in real trouble. If they dropped too far there would be an almighty pile-up. Summoning alertness from that amazing resource which had been plumbed to the depths during the Battle of Britain, David revved up to full power to maintain height and called his navigator.

'Brian, the flaming de-icer's gone for a burton. Where are we?'

'Just coming up to the last check before Frohnau, Skipper. Will we make it?'

'Ask a silly question,' he grunted, busy fighting the controls. 'Let me know when we're approaching the beacon.' A spasm of coughing just then prevented him from putting in his usual call to tell Gatow his position and cargo, but as soon as he recovered he got in touch with Ground Control in tones which betrayed his tension, and told them the situation.

'I'm eighteen miles from Frohnau Beacon and my de-icer's packed up. I'm now at four thousand five hundred and very slowly losing height. Can't retain full power for too long. I've half a coal mine on board.'

The ground controller responded with a request for identification, and David snapped, 'I've had so many different Daks I've lost track of which one I'm flying, for God's sake. Look on your bloody screen. I'm the dot that's lower than it should be and will soon be flying into any dots heading in the opposite direction.'

'Keep your hair on,' said the overworked man on the ground in a reasonably calm manner. 'Please give identification.'

The navigator told David their number which was written on his flight schedule, and David repeated it feeling certain he

265

had heard it somewhere before. Ground Control then assured him he would be given priority landing instructions, adding that it was snowing hard over Berlin and all departures had been cancelled so he need not worry about outgoing flights.

'Make contact again when you reach the beacon, KN 921.'

Still flying on full power and wondering if the engines would stand the strain, David muttered savagely that it was all very well for him to halt all take-offs, but what about those already airborne? It was a sign of his exhaustion that he questioned the controller, who had a screen showing the position of every aircraft within a radius of forty miles and could make contact with each and every one of them, if necessary. Trouble was, *he* could not even see the lights of the one ahead of him now, much less a dozen or more all packed into that narrow corridor. Sitting in a freezing cockpit layered with coal dust, staring at lights on an instrument panel with sore eyes, and with an eternity of snow-filled night sky right outside the perspex – *a night sky over Russian territory* – was nowhere near as comforting as sitting in a warm room on the ground, watching dots on a screen. David felt the controller had not fully appreciated that fact.

'Just approaching the beacon, Skip,' said the navigator over the inter-com.

'Roger.' David knew what he must now do and rolled into the turn holding the control column with all the power of his wrists. As he had feared, the Dakota did not take kindly to banking and lost height dramatically while he struggled to bring them back on even keel before they plunged into a dive. He had been quite good at cricket at school, but had never entered the tug-of-war. He wished he had now, because pulling the control column was very much like that activity – heaving with all his might with heels braced on the floor.

They were well into serious snowfall now. It was like flying through cotton-wool and he was relieved when the ground controller's voice came at him with news of where he actually was. His position was not exactly a cause for alarm, but at the rate they were dropping they could be on the ground short of the runway. That would not help anyone, not the line of aircraft behind and, now, above him, not the Gatow unloaders, and especially not David Sheridan who was an inspiration to a young Estonian girl. Monika had beautiful expressive eyes. She had beautiful everything.

'Come in, KN 921. How do you read me?'

David realized his mind was wandering and hastily acknowledged. 'Loud and clear.' He was very, very tired and his eyes were so sore the instruments looked blurred. Had he lowered the undercarriage and flaps when reminded by that calm voice from the ground? Yes, he thought so. Better check. The cotton-wool was getting thicker so it was much lighter in the cockpit now, but it produced the situation pilots dreaded. He would not see the ground coming up until his wheels were practically touching it. There was no alternative but to put his life and those of his crew in the hands of that anonymous man watching a dot on the screen.

The engines were starting to play up, but he dared not reduce power too dramatically. He suffered bouts of coughing so that the controller often had to repeat his instructions for acknowledgement. Seeing that he was now below two thousand feet he told himself he must have dropped through a convenient gap in the outward flow, too weary to realize none would be coming now take-offs had been halted. He longed to rub his eyes again but could not hold the column with one hand. It was difficult enough with two. The instrument panel appeared to be dancing up and down. The entire aircraft was shaking quite violently.

'KN 921, you are approaching the glide path,' said the voice from the ground. 'Turn left at zero nine two degrees. You are coming in too low. Decrease your rate of descent!'

'I can't bloody decrease it,' David swore. 'How about pushing the end of the runway half a mile towards me?'

The calm voice then told him emergency services would be standing by at the end of the runway, which he would not reach by about two hundred yards unless he could maintain his height for the next mile. As he knew he could not, David simply corrected his line of approach when advised to and tried to concentrate on making a landing in the rough as safely as he could. There were no high obstacles to the approach, for which he was thankful, but putting down on soft ground was always hazardous, particularly when it was covered with wet snow. He felt no fear. A pilot was always far too busy for that in tricky situations.

They rushed forward, guided by the ground controller and, next minute, faint light became visible through the density of snowflakes. The headlights of the crash waggons and ambulances were illuminating that white stretch just inside the perimeter wire which they were going to reach very soon. Still competing with the control column, David fought to urge the Dakota as far forward as he could before hitting the ground. The aircraft had had enough, however. Travelling sluggishly, it gave up the ghost and pancaked well before the spot where the vehicles waited, then slewed violently to port. David was so tired he forgot to close the throttle. In any case, he was tug-of-warring now with superhuman strength to keep his aircraft from charging full-pelt across to Staaken, the Russian airfield almost next door.

There was a terrible screeching. The entire fuselage shook and rattled as the machine swung back in the opposite direction when David struggled to correct his approach. Had they done this at Lübeck, returning empty, they would have been in far worse trouble, because the half coal mine David had reported carrying now acted as heavy ballast. His last sight was of lights racing towards him before they exploded in a shower of beautiful colours all around, like a Christmas tree in the snowy fairyland he had entered.

When he came to, his initial terror was banished by the sight of a snow-covered tree just outside the window by his bed. There was no snow in Singapore. Most station hospitals looked the same, anyway. His pulse-rate returned to normal, but the bad moment started off a bout of coughing which brought the present back and drove away fear from the past. His arms ached so badly he could scarcely lift them in order to feel the outline of his body. Every part of it was there, so he must have come out of the crash pretty well. He then began to worry about his crew. Strangely, he could not think of their names or even recall their faces, yet he must have had others with him. In a Spitfire a pilot was solitary, he could curse, panic or make errors which bothered no one but himself. In a Lysander, he had no crew, but there had been pasengers to be responsible for. In a bomber or freighter he relied on his crew for help, but the onus of getting airborne and safely down again was ultimately his. When that proved to be virtually impossible, he was supposed to set an example and give them encouragement. Had he done that? David fell asleep before an answer presented itself.

It had stopped snowing when he awoke, although low cloud suggested it was cold outside. A calendar on the wall facing him reminded him it was only September. Why had it been snowing? The mountain scene on the page was quite spectacular, but he would have preferred a pin-up girl whose breasts were falling out of her chemise. The thought made him amazingly randy, which took him by complete surprise. He had not felt the least stirrings of lust since . . . Recollection of that night in Singapore speedily had him back to normal again. Yet it was not long before he was thinking of Monika and the way her small breasts in the soft blouse had appealed to him. Everything about her appealed to him very strongly and he was soon thinking again about breasts falling out of chemises.

Another bout of coughing racked him and brought an orderly to the room with a kidney-shaped bowl. 'I thought you was being sick, sir,' he said, almost regretfully.

'No, it's *Luftbrücke* laryngitis,' he rasped, feeling weak from the effort. 'How about a socking great cup of tea? That would help no end.'

'Medical Officer's on his rounds now, sir. Can't do nothing till he's finished. Might manage a cup for you then, but dinner'll be on its way soon after.' The orderly's red-rimmed eyes acquired a slight gleam. 'That was a spectacular landing you made last night. Everyone these days is coming in like they was some kind of stunt men. There's been belly flops, kangaroo hops, racing skids, crab crawls, some who come down thinking they're flying helicopters, others who forget they're flying *anything*. Last week one landed, and when the unloaders reached it they found the whole crew fast asleep.' He gave a bark of laughter. 'Wonder how long they'd been like that? Anyway, you gave us a new variation. Talk about "The Skaters' Waltz"! You was gliding about all over the place chucking out sacks of coal as you went. There wasn't a lump of it to be seen soon after. All the Germans working here had it in their pockets to take home.'

David gave a grin. 'Maybe they'll offer me a medal for working out how to cut costs and speed everything up. Easiest way to distribute coal. No unloading necessary. Gets straight to the consumer.'

'Ha, that's a good one, sir, that is,' agreed the orderly, knowing pilots were a strange breed, and particularly so after crashing. It was best to play along with them.

The medical officer who entered was not prepared to play along with flippant pilots. Like everyone else connected with the airlift, he was not getting enough sleep and was overworked. He had not seen his wife and baby son for almost ten days, and he was very worried. As a doctor he considered the airlift to be inadequate and a dangerous form of bluff. Aircrews were becoming impossibly stressed, and he foresaw accelerated loss of life if it continued. This patient, for instance, with ample evidence of serious injuries, had surely given all he could by way of duty during the war. What was he doing here taking part in a lunatic scheme which could not possibly succeed in a hundred years? He could easily have been killed out there on the snow last night, and all for the sake of sacks of coal which were a mere drop in the ocean.

Those were his thoughts as an RAF doctor. As a husband and father he wanted to send his family back to England so that he would know they were safe from Russian aggression. As an Englishman he believed as fervently as the next that Berlin should not be surrendered to Stalin. It was an uncomfortable triple opinion to hold, so the sight of his orderly laughing with a man who surely had nine lives irritated him no end.

'Have you something useful to do with that vomit dish, Perkins?' he asked crisply. 'I suggest you do it, or get on with taking the evening temperatures.'

'Yessir,' said the red-faced Perkins, and went out.

'How are you feeling?' he then asked David.

'With difficulty. My arms are like lead weights.'

'Umm.' He did not seem too interested. 'How's your vision?'

'It comes and goes,' David admitted. 'It's the bloody coal dust. We're all the same.'

'Umm. I'll give you some eye-drops, if we have any left. We're waiting for another batch to come in.'

'Shouldn't count on it. Fertilizer, petrol, tinned fish, packets of POM, even lavatory paper, but not sure about eye-drops. They're a luxury.'

The man frowned. 'Are you one of those jokers who still think this is a kind of "Biggles" escapade?'

David took exception to being spoken to in that admonitory fashion. 'Does it matter what kind of chap I am so long as I fly the stuff in?'

After a moment the MO let out his breath on a sigh. 'No, I suppose it doesn't . . . but you won't fly much more in if you land two hundred yards ahead of the runway again. You were damned lucky.'

'How about my crew?'

'They were damned lucky, too.'

David relaxed. 'What's the damage, then?'

'To the aircraft, or to you?'

'Both.'

'The Dak won't fly again for some time. You will if you're determined to . . . but not for a week or so. You've concussion, severely bruised ribs and muscular fatigue in arms and wrists. I want to keep you here for another thirty-six hours, then you can go and please yourself what you do.' He tested David's blood pressure, looked into his eyes with a pencil torch, and listened to his chest. Then he straightened up and studied him carefully. 'I've just remembered where I've seen you before. The name rang a bell, but I didn't manage to put two and two together until now. I was a member of your medical board sometime in forty-three. You were keen to get back into a fighter, but we all realized that was out of the question. I believe we recommended limited duty, which we guessed wouldn't satisfy you. I heard later that you had somehow wangled a place in the special squadron at Tangmere, flying Lysanders over to France.' He smiled rather sourly. 'The nephew of "Sherry" Sheridan, I heard. You *are* the "Biggles" type, aren't you?'

'And you're the type who allows his supply of eye-drops to run out,' David retaliated sharply, as one squadron leader to another. 'Now we've summed each other up, I'd like a cup of tea . . . if you haven't run out of that, too.'

David slept, waking only to eat until he was discharged by the

MO who had finally spent a night with his wife and so was feeling much better. Repeating his stricture on being grounded for a further ten days, he arranged for his patients to be taken as passengers on a Dakota returning to Lübeck. Everyone was shunted away from Gatow as soon as they were fit to travel, because they were eating the very supplies they flew in, which defeated the whole exercise. Brian, the navigator, had a broken arm; the wireless operator was badly cut and bruised. As they waited for transport they all expressed gladness at the prospect of some time on the ground when they got back.

In the event, the Dakota taking them to Lübeck was flown there by David, because the pilot slipped and fell whilst climbing in, cutting his head so badly the bleeding could not be stopped. When the man was carted off to the hospital, it seemed sensible for David to volunteer to take over. He soon regretted his offer, because his arms were not yet back to normal. But whose arms were these days? They were carrying a backload of mail, which was cleaner and lighter than the coal, and all went well until they neared Lübeck when one of the engines began stuttering. David's own crewmen and those he was now flying with were deeply worried. The border was a bare two miles from the airfield. A forced landing short of it would put them down in the Soviet zone, and no one wanted to be *there* for a rest.

Visibility was good, however, and David was a very experienced pilot. What was more he could see from the cockpit the village where Monika lived and at that moment knew he would go there again as soon as he had landed, eaten and gone off-duty. Worried though his companions were, their pilot was calm and confident as he brought them down on three-quarter power with skill learnt over eight years in the cockpits of all manner of aircraft. Fliers were very superstitious people and it would have been easy for his crew to believe David Sheridan had now acquired a jinx, but the fact that they had landed and survived twice against the odds suggested that he was well able to combat any jinx that came his way, and confidence in him was strengthened even further.

There were two letters waiting for David when he eventually reached his quarters. He opened the envelope addressed in Vesta's handwriting expecting to read that she had married the man she was with. Guilt touched him in those few seconds. He had no idea who her lover was; his name, what he was doing in Germany, how he felt about Vesta. Why had he been so uncommunicative when she had turned up unexpectedly at Fassberg? He had been exhausted, yes, but that had really been no excuse for the way he had treated her after two years apart. Before he pulled the written sheets from the envelope he noted an address on the back of it, and was glad he could send congratulations. There were none to be sent, however. His sister's letter was chatty and uncomplicated, giving an account of the work she was doing in Fassberg, the news from home, and a sincere hope that he was taking great care.

> You looked so tired when I saw you, and so unhappy. I telephoned but they said you'd been transferred so I hope this will reach you, David. I promise not to ask any questions you find too painful to answer, so couldn't we meet when you get some leave? At least write and let me know you're alive and kicking. We were always such good friends. Whatever happens to either of us shouldn't drive us apart. Don't get so tired you start making mistakes in mid-air. We all think you're doing a tremendous job, and I do so hope you're doing it for the right reasons.
>
> Much love,
> Vee

He put the pages aside thoughtfully. How perceptive of her to suspect his motives. Back in Fassberg he had been doing it to counteract demons. In that moment he was aware that that was no longer true. He was now flying himself almost to a standstill partly because a young girl with brown eyes believed he was some kind of hero ... but mostly because she was some kind of heroine.

When he slit open the other letter, it was as if Monika had materialized from his thoughts. Her handwriting was thick and as erratic as her driving, full of energy. The note was short and asked him to come as soon as he could because there was something he must be told quite urgently. Her name was scrawled across the page with a flourish, and he could see her quite clearly, framed in the doorway that afternoon. Desire to see her flooded through him.

273

Stripping off the flying-suit stinking of coal dust, he then discovered his underwear also smelt of it. The row of showers worked only spasmodically. The water which gushed or trickled through was either icy or scalding. A comfortable compromise was rarely achieved, so he stood and shivered beneath a cold deluge while he soaped his body extravagantly in the hope of clearing away the last of the coal dust which had penetrated every pore. The cough was still with him – he could do little about that – but his eyes had improved. The MO at Gatow had found some eye-drops and they made a vast difference. He washed himself so vigorously that he winced over bruised ribs which would take a while to ease, but he reckoned his arms would function well enough to steer a bicycle.

He had no hope of a jeep. They were all guarded so closely, and were so constantly in use there was never a spare one sitting around with the keys in the ignition. Bicycles were much easier to come by because they were left lying around all over the place. If he could not get one by simply walking off with it when its owner was busy, he would pull rank and take one from beneath the rear of whoever rode up first. While he dressed in fresh clothes and brushed his hair he determined to reply to his sister's letter. It had contained a hint of wistfulness, he thought, and a longing for how things used to be. Well, everyone had that, but Vesta had had her future so well planned. His hand holding the hairbrush stilled. So had he . . . once.

The urge to get away from flying, from men smelling of everything under the sun, and from the constant roar of aircraft was too strong for him. Or maybe it was the lure of those brown eyes and a pair of enticing breasts above a shaped bodice which drove him from the building into weak late afternoon sunshine on the lookout for the means to see them again.

A bicycle was waiting to be purloined. It leaned against the wall outside his quarters, but not for long. David was on the saddle and pedalling towards the perimeter fence to look for a place to get through the woods behind the living accommodation. He banked on the present overload of work being responsible for laxer scrutiny of the fencing which would normally be inspected and repaired very promptly, and he was in luck. The constant rain had caused minor earthslips here and there, leaving big enough gaps beneath the wire for him to scramble through and drag the bicycle after him. It was late afternoon and growing very chilly, so he was glad of the exercise to keep him warm. The village was roughly four miles from the airfield. It seemed like forty to David. By the time he heaved his leg over the saddle and pushed the bicycle along the path between the houses to the one he remembered from four weeks – or was it five weeks? – ago, he was trembling slightly from effort and much less immaculate than when he had set out.

Halfway to the front door it opened. Monika stood there holding by the hand his half-sister dressed in a white nightgown tied at the neck and wrists with blue bows. David was struck by the contrast between the flame-haired child watching his approach with perfect composure, and the girl in navy blue dirndl with soft white blouse, who fairly glowed with vibrance as her dark eyes took in every detail of his dishevelled appearance.

'*Guten Abend*,' he greeted them quietly, coming to a halt with the bicycle.

'Hallo, David,' she said in her breathy voice. 'I thought you would never come.'

'I've been stuck at Gatow for a couple of days so I only had your letter this afternoon. Luckily, I've been grounded for a while.'

'What is this "grounded"? You must not drive a car?' She looked pointedly at the old machine he held. 'So you are not so clever at driving that you should say mine is not good.'

'May I come in?' He felt conspicuous on that grassy path, and it seemed even colder now he had stopped pedalling.

Monika led the way inside. Warmth greeted him as he propped the bicycle against the steps, followed her and closed the door. 'You would like coffee and cake?'

He nodded because now he was here he felt he should not have come. Nothing had changed. He was still not what she imagined and, even if he had revised his motives for flying the airlift, that did not wipe out the other reasons why he should keep away from her. When she went to the kitchen he was momentarily tempted to leave, but he was being fixed by two violet eyes and they kept him immobile.

'How do you do, my brother,' Mirjana recited with a small curtsey.

Disarmed, David said. 'How do you do, Mirjana. Where is your mother?' He crossed to her and squatted to repeat the question in German. It broke the barrier immediately, and the child told him that Sonja was visiting her friend in Lübeck and would not be back until after bedtime. Speaking in a more familiar language, Mirjana became a vastly different child from the formal little girl of his earlier visit. His lack of experience with children did not matter because she was enchantingly friendly. It did not occur to David that the peasant life might be restrictive for a naturally bright child, nor did he consider that this daughter of two talented, highly intelligent people would almost certainly be an exceptional character. He simply listened while she chattered about herself, her books, her lessons with her mother. Then he answered a barrage of questions about the big aeroplanes he flew and why they made so much noise all the time, and about the beautiful house in England where he lived.

It came as a slight shock to him to accept that she had been told a great deal about her grown-up brother, even before he came on the scene so unexpectedly. Sonja regarded her daughter as a member of the Sheridan family, that was plain. If Sir Christopher had lived what would he have done about this child of love?

'She has talked all the time about her so-big brother, ever since you came,' said a voice behind David, and he stood to find Monika had brought coffee and cake. 'Did you come now to see her?'

Breathlessness assailed David again as he looked at her. 'I came because of your letter. You wrote that it was urgent.' It was the first time he had thought of the contents of her letter. He had really come because he could not help himself.

Monika lit two lamps to brighten the dusk, and David watched her graceful movements with pleasure. Mirjana disliked having lost his attention and tugged hard at his hand, telling him to sit on the settee to eat cake. When he was there beside her, she did what any child would do and studied his deformed fingers with candid interest. Then she asked why his hands were so funny and why he had nasty marks on his face.

Monika made no attempt to silence her. She sat quietly in a rocking chair putting the onus on David to answer, and when his eyes met hers he knew he must reply as truthfully as possible in a way Mirjana would understand. It was not easy to think of the best words in a language he did not often use, but he eventually said, with his gaze still locked to Monika's, that he had been in a fight a long time ago.

'Have you seen cats fighting when they want something? They put out their claws and scratch, don't they? That's what happened to me. I would not give up what was wanted, so I got scratched.'

The reply appeared to satisfy the child because she then munched cake in silence, but an electric charge had developed between David and the girl. Soft lamplight played on her vivid face and her throat above the gathered neck of her blouse, and it was all he could do to stay where he was, drinking coffee, when he longed to reach out and touch her. She was equally aware of it. Recognition was in her gaze, which played over him in frank fashion. Neither spoke. There was only one thing to say and it had to wait.

Just as soon as Mirjana finished eating, Monika said it was well past bedtime and she must say goodnight to her brother. Naturally enough, having discovered she could communicate with him in German, the child was loath to end this enjoyable meeting and demanded that 'Dahveed' should put her to bed and tuck her in. Monika did not demur, so all three went up the staircase to the bedrooms. David saw the danger, but did nothing to avoid it. Like the crash landing at Gatow, it was impossible to turn back and he would either survive it or go under during the next half-hour.

Mirjana cleaned her teeth, knelt to say her prayers, then jumped into the wooden bed decorated with painted flowers which was already occupied by a family of rag dolls. She had beside her bed a small musical box, which Monika wound up to play, and on the chest of drawers stood a lighted candle within a protective glass bowl engraved with a moon and stars. The work of Sonja Koltay, without doubt. David tucked in the bedclothes as best he could, then was seized around the neck and kissed on his left cheek. That tender contact was fatal. Nothing could stop him now.

As they left the child settling with her eyes closed, David grabbed Monika's arm with a sense of urgency. 'Which is your room? This one?'

She nodded, and he steered her inside before kicking the door shut. In the near darkness he pulled her hard against him and kissed her without preamble. So worked up was he, and so certain it was what she also wanted, he went ahead with desire unchecked when her response gave him the right signals. It was a shock, therefore, when she suddenly fought free and backed.

He followed and grabbed her again. 'Come on! Downstairs just now you knew as well as I that this would happen. What kind of game are you playing?'

'It's no game,' she whispered, holding herself stiffly.

He was still highly aroused and tightened his grip on her arms. 'So what's this act of virtue in aid of?'

Held as if in a vice she gazed up at him stricken. 'When I was twelve Russian soldiers passed the field where we worked. They had had drink. We . . . we could do nothing.' Her head then dropped between his outstretched arms so that he could barely hear her add, 'I am ashamed. I am not *new*.'

As David realized what she was telling him anger began to replace his desire. Rape at twelve – probably multiple rape. Had it ended there? Dear God, how could she even bear him to touch her after that? Yet her overriding emotion was shame that her body had been used so violently. She thought it unfit to offer to him. As she continued to stand defeated, he was engulfed by compassionate humility. Drawing her against his tunic he wrapped his arms protectively around her and, in the darkness of that simple room, found himself confessing his own shame.

'I'm not new, either. I've been with a number of women, but all in perfectly natural situations.' He almost stopped there but forced himself to go on. 'Two years ago I met again a man I had known during the war. He had saved my life in a completely *un*natural situation. It had given him a kind of guilty sense of domination over me. At that recent meeting we both drank a lot, but I had a great deal more than he so I was hardly aware of what was happening when he took me to his hotel room.' He tightened his hold to draw comfort from her softness. 'Rape can be as degrading for a man as for a woman. I've been unable to be close to anyone since that night. Until now.'

Monika said nothing but her arms tightened around his body, too, so that they gave each other mutual comfort and understanding. As they stood close, David knew that the final defeat of what Kershaw and those unknown Russian soldiers had done to them would be to complete this loving union, here and now. Lifting her face up to his with gentle fingers he kissed her soft mouth, while his other hand slid down her arm to take hers in a warm clasp. The electric charge had burnt itself out to leave something less violent but infinitely more powerful.

CHAPTER FOURTEEN

THEY heard Sonja return in the little car, but they stayed where they were. Soon the house was quiet and they lay together listening to the roar of aircraft departing on the twenty-four-hour lifeline to Berlin.

For David that night was the salvation he needed. Holding Monika's slender body gently, entering her to create pleasure for them both, cleansed him of the humiliation of Kershaw's animal brutality. He perfectly understood Monika's sense of unworthiness. He had been similarly cursed. The relief of unburdening the fact to someone who would not be appalled or disgusted, and who knew the pain and self-loathing which followed, was heady. The delight in possessing this girl in the fullest possible natural way had been overwhelming.

From the time he had returned from the jungle of Sumatra, until those two stolen hours with Pat, he had just once paid a prostitute in order to discover whether or not he could still perform satisfactorily. Pat had more than proved he could. Then he had gone to Singapore. After that he had not trusted men, and had turned away from women. Monika had given him back the freedom to do what he had always done with enthusiasm and great enjoyment from the age of puberty. Four years of self-denial because Japanese soldiers had, in the space of three days, turned him into a broken, scarred shadow of what he had once been, had been followed by more years of it because of an Australian semi-madman. Tonight, an eighteen-year-old who had never known that willing surrender in love could bring her happiness, had released David from some of his demons. When dawn began to break and he saw that young face beside him on the pillow, he knew he must chase away the rest even if it meant losing her. If he did not speak of it now, it would be forever locked inside him.

He slipped from the bed and dressed in his shirt and

trousers to stand looking from the window. Cockerels were crowing; the people of the village were already up and about. A peaceful rural scene, yet the incessant roar of engines overhead was a reminder that peace was still an illusion three years after the war had ended. Turning, he looked back at the girl on the bed. Brown hair, released from its plaits, lay across the pillow in rippled swathes, and stranded over one bare shoulder. The coverlet exposed her delicate breasts whose nipples were still taut from his gentle bites and rougher handling. Her full lips were swollen from the pressure of his, and there were faint bruise marks on her throat. She slept, relaxed, breathing softly, totally vulnerable.

As David thought of this same girl – a virgin of twelve – being stripped naked by drunken soldiers, taken by force, then left in the fields while they staggered off laughing, there was born in him the kind of iron determination he had known after returning from the dead in 1943. Then, he had been set on rising above an experience which could well have destroyed him, and hitting back. Now, he would help this girl to show *she* had not been destroyed by what had been done to her, and he would hit back on her behalf by every means open to him.

Monika's eyes opened. For a moment she stared across at him as recollection came, then she gave a slow smile which further strengthened his decision to shed the rest of his demons. She trusted him, loved him, *believed* in him. He must tell her the kind of man he really was. When he had hinted to Vesta that he would probably not regain his freedom until someone motivated him to seek it, he had little thought the chance might come soon, and in such a manner. He must take it.

Monika came to him, slender and beautiful, before he guessed her intention. As she kissed him, her hands were pulling the shirt free of his trousers and unfastening the three buttons he had done up. He caught her hands and held them fast. 'Monika, I need to talk to you.'

Her eyes widened teasingly, as she broke into a stream of unintelligible words, which distracted him long enough for her to kiss him again.

'What in hell was all that about?' he asked roughly, enjoying the smoothness of her skin beneath his palms.

She laughed and pulled free to twirl around then fall back

on the bed with her arms above her head, her breasts high. 'I am telling you in my native language that I am ready to make love again from the beginning.'

'Go around saying things like that in words I don't understand, and you might find yourself making love from where we left off. That's when it gets *really* interesting,' he murmured as he sat on the side of the bed and ran a hand down her body from throat to thigh.

When he did no more than that she slowly sat up and studied his face. 'There is something wrong. I did not please you?'

He caught her against his chest. 'You pleased me more than I can say. You must have been aware of that.'

'Then is it that you must now go?' she asked, arching back to question him.

'Not yet. I need to tell you something first.'

'You are leaving Lübeck? You go home to England? You –'

He put his fingers to his lips to silence her, then wrapped her around with the coverlet. When he had finished his confession, she might no longer want him in her room, much less sit naked beside him.

'So serious you are,' she breathed. 'It cannot be good what you have to say.'

'No, it isn't ... but you deserve to hear it.' As she sat clutching the coverlet for comfort and watching him with those disturbing dark eyes, David began on an account of something which had turned his life around just as it was settling into place. 'I'm not sure how much you know about me –'

'*Everything*,' she interrupted passionately. 'Sonja has told me everything.'

'No, not everything.' He stared down at the floor beneath his linked hands, and travelled back in memory. 'I was young and in desperate trouble when I married a Chinese girl in Singapore. I thought it was love. She was what I badly needed at that time. I soon discovered she had married so that her husband could support and look after her seven brothers and sisters. When the Japanese overran the island she refused to leave, as I had arranged, unless I found places for all the children. It was impossible. While I was on duty at the airfield, she left our bungalow taking with her everything of use to her family. The lovely European things I had bought were left there to taunt me.'

Monika sat very still as he went on to describe how he had never known the name of Su's village, how he had financed her family but never met them. 'I was so hurt by her desertion I set fire to the building and everything in it, then went back to work until I should be taken prisoner. I never was. There were four aircraft left. Three got away safely. The pilot of the fourth was machine-gunned before he reached it. I flew it away from Singapore.' He drew in his breath as if to ease the pain. 'What happened next can't be put into words. You've seen my face and hands. Now you've seen the marks on my body. They were made by Japanese soldiers. Since that time I have had an uncontrollable hatred of Orientals.' He shot her a swift glance. 'No, *more* than hatred. *Terror.*'

He got to his feet and gripped the painted board at the foot of the bed. 'Such terror I almost lost my mind. It still wakes me in the night, sometimes, and I remember why.' He paused to compose himself, then continued speaking with his gaze on the wall. 'I planned to marry an English girl just as soon as I could find my wife and divorce her. It was very difficult because I had no idea where she lived, and the military authorities were too busy trying to trace missing servicemen. When I was offered a lift to Singapore by a friend, I was glad of the chance.'

He walked to the window and pushed it open so that he could feel the chill air rather than the remembered clammy heat of that island. Faint regret on having embarked on this made him pause, but it had to be finished now. 'I hadn't allowed for how I would feel on returning. The fear and hatred rushed back at the first Oriental face I saw. Nightmares returned so strongly I had to drink to withstand them. By pure chance I discovered the name of the village where the Lim family lived, and I went out there, very apprehensive.'

He was speaking now in flat tones and seeing from that window not chickens and geese running between German houses, but a tangle of jungle with a narrow path leading through it. His flesh was creeping with revulsion and he felt sick. 'They were aggressive. Said they had no time for an Englishman who had deserted his wife to save his own skin.

She had been made to serve a brothel until she died of fever. I felt nothing but relief at the news. Then they pushed two children at me. Identical twins who smiled like obscene Oriental dolls and followed me. They kept following me . . . and smiling . . . and I knew I had to get rid of them somehow. I sent my driver away and walked for a long way. Each time I turned they were there, smiling. Their black eyes seemed to mock me. Their smooth, flat faces terrified me. How could I have produced such creatures?'

His hands gripped the sill as if clinging to a ledge above a chasm. He was starting to shake. 'I walked into the jungle meaning to run off and leave them there, but I told myself they would be found. Their people knew who and where I was to return them to me. I thought how easy it would be to kill them. I almost did . . . but I would have been arrested and executed. Yet it would have been *so easy* to do it,' he repeated in monotones. 'After a while there was a fishing village. Boats. I watched for some time until I saw one preparing to sail off into the sunset. A big ocean-going craft. They . . . they were smiling as I paid the man with everything I had on me of value, and walked away. My children were probably still smiling as they were put to heavy work on some distant shore.' He swallowed noisily. 'They're always smiling, those people. *Always*. Even when you're screaming in agony, they continue to smile.'

From out of the life he had momentarily forgotten, someone came alongside him. A girl with dark eyes full of compassion and a body that was completely unflawed. She took hold of his arms and turned him to face her. Then she put up a hand and feathered away the tears on his cheeks.

'What else could you have done, *Liebling?*' she asked softly. 'They are with their own people, and you are with yours. That is always best.'

Holding her as if clinging to a lifeline, he buried his face in her hair and began to sob. She let him do so until he was exhausted, then led him back to the bed and made him lie down while she stroked his white hair and kissed each of his scars as if healing them. Before long he slept, and there were no nightmares to disturb his peace.

*

The deadlock showed no signs of being broken. In fact, Soviet attitudes had hardened further in the confident expectation that the airlift must fail when the Berlin winter set in. The scheme was now running to capacity. No matter how great the supply of all commodities needed, or how many new aircraft with fresh crews were available, flying to Berlin and back and loading and unloading had reached its zenith of speed.

Wizards of ingenuity had devised means of greater efficiency on the operational side. Aircrews experimented with parachute drops to save turn-around time in Berlin, but this was swiftly stopped. Packaging split on impact, boxes were damaged leaving perishable goods to be wasted, winds took parachutes so that vital supplies drifted down in the Soviet sector instead. There was only one solution to the problem facing the Western Allies. If Berlin could not be abandoned, yet could not be supplied with all that was needed, the people in Berlin would have to resign themselves to existing on less than ever during the severe weather to come.

Those who had witnessed the frenzied activity at airfields, seen the red-eyed, white-faced men who flew longer hours than safety regulations stipulated, or those people who had particular reasons for fearing Russians, braced themselves for the worst and appreciated what was being done for them by their former enemies. Those involved in the airlift gloomily accepted that they were in for an even more testing time in the grip of winter, and could not help wondering if the Germans would have done the same for them if victory had been theirs instead.

Vesta was deeply involved in gathering material for a set of paintings of the airlift activities at Fassberg, and could have got her hands on almost anything she wanted if she had let a few aircrew get their hands on her. Senior officers would give her no help whatsoever. She did not blame them. They were as impossibly overworked as the rest, and carried on their shoulders the responsibility for continuing this desperate operation to its uncertain conclusion. Small wonder they had no time for a female artist, and an English one at that. Even mention of Sir Christopher Sheridan – usually successful with a race who were impressed by titles – made no difference here. So the artist fell back on the Vesta Sheridan formula for getting what she wanted and now had quite a few useful contacts among the ground staff and aircrew, who had accepted, however, that she was 'off limits' so far as romance was concerned.

One day in early December she was driving her car towards the scene of a crash. They were becoming more frequent. Aircraft were going up in weather conditions which would normally ground them, so it was inevitable that weary pilots suffering from lack of sleep, persistent coughs and an overdose of coffee and doughnuts substituting for meals should over-shoot perimeter fences, or miss runways, landing instead where they believed them to be. The spate of accidents, together with the rumours of one or two suicides, worried Vesta.

David had looked ghastly on the day she sought him out. Having last seen him before he flew to Singapore, the differ-ence in him had shocked her. He was surely a prime candidate for cracking up. She had not seen him again, because he had moved to Lübeck. The letter she had sent to him there had not prompted a reply, but she still hoped for one. Knowing what it was like for pilots here, she allowed for the fact that her brother had little time or energy to put pen to paper. Still she worried. After coming through all he had suffered in the war, it would be terrible indeed if he fell victim to this mercy mission still alienated from all those who loved him. She had written to her mother and to Pat of their brief meeting, and left the onus on them whether or not to contact him. She suspected neither would. He had told them both pretty plainly to leave him alone. Paul advised her to do the same.

His posting to Fassberg had come at just the right time. It had been good to get out of stricken Hanover and to know that Paul would be in a safe administration job. He was still unaware that Vesta had witnessed the chimney bomb drama. She felt it was better that way. Jim had been posted to Aden shortly after Christmas, so he was also now safe. They both missed his cheery company.

As Vesta feared, Paul had wanted to be married as soon as they became lovers. He did not understand her reluctance in the face of her attitude about the way men used women. 'I love you. I'm begging you to become my wife, yet you seem to prefer being my mistress – a state you once deplored, if I recall.'

She explained that she had things to do before becoming an

army wife, with all the attendant restrictions. 'I'm very happy and fulfilled, and I'm doing some inspired work. I don't want to spoil that by taking on domestic responsibilities. I'm hopeless at running a home, I warn you.'

'You won't have to. There'll be a German maid.'

'I'll never be demure at cocktail parties to butter up your CO when I'm itching to finish a canvas. Please understand, Paul. I'll give you anything you want in bed . . . or out of it, so long as you choose somewhere warm and comfortable.'

Paul had accepted defeat when she agreed to wear his diamond ring which would at least warn men to keep clear, and they had spent his three weeks' Christmas leave in Switzerland in a state of great happiness. Once in Fassberg, Vesta had found another small apartment in a block used by the staff of a civilian welfare group, and Paul came there as often as he could. Vesta knew he was very deeply in love with her, and she made him happy in every way she could. Their only continuing cause of discord was when she needed to be alone to work. Paul resented being denied entry to her flat during those periods, and she refused to give in to his wishes. They discussed the problem in some depth, and agreed that when they were married she must have a room to which she could retreat without disturbance while painting. Paul was quite happy about that because she would still be under the same roof as him. It was the sense of being locked out he could not stomach.

The airlift paintings were going well, so they planned to get married early next year. The location was still undecided. Paul did not care where the ceremony took place just so long as she became his wife. Vesta dithered between going home to be married in the village church, as she always imagined she would be, or having a quiet ceremony in the military chapel before moving into officers' married quarters. She would have to make up her mind soon. In truth, she would have been happier to continue as they were. As Vesta Sheridan she could act as a free agent. Once she became Mrs Gaynor what she did could affect her husband's career. When a woman married a soldier she married the army, too. Paul had excellent prospects. It would become half her responsibility to ensure that he fulfilled them. Maybe she was afraid of that, afraid of having to curb her penchant for being unconventional.

David's marriage to Su Lim had barred him from the Officers' Club and every other colonial social sphere in Singapore. If it had continued there was no doubt his career would have gone into a backwater, despite his renowned name and flying skill. In service life attitudes were set and inclined to be narrow. While the man might sometimes be as eccentric and colourful as he wished – it got him noticed in the right quarters – his wife was expected to support him with impeccable conformity. Vesta was not sure she would always do that. She was supremely happy, at present. Paul understood and supported her determination to gain the material she needed for her work. He was impressed by the canvases she had already shown him, particularly so by *Betrayal*, which had affected him quite strongly. He was an exciting lover and, since moving to Fassberg, he had revealed an audacious, daredevil side to his personality which had clearly before been suppressed by unhappiness over their relationship and the strain of his work. Yet Vesta knew she could not keep him waiting much longer. The ambitious young captain's career would not be helped by a long-term mistress, he once told her in half-joking manner. She had swiftly pointed out that, as he was not married to another woman, she was simply a very generous fiancée.

The first set of paintings completed in Hanover had been sent to England, earning words of praise and a large cheque. The airlift collection was still under negotiation at present, but Vesta was so inspired by what was going on around her she was happy to go ahead without an actual commission. Her work was full of the colour and flair which had made her war pictures so successful, and there was no doubt they would sell to RAF sources and *aficionados* of dramatic events captured by a discerning eye. Vesta had, in fact, accepted three private commissions from American pilots with wealthy families, who would 'go just crazy' to have a lasting memento showing what their boy had done for Berlin.

She was not certain why she had decided to drive out to the site of a crash today. Three Americans had died in the C-54 which had plummeted shortly after take-off, and the cause of failure was being sought by investigators. In two minds about visiting the spot, Vesta had asked Paul's opinion at breakfast.

'Do you think it's too morbid a subject?'

'Not when you consider *Betrayal*. You're supposed to be doing a series on the airlift, and crashes are part of it. Propaganda will record the heroics. It's your job to record reality. You've always maintained that belief.'

Paul's judgement was usually infallible, and he remembered almost every word she said concerning her profession. He had found her a car of her own, which she ran with the added connivance of a young airman from Dixie who slipped her a can of petrol when no one was looking. The Americans were much more generous with commodities, which they had in ten times the amount issued to the British forces, Vesta soon discovered, and she brought home all manner of tasty fare she and Paul had not seen for years. They were also much more lax on discipline, and this meant she had no difficulty getting on and off the airfield. Dressed in khaki like the women in the forces, she was waved through the gates with a smile from men who were used to seeing her around and thought she had official status.

It was cold as she drove towards the field where the aircraft had come down during the night. Fog hung in patches over the open countryside so she took it slowly. Military drivers were notorious for racing around these roads in the expectation that they would be free of traffic. A US truck hurtling right at her out of the murk was what she dreaded. She had with her a thermos of coffee and some biscuits to tide her over in place of lunch. Sketching wreckage might take some time. She would have to do it now, because it would be cleared away as soon as possible. It was bad for aircrew morale to overfly a crash in which their colleagues had been killed. It was low enough owing to fatigue. The authorities wanted nothing to bring it down further.

Rounding a corner, Vesta braked hard. Dead ahead was a concentration of men and vehicles. Behind them she saw a broken wing sticking up into the greyness beneath low cloud: all she could see of the wreck. Despite this grim evidence she heard the roar of aircraft taking off and landing at five-minute intervals. The airlift went on regardless of tragic interruptions. Vesta pulled into a gateway clear of the lane, slid her sketch-book into her jacket pocket and left the car to approach the accident spot. It was an awesome sight. The C-54 had ploughed through the field leaving a deep gash in the earth, smacked into a group of trees which had snapped off most of one wing, then had tipped on its side to come to rest barely a few feet from the lane. The cockpit was crushed; one engine had been driven into the side of the fuselage by the tremendous impact. The tail lay several feet away in the deep rut. The aircraft's belly had been torn open to spill out part of a cargo of coal. It lay scattered all over the area, the dust from it now coating the damp fuselage so that it resembled charring from fire: an extremely sobering sight.

Vesta was moved but not horrified. She had seen worse things in Italy, and in the desert where she had once driven for miles through an area thickly scattered with burnt-out tanks, broken fighter planes and the skeletons of those who had once manned them. These things she painted because she wanted the world to know about them, because the people who had been part of them deserved recognition. There was no such motive behind pictures like *The Old Mill*.

After making several sketches from a distance, Vesta moved forward, pulling the collar of her coat up around her ears to ward off the cold. One of the drivers standing around recognized and greeted her. 'Hi, Vesta, shouldn'ta thought this'd be your kinda thing. How the hell can you make a picture outa this?'

She moved up beside him. 'The same way I make pictures of anything. How are you, Elmer?'

'Guess I'm kinda tired, like us all. Tired but sure as hell not beaten.'

'We heard the crash. Do they yet know why it did?'

He rubbed his chin with a grimy hand. 'Nope. But you can guess it was one of two things. A wore-out old plane, or a wore-out old crew.' He wrinkled his features. 'It's kinda hard to go out this way after fighting a war. Makes a guy kinda wonda what's it all about, don't it? How's your brother?'

'All right, so far as I know.' She gave a faint smile. 'I suppose *he's* a wore-out old pilot by now. Who are all those people beside the wreckage? Are they important, or can I go over there?'

'Nope, they're nothin' but newspapermen. They bin living

on the base since they caught on to realizing this airlift was kinda somethin' else, see. Get somethin' like this and they all come swarming around like blue-tailed flies.'

Vesta made an apologetic face at him. 'I'm just as bad, I'm afraid.'

He coloured slightly beneath his thatch of straw-coloured hair. 'I didn't mean nothin' disrespectful. You're different. These guys pick off any old carcase that's got meat on it, but you got *feeling* about what we're doing here. Nope, you're different, all right.'

'Thanks.' She spotted several uniformed men emerging from behind the wreckage. Not familiar enough yet with American insignia of rank, she asked, 'Are they generals or privates?'

Elmer grinned. 'They'd sure as hell *like* to be generals, but they're junior officers investigating possible causes. Go on over. You'll have them kow-towing in no time, knowing you.'

She laughed. 'You've never kow-towed to me, Elmer.'

'Yeah, but I'm not a lootenant. When a guy's at the bottom, like me, he don't kow-tow to no one because he cain't go no lower, see. Go on over.'

She went forward and through the open gate. Her flat shoes slipped on the coal lying everywhere. She guessed it was only still there because the area had been under guard. In Fassberg, coal was still a valuable commodity to local Germans. Twenty yards from the doomed aircraft, Vesta stopped abruptly as shock raced through her. Maybe as many as thirty seconds passed before he seemed to grow aware of her and glanced up from his notebook. They stayed as they were for probably another half-minute, and Vesta for the first time saw Brad Holland badly shaken.

He broke away from the other newsmen and came across to her, still looking as if he had seen a ghost. 'What in hell's name are *you* doing here?' he asked with considerably less than his usual assurance. For once, he was not on top of the situation.

'The same as I've always done.' She was amazed any words came out, much less that they sounded calm and reasonable. 'David's flying in the airlift. I'm doing a set of pictures.'

A man rarely thrown for long, Brad recovered quickly. 'You could have done that in Japan, or any place in the Pacific.'

'There was no airlift there. It was all horror and suffering. I didn't want that.'

'So you're going to make a picture of this, instead?' he asked sarcastically. 'Come on, Vic, that's no argument.'

His use of that name and the proximity of his five feet eleven, 184 pounds of dynamic aggression told her that all the old magic was still there. His brown eyes challenged, his quick tongue left her open to defeat, his immense virility threatened her survival every time. She fought for it now.

'It's just one aspect of what's going on here. I'm featuring them all. You, on the other hand, only appear when there's something ghoulish to record.'

He grinned, which was fatal. 'You haven't lost that upper-class haughtiness you put on when you're speaking to damn Yankees. You look just as I remember – workmanlike khaki, mussed hair, wide innocent eyes and pink, pink lipstick. And it still makes me want to break down that British reserve the way I used to.'

'Really?' she said with her best upper-class haughtiness. 'I thought you might have grown out of that by now. Iwo Jima, or was it Guadalcanal? I lost track.'

'You lost *touch*. Why didn't you answer my damned letters?'

'You appeared to be having too good a time with someone called Minnie Wing to bother with letters from little ole England.'

His eyes warmed with satisfaction. 'You always were the jealous type.'

'I was also the truthful type. What you damn Yankees would call "on the level". That always got under your skin, didn't it?'

'*You* got under my skin, Vic.' He was serious now and that made his impact even greater. 'You still are, damn you.'

This was terrible. Her composure was falling at her feet. 'What about the exclusive you've just *got* to get?'

'I've still got to get them. I guess I always will. You knew that from the start. Hell, you went with me to get some of them. I was completely "on the level" where *that* was concerned.'

Her only choice was to run. 'Well, I have to get some

292

sketches of this before they clear it away. It was nice seeing you, Brad.'

As she made to pass him, he gripped her arm. 'No, you don't. We're going to talk. We've a lot of catching up to do. Come on!' She was literally marched back along the path to a covered jeep and encouraged, none too gently, to get in. Brad went around the bonnet and slid into the seat beside her. Reaching into a front compartment, he withdrew a bottle of whisky and offered it.

Making no attempt to take it, she said, 'Still a hard drinker?'

'Always was; always will be. Couldn't get along without whisky.'

'Or without Rosa or Minnie?'

He lowered the bottle from his mouth. 'If you'd have come with me there'd have been no need for them. I told you that in Italy.'

She turned from the truth in his eyes and stared from the front window of the jeep at the bare trees and grey, foggy stillness ahead. She had felt as desolate as that scene after this man had gone out of her life almost three years ago. Why, oh why, had he come back?

'You had some exciting commissions, a prestigious exhibition in London, chances you couldn't pass up,' he reminded her. 'What are you doing here?'

'I'd completed all those things.'

'Then why didn't you join me?' When she made no reply, he said quietly, 'Minnie wasn't as good a partner as you were.'

'In or out of bed?' she asked sharply.

'Both.' He wiped his mouth with the back of his hand. 'Hell, it goes with the job. You know how it is – dingy old rooms in downtown hotels in the cesspits of the world . . .'

'You're beginning to sound like Humphrey Bogart in *Casablanca*, Brad. Don't spin *me* that line,' she said, rounding on him. 'I was there with you for almost two years.'

'And we made a great team, didn't we?'

Arguments with Brad always defeated her – at least they had done once they became lovers. Before that she had had her upper-class haughtiness to fall back on. All she could do now was change the subject. 'How long have you been on this assignment?'

'I flew in from Seoul two days ago. I'd been doing an in-depth assessment of post-war unrest and the influence of Communism on underdeveloped countries, but I sensed there'll be greater drama unfolding here within the next few months. It's a freelance job – I can auction my stuff around the class journals after that award for my work in Japan – and I don't mean to focus on the lines everyone else is doing, like this guy Helvorsen dropping candy on parachutes made of handker-chiefs for the kids in Berlin. *Everyone's* got that. I'm looking for an exclusive.' His smile hit her where it hurt most. 'See, I'm at it again.'

'I'm sure you'll find one,' she said faintly, wishing he would offer the whisky again. 'You always do.'

'You said your brother's flying in this circus. Where's he stationed?'

'Oh no, Brad. There's no way you're going to use my family again,' she told him, knowing that if he ever discovered details of her father's death he would have an exclusive of great worth which he would not hesitate to use. He had betrayed her confidences once before.

'I can soon find out.'

Before she could stop herself she became very emotional. 'For God's sake, leave us alone. We're not an exclusive. We're people who've been through enough without having it written up by the great and wonderful Brad Holland.'

There was a tense silence before he said quietly, 'That came from the heart. Care to explain?' He held up his hands. 'Off the record, I swear.'

She did not trust him, even on that. 'Leave David out of your search for a story no other journalist has unearthed. Why *not* do something on "candy for kids"? You'll find an angle no one has yet thought of.'

'Yeah, I guess I could.' He surrendered with suspicious alacrity. 'Are you working with anyone here?'

She shook her head. 'I wangled a commission for a set of pictures on the army of occupation in Hanover. I'm doing the same in Fassberg . . . and getting a few private orders from your countrymen whose parents have money to burn.'

'So you've been in Germany some time.'

'Almost two years.'

He took another swig at the whisky without offering it to her, so she asked for some. He handed the bottle over, asking pointedly, 'Can't stand the proximity?'

'Can't stand the *cold.*' She drank thirstily to prove her point.

'So what have you covered so far?'

Glad to get on to a safe subject, Vesta talked about her time in Hanover – the professional side of it – and described the night she helped catch a leading black marketeer.

'That's a line I thought I might follow here,' he said speculatively. 'Most guys are covering the schmaltz angles. I'd rather uncover what lies beneath.'

'You were never one for schmaltz,' she agreed with a touch of tartness.

'But my heart's in the right place, Vic. You should know. You discovered where everything else was.'

That was Brad. Lulling you into a sense of security then coming in with a whammer that undermined it. As usual, he followed with a line which continued as if he had never dealt the blow. 'Sure there's a lot of heroism and dedication, and good old-fashioned nobility of spirit – you're a sucker for that, I recall – but there are always people who trade on mercy. You can bet some guys are getting fat on stuff that's filtered off this airlift. Goods are delivered by road or rail to Fassberg. First chance to grab a box or two.' He held up one finger. 'They're stored on the airfield until needed.' A second finger went up. 'Third chance is when trucks are loaded up to go out to the aircraft. Can't do much finagling in mid-air except push it over the side, and they've proved that doesn't work, although small items like medicines or machinery parts could disappear into pockets on board. Then the schedule is repeated in reverse in Berlin. *That's* where the big rackets will be operating. Stuff is scarce there, so people will pay more.'

'Suppose you discovered some US airmen doing it?' she asked, seeing him as he had been in Italy – shrewd, calculating, keyed up – and reacting to his charisma as she had done then.

'So what the hell? I exposed corruption in the Senate in my youth and paid dearly for doing so, but those men never held office again. If some of our guys are flying this airlift for their own benefit, let's put an end to their game. I've never let patriotism blind me to the sins of my countrymen.'

295

Vesta knew that in this context he was speaking as a champion of justice rather than a seeker of an exclusive. Whatever else Brad did, he was unwavering in his hatred of those who took advantage of positions of power to line their own pockets, especially when they made a simultaneous public show of philanthropy.

'What I need to do is hitch me a ride to Berlin and do a bit of moseying around for a day or two.'

'You'll be lucky,' she told him with authority. 'I've been trying to do that for almost six months. If I could only go over on one of the missions, I'd be able to complete a range of pictures following a consignment from warehouses in Fassberg right to Berlin. With winter coming on, I'd be able to use snow to highlight the gaunt shapes of aircraft and blackened ruins in the background. I could simulate Gatow airfield, at a pinch, but I'd never get the sense of atmosphere which would make a competent picture sensational. And there's the actual journey across the *Luftbrücke*, as it's known. That's the link between the paintings, but I've never even been able to get *inside* a C-54, much less fly in it. I can understand why they've fobbed me off when the planes are on the ground. There's no time during which I could get in and do sketches. They've no sooner landed than they're being reloaded. Of course, it's out of the question for some English artist to float around with pencil and sketch-pad during that, but if they'd let me go over just one time, I'd have two hours to detail the interior of the aircraft and not be in anyone's way.' She sighed. 'They won't wear it though.'

'How about those machines out of service?'

'*They're* smothered in mechanics and engineers. You've only been here two days, Brad. It's a desperately frantic operation, believe me.'

'How about David? Wouldn't he take you over?'

'No, the RAF are much more starchy than your lot. He'd most likely be court-martialled and thrown out. Anyway, I wouldn't ask him, the way he is at the moment.'

'What way is that?'

Warning bells rang. 'Tired and flying himself into the ground, like everyone else,' she said carefully.

Brad studied her in silence for a moment or two. 'Who was responsible for bringing you to Germany?'

Determined not to bring Paul into the conversation, she said, 'Some of "Daddy's Connections". They were wonderful! Without their influence I'd never have cut through all the red tape, *or* gained a firm commission for the work I really wanted to do.'

He continued to scrutinize her, which was as unnerving as his potent nearness in that jeep. Then he said quietly, 'Now answer my damn question.'

'I grew tired of painting pretty pictures for clients who were dotty about some local beauty spot. When Mummy looked all set to marry someone she barely knew, I decided to leave home and give them a clear field for a while.'

'You don't care for her choice of second husband?'

Vesta was finding the meeting too much of a strain and wanted to end it. 'No one can replace Daddy.'

'I guess you always cared very deeply about him. Still wear that gold pendant he gave you when you turned twenty-one?' She nodded. Reminders of Italy were not helping her to survive this. 'Next to your skin . . . all the time?'

She reached for the door handle, but he caught her arm in a strong grip and held her there. 'Where's this "on the level" stuff now? You're lying through your teeth and you know it. If it was some guy you can't stomach as a stepfather who drove you away, why come to Germany? You could have traced me through the agency. We were a great team – in every way – and I still want you like hell. There's no Rosa or Minnie on earth can replace you, you know that damn well. Why didn't you come out to me, Vic?'

Frantic to get away before something disastrous happened, she cried, 'Why didn't *you* come home to *me*, Brad?'

'I had this assignment.'

'*Exactly*. Well, I have assignments, too. It cuts both ways. You never accepted that.'

'Yeah . . . but I know you. Who is it wooed you over here? Who's taken my place?'

'My work. An exclusive. Artistic fulfilment. Freedom to live as I choose,' she quoted wildly.

He released her arm with surprising suddenness. 'OK. Any one of them'll do.'

Now anxious not to spill from the jeep in an obvious panic

to get away from him, Vesta said, as nonchalantly as she could, 'Well, I have work to do, so I suppose I should be getting back.'

'Have they given you quarters on the airfield?'

'No such luck. I rent a room in Fassberg ... in a block occupied by women from a welfare service,' she added to give credence to her suggestion that she was heartwhole and married to her work. 'It's not the Ritz, but it's a lot better than the accommodation most Germans occupy.'

'And you've lived in some much tougher conditions,' he commented smoothly, as she vacated her seat and stood on the leaf-strewn ground.

'Yes.' She gave a light laugh to show him that water under the bridge affected her very little now. 'It was good to see you again, Brad. Good luck with your exclusive.'

'So long, Vic.' He gazed deep into her eyes. 'You always were a hell of a bad liar.'

She ran.

When Paul telephoned, Vesta offered the excuse of a really bad headache to get out of attending the Mess dinner that evening. 'I'm sorry, but it's so bad I've taken umpteen aspirin and plan to go to bed.'

He was clearly disappointed. 'I can't come over later tonight because I'm duty officer. Will you be all right, darling?'

'Yes, of course. It's one of the headaches which won't get better until morning, so it's just as well you can't spend the night here,' she told him. 'I'd be poor company for you.'

'I could have put cool towels on your brow. It's just a headache? Nothing more?'

'*No*, Paul.' He was constantly worried about making her pregnant in spite of his careful precautions. 'I'll be all right tomorrow. Go off and enjoy your dinner.'

'With a lot of boring brass hats? You were the only hope of making it bearable. Did you get what you wanted this morning?'

'Eh?'

'The crash. Was it possible to make some good sketches?'

'Oh, I ... I decided against using it as a subject. It looked so gruesome.'

After a second or two, he asked, 'Are you *sure* everything's OK?'

'Paul, I'll have to get to bed. My head's *thumping.*'

'Yes, all right. Try to get some sleep. I'll come over tomorrow, darling. Take care. I love you.'

'I love you, too.'

Vesta replaced the receiver and poured herself a second whisky. She did love Paul. She was going to marry him. It was simply the shock of coming upon Brad; the unexpectedness of finding him on her doorstep. There had been no time to prepare a defence.

During the next week Vesta applied herself to turning her sketches into paintings. She was unwilling to leave her apartment in search of new subject matter, although it had been her intention to do the ground work while rain held off, then sort through her sketches before choosing material for the series. It was not a happy decision, she discovered. Not only did Paul raise afresh his objection to her rule about solitude, the work she did do was totally uninspired.

'I don't see why we can't meet at all,' Paul complained on the telephone. 'You can't paint non-stop for days on end. I do understand that you work as the mood takes you, and that it's impossible to make fixed arrangements. I understand that, Vesta. But surely you could ring me when you've packed up for a rest, and I could come over for a while.'

'Unless *you're* on duty,' she pointed out.

'All right, I know my hours are irregular – any chap in the services has to put up with that – but I make every effort to see you whenever I'm free. Why can't you do the same?'

'Because when I pack up for a rest, as you put it, that's what I need. A rest.'

'We could rest together,' he said with intimate invitation.

'That'd be no rest.'

'I'd keep my hands off you . . . if you insisted.'

'Ha, I know you! If we were in bed together there's no way you'd keep your hands off me.'

'You're pretty "hands on" yourself, Miss Sheridan. Who took advantage of my broken arm and subjected me to a fate worse than death?'

She was in no mood for tender fun for once. 'Must we have

299

an argument every time I want to work? Yours isn't governed by mood, but by duty. When you're free you can switch on to something else. I can't. I *live* with my work until it's finished and I'm satisfied.'

He sighed deeply. 'Never fall in love with an artist. Or anyone whose job shuts you out of her life.'

His words touched her, and she felt guilty. 'You're not shut out. You're very important to me. Inspiration is all the greater because I know you're there.'

'But I'm not, am I? I'm somewhere else,' he pointed out. 'That's what I find difficult to take. I suppose I'll grow used to it, in time, but I need you so much I feel deprived when you put yourself out of bounds. Most army wives moan about the job taking their husbands away so often. I'll be the only chap doing the reverse.'

So Vesta gained her solitude, but found inspiration elusive. The weather worsened. Fog set in for several days in a row making the light bad. She was almost glad. The canvas she was working on had gone stale on her. How could she ever have believed that static trucks standing beside static aircraft would provide a compelling image? Leaving that aside, she started another when fog cleared to give half a day of cold winter sunshine. The roar of aircraft began again after a long silence. She knew the penalty of those two days on the ground for the crews. Time had been lost; the need was even more urgent. They would try to speed up the process to compensate, fly even longer hours. Already beyond the limits of normal endurance, the impossible would nevertheless almost certainly be attempted.

The relentless noise of the *Luftbrücke* made Vesta's own lack of achievement plague her more than usual. An artist who loses inspiration completely should do something quite different until it returns. Attempting to force it only brings deeper frustration, which drives it even further away. Vesta defied this wise rule. Day after day she sat dabbing colours on the canvas with dogged determination. Night after night she lay in darkness knowing why nothing she was doing was any good.

On the tenth day she awoke to pouring rain from low skies. The apartment seemed gloomy and stark. It was also cold. She got up, lit the stove, then made some tea. Warming her hands around the cup, she walked in her dressing-gown to the easel she had covered yesterday evening after working in fits and starts all day. The half-finished painting showed men grouped around a mobile canteen serving coffee and doughnuts to keep them going during their long, long shifts as loaders. Rain was slanting down as they huddled beneath the short overhanging roof. They wore oilskins with collars turned up around their ears, their faces betraying the strain they were under. Vesta had shown them incommunicado, each man locked away in his own exhaustion as he ate or drank, with haunted eyes staring into the distance. The background showed a rainswept airfield with dark, vague shapes of aircraft being loaded by dark, vague shapes of men. It was the picture she wanted, and yet it was lifeless. She was producing posters, not living paintings with the Sheridan flair, and she stared at it with a sense of desperation, certain *he* had not been in the least put off his stride by their meeting. Damn Brad! Of all the airfields in all the countries in the world, he had to walk into this one. Oh, God, now *she* was starting to sound like Humphrey Bogart in *Casablanca*!

A knock on the door heralded a fellow resident with a letter which had come with the main delivery. The woman was going to work so they exchanged only a few words before Vesta returned to her kitchen to pour another cup of tea drink while reading her letter. Only then did she realize it had come, via the Army Post Office, from Lübeck. Her spirits lifted considerably as she slit open the envelope and read pages written in the style of the brother she had once known. Astonishment grew as she learnt that he had crashlanded in snow short of the runway in Gatow, then had run into trouble on the return flight which he had piloted at the last minute because of crew shortages.

I had a third narrow squeak a few days ago when one of the engines cut out during take-off, and we couldn't reach our designated height before the chap on our tail started coming up in the belief that we were all right. Gave him a damn fright before we cleared out of his way. I've gained a reputation for having nine lives, so, despite the increasing number of accidents because kites are pretty well falling to bits for lack of regular servicing, crews are happy to fly with me. Must make Uncle Rex chuckle, don't you think?

The reference to his legendary uncle was the most heartening sign of all, Vesta thought, because David had always lived in Rex's shadow believing he must never let him down. Whenever he felt he had, her brother clammed up on the subject. The letter ended with an impassioned declaration that the airlift must go on, whatever the cost to machines, crews and everyone connected with it because the Russians could not be allowed to succeed in their scheme to dominate Europe.

We've been so busy fighting Hitler, his replacement has been setting his ghastly plans beneath our noses, Vee. How blind we were not to catch on before this to the fact that we now have an enemy quite as ruthless, cruel and greedy as the one we've just defeated. I for one will fight them all the way.

The letter was so surprising, Vesta read it through again. Its familiar enthusiastic style came over so strongly she could almost hear David speaking his written words. She had no doubt that he had emerged from the haunted state he had been in since revisiting Singapore, but was mystified over the cause of the change. Four months ago he had shocked her with his withdrawn, bitter attitude. He had been flying non-stop since then under incredibly difficult conditions, and had cheated fate on at least three occasions. Had he been right, after all, when telling Pat that he missed the excitement and danger he had known for six years and could not settle to marriage and breeding pedigree pigs? Had the airlift provided what he needed to be happy again? What other explanation could there be? Her gladness over David's evident return to his old self was muted by anxiety for his safety. Nine lives would not last for ever. She prayed he was not taking too many risks in his surprising fervour to hit out at the Russians.

While she was still contemplating this unexpected turn of events, there came another knock at her door. She went to open it expecting to be given a second letter which had been overlooked by the young woman who had sorted the pile earlier. Brad stood in the corridor, his coat soaked by rain, his dark hair slicked down by it.

'It wasn't difficult to find you. Apartment block used by welfare workers, all female, you said. It's known as the nunnery up at the base. Did you know that?'

'What are you doing here?' It was the most sophisticated comment Vesta could produce under the circumstances.

'If you'll let me in, I'll tell you.'

She stood her ground. 'This isn't nicknamed the nunnery for no reason. You'll have to leave.'

'Let's give 'em an exclusive, baby,' he drawled in an atrocious cinematic fashion, and manhandled her inside before shutting the door and looking her over with critical amusement. 'That's the Vic I remember: upper-class outrage at Yankee presumption . . . and loving every moment of it.'

He kissed her with the thoroughness she had never been able to resist, and there was nothing she could do about it now until he released her. Then she tried to gain control of the situation. 'I'm not Rosa or Minnie. I thought I'd made that perfectly clear on occasions so numerous only a fool would not have understood. Doubtless there's a Gretchen or two in Fassberg who'd be only too happy to give you the freedom of their simple rooms. I suggest you go in search of them, *right now.*'

Brad grinned as he relaxed back against the wall. 'How I've missed moments like this, when you put on that frosty voice and come out with touch-me-not speeches. They have quite the wrong effect on me. Gretchen wouldn't rouse me up half as much as you in this mood do.'

'Brad, I'm *working!*' she cried in desperation, tugging her dressing-gown back into place.

'OK.' He held up his hands in surrender. 'I know all about work, artistic fulfilment, the freedom to live as you choose. That *was* what you said had replaced me, wasn't it? See, I know this guy who flies C-54s to Berlin and back. He's on a twenty-four-hour stand-down, but I guess he'll take two unofficial passengers on one of his missions tomorrow.'

Vesta gazed at him in disbelief, 'Brad, you *haven't* wangled it?'

He moved towards her. 'Would I be here otherwise?'

'You're . . . you're . . .'

303

'Thinking of your work, artistic fulfilment, and so on?'

'You're *unbelievable*!' she cried. 'I've been trying for absolute *months* to get on one of these missions.'

'Yeah, well, you let too many things stand in your way. When you want an exclusive you have to go all out for it.' He perched on the arm of a chair. 'How about a cup of coffee?'

'You can have a whole potful,' she promised with mounting excitement. 'What are the arrangements?'

'When I get my coffee, I'll tell you.'

She ran to the tiny kitchen and put coffee on to brew. Feeling suddenly hungry she plugged in the toaster and slid slices of bread into it. Her mind was racing. This was the missing link she needed. Everything would fall into place once she had sketches of an actual flight, and of Gatow surrounded by the ruins of Germany's capital. Ideas were already flowing through her as she prepared breakfast in purely automatic fashion. She felt charged with new life.

When she carried the tray into the main room she found Brad had taken off his wet coat and was studying her painting of men around a mobile canteen. 'I'm not entirely happy with that,' she told him, arranging things on the small table. 'There's something missing, but I can't think what it is.'

'A dog,' he said.

'*What?*'

'That one you did of the desert campaign. You showed the grim reality of tanks around an oasis; men looking burned out and sort of listless. Then you had some guy in the foreground teaching an ugly little mongrel to beg with a biscuit on its nose. That gave the whole scene life. Hell, you've said often enough that you always look for the good shining through every situation. Where is it in this? You need a dog ... or a bird. Something that isn't part of the dramatic events all around. Some living creature untouched by desperation.'

Vesta went across to the easel. 'You're right,' she agreed, after a moment or two. 'You're *absolutely right!*'

'Do I get some kind of reward?'

She looked up into dark eyes full of invitation. 'Yes, toast with your coffee.'

'That's my Vic,' he said good naturedly, following her to the table and sitting while she poured coffee. 'You didn't make that bread stuff for me, surely? You should've known I wouldn't set out in the morning without ham, eggs, hash-browns and a plate of flapjacks.'

'No doughnuts?' she asked, using one of their private jokes without thinking.

'I ate them on the way over. Sure tasted good in the rain.'

They were laughing together when the front door opened and Paul walked in, rain dripping from the peak of his cap, his tunic soaked. He stopped two feet inside the flat, taking in the cosy domestic scene of Vesta in her dressing-gown eating breakfast with her former lover. She was shocked into silence, knowing how it must look to Paul. Although he had a key to her door she had certainly not been expecting him to come when he had been told she was working. He would never believe her now. No jealous man in love would. Before she could think of what to do, Brad took the initiative.

'Who the hell are you?' he demanded, still resting back in his chair.

Anger fairly blazed from Paul's eyes. 'I'm the chap who went ahead and cleared desert minefields so that you could advance and write your copy without getting blown to pieces, Holland. I understood you were away doing award-winning stuff in the Pacific.'

'I'm doing it here now.'

Paul advanced. 'Not in this apartment you're not. Clear out.'

Brad cast a significant glance at Vesta. 'Are you paying her rent?'

'You damned bas –'

'Because if you're not, you have no say over who goes or who stays. Until *she* tells me I'm unwelcome, I'll carry on drinking my coffee.'

Vesta had collected her thoughts by now, and got to her feet. 'Paul, it's not what you think. Brad came here to –'

'It's obvious what he came for,' stormed Paul. 'When I drove past and saw a military jeep outside, I thought there might be some trouble. I little realized what kind.'

'How come you have a key to her door?' asked Brad amiably enough.

Paul's expression hardened further. 'I'd be obliged if you'd stop referring to my fiancée as *her*. Where you come from it might be acceptable to treat women without respect, but you won't do so in my presence.'

Vesta was now as angry as he, but she was unsure with whom. 'Stop this, both of you! For heaven's sake, you're behaving like hooligans. I won't have it.'

Brad got to his feet wearing a curious expression she could not understand. 'You engaged to this guy?'

Why was it so hard to say yes? She nodded.

'Didn't I tell you you were lying through your teeth the other day?' He picked up his coat ready to leave, ignoring Paul, and made for the door. 'My offer still stands, Vic . . . and don't forget that dog.'

His departure left her with an impossible situation. How could she tell Paul this was their second meeting without his thinking, justifiably, that they were taking up where they had left off? Would he believe she had shut herself up with her painting in order to *avoid* running into Brad again? Would *any* man believe she had not given him her address? Most of all, she could not reveal the real reason for his visit, because Paul would ensure that she did not go to Berlin tomorrow . . . and she had every intention of doing so.

'*What* offer still stands, Vesta?'

'Paul, this wasn't planned, believe me.'

His mouth twisted cynically. 'So much for the "work" you needed isolation to do.'

'I have been working. *Don't look at me that way!*' She marched across to the corner by the large window and snatched up three canvases. '*There, there* and *there*,' she declared, holding each up in turn. 'And there's another on my easel. Don't you sneer in that cynical fashion.'

'*What* offer still stands?' he repeated, unappeased.

'Why are you here, anyway? You knew I was working.'

He walked towards her, raindrops glistening on the shoulders of his uniform. 'It seemed unusual for a jeep to be out at this hour, so I wondered if there'd been an accident. David. I couldn't just drive on without making sure everything was all right with you.'

She gave a long, heavy sigh. 'Oh, Lord, have you noticed that just as everything *seems* to be going right, fate invariably throws a spanner in the works?'

After a moment, he asked, 'Am *I* the spanner?'

'You both are. My concentration has gone, and any ideas I had have flown.' She put the canvases against the wall. 'I didn't ask him to come here. I don't know how he learnt this address. I didn't ask you to come either. Quite the reverse.'

Paul crossed and challenged her. 'If he comes again what will you do?'

'He won't,' she said hastily and with perfect conviction. 'Contrary to your very insulting remark, Brad has always respected me . . . which is why he had to wait several years.' She moved away. 'Please go. Neither of us is in the right mood for you to stay.'

'Before I arrived you seemed happy enough for *him* to stay.'

She spun round and looked him in the eye. '*That's* why I'd like you to leave. Nothing I say right now will satisfy you, and I truly can understand why. Let's leave explanations for another time, Paul.' As he hesitated, she added, 'We're too close for mistrust. If either of us feels it, I shouldn't be wearing your ring.'

He very obviously fought a battle with himself before accepting the point she was making. 'I love you, that's the trouble.'

'Love should generate trust.' Even as she said it she felt a craven hypocrite. She had loved Brad deeply, yet had been jealous of anything which took him away from her even momentarily. As Paul made to leave, looking very unhappy, her guilt deepened. 'I'll ring you . . . soon.' When he reached the door, she added, 'I had a letter from David this morning. It suggests he's somehow mastered whatever was bothering him. I was so delighted I read it through twice. That's why I was still in my dressing-gown.' He was halfway through the open front door. 'Paul, thanks for being concerned.'

He nodded. 'Yes.'

As the door closed behind him she felt like bursting into tears, but fought them back, marched across to her easel, and began, quite furiously, to paint a dog.

CHAPTER FIFTEEN

VESTA was at the airfield before five a.m. Waved through the gates in typical friendly fashion, she drove direct to Dispersal, where she expected to find Brad. She was disappointed, but the crews were not. Greeted by a chorus of wolf whistles and simulated cries of a real wolf, Vesta was angry with herself for attracting so much attention. She was certain it was necessary to stay in the background to prevent Brad's friend from being caught infringing the rules. Passengers had certainly been carried by airlift crews, particularly German civilians leaving Berlin on compassionate grounds, or children destined to stay with relatives in Western sectors during the emergency, but stowaways were different. She would have been taken up long before this if it had been generally permitted.

On the point of deciding to wait for Brad outside, Vesta was accosted by a lanky man in his late twenties dressed in flying-suit and khaki baseball-style soft cap. 'Hi, you must be Brad Holland's girl. I'm Chuck Peterson,' he said, chewing gum lazily. 'Wasn't too good an idea coming in here; but I guess everyone thinks you're my latest cutie.' He gave a grin which was lopsided because of the ball of chewing-gum in his mouth. 'Got a reputation. The guys all know that, so act like you think I'm kinda terrific while I tell you where to go.'

Unsure whether she was fooling anyone watching, Vesta tried to do as he asked as he gave her the number of the aircraft he would be flying, where it was parked and his departure time. 'Brad's already got that,' he added, then grinned again. 'I guess he'll look twice when you turn up. Didn't seem to feel you'd be coming, somehow. Get out there now. He knows what to do when the time comes.'

'I hope you're not taking too much of a risk,' Vesta said. 'I'm really terribly grateful.'

'Yeah, well I guess you could kiss me. Would look kinda natural to the guys watching.'

A chorus of howls and yahoos greeted her resigned kiss, then she fled to the dark morning outside. It took a while to find the aircraft bearing the number Chuck had given, then she parked her car well clear of the loading bay and was in the process of gathering together the things she had brought along when Brad appeared beside her.

'We're not going on an English picnic,' he said, nodding at her thermos flask and small packet of sandwiches.

'This is my breakfast. *I'm* not offered ham, eggs and everything under the sun, including chocolate fudge ice-cream, before I come out in the morning,' she replied coolly. 'I had no idea what time we'd be setting off, and it'll be a long hungry day if I have to act the stowaway the whole time.'

'Gee, that's all-fired too bad.' He always lapsed into exaggerated Americanisms whenever she became what he called 'frosty'. 'I cain't have mah li'l prairie rose goin' without her chocolate fudge ice-cream. Come over here, little darlin', and see what big Uncle Brad has brought you.'

Led by the arm to the back of the storehouse, Vesta found Brad's jeep parked there. From the rear seat he picked up a flask ten times the size of hers, and a canvas bag bulging at the seams. Opening the heavy zip fastening he took from it several aluminium containers, and removed their lids. One held soft rolls filled two inches thick with sliced ham, chicken and tomatoes. In the others were tarts and pastries smothered with icing, chocolate or caramel sauce. He offered her both. '*This* is breakfast, not that sparrow's food you brought. We'll get the chocolate fudge ice-cream at Gatow during the turn around. Go on, help yourself. It's surely better than that burnt bread *you* call breakfast.'

Vesta was relieved he was being light-hearted, but it was typical of Brad to act as if yesterday had never happened. Even so, for someone who claimed she was still under his skin, he was showing remarkable nonchalance over her engagement. They sat in his jeep to eat the rich goodies and drink better coffee than she was able to buy. She laughed when he said dinner was in the bottom of his bag, but he was serious. It was all in thermos containers to keep it hot.

'Small wonder your people called this Stalag Fassberg,' she told him. 'The RAF rations must have seemed like prison fare after food like this. David would give his eye teeth for some of it.'

'So what state is he in?'

Brad never let go of a lead, which was why he was so successful. This was one she was determined he would not follow.

'I had a letter from him yesterday.'

'I noticed it on your table.'

Surely he had not read it while she was making coffee. She would not put it past him. Thank heaven David had written in his old optimistic vein. 'He's had a few scares, but so has every pilot, I expect. Otherwise, he's fine.'

'Good.'

She knew he did not believe her, but he said nothing more because a glance at his watch showed it was nearly time for take-off. 'Ready?' he asked, climbing to the ground. 'Two and a half hours there, twenty minutes turn around, then two and a half hours back. Chuck should be touching down here again before noon. Give him a couple of hours for a meal and a rest, then he should be back to pick you up in Gatow around seventeen hundred. That be long enough for what you want?'

'Oh, yes.' She rounded the jeep to join him, shouting above the sound of engines revving up. 'Why did you say he'd pick *me* up? Aren't you coming back?'

'Not for a day or two – maybe a week. I need to get around Berlin asking questions. This thing won't be easy to uncover.'

'Be careful!' She was concerned after seeing signs of the underworld in Hanover, and Berlin was a more dangerous city. 'You can't simply wander around wherever you like.'

He gave her a patient look. 'Vic, I happen to know . . .'

'. . . a guy who'll take you around,' she finished for him. 'Tell him to be careful, too.'

A crew member appeared at the corner of the store and whistled with his fingers in his mouth. Brad took her arm and they ran forward to where the Skymaster was running all four engines ready to taxi to the runway. They were pulled up into the hold as men were preparing to close it.

'Who are *they*?' cried an astonished storeman.

'VIPs. Top secret,' yelled the crewman pushing Vesta out of sight. 'You ain't seen them. Got that?' The doors closed. Next minute the aircraft rolled forward.

'Hi, I'm Steve Polowski,' said the dark-haired young crew-man. 'Make yourselves at home. First stop Berlin. See ya!'

He walked forward and disappeared behind a bulkhead. Vesta wondered how she could accept his invitation because there was scarcely a foot of space to be found between the cargo. She would have to stand all the way to Gatow. Now she was inside one of the airlift machines, the true immensity of the operation hit her. It was one thing to watch boxes and barrels being handed through the loading hatch, quite another to be inside it. There must be fish somewhere, and something else smelling of sulphur. The entire aircraft reeked. Good thing the flight was a short one. She had never been a happy traveller by air or by sea, and there were no windows so that she could see what was happening outside. On that thought, she realized it was far too dark here to sketch anything well. She would have to do what she could and memorize as much as possible.

'Sit down or you'll be thrown about in a minute,' said Brad beside her.

'Where, for heaven's sake?'

For an answer he put his hands on her shoulders and pushed downwards until she took his meaning and sat on the floor in the gangway between stacks of containers confined by webbing straps. He sat beside her. 'You've grown soft, Vic. In Italy you'd have got down here right away.'

They were swinging around. The engine roar became deafening as they raced forward for take-off, and the entire fuselage began to shake. When the dread sensation of rising up while her stomach went in the opposite direction afflicted Vesta, she wondered very seriously if this had been such a good idea.

'You've been trying for absolute *months* to do this,' Brad quoted in her ear, 'so you should be looking happier than you are.'

She relaxed and smiled. 'Do you remember *everything* I say?'

'Pretty much everything. It's the way you say it I can't resist.' He shifted to a more comfortable position and closed his eyes. 'You're the one who wanted to sketch everything on board. Get started or we'll be there before you sharpen your pencil.'

For the first half an hour or so Vesta wished she had refused Brad's breakfast but, once she left the hold and moved to the crew's various stations, she grew absorbed in what she was doing and forgot her nausea. The men were friendly and helpful, delighted to be the subject of an artist's sketches, but they looked grey-faced and drawn now they were airborne and she noticed they all had nervous twitches of some sort. Chuck Peterson had lost his brash charm and sat soberly at the controls explaining to her how vital it was to keep to a designated speed and altitude when there were aircraft just five minutes ahead and to the rear, and others were returning not far away and just below them.

Vesta told him about David being at Lübeck, but soon realized he wanted no distractions so stayed quiet while she sketched him in the cockpit. A sense of achievement was inevitable while she was doing what she had longed for for so long. Her mind was full of ideas. She would need no dog in these pictures. There was life and drama enough within this rattling, smelly fuselage.

They landed late because the aircraft two spaces behind them developed engine trouble and had to be given priority. Vesta was glad to breathe fresh air and was thankful they would return with an empty hold. She understood why the men looked so unhealthy and coughed a lot. Travelling constantly with such odours was not a pleasant duty. Poor David was doing it, too.

Gatow was unbelievable. If she thought Fassberg was bedlam, the Berlin airfield was manic. It was similar to an ant colony under floodlights. Twenty-minute turn arounds were demanded, and everyone endeavoured to meet that deadline. No sooner had the aircraft halted than the hatch was opened and a team of men swarmed in to begin unloading. The crew dropped to the ground and climbed into a truck which rushed up to collect them. Brad pushed Vesta through the crew's hatch then followed her out and made for the truck.

'Who are they?' asked the driver.

'VIPs. Top secret. You ain't seen them,' came the reply again, before the truck set off along the perimeter track.

It drew up beside a mobile canteen and they all got out. Brad fetched four doughnuts with some coffee, and they stood close together against a wall to have it. Vesta declined the doughnuts and wished she had brought her packet of dainty meat-paste sandwiches, but the coffee was very welcome. While she drank she studied the scenes she would sketch whilst here. Excitement began to bubble in her. This was the heart of the airlift, the essence of its purpose. She was now in the middle of Russian-held territory, and the atmosphere was markedly different from that in Hanover or Fassberg. She felt it. She sensed it. It was vitally necessary to make her pictures of this place convey that difference.

Berlin was colder by far than Fassberg, and she shivered in the growing dawn. It was possible to see heavy frost glistening in the light thrown by powerful lamps on gantries. Two weeks and it would be Christmas. How on earth would Berliners keep warm this winter?

'Was it worth it?'

She came from her reverie to look up at Brad. 'Oh, *yes*. I could never have captured this without experiencing it. You know the way I work. If I haven't been there, seen it, *known* it, how can I possibly portray it to others? This is marvellous. Thanks for letting me in on it.'

He nodded, watching her closely. 'Does the Honourable Fitzroy know you've come?'

It was a long-standing joke, that name, and it hurt her where it was almost certainly meant to. 'I didn't want to worry him. He loves me very deeply.'

'But he'd have stopped you from coming. That kind of love's no good for someone like you.' He frowned. 'You don't say you also love him deeply.'

'I'm going to marry him soon. *He* doesn't chase all over the world after exclusives.'

'You wouldn't be here now if I didn't.'

'I've said thank you.'

'It's not enough. Why didn't you join me in the Pacific?'

She had been a fool to think he would accept her engagement without comment. 'I was angry and hurt, at first. When you wrote that you'd joined up with Minnie Wing, I told myself you didn't need me.'

'So you're going to settle for being Mrs Fitzroy and go to all the Colonel's cocktail parties and say the right things? It'll kill you. Where's the excitement, the challenge, the defiance of dreary normality? Where's the *spice*? Your life with him will be like that picture with no dog in it. It'll all be there, but it'll mean nothing.'

What a conversation to hold against the deafening roar of aero engines, the rumble of laden trucks, the shouts of men working flat out; what a time to talk about a passion that never slept, standing in a bitter dawn beside a mobile canteen on an airfield surrounded by hostile Russians. Brad never picked a time when she was prepared and could think. Right now he was shaking the very ground beneath her feet.

As always she fell back on evasion. 'Shouldn't you be meeting that guy you know who'll show you the underworld of Berlin?'

He looked surprisingly stricken before turning up his collar and dumping his canvas bag at her feet. 'Don't let dinner get cold. Chuck'll tell you what to do about the return flights. So long, Vic.'

Vesta watched him walk away and found she was crying. What had he expected her to do? She suddenly felt very alone and vulnerable without him and, for a moment, was tempted to tell Chuck she would go back with him right now. Then her fighting spirit returned and she listened to the pilot's instructions on where to wait for him from late afternoon onwards, before walking away towards the perimeter. By the time she reached it the hazy sun was just starting to brighten the dawn and illuminated the skyline perfectly. When you want an exclusive you must go all out for it, Brad had said. She must forget him and concentrate on work. There would only be this one chance, and Chuck would be returning within eight hours.

He did not come. Fog had descended by noon and did not lift for three days. All aircraft were grounded and visibility at Gatow was no more than ten feet.

The apartment was bitterly cold but, at two in the morning, Vesta could not be bothered to light the stove. She made a cup of tea, filled a hot-water bottle, put on every pair of socks she could find and went to bed in her dressing-gown. Only because she was worn out did she manage to sleep. Stranded in a place where she had no right to be, in freezing fog, she had had no option but to seek shelter in one of the warehouses. The first night had been cold, uncomfortable and full of regrets. What she could have done – *had* done – with Brad alongside was no fun at all on her own. It was inevitable that she would be discovered. Gatow was in the British zone and controlled by them. American aircraft were using the route from Fassberg to Gatow because it was a shorter distance than they must fly to and from their own sector airfield. Security was tight in Berlin. RAF and Military Police patrolled regularly with dogs. Vesta was discovered in the early hours of that next morning and virtually taken into custody.

Questioned by a senior RAF officer she had told him the truth, apart from a few white lies which had made her appear silly and gullible. Omitting any mention of Brad she said she had met an American pilot who offered to fly her over and back in a day, but she refused to name him no matter how pressed she was to do so.

'I've worked at Fassberg since the airlift began, so I've seen what these men are doing and what they're suffering for the sake of people who were bitter enemies a year or so ago. I'm certainly not going to land someone in trouble over something as ridiculous as this, when he's half killing himself on this mercy run,' she had said, in tones used to great effect in the past. 'I served in the ATS throughout the war, and I've seen a man who has come in after an eight-hour tank battle being dressed down because his tunic is not correctly buttoned. I discovered that the most successful commanders were those who managed to look in another direction now and again. If I told you this man's name you'd give it to your American counterpart, and the report would go from department to department until the poor devil was summoned to a disciplinary committee, and there'd be one pilot less at a time when we are all desperate for aircrew. It really makes no sense, does it?'

The wing commander had studied her with great amusement. 'You are very eloquent, Miss Sheridan. I can't, of course, *force* you to reveal the identity of your young man – we do not have thumbscrews on the premises – but you'll have to remain in custody until the fog lifts and you can be returned to Fassberg. I trust a day or two in the cells will give you time in which to reflect on the wisdom of not being taken for a ride by a Yank.'

The cell had been reasonably warm, and she was fed on basic RAF fare, but time had dragged and the out-of-date copies of *Picturegoer* one of the guards lent her held little of her attention. She certainly had had time to reflect on all manner of things, before being put on the first aircraft heading back to Fassberg when the fog lifted. She had endured a bumpy flight in an empty, freezing hold. Activity at Fassberg had been so hectic after three wasted days, no one bothered about a woman in khaki trying to start a car at midnight. After half an hour beneath the bonnet Vesta had got the engine running and had driven home with just one thought in mind. To curl up in bed and blank out thoughts with sleep.

It seemed no time at all before she was woken by someone shaking her shoulder with some force. The electric light almost blinded her as she tried to focus on the person bending over the bed. She put up a hand to shield her eyes, expecting to see one of the RAF policemen, but it was Paul. Remembering where she was, her heart sank. He looked extremely worked up and ready to do battle. She was not. Not nearly ready. She struggled into a sitting position, still fuzzy with sleep.

'What time is it?'

'I've been half out of my mind,' Paul said, his voice rough with emotion. 'Where the hell have you been?'

'Don't yell at me,' she snapped. 'And don't use that tone, either.'

'You've been away for *four days*! What was I to think?' he raged. 'Didn't it occur to you to let me know?'

She was awake now, and gathering ammunition. 'Yes, it occurred to me, and I decided not to, because I didn't expect to get held up. I'm sorry if you've been worried.'

'*Worried!* Have you any idea what I've been going through since I came here to talk things over and found the place empty and your car gone? One of your neighbours said she heard you leave in the early hours of Tuesday morning. After finding you here with him the day before, what was I to think?'

Vesta got out of bed in her crumpled dressing-gown and six pairs of assorted socks. 'That I had gone off with Brad

Holland. You were right.' She marched through to the main room and switched on the electric fire.

Temporarily silenced, Paul followed. When Vesta stood upright again and faced him, she was shaken by the dark rings under his eyes and the pallor of his skin. 'What are you doing here now?' she asked more gently. 'It's only six o'clock.'

'I made your neighbour promise to let me know the minute you returned – if you did – so she rang to say your car was back. I came over right away. I've been half out of my mind,' he repeated with deep feeling. 'If I hadn't known *he* was in Fassberg, I'd have set up a police search for you.'

She hugged herself tightly for a moment or two while she tried to decide how to handle the situation. His unexpected appearance had precipitated something she had dearly wanted to do with thought and understanding. She had not accounted for his knowing she had been away for days, although she should have guessed Paul was not the man to leave the situation he had discovered last Monday until she decided to contact him.

'Will you listen with an open mind while I tell you what happened?' she asked quietly.

'Has he walked out on you again?'

It was hopeless. He was in no mood to be reasonable, and she could appreciate why, so she plunged in with cold facts. 'I bumped into Brad when I drove out to that crash. We talked about the airlift. He came here on Monday to tell me he'd arranged a lift to Berlin with a pilot pal, who was willing to take me there and back the same day so that I could get the sketches I wanted. We flew over early on Tuesday morning. Brad went off to meet someone who was going to show him around Berlin, and I started sketching. Fog came down, grounding all aircraft. I was discovered by a police dog, but managed to keep the pilot out of trouble. I've spent the last forty-eight hours in a cell at Gatow. They flew me back late last night. I had no idea I would be away longer than a day. I'm sorry you've been worried.'

Her straight approach had not helped. Paul was paler than ever and considerably more worked up than before. 'The *bastard*! He took you on that aircraft knowing the terrible risks? My God, you even met up with him at the scene of a

317

wreck! They're going down all over the place, you know that, and he bloody well must have been aware that he was putting your life in danger all the way along the line. What if you'd crashed? What if you'd been forced to land in the Russian sector? Some have.' He swallowed hard, but was no calmer for it. 'Christ, I can't believe any man would have been so irresponsible! *Anything* could have happened to you after he went swanning off to Berlin. It did. He must have known you'd not be able to get back here once fog came down. I can't believe . . . I can't *believe* anyone with even a spark of decency wouldn't have come back to see if you were all right. I . . . I . . . it's beyond belief,' he concluded forcefully, taking off his cap and flinging it into a chair. 'What kind of monster is he?'

He was right. Every point he had made was a valid one. Yet she rose to Brad's defence. 'He knows I can look after myself. I went through far, far worse danger in Italy.'

'You're not in bloody Italy now. And you're no longer his mistress, you're my future wife. What flaming right has he to take you off beneath my nose and expose you not only to danger, but the humiliation of military custody? If I meet up with him again, I'll *kill* him!'

'Paul, please calm down. He didn't take me off beneath your nose, I went of my own free will, neither as his mistress nor yours. I went as Vesta Sheridan, the artist, because I dearly wanted to. Yes, I knew the risks, but I was prepared to take them.'

'Without considering how *I* would feel about it? Haven't you *any* idea of what I've been through these last few days?' he demanded, seizing her upper arms with a fierce grip.

'Roughly the same as I went through watching you defuse a bomb stuck in a crumbling factory chimney,' she flung at him. 'It's hell, but you get over it.'

His hands dropped away as her words made sense to him, and he said incredulously, 'You watched that? How?'

'Never mind how . . . but it was then I realized how much you meant to me.' He seemed almost dazed as he stood staring at her. 'I think we both need a drink,' she said. 'I know it's too early, but the time for whisky is when you need it, and we both do right now.' After pouring the drinks and handing him one, Vesta curled up in a chair beside the electric fire and took a good pull at her whisky.

Paul sat on the edge of the other chair, still very ill at ease and not touching his drink. 'Why didn't you tell me you'd met him again? Is that why you cried off the Mess dinner?'

She nodded. 'If I'd told you, you'd have been upset. So I kept quiet, and stayed at home painting so that I wouldn't be likely to see him again. I wasn't expecting him to come up here. When he told me I could get to Gatow so easily after all these months of trying, I didn't hesitate. How could I guess I'd be there so long? I believed I'd be back by that same night.'

'Would you have then told me about it?'

'Probably not. You'd still have reacted the way you are now.'

He twisted the glass around in his hands with nervous movements. 'Why haven't you told me before about watching that chimney business?' he asked quietly.

'For the same reason. You'd have been furious.'

'I'm not furious about it now.'

'That's because it's swallowed up in a greater fury.' She put down the glass and began what she must say. 'Paul, I need to be able to do what I want, have a free hand over my career. You refused to let me watch you deal with a bomb yet I was certain it was what I most wanted to portray. I had to go behind your back in the end, then found it so nerve-racking I knew I couldn't use it as a subject.' She managed a pale smile. 'I was so frightened, I was dreadfully sick all over the rubble.'

'Were you?' He spoke as if still in a daze.

'You had been right to say no, but I had to find that out for myself, not take your word for it.'

'Oh.'

'I also had to go to Gatow. Everything went wrong and fog prevented me from making sketches – I could do a pretty good one of a detention cell, mind you – but I couldn't have had you forbidding me to go. And you would have, wouldn't you?'

He sighed, still playing with the glass. 'Yes . . . yes, I would. You were lucky to have got off so lightly. They're doing a bloody difficult job which is of international importance. They can well do without civilians hitching a lift in order to fulfil an urge, and treating the whole business as a bit of a lark.'

That smote her, because there was a grain of truth in it. 'You don't take my career seriously, do you?'

'*Yes*. I always have. But I happen to believe that what we're doing out here is a bloody sight more important. Brad Holland writes with uncanny empathy – I've read his stuff on the Far East – but, when it comes to the crunch, it's not telling the world that gets things done, it's the blokes who get on and do them.'

They were quiet for a while, then Vesta put into words what she had thought in her cell at Gatow. 'I'd like to go home, Paul. For Christmas. I think I should make my peace with Mummy and Leo, and get away from ruins, rubble and aircraft.'

'And me?'

'I need to think in quiet surroundings. You see, I know you're right on so many issues, but those years with Brad taught me to look at things differently. From his viewpoint. If I'm going to become your wife, I'll have to sort myself out. I can't do it here.'

He came to squat before her, putting the untouched whisky on the table beside her and taking her hands. 'You've no need to sort yourself out. I love you just as you are. Everything was fine until he turned up. Let's get married right away, then he'll leave you alone. If he doesn't, I'll soon persuade him to.'

'No, you don't understand what I'm trying to say. I need to go home.'

'All right, darling, but wait just a couple of months until my long leave is due and we'll go together.'

This was the moment she had dreaded. 'Paul, when you were up that chimney I knew how much you meant to me and I then showed you ... but I've discovered Brad still affects me. He'll follow his story through to the bitter end, so I'd rather not be here for a while.'

It was clear he still did not understand. He stood up looking very upset. 'I'm not sure what you're telling me.'

'I'm trying to be honest with you. With us both.'

'You can't love two men at the same time.'

'That isn't what I'm saying.' She got up to face him. 'You're such a straightforward person I know exactly how I feel about you. Brad's complex. He's always one jump ahead of me, which is often exciting but leaves me in his shadow. I don't want to be there ... and yet ...'

320

'It seems to me you don't know what you *do* want at the moment.'

'That's why I need to go home, somewhere right away from all this so that I can think reasonably.' As he stood silently trying to accept her terms, Vesta slipped the ring from her finger and held it out. 'Would you prefer to hold on to this while I'm gone?'

He shook his head numbly. 'Not unless you're saying it's all over between us . . . but I don't think you'll solve anything by running away. The first rule when facing an uncertain adversary is not to retreat, but stay and find out what you're up against. If you're unequal to the job you call up reinforcements, or move to a stronger position. If you flee he'll simply come after you.'

'Not if he senses an exclusive, and there are none in Tarrant Royal right now.'

Marion replaced the receiver feeling decidedly apprehensive. Vesta was in London about to take a train to Greater Tarrant. It was the same old story. *I decided to come home for Christmas*, she had announced. Just like that. Eighteen months ago, on the spur of the moment, she had decided Germany was the place she must be and had taken off to meet up with Paul Gaynor. She was supposed to be engaged to him, yet she was arriving alone. What did it mean?

She sat in a chair by the desk and gazed at the arrangement of glossy leaves and berries she had set on the smooth round table yesterday. Life had been wonderfully serene since her marriage to Leo. She had never felt as loved as she was now. For almost the first time in her life she had someone to help her run the financial side of the estate. It was not that she had no idea how to do it – she had had the job for years – but it was so good to have someone to talk it all over with now it was running into debt. Someone to support her decisions. In short, another person who cared what she was doing with this house and land. The fact that he also cared for her was a bonus.

Leo had blossomed – if a man could do that – from the day he came to live with her at Tarrant Hall. He loved it the way she did, his interest in architecture and décor finding full rein in reviving that part of the house which had been handed back, polished and good as new, by the department he had worked for. Marion had brought out of storage those special items Chris had been unwilling to leave to the not-so-tender mercies of the RAF officers, and Leo had polished or cleaned those requiring only a layman's attention. The most valuable and delicate pieces he had taken to London, item by item, to be cleaned by experts. It had cost rather a lot, of course, together with new curtains and carpets in some of the rooms, but the Hall was back to its former glory and Marion now found it difficult to imagine how she had lived for so long in just a small part of it.

They had chosen as their bedroom a room at the rear of the house with long windows giving views over the rose garden and the distant hills. Marion did not want any reminders of nights with Chris – not that there had been all that many – and Leo's tender passion had awoken an exhilarating response in her. Suddenly, at fifty-three, she was young and in love. It was incredible! Leo played an active part in village affairs, and the Chandlers had taken him to their hearts from the outset. They had had two bad years, with the snow and then floods of 1947, followed by drought for successive summers. Crops had been meagre and they had lost valuable animals, but then so had most farmers. It was worrying, but the only real clouds on Marion's horizon were named David and Vesta, and they had been distant ones. Now, one would be arriving within a few hours and she felt, for some inexplicable reason, that her new personal serenity was threatened.

Leo came in bringing the fresh tang of aftershave. Even that formed part of her happiness – evidence of a masculine presence in a house too long without it. 'Hallo, what are you doing sitting there in deep reflection of a bowl of berries? You're not going all arty on me, I hope. One in the family is quite enough.'

She glanced up with a smile. 'Are you ready for breakfast?'

'I'm *starving*.'

'You sound so like David. It was almost impossible to feed him enough. Chris was quite different, but then he was a gourmet who treated food with something approaching reverence.' She got up and went across to him. 'Come on, let's tell Robson to serve before you die of hunger.'

He draped an arm over her shoulders as they walked to the dining room. The casual gesture never failed to thrill her. Having been neglected for so long she could not be touched by Leo often enough. In truth, she had discovered an astonishing passion for him. His body was hard-muscled and exciting to touch, despite the puckered marks on his chest and stomach which he said were the result of a serious fall whilst climbing. She could feel the firm warmth of him against her side as they walked, and revelled in it. A flutter of fresh apprehension touched her as she thought of the telephone call. Vesta had been so aggressive and suspicious of him. Would she break the gentle, delicate rapport she and Leo now shared by walking in with her heavy army boots? Why was she coming? Where was Paul?

They sat at a small table set in the window alcove. Leo had suggested the arrangement as more cosy than sharing a table equipped to seat at least twenty, and Marion wondered why she had not thought of it before. The view was panoramic, and the sun came through to bless them on summer mornings. Today, rain fell heavily against the panes.

This was one of the rooms they had refurbished. The rich furniture now stood on a pale blue carpet which enhanced its dark gleam, and the seats of the chairs had been covered in gold and cream striped brocade. Marion loved this room, which had been used as an ante-room by the RAF and had shown signs of their occupation until restored. As it was still dark outside, Robson had lit the small table lamp and the lights on the far wall to give a cheery atmosphere to this morning a week before Christmas.

Marion rang the bell to alert Robson, and they began on porridge from the heated serving bowl. Leo ate a spoonful, then gave a gasp as he burned his mouth. 'I think Cook imagines she's creating a new form of energy with this stuff, and brews it to a thermometer reading designed to explode within half an hour.'

Marion laughed. 'You'd be the first to complain if it was barely warm. Blow on it before you eat any more.'

'You're the most unsympathetic woman I know,' he grumbled, as men do when they know they are making a fuss over nothing.

She studied him with the eyes of love. In a colourful Norwegian sweater over a grey flannel shirt he looked robust, happy and far from starving. 'What are you planning to do today?'

'Organize the Christmas tree. Jack has already felled it, it's just a case of going out with him to see it loaded and brought in. I thought it would be nice to have it in the corner room this year. We rarely use it, and it has such charm. If we put the tree in there, it'll be a natural place to converge when others come.' He gingerly tested the porridge. 'That's better. We'll use it ourselves, too, if there are fairy lights and parcels to tempt us,' he added, munching his breakfast with enthusiasm. 'We could shift some of the furniture around and use it as our main sitting room, at least over the holiday period. What do you think?'

'Chris always thought the tree should be the first sight to greet visitors. We used to have an enormous one beside the staircase. He never did anything about dressing it, however. David, Vesta and Pat used to choose the ornaments and Robson went up the ladder to tie them on. When David was old enough *he* used to go up the ladder. David and Pat were all for putting on everything but the kitchen sink. Fortunately, Vesta's artistic eye curbed their wilder ideas. Even so, Chris invariably winced when he saw it. Each year – he made a point of endeavouring to be at home for Christmas – I had to explain that the children wanted something bright and colourful. He enjoyed the religious significance of the festival.' She was seeing it all in her mind's eye as she spoke. 'Yet he was not a particularly pious man. It was the purity of the Christian representation of Christmas I suspect he appreciated.' She smiled without realizing she was. 'He once told me he saw the tree as a symbol of friendship and unity. The trunk was the Sheridan family; the branches our ties with the many races of the world. It was all way over my head. Poor Chris! It must have been difficult for him to live in a world mostly peopled by simpletons.'

She was so far into the past it was a surprise when Leo said, 'Another instance of your exclusion from family activities. Did none of them ever ask what *you* would like to put on this tree which represented the Sheridan family?'

Marion coloured, as she always did when he picked on these

examples, and said, as Robson came in with a laden tray, 'I've never regarded myself as a Sheridan. I'm too mundane anyway. Mothers traditionally concern themselves with food at Christmastime.' She glanced up at the poker-faced Robson. 'When Mrs Parfitt arrives would you ask her to come and see me before she starts cleaning? I'll have a word with Cook after that.'

'Very well, madam.'

When the butler left, Marion expected Leo to make his usual comment about when the silly old man was going to accept a new master, but he was instead studying her with a creased brow. 'Is something wrong?'

She hedged. 'Why?'

He leaned on his elbows and fixed her with a shrewd look. 'All you've spoken about since I found you gazing at that bowl of berries are Chris and your children. You've been delightfully free of them for a very long period. Why have they taken you over this morning?'

It had been silly to delay telling him. He was no fool. 'Vesta rang from Waterloo Station. She's on her way home for Christmas.'

'Oh.' He took in the implications. 'Did she say why?'

'She thought she'd like to. The train was departing in a few minutes. She had to run, she said.'

'Is Paul Gaynor with her?'

'Not so far as I gathered.'

'I see. Why didn't you tell me right away?'

'I don't know.' She appealed to him. 'Why would she come home unless she was in some kind of trouble? She must have split up with Paul and is so heartbroken she can't stay out there where he is.'

'Now that's pure conjecture,' he said irritably. 'It's pointless thinking along any lines at all until she arrives and puts you out of your misery.' He began to serve himself with bacon and eggs in a determined fashion. 'Your daughter is a respected artist and a woman of almost thirty. She's been through the war and knows how to look after herself. She also conducted a very close liaison with Brad Holland for a year or more before splitting with him and, doubtless, has had the same relationship with Gaynor. Vesta seems unable to commit herself legally to any man, but that's her problem, not yours.'

325

Marion was outraged, forgetting her own youthful folly. 'Vesta's not the kind of girl to do what you've just suggested. She *worked* with that American during the war, then they decided to get married once he was divorced. When he went off to Japan I wasn't sorry. He was quite unsuitable for her. Paul's different. He's been very fond of her from the start, and would have married her long ago if it had been up to him. He's extremely honourable.' She frowned. 'Vesta's my daughter, so her problems must concern me.'

'Why? Yours have never concerned her. That was very evident to me from the one short meeting we had.'

'She wasn't herself then. She's normally very sweet and understanding . . . and extremely *moral*,' she added firmly.

'Then why are you so worried about her imminent arrival?'

When her husband was in this mood Marion always felt at a disadvantage, despite knowing it was his defence of her for which she should be grateful. 'You're sometimes very hard, Leo.'

'And you're much too soft, my dear. You've allowed your family to dismiss you as unimportant, then agonized over their troubles. They've had their share, I agree. David had the right idea and took himself off to sort it out. Perhaps Vesta did the same by going to Germany, and there could be a very happy reason for her visit. It *is* only a visit, I hope.'

'This is her home,' Marion reminded him.

'Sorry. Yes, it is. And she's your daughter, not mine.' He sighed. 'But you're *my* wife, so I'm entitled to step in if I feel you need support.' He put down his knife and fork. 'You've made me so very happy, given me back so much I thought gone forever. Let me do what little I can for you in return.'

Anxious to regain their serenity, Marion poured coffee and changed the subject. 'I think that's a lovely idea to use the corner room over Christmas. The tree will look just right between the high windows on the west wall. We'll add those two settees from the middle room and the set of walnut tables from the corridor.'

'And I think *you* should dress the tree for once.'

'Heavens, all those old ornaments from the attic.'

'I bought new ones last year, if you recall. Do it with Vesta to add artistic inspiration.'

'You will be nice to her, won't you?'

'I was nice last time. It was she who pitched in at me.'

Despite Leo's confidence, Marion fidgeted all morning, looking at the clock every fifteen minutes or so and wondering what was about to happen. The days would become unbearable if Vesta still resented Leo. He was out with Jack for most of the morning, and Marion hoped her daughter would arrive before he came back with the tall fir destined for the corner room hardly ever used in Chris's time. She told herself she must stop using that expression. It suggested an era or a reign in this house, which was quite wrong. Tarrant Hall was the Sheridans' property. Always had been; always would be. She had never felt herself to be one of them, and did not even bear their name now. As Mrs Roberts she was even less entitled to put Chris into a time bracket. This place would be his until his son took it over.

Vesta's room had been prepared by the daily cleaning woman and a fire lit there. Lunch had been set for three people. The new day-dress Marion had bought for Christmas was on her now and she wondered uneasily whether it would have been wiser to stay in her tweed skirt and yellow jumper. As she dithered she heard car tyres on the gravel and guessed it was the village taxi. She *should* have stayed in the skirt and jumper. But at least Leo was not back yet. She went to the door herself. Vesta was paying Bob Sandalwood, and Marion felt terribly overdressed against a daughter clad in crumpled khaki with tall black boots and a black knitted hat. Then Vesta turned and came towards her with a wide smile.

'Hallo, Mummy. It's *marvellous* to be home.'

They embraced, then went inside each with an arm around the other's waist. Marion began to relax. Perhaps it was going to be all right. Robson appeared as Bob brought in items of luggage.

'Hallo, Robson,' Vesta greeted him cheerfully. 'My goodness, you look very hale and hearty.'

'Don't go by looks. I've been under the weather lately,' he replied. 'Welcome home, Miss Vesta. It's very good to see you've come back safely from that terrible enemy country.'

They went through to the small sitting-room they had used during enemy occupation, as Leo termed the requisitioning of the house, and Vesta said immediately, 'Where's *The Afterglow*?'

'In the larger sitting room. Le – I thought it would be better there now we've the whole house back,' Marion told her, perturbed by how quickly she had noticed the change. 'You don't mind, do you?'

'Of course not. It's yours . . . ours . . . the whole family's. It doesn't matter which room it's in.' Vesta tugged off her close-fitting hat and thick jacket. 'You've put on new loose covers.'

'No, they are the chairs from that small bedroom next to the one Pat used to use when she came to stay before the war. The ones from here are now in the corner room.'

'Where Daddy used to keep his Sonja Koltay engraved glass because the light is so cold in there?'

'That's right.' Marion decided not to say that Chris's prize glassware was also in another place. She had had no idea about the cold light in that room. Was it cold enough in the rear corridor? Vesta resembled some kind of shabby female mercenary, or one of those intrepid women who travelled through darkest Africa. Totally out of place in elegant surroundings. 'My goodness, dear, you look very tired and crumpled.'

'So would you if you'd come from Hamburg on a ship packed with troops while a storm raged. It was hell. I was as sick as a dog.'

'Does that mean you're not hungry? I've organized lunch for one o'clock.'

'No, I'm ravenous after throwing up last night's dinner. What I really want more than anything is a long, hot bath and to wash my hair. I seem to have been travelling for ever.'

'I told Robson to bring coffee as soon as you got here.'

'I'll have it upstairs. Oh, you've split up that pair of Dresden figurines,' she commented, still looking about her. 'Daddy always had them standing together.'

'Yes, he did.' Marion had not realized how much they had changed things. 'Leo . . . we thought they looked more impressive at opposite ends of the room.'

'Mmm, actually they do.' Her searching gaze finally swung back to Marion. 'I must say you're awfully swish in that frock, Mummy. If I tell you you look very fit and most

328

disgustingly young, you won't copy Robson and say you've been under the weather lately, will you?'

Marion laughed over her impersonation of Robson's mournful tones. 'He's really beyond it, of course, but he's become such a part of the Hall it's impossible to pension him off.' She broached the tricky subject. 'Paul wasn't able to come with you, then?'

Vesta shook her head and said, calmly enough, 'A soldier's life is not his own. He's probably coming in February when he'll get long leave.'

'That'll be nice.' Marion did not have the courage to ask if they were planning to be married in the village church when he came. Take a little at a time. If he was coming to join her there was nothing to worry about. 'Look at us standing in the middle of the room as if there were no chairs,' she said with a smile.

'I've been sitting for two days. It's nice to stand for a while. Anyway, I want to change into something more normal. I've worn clothes like this the whole time, except in the evenings. For one thing, they fool people into thinking I'm in the army so that it's easier to move around, and for another they're a better deterrent to amorous hopefuls on trains and boats. But khaki seems very out of place in this gorgeous room. Almost an insult.' She gazed around once more. 'I've forgotten how beautiful home was.'

Robson brought coffee on a tray. Vesta poured some right away, picked up the cup and saucer, scooped a handful of biscuits, and said, 'I'll go and make myself presentable for lunch, if you don't mind. We'll have a lovely long talk then. There's so much news to catch up on. What were those ghastly huts on the edge of the village? Then I must ring Pat and tell her to come over tonight. Tell all three to come. I'm dying to see them. I *must* clean up. See you later, Mummy.'

Marion followed her daughter through to the hall just as the side door opened to admit Leo, minus green boots and jacket which he had left in the outer cloakroom. He pulled up short on seeing Vesta. Colour drained from his face as an expression of inexplicable shock crossed it. The pair studied each other in silence, apparently unable to break it.

'Vesta's going up for a bath before lunch,' Marion told him nervously.

'Of course.' Silence. 'Did you have a good journey?'

'Yes . . . thanks.'

'You're staying for Christmas?' Leo seemed to be slowly returning to normal.

'Through till February, at least.'

'Ah, I see.' Another long silence. 'In that case, we'd better become friends, don't you think?' In the face of *her* silence, he added, 'I'm wearing my own pullover this time.'

'It's very nice.'

'Thank you.' Again a pause until he said quietly, 'That coffee will be cold unless you drink it soon.'

Vesta looked down into the cup then back at him. 'I'm afraid I can't possibly call you anything but Leo.'

'That's all right by me. It's better than Major Roberts.'

'I'll . . . I'll be down for lunch. Looking a bit more human.'

As Vesta moved away towards the stairs, Marion knew there was, after all, something to worry about. It was none of the things she had imagined. Loving Leo as she did, instinct told her something had sprung up between those two that she did not understand or share in.

CHAPTER SIXTEEN

WHEN Vesta descended for lunch she did not look the same girl. Her cap of light brown hair was soft and shining around a clean face enlivened with very pink lipstick, and she wore a sherbet-pink sweater with a swirling black wool skirt. Although she seemed thinner and a little taut, Marion realized her daughter had become a very striking woman. The only giveaway to offset her outward confidence was a sadness in her eyes, that appeared even larger than before. Marion dismissed the notion that Vesta had gone away a girl and come back a mature woman, and instead acknowledged that her mother's eye had seen a girl before because it had blinded her to an unwelcome truth.

During the meal they talked of local matters, giving the returning villager news of how things had changed. Leo explained that the 'ghastly huts' she had passed in the taxi were bungalow homes known as prefabs, either in affectionate or derogatory terms depending on one's outlook.

'They're springing up everywhere,' he said. 'We're told they're a temporary measure to house all those whose homes were destroyed, but it's going to be years before this country is anywhere near being rebuilt – we seem to be more intent on doing that in Germany at the moment – so I think our prefab colony will be a blot on the surrounding countryside for a long time.'

'People have to live somewhere,' Marion pointed out, as she frequently did when elderly villagers complained about the sprawl of residences which more nearly resembled the RAF huts on Longbarrow Hill than homes. 'We thought families were going to be moved up to the old airfield at one stage, Vesta, until the Parish Council pointed out that the only access was a lane and that schools, shops and the doctor were all down in the valley from which Longbarrow Hill could be cut off by snow.'

'Of course, the village school grew so overcrowded it was impossible to teach anything. There's now an overflow school in the village hall until better facilities can be built.' Leo pulled a face. 'That's merely a grand phrase to describe a prefab of larger size than the rest, no doubt. But what's the alternative? The stalwarts of Tarrant Royal, of which your mother is one, deplore the influx of people who have no ties with the village and expect things to be run as they are in cities. There have been protest meetings over all manner of issues – the infrequency of buses into Greater Tarrant, waiting time at Dr Bletchley's surgery, lack of a cinema within easy distance, the hostility of farmers, and so on. What we're afraid of is industry moving out to these workers who find it so difficult to get into nearby towns each day. Not only difficult, but expensive. Once that happens, the village will never be the same again.'

'It isn't now,' claimed Marion. 'Children of people who've lived here all their lives want the same things. Would you believe, they're campaigning to hold twice-weekly dances in Ron Pilger's old barn. They're repairing it at weekends, and have bamboozled the poor old man into signing an agreement to let them use it on Wednesdays and Saturdays. There's nothing the Parish Council can do. It's his land and buildings, and Reginald Tait had to admit that the document is legal enough because Pilger sticks by it. Reginald suspects Terence of being behind the whole affair and copying the wording of official forms in his office, because the boy has returned from his four years in the navy – where he apparently learned to play the saxophone – and is wasting his talents, with two or three of his chums, trying to set up as a dance band instead of following his father into the legal profession. All the young people seem to want is *fun*. Jim Parkins and Seth Oates have already gone off without a penny in their pockets and with no fixed idea of what they want to do, leaving their fathers with no one to take on the farms when they're too old to cope with them. None of the young men want to farm after driving a tank, firing torpedoes from a submarine, or dropping by parachute on some enemy outpost. You'd think they'd welcome getting back to something normal like that, wouldn't you?'

'No, Mummy,' said Vesta, who had been quietly listening to all this. 'In a curious way they felt vital and important doing all those things. Milking cows really isn't an attractive alternative.'

Leo smiled across the table at Marion. 'We who have been through two wars very definitely think it is, my dear. Give them time, or a fresh conflict, and maybe they'll feel the same.' He turned to Vesta and embarked on a tricky subject. 'Since the house has been restored certain things have been done to it, you'll notice. Change is not confined to the village.'

He went on to outline the alterations they had made, and Marion felt he was defying Vesta to object. She gave no sign of wanting to, however. There was no evidence of resentment or suspicion, no hint of the bitterness with which she had once attacked Leo; and Marion was deeply thankful that her daughter appeared to accept his right to make decisions in the home Chris had loved but so rarely visited. Even so, there was still a curious facet to Vesta's treatment of her stepfather which she did not understand. It was not wariness, nor shyness. It appeared to fall somewhere between the two.

Leo was his normal self again and treated Vesta with easy friendliness. When Marion had questioned his initial reaction to her he had explained with frankness.

'I've only met Vesta once before; extremely hostile, haughty and ultra-glamorous. Coming indoors and seeing a dishevelled pale-faced woman in worn khaki and black boots, looking strained and exhausted, gave me a shock. I saw a number of young women like that in Norway during the occupation. Some vanished without trace, some were tortured and shot. It's impossible to forget them. For a few moments, Vesta took me back to those days, that's all. I've been foolish. Although I knew she has been quite as intrepid as many others, and has experienced the horror of conflict in various parts of the world, my idea of your talented daughter was based only on the evidence of my eyes. A temperamental, passionate beauty sensitive enough to paint a masterpiece like *The Afterglow*. She has, of course, much greater depth of character, which I hope she'll allow me to plumb while she's here.'

His words added to Marion's acknowledgement that she had previously been unwilling to accept the things he had just mentioned; had not wanted a daughter so divorced from the one she needed. Now she had Leo her needs were fully satisfied, and she would have to plumb the depths of Vesta's personality, too. There was little opportunity that afternoon, however. When Leo asked if she would care to trim the Christmas tree, she declined.

'I think you and Mummy should do that, as it's your first time together.'

'It's our *second* Christmas,' Leo pointed out.

She looked upset. 'Heavens, so it is. How could I have forgotten? I've been away longer than I thought.'

'Too long?' he probed gently.

'I've been working hard.' It was defensive.

'Your father used to say "I've been phenomenally busy" whenever he discovered he'd been absent for every birthday, anniversary and holiday,' Marion put in. 'Like you, he was always abashed by the fact that he hadn't noticed time passing.'

'It's different over there, Mummy. People are dying of starvation and cold, our troops are risking their lives in an effort to rebuild what they knocked down several years before, and if you had ever seen Fassberg or Gatow airfield you'd understand why birthdays and anniversaries slip past unnoticed. Or why they no longer seem important. Not every place is like Tarrant Royal, you know.'

'Without people like your mother it wouldn't be the haven it is,' Leo pointed out. 'We all have our part to play, Vesta. You and I are thankful presently to be in a place where ordinary life is important, aren't we?'

Vesta gave him an inscrutable look before saying quietly, 'Yes. Yes, we are. I'll look forward to seeing the tree in all its glory by tonight, when the Chandlers come. I'll go off and ring them now.'

They waited for their friends in the corner room where the tree stood in silver and white splendour between two long windows. New raspberry-pink curtains added warmth to the original grey carpet scattered with Chinese rugs, and a mixture of chairs took away the formality of a room that had, in the past, merely been walked through to get elsewhere. Vesta exclaimed on the charm of the tree before asking the

334

whereabouts of her father's beloved Sonja Koltay bowls and goblets. She accepted the explanation without further comment, but Marion felt faintly guilty, nevertheless.

When the Chandlers arrived it was like a small circus coming in. There were cries of delight and hugs all round, the booming bass of Bill, the quieter excitement of Tessa and the uninhibited pleasure of Pat. They all asked questions at the same time, which Vesta was too bewildered to answer, until Leo cut across the babble with an invitation to find a seat and name their poison.

'Well, well, this has taken us all by surprise,' said Bill, still on his feet beside the blazing fire. Then, with typical Australian bluntness, added, 'Do we have to dig into the coffer to buy a toastrack or a set of fish knives?'

Marion almost held her breath. Vesta was wearing a diamond solitaire on her left hand but had said nothing about a spring wedding. She now sidestepped the issue very neatly. 'I'd rather have something more glamorous for Christmas, Uncle Bill. You're always making knowledgeable comments about women's nifties, so how about some of those?'

'What the hell are nifties?' asked Leo with a laugh.

Bill winked. 'I'll take you aside later, son, and explain.'

'Don't listen to him, Leo,' Pat advised. 'It's all bluff. He'd run a mile if he ever saw any but those on our washing line.'

The conversation was light-hearted until they sat down to dinner prepared by Cook with much complaint about last-minute guests. Only then did Vesta reveal something of what she had been doing in Germany, in response to Bill's prompting. Marion sat aghast as the slender, attractive creature in a dinner gown of blue velvet related how she had helped capture a leading black marketeer in the ruins of Hanover.

'The man who took you along would have been court-martialled, I take it,' said Bill.

'No one knew I went. He swore everyone to secrecy and his CO was on compassionate leave to sort out his wife who was so often in the American sector Billy said she must have stars and stripes on her underwear.'

This prompted further questions and the evening passed in the manner of old times, when the entire Sheridan family had been home. Vesta was the focus of attention as she kept

everyone entertained and amazed by what she had been engaged in since leaving home at the receding of flood water
more than eighteen months ago. Leo and Bill were deeply
interested in the political aspects of all Vesta had experienced,
and she was able to answer their questions fully enough to
encourage further discussion. Marion said little. She was not
sufficiently versed in the complexity of post-war Germany to
contribute.

When Vesta eventually revealed, after they went back to
the corner room, how she had stowed away on an American
aircraft to Berlin, had been forced to hide in a store when fog
halted all flights, then had been arrested and kept in a detention cell for two days, Marion had to face the fact that she did
not know her daughter at all.

'So you were unable to sketch Gatow,' said Leo with the
rapt interest he had shown all evening. 'Does that mean that
you can't complete your set of airlift paintings?'

The glow of life in Vesta appeared to dim suddenly. 'Some
of them weren't any good, anyway. I'm inclined to abandon the
project.'

'You don't seem to me to be a person who abandons
something she's gone through considerable risk and discom-
fort to achieve,' commented Leo, getting to his feet to recharge
glasses. 'Have you brought the canvases with you?'

'They're not up to a standard to offer anyone.'

'Perhaps you'll improve on them while you're here.'

'I shouldn't think so,' she said, watching him pour gin in
her glass. 'Once a theme dies on you, inspiration rarely
returns.'

He glanced at her with shrewd interest. 'Does that mean we
won't have the pleasure of seeing any of the work you did out
there? It can't all have been sub-standard.'

Again that suggestion of curious shyness with him. 'I sent
over my set done in Hanover, and banked a nice cheque.
There are one or two other pictures I have with me . . . but I'm
not sure I'm yet ready to show them to anyone.'

Leo smiled. 'Artist's temperament rearing its head?'

'Unwillingness to let outsiders into my private world,' Vesta
replied.

'Message understood.' He moved away.

'I didn't mean it that way,' she protested with a surprising hint of real distress, which halted Leo. 'It's simply that sometimes an artist completes a canvas then sees that she's revealed more of herself than she intends to. It was ages before I let anyone see *The Afterglow* – even my family.'

Leo stood with decanter poised over Bill's glass. 'Poor you, *compelled* to put your emotions on canvas, then feeling terribly exposed to the world.' He smiled at her. 'That's probably why I became a schoolteacher instead. If things started growing too personal I could always give someone six of the best to take off the heat.'

Everyone laughed and the strange air of tension vanished, but Vesta was quiet after that and very soon said that she was rather tired and hoped no one would mind if she went to bed. The evening broke up then, with Pat pressing Vesta to ride across to Wattle Farm tomorrow for a girls' chat.

Leo was deep in thought as he prepared for bed, which increased Marion's inexplicable uneasiness. He appeared to have become a different person in a guise which somehow excluded her. With Chris's guests she had been entirely out of her depth. This evening she had again certainly been on the fringes of the deep end.

When they were in bed Leo seemed disinclined to turn out the light, yet made no start on a conversation. Marion could not stay silent. 'If I'd been aware of half the things Vesta had been doing, I'd have been beside myself with worry.'

He continued to stare at the ceiling. 'Then it's just as well she sent so few letters, each so short.'

Marion tried again. 'You're not upset that she's intending to stay until Paul comes in February, are you?'

'Of course not. It's her home.'

'I haven't plucked up the nerve to ask if they mean to get married then, and she hasn't said. Even Bill failed to find out.'

'I can't see it happening,' he said absently. 'If she's afraid of giving her true self away in a painting, she certainly won't do so to any man. Until she can, there'll be no wedding.' He turned his head on the pillow to face her. 'What's she afraid of? Did she have a bad experience when she was young?'

'Only the war, and everyone shared that.'

'Mmm.' He resumed his study of the ceiling. 'She paints *The*

Afterglow, which is sheer brilliance, then runs off to do a series of grim studies of a life completely lacking in romance, and involves herself in the masculine world all around her. It suggests that what she's frightened of is being a woman.'

'That's nonsense!' To change the subject she was finding once more beyond her, Marion slid her arm across his stomach and felt the hardness of his hip. 'The tree looked so right where you put it. With the additional furniture, that room makes a perfect place to entertain guests. Not that the Chandlers can be called that. I had no idea how attractive that corner room could be. Chris used it merely to display that expensive engraved glass he was so passionate about, and it always struck me as slightly forbidding and chilly. You've worked a miracle in there.'

'Hardly that,' he murmured, 'but I'd like us to use all this house, not keep half of it as a kind of museum. I'm glad you're pleased with my brainwave. I'm not so sure Vesta was. She noticed the glass had gone the moment she walked in.'

'It was only a comment. She didn't really mind. In any case, we're the people living here. She's just passing through.' Snuggling closer to his warmth, she said, 'I'm afraid we'll have to decide tomorrow about the Christmas donation to the church, and whether or not we can continue to fund the maternity ward at the Cottage Hospital. Although there are only four beds, costs are rising with dismaying speed and our income is decreasing at the same rate. The Rector and the village council are coming for coffee in the morning. They'll be expecting my answer and I really don't know what I'll say.'

When his silence continued too long, she raised her head to find that he had fallen asleep. Too warm and comfortable to get out and switch off the light on his side of the bed, Marion lay wide eyed. It was an elegant room in lime and gold, with French-style furniture and a carpet of cinnamon wool. Leo's maroon dressing-gown across a pale chair added the masculine touch her bedroom had for so long lacked. All at once this harmony seemed threatened; this harmony which had arrived so late in her life. Vesta's arrival had shifted the focus of a familiar routine; had brought into it the stark grimness Leo claimed she was painting. The war was over. Marion did not want its aftermath intruding upon her new-found happiness.

There was enough to worry about here. Fresh ministry demands, more paperwork, smaller rations, unemployment, divorce rate soaring, social unrest, old traditions vanishing. She did not want to shoulder her enemy's problems as well.

All the talk this evening of whole cities of rubble with children living beneath it and feeding on rubbish taken from dustbins upset her. She did not want to hear about dens of vice where anything could be bought for a few British or American cigarettes. Nor did she need descriptions of skeletal old women searching through dangerous ruins for scraps of wood to burn for warmth at night, or unmarried mothers selling themselves to buy food for some passing soldier's bastard. Most of all she had not wanted Vesta's account of the airlift in which David was taking part. She had not realized the dangers involved in something she had thought was little different from the transport job he had been doing since the end of the war. She had agonized over her family's safety throughout six years. *The war was over.* The Allies had won. That should be the end of the matter.

As sleep fast retreated from a brain churning with unpleasant thoughts, Marion returned to the problem of finance. Chris had instigated numerous philanthropic gestures at a time when Tarrant Hall Estate could afford them. She had determined to maintain them after his death. Indeed, some were tied to his will, which left the land and property to David with Marion as custodian until he took over. Those donations could only be discontinued on David's written authority, and how would she get that at the moment? Others within her power to stop were projects dear to Chris's heart. Such was her sense of duty to him she still honoured his wishes, even though the money could be ill spared. The family at the Hall was expected to provide. It always had, so she must make sure it carried on doing so.

Now her mind was on the worry-track, she thought of the bills for furnishings and carpets run up when opening up the rest of the house. Perhaps they had been too extravagant. Leo had had very little money to contribute. The sale of his cottage had reaped a disappointing amount, and he had lost on investments made during the war in a company which proved unsuccessful in the transition from making parachutes to making female fashions. Dior's New Look had transformed style and small firms went under. Bad harvests, animals lost, blight which had attacked their trees in the forest had all cut down their income, and the Labour government had introduced better pay and conditions for workers. All these had been a drain on the estate. How could she explain it to David when he finally came home?

Thoughts of David brought Marion back to the worry of the airlift. Suppose he crashed in fog? Suppose he came down in the Russian zone and was never heard of again? Beset by sudden agitation she shifted quite deliberately in the hope that Leo would be woken by her movements. He slept on, and Marion watched him with a niggling ache in her chest. He had been different tonight. It was as though he had jumped the wall to join the others, leaving her on the shady side of it. This morning she had awoken feeling secure because she had love and harmony. The financial problems had become much less burdensome because Leo was beside her. Then the telephone had rung, and everything had changed. Even Leo. That was another thing to worry about.

Vesta slept late, so Marion breakfasted with Leo at their small table beside the window as usual. She was glad. After a night of lurid dreams, she had woken with one of her headaches hovering. They had been her constant companions from the time of David's shocking announcement of marriage and his consequent presumed death. Since Leo came on the scene, they had been rare. This one had clearly been induced by Vesta's talk of life in Germany, and by the chain of worries her arrival had forged. It had always before been David who caused anguish and concern. Vesta's attachment to Chris had kept mother and daughter partially distanced. Vesta had always been a dreamy child, whereas David had been an extrovert. The pair seemed to have changed personalities over the last two years. Marion could no more understand this daughter who stowed away on an aircraft and got arrested in Berlin, than she could the son who had turned his back on all he loved.

Studying her husband across the table it occurred to Marion that she had had enough of her children. Until she had met

Leo her family had been of supreme importance to her. Now she had a life and love of her own, she wished to be left alone to enjoy it. David's conception had created aggression, anguish and humiliation. She had then been eighteen. Surely, at fifty-three, she was entitled to relinquish him and the girl born as the result of determined efforts to make a doomed marriage work. Both seemed destined to make life as difficult as possible for themselves, so they must sort it out without involving her and Leo. Everything had seemed so simple at the end of the war, but it might as well not have ended for all the happiness and contentment her children had found with peace.

'You're very thoughtful.'

Marion smiled. 'And you're very intent on your bacon and eggs. Have I ever told you how much I enjoy our breakfasts together?'

'No, but I'm happy that you've told me now. So do I. Even more so in summer, when the curtains are back and the sun streams in. We've made this into a most attractive room, haven't we?'

'Yes.' She refrained from mentioning the expense. 'Leo, what am I going to tell the Rector and the committee members this morning?'

He sighed. 'I don't see how you can discontinue your habit of giving to these people what they're probably banking on.'

'But we've made a loss two years running. They must be aware of that. The farming community as a whole has suffered. If we have another severe winter followed by drought it will really begin to worry me deeply. Everyone's struggling.'

'Including these people who rely on handouts from you.' He helped himself to more scrambled egg, then gave her a straight look. 'See it from their angle. Times are very hard. I know the estate has taken a bit of a beating, like everything else, but people from the village come up here for meetings, and so on, and see these rooms filled with priceless works of art. They're given coffee to drink from Spode or Royal Doulton, and scones made by one servant and brought by another. Can you reasonably tell them this morning that you can't afford your usual donations?'

She gazed at him, stricken. 'All those things were bought with Sheridan money – Chris's money.'

341

'So they might have been. You're so immersed in your belief that you've never been a real Sheridan, you must nevertheless accept that Chris's treasures are part of the estate you're managing. They're *assets*, my dear, just as much as tractors and herds of cattle. The home farm and forestry might have made serious losses, but all those ornaments and paintings we've been moving around the house are worth several fortunes rolled into one. You *can't* plead poverty to the Cottage Hospital committee and the poor old Rector. You just can't, Marion.'

A surprising sense of distress assailed her. 'I'm not sure what you're saying. They're not assets, Leo, they're David and Vesta's inheritance.'

His hand closed over hers playing with her teaspoon. 'I know how you feel about being a caretaker for David. But there's no indication of an imminent change of attitude from him, and he's prepared to let you continue to run things until there is. You are an extremely astute countrywoman. I keep telling you that. You instruct Jack Marshall to buy and sell livestock and machinery. Why not valuable items from *inside* the Hall? The land and forest are just as much David's inheritance as Chris's aesthetic indulgences are. If we have another bad year you might well have to consider putting some of this stuff to auction. That collection of Koltay glass alone would fetch more than a hundred thousand. Would your children really care if it was no longer here?'

'Vesta straightaway noticed it had been moved,' she said in troubled tones. 'She knew Chris particularly loved that glass. It *is* very beautiful.'

'Chris also loved his home, the church and the village. That's evident by his generous covenants. But would he see all those things diminish while clinging to several engraved bowls and goblets? I don't think so.'

The headache had fully developed now; the tranquillity of the morning had flown. 'Let's not discuss it any further,' she said. 'I'll give the usual donations, of course. That'll please everyone in time for Christmas. I thought we might drive to Bournemouth tomorrow to do our shopping.'

'Why not go with Vesta, instead? Pat and Tessa, too, if they can tear themselves away from sheep dip and fertilizers.

It would do you good to have an all-girls outing, and it might help Vesta loosen up a bit. She's been through quite a grilling time, I imagine. All self-inflicted, of course, but very much in earnest.'

'Yes. I'll see if they'd like to do it,' said Marion, longing to confess that she'd much prefer her original plan of a day out with him and lunch at Bobby's. It had been so enjoyable last year.

As they left the table Leo slung his arm around her shoulders in the manner she loved, and pulled her close to his side. 'Make sure this shopping spree really is one. Your wandering daughter is home for Christmas, and you are nowhere near the poverty line, madam. Go to Bournemouth tomorrow and splash out on a celebration together.'

They walked through to the hall and Marion said as lightly as she could, 'Yesterday you were hoping Vesta was planning no more than a flying visit.'

'That was when I expected the hostile, haughty, ultra-glamorous creature I first met. I think she has accepted me for some reason, and I look forward to discovering what's really behind her visit. I don't believe she just couldn't bear another Christmas away from home. She might not like revealing her innermost self to others, but I'm going to have a shot at achieving just that.'

The meeting followed its usual pattern with Marion playing what Leo called the gracious lady of the manor, dispensing coffee and scones whilst offering knowledgeable and shrewd solutions to subjects discussed by people like herself who had served the village faithfully for years. Everyone was suitably grateful for the money they were very definitely expecting, and they departed with reminders to Marion of the various Christmas functions they hoped she would attend. Perhaps Miss Sheridan would honour them with her presence, too, and judge the Sunday School children's painting competition, the subject of which, this year, was the Berlin airlift – love thine enemies. Marion agreed to it in order to get rid of them. Her headache had become really bad, and she had worried all through the meeting about the Royal Doulton and the scones made and served by her servants. Chris had believed in the gracious life and impeccable manners, not as symbols of status

343

but because he was firmly convinced that gentleness and beauty created serenity, which was the basis of peace. Did people from the village whom she had known all her life come to the Hall and resent what they saw? Maybe the prefab dwellers would, but not the old stalwarts who respected the family there.

When Vesta joined them for lunch, also served on Royal Doulton, Leo immediately raised the subject of the shopping excursion on the morrow. She was enthusiastic.

'I'd love it. I'm going across to Wattle Farm this afternoon, so I'll put on the thumbscrews until Pat and Aunt Tessa agree to come. It'll be absolute bliss to browse in real shops instead of the NAAFI. Their stock was pretty good, but women ended up wearing the same things and using the same colour lipstick. Oh, Mummy, it'll be *fun*! We'll have lunch in Bobby's, then you and Aunt Tessa can go off and look at the corsets and sensible shoes while Pat and I buy silly extravagant presents for everyone.'

Leo was busy removing a bone from his plaice when he said casually, 'Your mother doesn't wear corsets, Vesta. They're for old ladies.'

To Marion's amazement her daughter flushed darkly. 'It was a joke, that's all.'

Leo glanced up at her and smiled. 'Ah, I see.' He turned to Marion. 'Have you mentioned the painting competition? Oh, of course, you've had no chance. Shall I?'

As Marion herself felt slightly embarrassed over the corset issue she nodded, and Leo passed his attention back to Vesta who was still gazing at him in a mysterious fashion. 'It is earnestly hoped that the renowned Miss Sheridan will consent to assess the Christmas paintings done by the Sunday School classes. I'm afraid we've let you in for it by agreeing more or less by proxy. The subject's the Berlin airlift. Something you're particularly qualified to judge.' As she gave no response, he continued smoothly. 'God knows what images you'll be faced with. During my time as a schoolteacher I saw Pontius Pilates wearing flying helmets, holy lambs with bare patches in their fleeces, and archangels sitting alongside Noah on wooden boats. Children associate their ideas with the things they know, don't they?' He chuckled. 'Don't be surprised if there's

344

one showing a bald man with a wig an inch above his head. They'll have heard of a facelift and will adapt it to someone's hair.'

Marion laughed, but Vesta did not seem to think it funny. 'Surely they'll have seen footage of it on newsreels at the cinema. If they haven't, I'll very soon enlighten them. Everyone in this country should know the sacrifices being made to keep it going.'

'I'm sure everyone does, but children don't always understand, Vesta. I'm all for keeping it that way. We learn about war and inhumanity soon enough. Let's preserve innocence while it lasts,' said Leo.

'Daddy could have said that line,' mused Vesta, abruptly changing her approach. 'You're both right. I'll judge the competition light-heartedly.'

When they sat with coffee at the end of lunch, Leo returned to the subject of the airlift as he glanced at the newspaper. 'There's an item here about something they call Operation Santa Claus. They're flying in sweets and presents for Berlin's children. The Yanks, of course. They're the only ones with the wherewithal to do anything like that.' He glanced up at Vesta. 'From Fassberg, too. There's a missed opportunity for you.'

She shook her head. 'One box looks like any other. Unless I dressed the crew as Father Christmases and showed lollipops or teddy bears tumbling from one of the packages it would look no different from the pictures I've done already.'

'You wouldn't like Father Christmases and teddies?'

'I paint reality, Leo, not fairy tales. They're for amateurs.'

He smiled and folded the paper. 'OK, so now we're even.'

After a moment, Vesta smiled back. 'It wasn't deliberate, but, yes, we're even.' Taking something from the pocket of her beige skirt, she turned to Marion. 'As we're on the subject of Berlin, I think it's a good time to give you this, Mummy. I hope you received my letter telling you David had moved to Lübeck – the RAF and the Americans weren't terribly compatible and Fassberg became impossibly overcrowded, anyway. He sent me this last week. It's quite amazing. He writes like his old self. Read it.'

Marion took it with a sense of reluctance. She had had no communication from her son since the day he came here to tell her why he had flown away leaving Chris mortally wounded. The formal card of congratulation and a cheque when she and Leo had married could have been from anyone. It had meant nothing. She was not sure she wanted to read this letter written like his old self. After much pain she had been able to accept the new, aloof David. If the old one was back what would it entail?

Vesta was right. As Marion read she could picture the laughing, boisterous young man who had been the love of her life in place of his father; the young man who had not yet travelled to Singapore. She handed the pages back to Vesta without comment, feeling agitation gather once more. Had he recovered from whatever had made him hostile to them all? If so, would he soon be leaving the RAF and coming home? Where did Pat now stand? What was going to happen to the Hall? She faced the incredible truth that the only emotion she presently felt was fresh fear for her own happiness with Leo.

'I've no idea what caused the great change,' Vesta said. 'When I met him at Fassberg he looked ghastly. I was shocked because I'd not seen him since he returned from Singapore, as you had. He was very tired, of course, and showing signs of strain from so much flying, but he was also withdrawn, all tied up inside. Four months later this came. Mystifying, isn't it?'

'Did you reply?' Leo asked.

'Didn't have time. I flew to Gatow the following day and ended up in the clink. I'll do it tonight and pop in a Christmas card. Why don't you do the same, Mummy? I'm going to show Pat the letter. The rest is up to her.'

'It's addressed to you. If he writes to me, I'll reply. Not before,' Marion heard herself say.

'I think you should write,' put in Leo from his corner. 'If he's coming out of it he'll need his family to support him.'

'He told me in no uncertain terms that I had never understood him and was little more than a country bumpkin,' she protested hotly.

'We've established that the latter isn't true, haven't we? I know very little about his youth, except that you and he would seem to have been very close, sharing an extremely warm relationship. That doesn't suggest lack of personal understanding. He was probably referring to much more recent

346

times, and I'm afraid he's probably right. But it's through no fault of yours, my dear.' He got up and moved to sit on a footstool, facing them both. To Vesta he said, 'I'm glad you're here to listen to this. I've known for some time, but decided against telling your mother until the moment seemed right. I believe that's now.'

Marion knew instinctively that she would not want to hear what he was determined to say, and agitation became a pain in her chest as Leo told a hideous story concerning prolonged torture by the Japanese, and the kind of terrible journey through hostile jungle that belonged to the world of fiction.

'Only because of my links with SOE have I been able to discover this,' he said with great gentleness, holding Marion's hands between his own. 'Chris probably knew but could say nothing. All he could do when David returned broken and shattered was to acknowledge that it was no more than a setback to his son's life. Which it was. David soon proved he could still fly, and set about wreaking the only revenge for his torture he could manage by continuing to be a Sheridan, through and through. Not knowing meant you *could* not understand what he then needed. You did what most mothers would do: tried to kiss him better and keep him from further harm.' He put out one of his hands to take Vesta's before saying to them both, 'Going back to Singapore, seeing Oriental faces everywhere, would have brought back unacceptable memories. He had challenged his fate and won through, but it came back to torment him.' He sighed. 'It was a tragic mistake to go back there. Small wonder he wanted isolation from all those who had promised him a good future. Recollections soiled those plans, I suspect. If Chris had been alive he might have been able to help him, but you two couldn't possibly. Nor could Pat. Especially Pat.' He paused and seemed to be far away as he added, 'Torture is the basest form of degradation. It takes away a man's very soul.'

Vesta got up rapidly and hurried to the window where she stared from it, shoulders shaking gently. Marion merely gazed at Leo, feeling numb. Although he was gripping her hands he appeared to be looking right through her. Silence reigned for a long time, until he swallowed and focused on her face again.

'I think you should write to David. Just a friendly, chatty

letter as if nothing had changed. He needs that right now, take my word for it.'

'You must be mistaken,' she whispered. 'All that couldn't have happened without my knowing. I would have sensed it. He would have told me.'

'He *couldn't* tell you; couldn't tell anyone.' Leo's brown eyes were full of compassion as he studied her. 'It actually happened almost seven years ago, my dear. David survived and defeated it. You must see it as something in the past and now concentrate on his future. If that letter suggests he's bouncing back again, we must all be ready to offer help when he needs it.' He squeezed her hands. 'Write to him, Marion. Send a jolly Christmas card and all the village gossip. He'll then know everything's all right between you, and that'll be of utmost importance.'

Vesta turned back into the room as Marion remained in her state of numbness. 'Thank you for finding out, Leo. David might prefer us not to know, but it's such a relief to understand why he changed so drastically.'

The pain gathering inside Marion was unbearable. 'What would the Rector and the village committee make of the Sheridan family if they knew, do you think? Perhaps they'd no longer resent the Royal Doulton.' She burst into tears, rocking back and forth hugging herself to ease the anguish which had spread up through her chest to her throat. It stood like a great wall between herself and eighteen months of happiness with a man who meant everything to her.

They went to church on Christmas Eve, as usual. There were a few new faces; some old ones were missing. People from the prefabs all sat together, and were mostly ignored by villagers. It was sad that the clash of two cultures should be evident in the one place where brotherhood was encouraged. Vesta could not help thinking that her father would have done something about it. He would not have tolerated this veiled hostility, and would almost certainly have made a point of talking to the new residents of the area and drawing them into the rustic circle. Vesta was subjected to some scrutiny, but she did not fool herself that it was because these strangers knew of her pictures. It was much more likely that they were resentfully curious about the daughter of the family which had such wealth and influence in this small corner of Dorset.

There were other tensions to mar that familiar annual routine. Marion was still upset over what she had been told about David. Vesta had been taken aback by her mother's vivacity and youthful appearance on first seeing her again. The change marriage to Leo wrought in her was incredible. Now the light in her eyes had dulled and she was much more the woman Vesta had always known. She was still wearing her new smart clothes, but age seemed to have crept up on her again. Tonight, the cherry-red coat with a fur collar she claimed to have bought in Bournemouth with her supply of clothing coupons last Christmas looked too bright and gay for its wearer. The shopping trip had not taken place three days ago. Marion had spent the day in bed nursing a migraine. She did not look much better tonight.

Vesta had managed to come to terms with Leo's revelation only because she was more hardened to such things. She was also grateful that she knew and could offer support to her brother without necessarily betraying the fact. She was certain David would be upset if told Leo had spoken of his horrific experience, but the knowledge made his recent rejection understandable. Curiously enough, Vesta's distress on hearing the truth had been compounded by Leo's final words: *Torture is the basest form of degradation. It takes away a man's very soul.* She knew he had spoken from personal suffering, and David's agony had somehow merged with his to become one in her mind. She had seen in that moment that *Betrayal* could not be exhibited and never, ever given to Leo as a tribute of apology.

Leo was proving a greater problem than expected. Far from creating resentment and comparisons with her father, he appealed to her more strongly than a stepfather should. There were elements of Brad's mastery and challenge in the way Leo leapt to her mother's defence, and an impression of purpose which would not be deflected in all that he did. Leo's eyes did not contain the sizzling intimacy of Brad's rich brown ones, but she recognized the challenge in them whenever he and she clashed momentarily. Overpowering guilt had been responsible for her painting *Betrayal*. It had been intended to get Leo out of her system. It had, and she had let Paul become her lover.

349

She was uncertain now whether Leo was in danger of haunting her again, or whether it was simply that he reminded her too well of Brad, who clearly was *not* out of her system. She did not think a painting would do the trick with him.

Coming home had been intended as an escape. It was proving to be anything but. Leo's torture had become David's; Brad was turning into Leo. Paul stood out on his own. There was only love and concern in his clear, frank eyes; exciting satisfaction in his arms. She had run to him for the very things he had given her, then been reluctant to take them because she could not give them wholeheartedly in return. She loved him too much to be unfair to him. Coming home was to have given her the chance to put everything into perspective. So far there was no chance of it.

After the service they lingered to chat while the prefab dwellers walked past them into the night. Vesta's conscience told her she should speak to them, but her inclination was to let someone else be the good Samaritan. In the churchyard Marion turned to Vesta, handing her a candle and a box of matches.

'You do the ritual, dear. You're the only Sheridan here. I felt awkward doing it last year, but there wasn't anyone else and we haven't missed a Christmas since she died.'

Vesta took the things, saying, 'Don't be silly, Mummy, you'll always be one of the Sheridan family. Leo would be the first person to agree.'

'Of course, but your mother's right. You should do it as you're here.'

Although it was cold there was little wind so the candle lit straight away. Vesta put it carefully beneath the protective glass bubble at the foot of Laura Sheridan's grave and stayed a while there thinking of the three brothers whose passing was marked by simple crosses in the French countryside. She thought in particular of her father, who had loved Rex's wife so much he had instigated this ritual. A lump formed in her throat as she remembered the single set of footprints she had painted, and the fact that her mother had never understood that they symbolized the last of the brothers going to join those already with Laura.

They walked up the hill arm in arm, two of them silent

because of their memories, and Leo respecting the fact. At Marion's request Robson had not stayed up, but he had left lights burning in the hall and in the corner room which had somehow become the place to gather this Christmas. There was the usual mulled wine and mince pies set out for them. Vesta sat near the fire with a pie on a plate while Leo poured wine into the antique goblets used every year for the purpose. Marion chose not to sit and, after only a sip of the wine to herald Christmas in, she announced that she was very tired and would go to bed.

'Please stay and enjoy the occasion,' she said to Leo. 'I am sure you and Vesta can find a great deal to talk about.'

'You're all right?' he asked solicitously.

'Just tired. That hill seemed particularly steep tonight. I must be getting old.'

Leo kissed her with tenderness. 'Not you, my dear. You've simply had a hectic few days being the lady of the manor to all and sundry. I've hardly seen you alone. I'll just have some wine then join you.'

Vesta looked away into the fire. Just as her mother had been uncomfortable when David kissed Pat in her presence, so she felt now watching them. A kiss on the cheek from Leo would have been acceptable, but a lingering one on her mother's mouth was slightly embarrassing, along with his promise to join her shortly. Vesta recalled Paul speaking about how shocked children could be on realizing what their parents had done in order to give them life. She pushed away a peculiar yet similar sensation at the thought of this man going to bed with her mother. She was not so naïve she could not believe they ever indulged in sexual expression, but her mind shied from the notion.

After Marion left, Leo came to stand beside the fire but did not drink from the goblet in his hand. 'I think I made a bad error of judgement in telling her what happened to David in the Far East. She's taken it very badly.'

'Of course she has,' Vesta said with emphasis. 'Forgive me, Leo, but you're so keen to impress upon everyone what a sterling job Mummy did here throughout the war and continues to do, how vital she is to the local community, and so on, you've completely overlooked the fact that she nevertheless has had very little personal experience of pain, and has witnessed nothing more dramatic than a German bomber crashing into the village church. Whereas you and I can eventually come to terms with such knowledge, poor Mummy can't. It's not her fault, it's just the way she's lived.'

He sighed. 'I thought it would help her understand David better, minimize the hurt his rejection caused.'

'I know. You did it for the very best motives. I now have to decide whether or not to tell Pat. Will it help, or hit her the way it has Mummy?'

'I should leave well alone, if I were you. That girl loves him very much. He once loved her the same way – probably still does beneath it all. If he stays away, the knowledge will put on her an additional burden of devotion and loyalty which will ruin her whole life. If he comes back to her, he'll want to tell her himself or keep her in happy ignorance. It's his agony, so it's his choice.'

The emotive atmosphere which had sprung between them, the cosy normality of that room in a house where she had grown up with a brother unaware of what horror lay ahead for him, and the overtones of fellowship in the early hours of Christmas morning, all led Vesta to speak.

'I should never have accused you the way I did,' she began quietly. 'At that time I truly believed you were up to no good. After Sheridan money. Out to get your hands on everything we had. That business of arriving on skis during a snowstorm! I thought it ludicrous; a trick to win over a lonely, gullible widow. I was certain Mummy was being taken in, and furious because she couldn't see through you.'

'Yet you went off to Germany and left her at my mercy,' he said.

'She told me to accept you, or leave.'

'Ah, I see.'

She studied the dark wine in her goblet. 'But I didn't leave things as they were. Paul's father worked for SOE in an administrative capacity towards the end of the war ... so I asked Paul to write and get Colonel Gaynor to trace some facts on you.'

'My God, *you didn't!*'

When she glanced up it was to discover he looked deeply

shocked. 'When you told us what David's ordeal would have done to him, you spoke from experience of your agony in that mountain hut, didn't you, Leo?'

He was quiet for so long as he gazed into the fire, Vesta thought he was refusing to answer. Then he murmured, 'Those secrets we were once expected to give our all for are now being spilled with ease.'

'I'm sorry, so dreadfully sorry,' she said in a mere whisper. 'It's no worse than you probing David's hidden years, is it?'

Shock still appeared to govern him, as he asked, 'They accused me of being a traitor, did you know that?' At her nod, he continued. 'What happened in that hut will be with me for the rest of my life, as it will be with everyone who suffered in the same way, but we had been trained to expect torture if we were caught. The fear was constantly with us. When it follows false accusations and internment by your own people, who then, in order to see whether or not they're right, trick you into undergoing agony almost to death to protect worthless plans, there's no way you can go on living as before. I lost faith in God, in my fellow men, in everything. I saw no future; *wanted* no future.

'Then I was given the task of inspecting property which had been commandeered, and became interested in country houses. When I was told to come here, I realized it was the house of a man I had known and respected. A man who died under tragic circumstances. I was keen to see Tarrant Hall. When I did I knew I had been given my one chance to be human again, and I went all out for it.'

He paused momentarily, watching Vesta closely. 'I *did* regret unwittingly betraying the truth about your father's death and David's involvement in it, but it gave me my perfect opportunity. I admired what your mother was doing here and I could see she was lonely and suffering greatly from the penalties of being an agate among diamonds, so I exploited those weaknesses. Before I could return, the big freeze set in, so I set about performing my rescue act. You're right, it *was* ludicrous. A trick to win over an unhappy, gullible widow. I would never have done it if I hadn't decided I wanted to live in this house more than anything in the world. I saw Tarrant Hall as my haven, and worked hard to enter it.'

As Vesta sat rooted to the spot, Leo walked across to her. 'I don't love Marion, but I'm fond enough of her to make her believe I do. I happen to think you've all been thoughtlessly unkind to her and are mainly responsible for her sense of inferiority, so I try to bolster her self-esteem. I'll defend her against anyone who tries to hurt her, and I'll be loyal because being here has given me something to live for. I know it's all legally David's. I've no designs on *stealing* anything from you. I just need to borrow it; to be able to live in this splendid old house overlooking peaceful hills for as long as I'm able. In return, I give Marion what she never had from your father. I believe that's a fair bargain, don't you?'

It was Vesta's turn to be shocked, not so much by his admission but by his decision to make it. Why? She had been eating out of his hand. 'What's made you choose to tell me all this?' she demanded shakily.

He took the empty goblet from her hand and went with his own to the large silver punch-bowl to refill them. He returned to hand her one, then sat on a nearby chair. 'When you swept in from Salisbury that day you threatened all my hopes, my one chance of survival. I had to play on your mother's sympathy to strengthen my defence. When I learnt you'd gone to Germany, I couldn't believe my luck, so my heart sank when Marion said you were arriving at any minute. I was prepared for hostility, but was greeted with acceptance; a brand of puzzling friendship almost smacking of admiration. It didn't make sense, but it has allowed me to get to know you a little. I see a very lonely young woman who has learnt in the school of experience to be shrewd and resourceful. You have fought with the rest of us, and have mixed with other nationalities and all ranks of society. You've achieved artistic success in an unusual medium. In other words, a person to be reckoned with. Why, then, should such a person have swung from one extreme to the other for no apparent reason, I wondered?'

He drank some wine, leaving that question in the air a while as he watched her closely. Then he said, 'What you've told me tonight has given me the possible answer. I suspect, Vesta Sheridan, that you are an incurable hero-worshipper. First it was your father, then a gallant brother. Brad Holland's personal daring and outspoken journalism made him a candidate, without question. Paul Gaynor must have touched the right chord somewhere. When his father tells you of one small fraction of my life, *I'm* suddenly on the list.' He shook his head. 'I can't tell you what to do about the others, but you must cross me off. I've just revealed why you should.'

This was far too much like the cynical challenging superiority of a man from whom she could not entirely shake free. It spelled danger, so Vesta reacted as she always did to Brad. Sipping her wine coolly, she said, 'Congratulations! You've worked hard for what you've got. I won't rat on you, but I'll be interested to see what happens when David comes home . . . which he will.'

Leo eventually gave a rueful smile. 'You're quite a girl! Don't worry about me. I live one day at a time and feel thankful for it. You're the one who needs to think of the future.'

CHAPTER SEVENTEEN

FOR David this time of year had once meant carol-singers from the village, church on Christmas Eve, mulled wine and mince pies in the early hours, laughter, kisses under the mistletoe, extravagant presents, a great deal to drink, family warmth and dinner with the Chandlers. Since those days he had celebrated in a number of different places, with all manner of people and in a variety of moods. This Christmas of 1948 would be spent flying to and from Berlin if an aircraft could conceivably be taken off the ground.

The start of his forty-eight-hour stand-down period saw him in a jeep, whose driver promised to drop him just a mile from the village where he intended to stay with those he had come to regard as his second family. In his bag were gifts wrapped in coloured paper, along with food and chocolate from the NAAFI. When on leave, or the brief stand-down periods, aircrew either slept, got drunk, or found a woman in Lübeck. David knew he must be the only one going off to celebrate an early Christmas with a family, and a girl who occupied a special place in his life. They must all envy him.

It was bitterly cold, but he knew Sonja's house would be warm and welcoming so he walked briskly after the driver said that was as far off course as he would go. The pine forest on each side of the road smelled good but reminded him of his days in Scotland. That period of self-isolation resembled a dark grey area from which he had now escaped because of Monika. Kershaw's brutal onslaught continued to diminish him whenever he remembered that night, but he no longer felt unclean or unable to indulge his own desires. In time, he knew he would fully conquer the sense of shame and anger.

As for the Chinese twins whom he had given, along with his watch, gold pen, a signet ring and several hundred dollars, to a toothless seaman bound for some unknown destination, their identical smiles now rarely haunted him. Monika had asked what else he could have done, and he had been asking the same question ever since. The villagers who had thrust them at him would not have taken them back, and he could not possibly have installed them at Tarrant Hall to be hated by him and his mother, cold-shouldered by the villagers and isolated within a race and creed so far removed from those of everyone around them.

Monika had been right to say they were better off with their own people and he with his. He now questioned whether they had actually been his children. No one from that jungle village had tried to trace him as their legal father so, if he had not turned up out of the blue, the twins would have spent their days among the pigs and chickens unaware that he was still alive. David was inclined to the opinion that he might have been seen as a means of ridding a poor community of two extra female mouths to feed. The Chinese were great believers in Providence solving problems. He would never be certain, of course, whether or not he had fathered those two, but he now accepted that they had been victims of machinations which had had no possible fairy-tale ending.

Monika had been watching for his arrival and ran out from the house the moment she saw him coming along the grassy track. She arrived before him breathless. 'Every time we say goodbye I think perhaps we will never say hallo.'

'Then you're very foolish,' he told her roughly, putting an arm around her as they walked up to the house. 'You should know by now I have nine lives.'

'Some have already been used, *Liebchen*. I will not let myself think how many.'

'Look my girl, if I'm going to die it won't be at the controls of a Dak, but as a passenger in your car. When we go back to the airfield tomorrow evening, *I'll* drive.'

She chuckled. 'I think in English you are called a scared cat, is that right?'

He hugged her tighter. 'I'll tell you tonight what to call me.'

She glanced up at him, her eyes glowing. 'Miri is having a short sleep and Sonja is working and cannot be disturbed, so we can love as soon as we are just inside the house.'

'I'm certainly not going to do it out here,' he told her with a grin, delighted by the news.

357

After an unusually hectic period when their hunger for each other seemed impossible to satisfy, David must have fallen asleep, because it was dark when he next remembered where he was. They dressed hurriedly and went downstairs to find mother and child playing with farmyard animals. Coffee and cake stood on a low table.

Sonja looked up with a smile, but Mirjana jumped to her feet and hurled herself at David with a shriek of pleasure. She spoke to him in German despite the two women's efforts to teach her English. What she had to say was too important to translate into another language. 'I have a little cat. Herr Stamm gave it to me. I called it David, but Mummy said it's a girl and must be Davida.' She pronounced it 'Dahveeda'. 'Will that be all right? Come and see her.' She led him to the kitchen where a white kitten lay asleep. It was ruthlessly pulled from slumber and put in his arms. 'See, she has white hair like yours. Has she been scratched in a fight like you, do you think?'

He shook his head, astonished that this child had remembered the explanation of his scars he had given her weeks ago. In truth, knowing nothing of small children, he gained enormous amusement from the revelations of a half-sister young enough to be his own child. 'I think Davida is too small to have been scratched in a fight, don't you? She needs to be loved and kept warm, so you must make her stay inside for a while. I think she is more beautiful than any little cat I have ever seen,' he added, setting the kitten back on its bed of straw, 'and I feel honoured to have her named after me.'

Mirjana found that speech amusing and chuckled as she took his hand again. 'You say funny things sometimes. Now I must show you our tree for Saint Nikolaus. It was quite a surprise. When I went to sleep last night it wasn't there, but this morning it was. Have you ever seen one?'

'Certainly I have,' he said, returning to the main room in a state of lethargic happiness. 'We have them in England, too.'

'Good. Everyone should have them, don't you think? But not more beautiful than ours.'

'Oh, no. That would be very unfair of everyone.'

Mirjana chuckled again then stopped and indicated, with a thrown out hand, the decorated fir tree. It was small and topped with a silver star, but what made it exceptionally attractive were ornaments of frosted glass individually etched with designs of animals and birds, which hung amidst tiny white candles standing on circles of holly. These Christmas ornaments must be the most valuable he had ever seen, he reflected.

'My father would be utterly charmed by this,' he murmured.

'And you?' asked Sonja.

He turned to her. 'I might never have known about it, about Miri and Monika, if the Russians hadn't decided to blockade Berlin. It seems wrong to thank the Lord they did, but I do. I think Father would feel the same.'

'Come and have some Stollen,' she insisted, her eyes bright with fondness. 'I would like to boast that we made it, but I am no cook and Monika has other things to do. Frau Stamm sent it when we were given the kitten.'

David sat close beside Monika, wanting to feel her body touching his. He was always the same after lovemaking; loath to be apart from her. 'At Tarrant Hall there's a considerable collection of your work. Did you know?'

'Yes, he told me.' They spoke in English, but Mirjana was too intent on her cake to worry. She had had her moment.

'You're working on something now?'

'I finished it an hour ago. It's for you, my dear, and, therefore, for him.' Sonja took from the floor beside her chair a plain box. 'We shall not have you here on Christmas morning so you must be given it now.'

Inside the box on a bed of straw lay a goblet of finest glass. On it was an oval frame surrounding an engraving of a house standing between trees. As David recognized it a lump formed in his throat.

'Chris was strangely disturbed when I once told him I had visited Tarrant Royal,' Sonja told him quietly. 'I thought at first that he had resented what I had done, but he was upset because he had not been there to see it with me. I made a sketch of his home, meaning to use it one day for him. I give it to you, instead.'

Overcome by the gift and her motive for making it, David could only say, 'You should be in Paris using your magnificent talent to the full. I shall add this to his collection. "Thank you" seems inadequate, somehow.'

Mirjana had finished her cake, and understood the giving of presents in any language. She went to take from beside the tree an oblong wooden box of typical Germanic style painted with flowers, and gave it to David. '*Herzliche Weihnachten!*' she chanted with a smile, and curtsied like a true European before standing, eyes wide with anticipation of his reaction to what was inside.

David made a great business of opening the box, enjoying the child's expression. Inside was a miniature scene made with tiny pebbles, straw, feathers and coloured paper – the kind of artwork children did in kindergarten. The underside of the lid bore his name painted in uneven capitals.

'Well, now,' he said in German, 'I think I must be the most fortunate brother in the world to be given such a beautiful present, as well as having a kitten named after me.' He stood up and bowed. 'Will you dance with me at the ball tonight, Miss Mirjana?'

The little girl burst into laughter and nodded, pleased with a response which was all she had hoped for. David then fetched his bag and took from it several packages for her. His own sense of anticipation as she tore off the wrappings was equally high and equally satisfied. A clown puppet, a tiny fur monkey, some colouring pencils, a striped ball and, causing most excitement of all, a book with a cut-out doll on the cover and sets of clothes that could be fastened on to her with foldover tabs. A woman in the NAAFI had told David *all* little girls loved that sort of thing. Mirjana's expression told him she was right.

He gave Sonja a silk scarf and some perfume, knowing the gift in no way compared with hers, but he also had with him coffee, chocolate, jam, biscuits, flour and some dried fruit, all of which were highly prized by her. Finally, he gave Monika two parcels he would rather have handed over when they were alone. One contained a bright red cashmere sweater, and the other a nightgown and negligee in apricot silk trimmed with swansdown. He had bought both at highly inflated prices from an American pilot taking orders last month during the twenty-minute turn-around time at Gatow. David did not know or care where the stuff had come from, and neither had other British aircrew eager to get hold of luxury items their womenfolk had not seen for years.

Monika tried hard to be enthusiastic, but David knew she did not feel the way he hoped and was deeply disappointed. Her simple gifts to him of a cowhide stud box and a thick blue scarf knitted by a woman in the village somehow made his seem over elaborate.

He could do nothing until they went to bed tonight, so he tried, as she did, to enter into the spirit of the season and enjoy the meal of thick soup, roast goose and a dessert made with the ground almonds, apricots and tinned cream he had brought on his last visit in answer to their request. After the meal Sonja lit the tiny candles on the tree, and the frosted glass baubles which would have fetched a tidy sum in Harrods then glittered and twinkled enchantingly. Mirjana went to bed full of happiness. When David followed to tuck her in, she had the cut-out doll wearing a yellow hat and coat standing beside her bed, and she extracted a promise from him to cut out the other outfits in the morning. As he kissed her goodnight he had the notion that his father was smiling on them both.

It was a clear, cold night so the constant roar of aircraft disturbed the silence more than usual. Because of the season and, perhaps, in an effort partially to drown the reminder that peace on earth was still a distant hope, Sonja sat to play the piano she had recently acquired. It was no more than a standard upright, but she drew magical sounds from it.

'Chris would sit quietly for half an evening when I played,' she told David between pieces. 'He loved music. Said it saved his sanity. I believed him. He was quite passionate in his support of international concerts, because he felt that music was a great peacemaker.'

David shook his head. 'That was another of his idealistic theories, I'm afraid. Some of the most violent men in history have loved music.'

'Some of the most violent have written it,' she replied. 'But we must all maintain our ideals or there would be no sense in what we do. What are yours, David?'

He was nonplussed. 'I haven't any.'

'What will you do when the airlift ends, as it must?'

'That depends on *why* it ends. If the Russians attack, I might soon be flying bombers in another war. Ideals will then be useless.'

'They will not attack,' put in Monika, who had not spoken for some time. 'They are afraid of the atom bomb. It is that they hope you grow tired and stop the *Luftbrücke*. They do not want war; they want to march in and take. That is their way. They think winter will stop you. They think the people of Berlin will not survive the cold, the starvation, and will then say they wish to be Russian. They will not attack, I tell you. They are waiting. This I know.'

David grew immediately angry. 'You have been over there again, haven't you?'

'Yes. But not many times a day like you,' she returned.

'What I do is open and above board. It's also governed by a code of international law. What you're doing is dangerous and punishable by long imprisonment or death. Monika, *when* are you going to listen to me, and give this dangerous business up?'

'I listen,' she told him.

'But you still continue!'

'Of course. I shall go again tomorrow night.'

He gazed at her. Monika, wearing a dark green jumper and homespun skirt, was curled up in a rocking chair challenging him with every inch of the body she gave to him so freely, and David knew why she had not appreciated his gifts. This slender young creature was no glamour girl. She was a fighter. Recognizing the inevitable, he nevertheless found it unacceptable.

'What if I asked you not to?'

'I still will go.'

'But it's Christmas Eve,' he protested hotly.

'You will fly there on Christmas Day. Never have I asked *you* not to go.'

'I've already given you the reasons why what I'm doing is acceptable and yours is not. You could be *shot* if you're caught!'

'You could crash and die. Some already have.'

She was impossible in this mood. Knowing misplaced admiration for what he had done in the past was partly responsible for it made him feel even more impotent. He appealed to Sonja. 'Can't *you* stop her?'

She studied him for a moment, her classic features and

362

titian hair enhanced by the lights on the Christmas tree, making it hard for him to think of her as the Free French agent 'Mirjana' who had operated in occupied territory for more than four years. 'You don't really mean to ask that question of me, David.' She got up from the piano stool and walked to the side table. 'I cannot leave you two angry with each other. We shall have some more of the wine you brought us, and speak of other things. Tell us how you spend Christmas in that lovely house on a hill, my dear.'

They drank by the low light from the decorated tree, and Monika moved to sit within the circle of David's arm on the settee while he described the festive season in his home. As the level of the bottle grew lower, and the two women sat quietly listening, he travelled back to the place he was speaking of and, for a while, forgot that he was in the heart of a German village just a mile or two from the urgent activity he must soon return to.

When they eventually blew out the little candles and went upstairs, reminiscence had diluted David's anger but left him nostalgic for a time when fear had been a stranger. He did not immediately undress, but stood looking from the window at a cold moon silvering the sky. For once, this did not remind him that on nights such as this his squadron had operated between England's south coast and occupied territory; his thoughts were still in that house on a hill from the windows of which he had so often seen the moon gleaming from a cold yuletide sky. He should have written to his mother for Christmas. It was the time for reaching out, for making amends. Perhaps he would write a quick note when he got back tomorrow. She would get it in time for New Year. Nineteen forty-nine. The last year of a decade which had snatched up the world, tossed it around, then let it fall higgledy-piggledy. Would these next twelve months see it all back in place, or in even worse confusion?

Arms slid around him and Monika's body pressed against his back. 'You have gone from me. Come back, David.'

He turned to find her wearing the silk lingerie he had given her. He touched her long, dark hair with caressing fingers. 'Take them off. I should never have given them to you. They're only for floosies.'

Her eyes were troubled as she gazed at him in the darkness flooded by moonlight. 'But this is what you like?'

'I *used* to like.'

He thought he meant what he said, but the act of slipping the soft silk from her body to drop in a fluid heap around her ankles nevertheless gave him erotic pleasure. When he began to kiss her shoulders she stopped him and walked away to pick up the coverlet for warmth. He followed in some concern. 'It's all gone wrong this evening, hasn't it? Those damned unsuitable presents! I could see you were upset.' He sat beside her on the bed. 'It *is* that, isn't it?'

She spoke without looking at him. 'I think you are very much like your father. He was with Sonja for three years and was so happy. Then he found she was an agent, and became very angry. He could love her when he did not know the truth. Afterwards, it was not the same. He said she must stop it; it is too dangerous. She could not. There is a need to hit back.' She glanced his way then. 'You know this. You understand. You can do it and it is all right, but I cannot. Sir Christopher could do it, but Sonja could not.' As he made to reach for her, she stood up and walked away clutching the coverlet around her. 'These things you have given me, all you have said just now about your home and family, I see that this is what you really need, David.'

'No, you're wrong.' He got to his feet in protest, yet a tiny part of his mind could not go along with it.

She turned to regard him across the moonwashed room. 'We are the same now because we have had violence – you so much more than me – and we now are together in this drama over Berlin. We give each other comfort, and it is very good, very wonderful. But it is for different reasons.'

He went to her. 'Monika, please . . .'

'Listen, David. I wish you to listen.'

He stood not touching her. 'All right, so long as it clears up the problem.'

'The problem is that I love for what you are . . . but you love for what you would like me to be. I am not that. I cannot be that.'

He sighed. 'I knew as soon as you saw those things that I'd been a bloody idiot to give them to you.'

'Not idiot, just a man who likes such things. Your father was in love with Sonja Koltay, a very beautiful person who makes very beautiful things. Sonja tells me this many times. She is what he needs when his life is bad and full of . . . how you say, *die Qual*?'

'Anguish.'

'When he finds she is doing this same dangerous, ugly work it spoils everything. He tries to stop it and have only the lovely part. But she is also "Mirjana" the agent. Because he cannot stop her he thinks to help. And he is killed for it.'

Knowing that what she was saying was true where his father was concerned, David nevertheless defended himself and tried to lighten the situation. 'I'm not planning to go to Russia with you tomorrow night. I'll be too busy flying coal to Berlin. My famous uncle apparently wore a silk scarf which popular fiction turned into the nightgown of a countess he had charmed.' He tried a light laugh. 'Maybe I should wear that thing on the floor around *my* neck.'

It failed to work. 'I think you should give it to that girl at home in your charming village. When you spoke of it I saw that is where you belong, *Liebchen*.'

Dismayed by her reference to someone he had resolutely thrust from his life, feeling unworthy of her, David tried to recapture something fast slipping away from him. 'This is where I belong,' he murmured against her soft mouth, pushing away visions of a girl with silver green eyes. 'I'll soon convince you I'm right.'

'You are *wrong*,' she insisted softly. 'When the *Luftbrücke* ends, you will be sent home where your family waits. I have no family, just Sonja and Miri, and I shall do what I do for as long as they ask. Love me for that, David. Just for that.'

He was unable to love her that night for any reason. The mood had been broken and his passion of the afternoon could not be revived. This failure, together with the troubling issues she had raised, kept him awake long after she slept. He left earlier than planned after a day during which he felt guilty, unhappy and uncertain. Even Mirjana's childlike charm failed to lift his spirits, and neither Monika nor Sonja attempted to jolly him out of his introspection. They were wise women.

After driving Sonja's car to the airfield, he turned to Monika. 'When will you get back?'

She shook her head. 'I will let you know with a letter.'

'May I come again then?'

'Yes, oh yes! David, you are *very* important to me.' She seemed distressed. 'I spoke about your father. Sonja also tells me she would say to him: Think of now, not for ever. I say this same to you. It is still now, *Liebchen*.'

The guard at the gate was very interested in what followed, but it was restricted due to lack of space and David soon untangled himself from Monika and the wheel then scrambled from the car. He did not dare to tell her to watch her step and refrain from doing anything risky. It was essential, he felt, to feign cool acceptance of her work. She, on the other hand, managed it more naturally.

Leaning from the car, she called out, 'Take great care of yourself.'

'That's why *I* did the driving,' he returned with a grin, assuming a lighthearted manner.

When he flew to Gatow in the early hours of Christmas morning, he was not thinking of the usual ritual at home but of a young girl who had spurned the expensive clothes most would adore. She would now be somewhere in the dark, freezing forest preparing to cross into the Soviet-held territory he was presently overflying. He worried about that all the way to Berlin and spoke only to Ground Control and his crew when passing on information. No one cared. They were all tired and fed-up anyway. What a way to spend Christmas Day!

When David landed, one of the Dakota's threadbare tyres blew and he ended up doing the Skaters' Waltz over the snow-covered airfield once more. When they finally came to a halt they were blocking the take-off runway and had to be towed free of it. As he climbed from the cockpit, numb with cold and heavy-hearted, he muttered, 'There's another of my nine lives gone.'

His weary brain could not assess how many he had left.

On New Year's Eve trouble sprang up in Tarrant Royal. It had been threatening for some time and came to a head when a group of the 'prefabbers', as they were called in the village, wandered into the George and Dragon to celebrate the arrival of 1949. The village pub was a second home to Royal stalwarts and they resented this intrusion from virtual foreigners on the night they held the last darts match of the year to decide on their new champion. The prefab dwellers had so far used the Black Ram, an inn several miles along the road to Greater Tarrant, which had few regulars but picked up passing trade because it had rooms enough to do bed and breakfast. The Ram was nearer the chalet-type houses, and the landlord had his eye to the best chance by making the new residents welcome there.

On December 31 a family of them had booked a wedding reception at the Ram, so normal revellers were crowded out of the two bars. They piled into cars and moved on, some into Greater Tarrant, some in the opposite direction. The trouble began with a few loud derogatory comments about the teams; then, as beer flowed, the intruders began to distract players about to throw their darts. Inebriated tomfoolery turned into nastiness when the landlord refused to serve the ringleader. These men had recently been through a war, which had trained them to be tough and aggressive; they were contemptuous of those who set great store by insignificant little rituals. They set about showing the 'dumb old yokels' what was what. They clean forgot that many of these farmhands had also been through the war. Some had been through two. They *really* knew what was what.

Sergeant Medley and Constable Hall had to be called from their family parties, and the Black Maria was fetched from Greater Tarrant to take the troublemakers to the three small cells for the night. The greatest mistake of the night, however, was for Sergeant Medley to lock up the prefab rowdies and merely send home those from the village. The George and Dragon closed in order to sweep up and count the cost.

Another war started after that night. It began in subtle ways and progressed to overturning display racks outside the village shop, and leaving tractors to block lanes leading from the new, hated community so that cars could not pass. The Rector tried, Sergeant Medley tried, the Parish Council tried to put a stop to it, but the participants did not want to stop. A general meeting was held in the Church Hall. Half a dozen people turned up, and they only went for the tea and biscuits at the conclusion. When chickens and ducks began disappearing, three of the prefabbers' worst hooligans were picked up by Constable Hall as they left school and taken to the station for questioning. Their parents were charged with disorderly behaviour after they stormed in and demanded their boys' release. When the culprit was revealed to be a fox – the most obvious thief, of course – it put a match to the tinder. In the third week of January, the George and Dragon was set alight in the early hours. This act of arson, which could have claimed lives, shocked everyone involved in the feud. It had now gone too far.

Marion was deeply upset by what was going on. Her village had picked itself up after the Great War, and continued as before. It had resisted those who preached modernization, and cherished the old traditions. Families had farmed there for several generations. They were peaceful folk, on the whole. She knew them all. Since this latest war ended the face of Tarrant Royal had begun to alter. Jeeps were everywhere. A plodding horse and cart were rarely seen now, although the ploughing competition survived along with other long-standing traditions. Certainly, many of the village sons had deserted for the dubious excitement of cities, but the old families remained. The burning of the George and Dragon was comparable to the German bomber crashing into the church, so far as Marion was concerned. The George was just as much a hub of village life. For someone to attempt to destroy it was sacrilege.

Unreasonably, Marion linked all those things with Vesta's return. Nothing had been the same since that day. Leo was different in a way that she could not put her finger on. The girl herself had become moody and uncommunicative, spending most of her time riding on Longbarrow Hill or shut up in her studio. Whether or not she was actually painting anything was debatable. Marion was convinced there was still something going on between Vesta and Leo, although it had altered. Vesta now treated him in a cool, businesslike manner which appeared to amuse him. It was as if they were conducting a private contest of wills which was beyond Marion's comprehension.

The black shadow of David's ordeal in the Far East still darkened Marion's days, and the bills kept coming in. Now there was a sinister force at work in the village she had loved all her days. Day after day she longed for the peace she had shared with the man she loved before Vesta had telephoned from Waterloo Station. The headaches were becoming more frequent, she had a constant pain in her chest, and she was not sleeping well. Leo eventually suggested that she should see the doctor.

'You can't continue as you are,' he pointed out over break-fast. 'Three days last week you stayed on your feet through sheer determination, but it will take its toll. You're looking tired and washed out.'

'You mean *old*,' she snapped. 'Why don't you say so?'

He put down his coffee cup. 'I mean tired and washed out. Don't put words into my mouth.'

'Sorry.' She played with her spoon. 'I shouldn't take it out on you.'

'Take *what* out?' he probed. 'Look, I realize I miscalculated when telling you about David, but there's something else behind all this, isn't there?'

He looked so solid and dependable across the small, intimate breakfast table, so attractive in the cream pullover she had given him for Christmas, she found herself confiding in him. 'I wish we were alone again. Everything was wonderful then.'

'Yes, it was. It will be again when you've seen the doctor.'

She regretted her words as soon as she had uttered them: 'A few pills won't make Vesta marry Paul Gaynor and go back to Germany.'

'I see. *That's* the problem, is it?'

'Don't you think so?'

'She's not happy, that's obvious. I shouldn't bank too much on her marrying Paul, if I were you.'

'Oh?' Her voice rose more sharply than expected. 'You seem to know more about my daughter than I.'

'I probably do,' was his calm response. 'The Sheridans are a fascinating family to the eyes of an outsider who sees things they can't because of their closeness. I've also assessed many of your words, and Vesta's, then added that to what the world knows of you all, and come up with a conclusion I believe Bill Chandler would echo.'

Marion was further irritated. 'I much preferred it when you

concentrated on me and our life together. I don't want an analysis of the Sheridan family. I had enough of that clever talk from Chris.'

'All right,' he agreed amiably. 'I'll go back to concentrating on you and suggesting you see the doctor. *You* were the one who fobbed me off and introduced Vesta into the conversation.'

'I can't imagine how I got through those years before you arrived on the scene. Remember how I came in soaked, not expecting you until the next day?'

He smiled. 'I've never known a woman smarten up as fast as you did.'

She smiled back. 'You made quite an impact at first sight. That's why.'

'So did you,' he returned with a laugh. 'Lady Sheridan of Tarrant Hall looking like a drowned rat.'

'I love you, Leo,' she said with a curious lump in her throat.

'So will you see the doctor?'

She nodded. 'It's all this business in the village that's upsetting me. Where will it end?'

'I think it has.' He resumed eating his breakfast. 'That attack on the George and Dragon will have brought everyone to their senses. Such a pity. It was a lovely old inn. The way things are going we shall have to hang on to our old buildings tooth and claw, because the wind of change will bring a new era. So much of this country has to be rebuilt – great chunks of cities, in many cases – and it'll be done quickly and cheaply. Architecture will adapt, and I fear it'll never again produce the beauty of line and colour our ancestors enjoyed. This house, for instance.'

'You love it, don't you?'

'As much as you do.'

'What will happen when David comes home?'

He glanced up swiftly from cutting his bacon. 'That's an unnecessary worry, my dear. Get the doctor to sort out the ones you presently have, and leave future ones *to* the future.'

'My father was once the village doctor, and I his receptionist,' Marion told the young man opposite her. He had become a naval surgeon as soon as he qualified, and the job at the Cottage Hospital was his first civilian post. He had yet to get used to dealing with middle-aged women who regarded him as a callow youth. They made him nervous. He was a good doctor and knew what he was talking about, but these kinds of county ladies made him behave as if he did not, and this one was on the hospital board.

'Oh, yes?' he replied pleasantly.

'So I know what it is that you've just put into medical jargon. Please don't try to pull the wool over my eyes and pretend it's no more than menopausal symptoms.'

He fidgeted with the papers on his desk; the results of Marion's tests performed the week before. 'Medicine has changed, become more updated, Mrs Roberts.'

'Heart conditions haven't.'

His fair skin turned slightly pink. 'No. No, you're right. Um, they haven't.'

'How bad is it?'

'Well, it depends . . .'

'The truth, please.'

He ran a hand over his bright ginger hair and leaned back in his chair, abandoning his conciliatory attitude. 'It's quite serious. Your blood pressure is high so I'm surprised you have been as well as you have, but the count could have increased only recently due to the worries you mentioned to Dr Craig. We can bring that down to a more satisfactory level for you, and give you a couple of additional drugs which will ease your symptoms, but . . . the rest is up to you. You must take life easier, cut down on your responsibilities, try not to let things get on top of you.' He gave a forced smile. 'Worry never solves anything, you know.'

'Well, we all live and learn,' she said dryly to this man half her age.

His faint blush became more pronounced. 'I . . . I understand you've recently married. It's probably not necessary for me to say this but . . . um . . . you shouldn't indulge in too much . . . ah . . .'

'You'll have to get used to putting things into words, Dr Waters,' she said quietly. 'Farming communities might not be highly sophisticated but they're very, very familiar with the basics of behaviour. If you um and ah too much they'll never catch on to what you're trying to tell them. Speak to them as you did to sailors and you'll be all right.' Getting to her feet, Marion asked the vital question. 'How long have I got?'

He shook his head as he stood. 'It's not a question of time, Mrs Roberts, but commonsense. That heart of yours can cope with a good number of years yet. How many rests in *your* hands. This medication will control the problem, providing you are sensible and make considerable changes to your life. If you overwork that poor old ticker, it's going to go on strike.'

She managed a smile. 'That's better, Doctor. You're now calling a spade a spade. Thank you for your advice.'

'The best medicine would be a long holiday. When did you last take one?'

'When I was twenty-five.' She left before her courage failed.

The brave act she had put on for someone more used to treating war wounds, shell shock and VD deserted her once she sat in her car. She had all along believed they were menopausal symptoms, but would not say as much to Leo because it suggested ageing. She was very aware that he was four years younger than her and in the peak of condition. The news had shocked her, but she thought she had hidden it well. Now there was no need for that and she found that her hands were shaking. She would like a cup of tea, but the prospect of going to the Punch and Judy Tea Rooms where there were bound to be people she knew was too daunting.

When she felt able to start the car she headed for the lane which led up to and along Longbarrow Hill. She would rather have taken her mare up there, but that would mean going home first and she could not face Leo yet. It was very blustery and she was not dressed for country walking, yet she left the car and made her way across the turf to where the old hangars still stood. She held her fur coat across her body with her arms as she walked into the wind; her hair was blown into tangled strands around a face that felt stiff and set.

This hill had played such a great part in her life. She had ridden here with Chris in the early days after that first terrible war, when they were both barely into their twenties and trying to create something good out of all that had happened to them. They probably had. Yes, of course they had. Later,

David and Vesta had ridden with them along these well-worn tracks, on ponies that grew in size with the children. Various dogs had joined in the fun.

As Chris became more in demand and increasingly lured away by issues as dear to him as his life, Marion had still come up here whenever she could. Vesta had preferred to dream and draw indoors, but David had loved chasing along here with her until they were both laughing and rosy-cheeked. So like Chris had been as a youth, David had become as vital to her as breathing. He had adored her in return.

Marion walked on seeing little of that cold, early February day as she returned to other times. David's squadron had landed here during an emergency – what had remained of his squadron. Spitfires had dropped down from an autumn sky to run along this ancient turf and come to rest beside the little clubhouse, which had been knocked down to make room for runways, hangars and huts. Half their doors were now hanging on one hinge, and most of the windows had been smashed by boys with slings and stones. So many young men at Tarrant Hall had used this hill for deadly purposes, and for lighthearted courting. Pat Chandler must have been kissed up here a good many times, but never Vesta. She had been in the desert painting. Or driving around Italy with a married American. Had she really conducted a sexual affair with him, as Leo suggested? She did not know her daughter well enough to be certain she had not.

It had been after a canter along here that she had first encountered Leo, Marion mused. After so many solitary excursions in sight of those distant hills, she then had a companion. A *beloved* companion. Leo was not an expert rider, but he enjoyed bringing a gelding up to canter with the wind in his hair and the valley at his feet. Marion halted and gazed around with a renewed sense of shock. Not to ride up here would be unthinkable. Not to race until she was breathless would be a severe penalty.

She began to evaluate the others. Resign from the board of the Cottage Hospital, give up the presidency of the gymkhana committee, abandon the demands of the Church Fellowship, discontinue the weekly visits to the Dorchester Alms Houses. There were other local women who could do that. She must never walk up to her home from the village – too big a strain on her heart. Restrict the number of times she went up and down the many stairs at Tarrant Hall. Put an end to vigorous hoeing and weeding in the rose garden. She must employ a secretary, a perky girl with too much lipstick who would say 'OK' to everything. Expenditure would have to be curbed to prevent worrying bills; Leo, the children and her friends must keep from her any news which might upset her. Life must be smooth and untroubled. A nap every afternoon; feet up on a stool all evening. Fewer glasses of wine, nothing fatty or covered in cream, no boxes of chocolates. Separate beds . . .

Agitation set Marion walking again. Was she going too fast; being too energetic? Did it really matter? Time passed and she came to a halt in the lee of some brambles. Anyone driving along the top lane would see a mad old biddy wandering alone in an expensive fur coat. She gave a shaky laugh as she thought that was what she would eventually become, if the ginger-haired doctor had his way.

That led her to memories of Laura and her flame-coloured hair – passionate, vital, so in love with Rex she was terrified of becoming one of the sad creatures who studied the casualty lists each morning. Laura – beautiful, talented, keeping morale up by singing and dancing to show she defied fate to take away the husband whose exploits in the air thrilled and encouraged a nation. Fate had taken pity on them and neither had felt the loss of the other. Death had been instantaneous for them both. So young, and yet they had dazzled during their brief lives.

Roland had been lost only a year before. Quiet, moral, devoted to the English way of life, he had been killed by a mine while trying to rescue a battle-crazed horse. Only twenty-six, he had left to those who survived a book of letters from the trenches, which had been hailed as a brilliant testament for peace. Chris had done more than any of them; he had made his mark in so many different spheres. His work would be valued for years to come. Marion now knew he had been shot in France; had died a hero's death. Swiftly. Aged forty-eight. Four Sheridans, the afterglow of whose brilliance would remain for ever, each of them gone in an instant.

What of the woman who had borne their name but never

really earned it? Was she going to die very, very slowly, becoming a careful invalid who was a burden on all those around her so that a great sigh of relief was felt when she finally expired? Was she going to give up those few things she had accomplished with her life in order to prolong it for as many years as possible? Was she going to abandon true happiness now she had found it and become a slave to pills? Was she going to sacrifice her one chance to show gratitude for sharing the lives of those others who had done so much? David and Vesta had already more than earned their place in this talented family. Was she going to shrivel carefully into old age without even trying to?

When she reached the Hall it was beginning to grow dark. Dusk came early in February. Leo walked through from the rear of the house, with tousled hair and a cloth in his hand. 'Hallo. You've been so long I was about to send out a search party.'

'I encountered the Rector. He's so difficult to get away from. What have you been doing?'

He grinned. 'Trying my hand at French polishing. They charged so much for that three-legged table, I thought I'd save us a few bob by doing the escritoire myself. I'm rather enjoying it.' He looked at her keenly. 'What did he say?'

'Oh, everything's fine.' She smiled. 'It's just the penalties of being a woman, which a few pills will sort out.'

'Splendid! Aren't you glad that I bullied you to go?' He slung an arm across her shoulders. 'Let's have tea. Robson has been hovering ever since four o'clock.'

Marion turned to face him. 'I was rather nervous about going today. After tea I'd like to celebrate with you . . . upstairs.'

'Good Lord! Do you mean what I think you mean?'

'Would you rather not?' she asked anxiously.

His look of surprise faded into one of amusement. 'Ask any man whether he'd rather do French polishing or that, and it's a safe bet the furniture will stay dull.'

It was the first time they had made love on impulse. Where they usually fell asleep afterwards, the early hour meant they simply lay lethargically in each other's arms.

'We must do this more often,' Leo murmured with a contented sigh. 'If it's the result of one of the penalties of being a woman, I'd say it's a very attractive penalty.'

'As long as you're happy.'

He kissed her temple. 'You make me happier than I deserve to be, you know that ... and now you've sorted out the problem, you'll be able to enjoy everything again. That's what you wanted, isn't it?'

After a moment or two, Marion said, 'I've been thinking about the trouble between our villagers and the new people. Perhaps the partial destruction of the George *has* brought it to an end, but there's nothing to prevent it from starting up again over some future grievance, is there?'

'I suppose not.'

'The real problem is that the villagers regard everything here as theirs, and resent outsiders elbowing their way in. But there's nothing else for the prefabbers, is there?'

'There will be, in time, I suppose. Trouble is there are far greater priorities, and the government is broke.'

She turned in his arms, loving the sensation of his hard strength beside her. 'We can't afford to wait. Half the village may have been burned down by the time something is done, so I've decided to do it myself.'

Leo raised his head to glance at her face, then pulled himself into a sitting position still looking at her curiously. 'This female penalty appears to be having a very strange effect on you. What's this idea you've had?'

Marion sat up, too, pulling the bedclothes over her breasts for warmth and covering the scars on Leo's torso with them. 'I think it's essential to keep the younger people from leaving Tarrant Royal and the other villages around. The old ways will be completely lost, otherwise. Darts, cricket, the church social, the annual fête are no longer enough for men and women who've been all over the world and done so much. But those activities are the backbone of English country life, and I can't bear them to be lost. The older people maintain them and, as their children grow to middle age, *they'll* enjoy such things. We need to give them something for now, which will keep them happily occupied and away from each other's throats until they become parents themselves.'

'And how do you propose to do that?' he asked, bemused, but seriously interested in what she was saying.

'I'm going to build a clubhouse on that far meadow nearest

376

to the prefabs, and I'm going to fill it with equipment for all kinds of activities. They can have a dance every Saturday – young Terence Tait and his band can play for it – and sports tournaments. I'll get the WI to provide refreshments. We'll erect a small stage in it so they can put on plays. The village hall isn't really big enough. And you, my dear Leo, can help organize it. You used to teach so you'll know exactly how to sort out young people.'

'Hey, hey, slow down,' he said, putting a hand on her shoulder. 'Suppose you do offer that meadow, who do you think is going to build this marvellous place?'

'Frank Carter in Greater Tarrant. He was telling me several weeks ago that his two lads were talking of leaving because there's not enough work here. The prefabs have almost put them out of business. He's very upset. His great-grandfather started it, and Frank had set his heart on his sons keeping it going. This job will help. Oh, and I'll ask Bill Dwyer to do the thatching. You see,' she added enthusiastically, as she clutched the covers beneath her chin, 'I won't have an ugly building to mar the landscape. It'll be of local stone with a thatched roof. The youngsters themselves can choose how they want the interior, but the outside *has* to blend with the village.' She smiled. 'It won't offend your eye for architecture, either.'

After a moment or two during which Leo studied her in a puzzled fashion, he asked, 'How long have you been thinking about this?'

'For some time,' she lied.

'And where's the money coming from?'

'The sale of some pictures. There are half a dozen abstracts here I've never liked, nor even understood. Insurance is costly, so auctioning them will also cut down on expenses. They ought to raise enough for this project. If not, I'll select a few others.'

Looking as if he had hit a rubber wall, Leo asked, 'What about your children's inheritance?'

Marion shrugged. 'David's never shown any interest in the abstracts, and Vesta paints her own pictures. As you said, they're just assets like tractors and harvesters.'

Trying to assimilate the astonishing ideas she had put to him, her husband regarded her with a frown. 'You're proposing this because Chris would do anything to prevent what's going on in his beloved village, aren't you?'

'No, I'm not,' she said calmly. 'Chris would certainly act, there's no question of that, but he'd build a language school or set up an art gallery. He believed culture led to universal understanding and, therefore, to peace. What's really wanted is a place where the new generation who've survived the war can continue to let off steam and feel important according to their talents. That's what the Sheridan Centre will be, and it's what *I* want.'

'But you've never been a Sheridan. You've told me that so many times.'

'I was wrong. I suppose I've simply been waiting for the right time to prove it to myself.' She swallowed back tears. 'You *will* help me, Leo?'

He nodded, a slow smile dawning. 'I suppose I'll have to.' He kissed her. 'Shall we celebrate some more?'

'Yes, please,' she said. 'To hell with Robson's timetable for dinner.'

CHAPTER EIGHTEEN

'I WISH you'd put down that pail and listen to what I'm saying.'

Pat glanced up at Vesta in the barn. 'I'm working.'

'Can't you stop for ten minutes or so? I've been standing here *ages*, and I'm frozen.'

Pat grinned. 'Pick up a broom and get cracking. It'll warm you up.'

'Come on, Pat,' she urged, hugging her jacket around her shivering body. 'Let's go in for some coffee.'

Her friend surrendered but, as they walked across to the large house, said, 'When *you* work, you shut yourself away and no one's allowed to go near you for days. Fat chance of dragging you away for a coffee *any* time of the day.'

'That's different.'

'No, it isn't. Work's work no matter what form it takes. Days are short in February. We have to make the most of the light.'

'I really need to talk to you,' Vesta said, feeling the icy wind cutting her face as they hurried across an exposed section before entering the warmth of the huge kitchen.

Pat halted to take off her gumboots. 'Put the kettle on, Vee. There's some fruit cake in the tin. Cut a couple of thick wedges.'

Vesta got busy. 'The way you eat I wonder you're not eighteen stone.'

'I work it off.' She came forward in trousers and a thick Aran sweater, rosy and glowing. 'Remember how podgy I used to be when I was younger? David once said to me if I got any fatter I'd resemble a ball on legs.' She grinned. 'He used to be horrid to me then.'

'He's being pretty horrid to you now.' Vesta paused on the

379

point of cutting a second slice of cake. 'Pat . . . he had reasons for what he's done.'

'I know that, you idiot.' Her friend spooned coffee into large cups. 'No one changes so dramatically without *reasons*. I suppose it's the fact that he doesn't feel he can tell any of us – me, in particular – which hurts.'

Vesta sat at the big, square table with the cake on two plates while Pat carried the cups across. 'I wish I was like you. You find life so simple.'

The other girl put a cup in front of Vesta very forcibly. 'Do I hell.'

'Sorry,' she said with immediate sympathy. 'I know you've been waiting five years for David already . . . but you know he's the one you want and never have any doubts over it. That's really what I meant. You want David, you want to live here, you want to farm. I suppose you want children and grandchildren – all the usual things? You've never deviated from that, have you?'

Pat was already munching cake and removed a crumb from the side of her mouth with her little finger, as she said, 'I was engaged to Dirk van Reerdon, who would have returned to South Africa at the end of the war. I was very, very fond of Dirk, Vee, but whether I would have gone there to live with him I'll never know. David came back from the dead, and I then saw that I'd never be happy with anyone else.'

'He'd been through a *terrible* time,' Vesta emphasized, torn between telling her friend or taking Leo's advice to leave that option to David himself.

Pat put her cup in its saucer with a bang. 'Vee, *I* was the one who fetched him from the station. It was on *my* lap he broke down and sobbed because he found that nothing at home had changed while he had been suffering unimaginable anguish and fear.' Her lovely eyes were bright with unaccustomed anger. 'I believe you actually think I'm the village idiot because I haven't seen the world and done things you have. I read the papers, I see the newsreels at the cinema. I know what went on in the Far East. Half Daddy's patients were POWs, and young Billy Turner was captured in Burma. Every time I go in the butcher's shop I see his blank eyes and feel for him. If you haven't realized ages ago that, somewhere along the line, David was caught and tortured, you must be in another world. I've never said as much because of Aunt Marion. *She* very obviously hasn't cottoned on, but you should have done. You didn't see him when he came back. *I did* . . . and I've never forgotten how he hung on to sanity by the skin of his teeth. Life's not simple for me, as you claim, but it's uncluttered by the issues that bother you so that I see things in a more straightforward way. Farmers aren't dimwits in smocks, as many seem to think. In the course of a year we suffer the full range of life and death, success and failure, hope and fear, creation and destruction. If we have a serious failing it's that we accept it all more easily than most. At the risk of sounding priggish, nature is a comprehensive teacher.'

Vesta was upset and pushed away her cake. 'I didn't mean to be patronizing. There's no need to fly at me. I know you're *au fait* with what goes on in the world. Aunt Tessa's terribly well informed and' – she gave an emotional giggle – 'Uncle Bill's too clever by half.' She played with the spoon in her saucer. 'You're right about David. Leo found out what happened. It was pretty horrific, Pat.' Tears seriously threatened now. 'He said I should leave David to decide whether or not to tell you. Like you, I'd guessed he'd been ill-treated but shied from thinking about it too much. Mummy suspected he'd been attacked by animals.'

'He was,' said Pat, also abandoning her cake.

'When Leo told us the details she was dreadfully upset. *That's* why we cancelled the shopping spree to Bournemouth, and why she was so moody over Christmas. Leo said he'd miscalculated and shouldn't have told her.'

'I agree. He shouldn't have.'

'He thought it would help her accept his reaction to going back to Singapore.'

Pat shook her head. 'She got over that when she married Leo. He was daft to raise the issue again. I thought he had more sense. I certainly never want to be told the exact details. I couldn't bear it.' She sighed. 'It happened seven years ago, and poor David has been through even more horrors since. I think we should concentrate on being wonderful to him when he's ready to love us again, rather than get upset over something he dealt with long ago.' She bit her lip. 'He's been *so* courageous, Vee. Just like Uncle Chris. I can't wait for him to come home. From the tone of that letter he sent you before Christmas, it might not be too long before he does. If he's more like his old self I'll be able to talk to him, thrash it out in a reasonable manner.'

'You're so loyal,' Vesta said with warmth.

'I love him.' She picked up her cup and saucer. 'This coffee's lukewarm. I'll make some more.'

While Pat set about making fresh drinks for them both, Vesta said, 'He wrote to Mummy just after Christmas. A chummy letter hoping she was well and wishing her and Leo a happy new year.'

Pat glanced round. 'She didn't say anything to us.'

'I know. You'd think she'd be over the moon. She wasn't. David had addressed it to Lady Sheridan because he'd forgotten her new married name, and she felt Leo had been slighted.' Waiting until Pat returned with the coffee, she added, 'She's really dotty about him.'

'Of course she is. Apart from being very easy on the eye, he's dotty about *her*.'

'No, he isn't.'

'OK . . . he isn't,' agreed Pat, studying her closely. 'To be honest I thought *you* had a bit of a thing for him when you arrived for Christmas. Lately, I've not been so certain.'

'Then you *are* a dimwit in a smock,' Vesta snapped.

'I'll put it on in a minute,' her friend said smoothly. 'Come on, Vee, out with it. What are you really here for?'

After all the preamble, Vesta was doubtful about discussing the issue with Pat. She was so down to earth and sensible, which often made Vesta feel inadequate. Emotionally, certainly.

'*Come on!*'

Thus urged, Vesta said, 'I heard from Paul this morning. He's not coming on leave. There's a flap on over the Russians, who are either mounting a gigantic bluff or preparing for battle. Paul's been sent to Berlin to replace a captain who's been injured in a jeep smash, and he's overseeing repairs to the runway at Gatow. It's breaking up under the wear and tear of the airlift, so it's imperative that it's available for future use. We may be flying in extra troops soon.'

'Oh Lord, is it getting serious?'

'Looks like it. Worrying, isn't it?'

Pat resumed eating her slice of cake. 'What are you going to do now?'

'I don't know.' She got up and began to pace restlessly. 'If he had come as planned, I expect we'd have got married and that would have been that. This delay seems like an omen.'

'An omen of what?'

'That it's not meant to be.'

'Rubbish! You're the only one who can make it happen or not. You always imagine such mystery to life. It's black and white, Vee. Either you love him, or you don't. Either you love Brad or you don't. Make up your mind which one you want. If you don't want either, send them packing and find someone else. That new young ginger-haired doctor at the Cottage Hospital has been chatting me up at village dos. He's lonely. How about him? You could paint his operations. Plenty of action and drama.'

Vesta pulled on the jacket she had taken off on entering. 'Thanks for the coffee. Don't eat any *more* cake or you really will be a ball on legs.'

Pat stopped her at the door. 'Come on, Vee, pull yourself together or you'll never be happy. I was only trying to help.'

Vesta thrust her hands in her pockets. 'I don't *know* what I want. Yes, that's a boring and irresponsible thing to say, but I don't. *I just bloody don't!* It was obvious from the moment I arrived that Mummy resented my intrusion into her love-nest. Now she's been told by your ginger swain that she's merely going through the menopause, she's doing the craziest things. Selling paintings for money to build a youth centre on our far meadow; riding over Longbarrow Hill with Leo at all hours of the day. She's so fizzy with life I think she'll go pop before long.' She frowned. 'I'm in their way, Pat, but I don't know where to go next.'

'You can come here, if it helps.'

'Thanks, but it wouldn't. I've got after-the-war blues, like so many others. I haven't found a comparable substitute yet.'

'Maybe you should join another. There are plenty going on around the world. Go back to Berlin. One might be starting up there before long . . . and you know the ropes in that area already.'

'Yes . . . Thanks, Pat. Sorry I held up your work.'

She smiled sympathetically. 'That's one advantage of nitwits in smocks. They're far too busy to analyse life and make it complicated. Don't fret, Vee. It'll come right in the end. Just put your sense of the mystery of life on canvas. That's the best place for it.'

Vesta rode home slowly despite the raw coldness of the day. The visit to her closest friend had solved nothing; merely increased her irritation with her own inability to sort out her career, her emotions and, ultimately, her future. Pat was practical and full of commonsense, but then *she* could not possibly paint a haunting picture like *The Afterglow*. Where was the afterglow to be found? Only when life ended? There must, there surely *must* be an afterglow to follow the years of devastation and loss. Had they all hoped for it too soon? Her mother and Leo appeared to have discovered it. Marion had taken on a new lease of life which Leo apparently found irresistible. He was not behind the astonishing disposal of six of the modern paintings hanging in the long corridors of Tarrant Hall. Marion had made it perfectly clear that it was her decision alone. She had grown amazingly assertive. If the menopause did that for a woman Vesta longed to suffer it herself. She needed *something* to drive her out of her present mental inertia.

Paul's letter this morning had come as a blow. She had been expecting him to arrive on leave within a few days, and hoped that seeing him again would make everything fall into place. The tone of the letter had not been encouraging, either. He was disappointed that she had not written as often as he had, which suggested she was still uncertain about their relationship. He hoped she would not keep him on a string too long because he would like to know where he stood now. No one knew how serious the present Russian threat was, or what was liable to develop, but he was unlikely to be given leave for a while. He hoped his absence would make her heart grow fonder, but if it did the reverse he would like to know as soon as possible.

Vesta had missed Paul a great deal; had banked on his February leave solving everything. Coming to Tarrant Hall had been a great mistake. Leo had played havoc with her opinion of him, and she now felt an unwanted third in her own home, mainly due to her mother's new attitude. They were so happy together, so full of plans which no longer appeared to consider David's return to take up the reins one day. Vesta knew she must leave, but could not think where to go. Perhaps she should buy a studio apartment somewhere in Cornwall and paint rugged landscapes. The problem with that was that too many artists had already done them.

It was almost time for lunch when Vesta reached the Hall, so she went to her room and changed out of her riding-clothes. When the gong sounded – Marion had reintroduced that fashion – Vesta descended to join her mother and a man she would never regard as a stepfather, feeling even more strongly that she must make a positive move to end the hiatus she was presently allowing to continue.

Leo came from the sitting room with his arm across Marion's shoulders. 'Hallo. Did you enjoy your ride? How is the luscious Pat?'

'Up to her knees in manure,' Vesta replied shortly, irritated by their togetherness.

He laughed. 'Any woman who can look as lovely as she does in gumboots and layers of dung-coloured clothes is a marvel. David's a very lucky man. I hope he soon realizes it and comes home to her.'

They sat at the table and Robson served tomato soup. Vesta declined. It was not one of her favourite flavours at the best of times, and she had little appetite this morning.

'You should eat, dear,' Marion told her in a vague maternal fashion. 'You look rather thin these days.'

'Against the luscious Pat, I suppose I do.'

Leo gave her a keen glance. 'Pity about Paul's cancelled leave. A rather worrying situation, too. Wrong time to get a posting to Berlin.'

'He's been in worse spots.'

'The desert?'

'And up a broken factory chimney with an unexploded bomb.'

He nodded sagely. 'Ah, *that* was what did it, was it?'

Vesta glared at him. 'I'm not an impressionable child, Leo. *Hundreds* of men have done courageous things when I've been around. I really *don't* go ga-ga over just one example of

385

heroism, you know. I suppose you could say I saved Brad's life at Monte Cassino, but I haven't put myself on a pedestal.'

'*He's* a lucky man. By the by, you didn't say he was in Germany when you were there.'

Vesta felt the colour deepen in her cheeks. 'I . . . How do you know?'

'There's a double page exclusive of his in one of today's more radical newspapers. Ill-judged timing, just as the Russians are mounting what we hope is no more than a massive bluff. It hurts the Allies' image as upright saviours of the downtrodden, but Brad Holland has never been a man to fight shy of the truth, and editors are always eager for sensation to increase circulation.'

'Did you meet him?' asked Marion. 'I thought he was in the East. Why didn't you mention that he had come back to Europe?'

'What is this; the third degree?' she cried. 'Yes, he was there; yes, I met him. In fact I flew to Gatow with him. Then he vanished into Berlin itself to investigate black marketeering. That's all I can tell you, I'm afraid. Why the sudden interest? I thought you disapproved of him.'

'That's what his exclusive is all about,' put in Leo smoothly, as if she had not made that outburst. 'It's an exposé of money-grabbing among Allied troops, aircrews, civil servants and even some diplomatic staff. Goods are being siphoned off the airlifts and sold for inflated amounts in Berlin. He's even uncovered one set-up where the stuff's being sold to a contact in the *Soviet* sector. He should be very certain of his facts to make public such a claim, but the whole investigation must have endangered his relations with those officials who have previously given him *carte blanche*. He's treading on very thin ice in his bid for journalistic acclaim.'

'It's not that,' said Vesta fiercely. 'He simply has a strong aversion to people who act the part of benefactor while lining their own pockets. Brad might have his faults, but that isn't one of them.'

'Yet he's accepting a very large sum for doing this favour to mankind,' Leo pointed out.

Furious, Vesta said, 'You should know all about that, Leo. You're doing much the same on a smaller scale here, aren't you?'

There was an electric silence as they looked at each other over the table. Then Leo said, '*Touché*. I thought he was a back number where you're concerned.'

Before Vesta could deal with that, Robson appeared at her side. 'There is a long-distance telephone call for you, miss.' His expression lengthened with disdain. 'From *Germany*, I understand.'

She jumped up filled with relief. Paul would not ring her unless he had some good news. He must be coming home as planned. As she ran through to the sitting room she offered up a prayer of thanks. The hiatus was over. They would get married in the village church during his leave, and all her uncertainty would be over.

She snatched up the receiver. 'Hallo, darling.'

'Hallo, Vic,' said Brad's voice into her ear. 'I don't have long. The operator is licensed to cut off calls if they exceed the limit. I've fixed for you to go with me on an exclusive. There's a group of Japs in the Malayan jungle who don't know the war's over. They've been seen twice but vanish each time. There's a British patrol out searching for them. I want that story and you'll get great material. It's new ground for us. Now, listen here. This guy I know runs a charter freight company. There's a plane leaving Northolt tomorrow morning seven hundred hours, heading for Singapore. A seat on it is booked for you. I'll pick you up in Frankfurt. Ask for Clem Bastido. He'll do the rest. Got that OK?'

'Brad, how did you know I was here?' she asked faintly.

'They told me at the nunnery . . . after I saw the Honourable Fitzroy in Berlin looking distinctly unhappy. Put two and two together. See you in Frankfurt, Vic.'

'Now, just a minute –' The call was cut off.

Vesta sat on a chair very quickly because her legs suddenly gave out. A minute ago she was all set to marry the Honourable Fitzroy and now . . . She covered her face with her hands unsure whether she was laughing or crying. How *could* she use that silly joke name for Paul, whom she loved? He was too splendid a person for that. Yet just the warm, transatlantic tones of Brad's so-familiar voice had charged her with excitement. Singapore! The city of her brother's dramatic marriage and escape, the place which had been so emotive it had changed his life around a second time. Japanese soldiers still armed three and a half years after the war ended? How bizarre! A British patrol stalking them through the jungle? Their eventual capture and stupefied expressions when they learnt the truth!

Pulling herself together, she grew angry. How typical of Brad. He had seen Paul in Berlin looking unhappy – of course he was; his leave had been cancelled – and jumped to the conclusion that they had split up because she was presently in England. Did he think he would take up where they had left off? What a nerve! He knew a guy with a charter freight company. He *always* knew a guy. She began to smile. Working with Brad was so much easier. He smooth-talked his way into everything he wanted. The smile froze momentarily as she thought of his ability to get *that* whenever he wanted it, too. There was always a Rosa, Minnie or Gretchen only too eager. He had had to fight for Vesta Sheridan, however. He would have to again on this trip.

So she was going? Getting to her feet she paced the room in indecision. Pat thought in black and white. Either you want this man or that one. If you cannot decide, find a different one. It was not that simple for Vesta Sheridan. She did not want a different one. She loved two already. Stopping by the sherry decanter she poured a generous amount into a glass and drank it very fast. The resulting warm glow enabled her to see that the decision had been made for her by fate. If Paul had been on the other end of the line she would now be off to buy a wedding-gown. The result had been as close as that.

Robson appeared. 'Will you be requiring the glazed lamb chops, miss? Cook is ready to serve.'

'Yes, Robson, I'm famished,' she said, passing him in the doorway.

Two faces looked at her expectantly as she resumed her seat at the table. 'I'm flying to Singapore with Brad at seven tomorrow morning,' she announced with smug pleasure. 'You'll have the place to yourselves again.'

'Why Singapore?' asked Leo with genuine interest.

'He's chasing an exclusive, as usual.'

'How long will you be away?' Marion asked, surprisingly unflustered by her daughter's news.

'No idea.' She helped herself to vegetables. 'It just depends on how long the story takes to break.'

'Are we allowed to know the details?'

'Sorry, no. That's what makes it an exclusive.'

He smiled at her. 'Good luck, anyway. I look forward to seeing the subsequent pictures.'

All smugness left Vesta. 'Leo . . . what I said to you . . .'

'No harm done. Brad is a lucky man. If he could see the difference his call has made to you, he'd be certain of his best "exclusive" by making you Mrs Holland the minute you land in Singapore.'

'What are you going to do about Paul?' her mother asked.

'Play fair and send back his ring.' Her slight sense of misgiving at that prospect was quickly banished by the realization that a fateful telephone call had solved all her problems in one fell swoop.

'The poor man is certain to be upset, but he's young and has years ahead of him to find happiness elsewhere,' mused Marion. 'You must seize every chance that comes your way. Life's too short for missed opportunities, isn't it, Leo?'

'That's for sure,' he replied with a loving smile. 'We're not going to miss a single one, my dear.'

'You'll be going up to stay overnight in London, I suppose,' Marion continued. 'We've an appointment with an architect in Dorchester to discuss the youth centre, but we should be home by six at the latest. You'll still be here then, won't you?'

'Heavens, yes. I've packing to do, letters to write. I'll arrange for the ring to be delivered to Paul's family. It's too risky to send it to him in Berlin.'

'Of course, he has been sent there because of the dangerous situation. Oh dear, what a time to give him such news!'

Vesta heard Jim Shannon's voice: *When a chap has personal problems it means his mind's not entirely on the job, and he can get careless.* She said swiftly, 'He's been trained to deal with dangerous situations. And don't forget David's also out there in the thick of it.'

'He's been similarly trained,' asserted Leo. 'I don't think we need worry about either of them. Now then, I suggest we call Robson to bring our pudding or we'll be late for our appointment in Dorchester.'

Marion rang the little bell while explaining to Vesta her hopes that Duncan McCloud was the right man to design her youth centre. Talk of that dominated the remainder of the meal, and Vesta settled to her own many tasks marvelling over her mother's acceptance of what she had been told without the usual myriad questions on where she would be living, had she the right clothes, what about money and would she be marrying Brad after all?

Learning from experience to travel light, Vesta dragged from her wardrobe several sets of lightweight shirts and trousers, and the minimum amount of underwear to pack in her holdall, then went along to her studio. It was much more essential to load up with paints and canvases. Singapore might provide such things, but the heart of Malayan jungle would not. The unfinished set of paintings of the airlift made her pause with a touch of sadness. Would she ever recapture the right mood to finish them? Still in pensive frame of mind she uncovered *Betrayal*. It contained all the hallmarks of her individual style, and as an evocative image it was brilliant, but it now held undertones of her brother's days of torture. She threw the cover over it again. At some time in the future when she could face it without personal associations, it would remind another generation of the sacrifices made by her own.

Excitement flooded her. The Far East: new ground, as Brad said. Tropical landscapes, gentle people in bright, swathed clothes, brilliant birds. Hot, dazzling sunshine, relentless rain that began and ceased in an instant. Swollen rivers, lonely shores. Brown-sailed junks, graceful dhows, rocking sampans. Unbelievable blood-red sunsets. Sudden chill replaced her excitement. A place where men had suffered so cruelly they could never forget it. David was one of that legion who continued to have nightmares.

She collected her things together and returned to her room where she wrote to her brother as if she were staying at Tarrant Hall. The letter contained a pack of lies about herself, and ended with a subtle hint that Pat was interested in what he was doing so why did he not contact her and save his sister from relaying all the news secondhand. The letter to Paul proved more difficult than expected. She made three attempts, then wrote a short note saying she was deeply, deeply sorry and thanking him for two marvellous years. She boxed the diamond solitaire, addressed it to Paul at his parents' house, and left instructions for Moses Hopkins, who brought the mail, to have it sent by registered special delivery.

She next telephoned Pat. Her friend listened quietly, then said her bet was still on the ginger-haired doctor.

'I'm so glad I'm not an artist, Vee. I'd hate to lead a tortured life. Give me sheep, gorgeous green countryside and plenty to eat and I'm satisfied.'

'What about David?'

'You know what about him, idiot. I'd swap all the rest for him.'

'Dear Pat, you're so uncomplicated. That's why we all love you so.'

'Go on, say it,' she grumbled. 'What you really mean is I'm "nice". What an epitaph I'll have. *Here lies nice Pat; whose only vice was being fat.*'

They both laughed, and Pat said, 'Take care, Vee. I wish you all you wish yourself.'

'Bless you. And I wish it for you.'

'Do you think we'll actually get it one day?' Pat asked on a wistful note.

'Yes, of course we will . . . and it won't be with the ginger-haired doctor, I promise.'

'My love to Brad. And give him what for this time.'

Brad was not at Frankfurt. Clem Bastido was handed a message saying he had hitched a ride with someone else and would have everything organized when Vesta arrived in Singapore. A seat in a freighter is not the most comfortable way to fly to the other side of the world, and Vesta suffered from motion sickness most of the way. Clem's cargoes caused delays *en route*, and the smell from some did nothing to help banish her nausea. The pilot was helpful, and full of bluff charm but by the end of the third day Vesta was aching all over, wondering if her stomach would ever hold food for more than an hour, and longing for a bath and a bed with cool, clean sheets.

Because of several problems with off-loading and taking aboard merchandise, they arrived in the evening almost twelve hours late. Clem went to the cargo building with his flight log and clearance papers, while Vesta assembled her baggage. As she was not on a normal passenger flight she was made to wait in a bare office while lengthy Customs formalities were carried out. A ridiculous argument was then conducted over whether or not *she* should be treated as freight. The raised voices faded into a distant sound as she sat beneath a lazily turning fan in a near stupor, certain the room was actually going up and down. Despite the fan, the office was sweltering. Perspiration ran down her face and legs. Her shirt was sticking to her back, and every bone and muscle ached. Her numbed brain asked why Brad had not known a guy here to smooth the way, and thought of the ginger-haired doctor who was Pat's best bet for her.

'Geez, you look pretty beat up.' Clem stood before her, unshaven, red-eyed and with dark patches all over his shirt and shorts.

'And I return the compliment,' she murmured. 'Are we free to go?'

'Sure are. There's a truck outside to take us to the main building. Here, I got your bags. Just get out there and down the steps before you nod off.'

The evening was so sultry it was difficult to breathe. Humidity filled her nostrils and lungs. It had been hot in the desert, but never like this. It had been hot in Italy without the sensation of being crushed by a blanket of dampness. The night was clear with a multitude of stars. Lights around the perimeter illuminated palm trees and not much more. There was an indefinable smell about the place, not exactly unpleasant, yet alien.

When they emerged from their final check by airport authorities there was no sign of Brad. The clock showed it to be almost nine. They had been expected at seven this morning. He would have tired of waiting, naturally, but would have left a number where he could be reached. Vesta stood (only because if she sat it would be on the floor, from which no one would persuade her to get up until morning) while Clem made some enquiries. He returned within five minutes accompanied by a young man in creased white trousers and loose tunic, with a sort of black forage cap on his head. Clem looked apologetic.

392

'Vesta, this here is Ahmed. Brad waited until noon, then went ahead. Ahmed's all set to take you up-country now, but I guess you'd like a hotel room for the night and then to set off around dawn. I'll fix it for you.'

Her brain was not so numb it could not work out the obvious. 'No, I'll go off with Ahmed now. If I wait until morning, Brad will have moved on again and I'll never catch up.' She did something uncharacteristic: going on tiptoe, she kissed him. 'Thanks for everything. Good luck.' Turning to the Malay, she gave the best smile she could muster. 'I'm sorry you've had such a long wait. Give me ten minutes to freshen up and we'll be on our way.'

In a cramped toilet cubicle favoured by cockroaches, Vesta scrambled into fresh clothes after the most comprehensive wash she could manage in the circumstances. Knowing better than to spray herself with perfume after her desert experiences, Vesta had nevertheless been very liberal with talcum powder, little realizing its effect would not last long. Ahmed was waiting beside her bags, seemingly unperturbed by the passing of time and the drive ahead of him. Vesta dared not ask how far they would be going. Better to remain ignorant.

Transport was a small saloon painted black and yellow. Vesta climbed into the rear, resigned to curling up on worn leather with one of her bags as a pillow, but Ahmed had a surprise in store. He opened the boot to put in her luggage, first taking from it a pillow and multi-coloured cotton throw-over, a large thermos, and a canister with bowl and spoon.

'Mr Holland say look after you, Mem,' he explained very seriously. 'Here is bed, rice, tea.' Reaching into his pocket he brought out an envelope. 'This from Mr Holland.'

Overwhelmed by the Malay's simple provision for her comfort, Vesta opened the envelope while Ahmed stowed her bags and prepared to depart. Inside was a Press pass bearing her name, and a single page.

The only way you'll get around here is with this, but don't let anyone examine it too closely. I hope to God you haven't brought that Edwardian pith-helmet.

That was Brad. No apologies. No 'sorry I missed you'. No 'longing to see you'. Mention of the solar topee she had

393

arrived with in the desert said it all. As the car drove between dim shadows of huts set between trees, and the shrill chorus of cicadas became almost deafening, Vesta drank some of the curious pale tea, took one whiff of the curried rice then put it away in a hurry, and settled thankfully on the pillow to sleep. Not once did it occur to her that she was alone with a male stranger who was driving her to an unknown destination through terrain inhabited by snakes and other poisonous creatures. Vesta Sheridan could look after herself in any situation. That was why she and Brad made such a good team.

A hand shook her awake none too gently. She found herself looking up at a red face topped by a khaki hat turned up on one side and adorned by a military badge. No more than nineteen, the soldier had one blue eye and one green. Vesta gazed at them in fascination.

'What's goin' on 'ere?' he demanded, quite as fascinated as she by what he saw.

She smiled sleepily at this boy born within the sound of Bow Bells. 'You're looking at me and I'm looking at you.'

Annoyed by her flippancy, unhappy over what he would call her 'posh' accent, he adopted a pugnacious expression. 'One of the funny ones, eh? I'd like ter see some identification, miss. *If* it's not disturbin' yer too much.'

Vesta frowned at him now. 'Who are you? Where am I? What's the name of this place?'

'Don't pull that one! I've 'eard it all before. Come on, out yer get and we'll see what me sergeant 'as ter say.'

The sergeant had plenty to say, all with a broad grin on his face. 'We've been expecting you since yesterdee. Cheered the lads up to think we'd have a woman here for a day or so. Sobered up a bit when they learnt you was already spoke for, but the eyes'll shine when they see you, ma'am. Not much fun, this patrol duty. The lads don't go much on it. It's hot, it's stinking and it's downright poisonous. Still, you'll find out for yourself soon enough.'

'Yes, I expect I will,' she said vaguely.

Having been practically pulled from beneath the cotton cover in a half-comatose state with her shirt loose and unbuttoned and nothing on her feet, Vesta now stood in what she supposed was the guard-room of a small military post somewhere up-country. She still had no idea where she was, and it was not easy to be rational, especially after three days on a cargo aircraft which had crossed the dateline somewhere *en route*.

The sergeant turned on the soldier with odd eyes. 'Never thought brains was your strong point, Fletcher, but you've excelled yourself tonight. Where was you when Lieutenant Chard told us all the lady was coming to join Mr Holland? 'Oo did you think she was, eh? A Communist rebel?' He guffawed. 'Or one of them Nips as is hid out around here? Get back to your post, numbskull.' Thus humiliated, Private Fletcher returned to his uncongenial duty in the sweltering night, and the sergeant spoke into a transceiver of the type Vesta knew well. 'Sorry to disturb you, sir, but the lady's arrived with a Malay in a beat-up old car. All right to send 'im on up?'

A voice mumbled a reply which must have been satisfactory, and Vesta was told her driver could follow the track through to where their CO would be waiting to welcome her. 'Sorry about the way Fletcher treated you, ma'am. National Service-man. Got no idea, most of 'em.'

She paused on the threshold. 'I thought he got the idea very well. No one would easily slip past him.'

Ahmed brought the car forward beneath the barrier Fletcher raised. Vesta scrambled in to do running repairs to her appearance, then decided it was a vain hope. Brad was used to seeing her resembling a homeless waif, and Lieutenant Chard was unlikely to want a living pin-up on camp. He would almost certainly also be doing his national service – very young, very nervous and irritatingly pedantic, with a pert fiancée waiting for him to become an estate agent and marry her. She knew the type well.

The outpost was set in a clearing and consisted of no more than a dozen huts raised on brick supports, with shuttered windows and wooden verandahs. Each had outside lights powered by a generator whose throbbing vied with rhythmic shrilling of cicadas. Jungle surrounded the huts and two large open sheds housing vehicles. A guard sauntered in bored fashion before these, but did not seem unduly concerned with the arrival of a civilian car at three in the morning. This place was very definitely an outpost, and Vesta easily believed the sergeant's description of hot, stinking and downright poisonous. It was hotter here than ever, and there was an overwhelming aroma of rotting undergrowth, cooked cabbage and latrines. She accepted the poisonous aspect on trust as her heart sank. Where were the stately dhows, the gentle people in bright clothes, the brilliant birds, the blood-red glorious sunsets? As she gazed at the encroaching trees a shiver raced up her spine, making the hair on her neck rise up. David had been in places like this for seven months, hanging on to life against all odds. Small wonder he still had nightmares.

She had been completely wrong about the CO. Lieutenant Chard was a gaunt man of around forty who must have been commissioned from the ranks. He had iron-grey hair, black staring eyes and a smile which came and went as fast as a lizard's tongue. Beneath his abstract gaze Vesta felt she became depersonalized, so his official welcome came as a strange contrast. Fully dressed to the extent of cap and Sam Browne with a revolver in its case, he met Vesta on the steps of his office with an outlandishly flamboyant salute.

'I'm Brian Chard. Welcome to Tanjong Kayu, Miss Sheridan.' The smile appeared and vanished. 'Your husband said you prefer to use your professional name on assignments. He's just getting dressed. Would you care for some gin or whisky?' Smile. 'I'm afraid I'm out of tea.'

This was so totally bizarre Vesta was scarcely angry that Brad had pre-empted their marriage by announcing it as fact to this unnerving man. Three a.m. A hut in a jungle clearing, furnished with the minimum office necessities, an easy chair in cane with floral-patterned cushions, a collection of gin and whisky bottles, mostly empty, and a large picture of the King and Queen on the wall. Add that to a fully-uniformed, armed officer, who was surely eccentric to the edge of actual madness, and it was not surprising that she should feel she had wandered into a dream.

'Whisky would be lovely,' she said, and then goggled as Chard sploshed the spirit into a tall glass as if she had asked for a long, cool lemonade.

'Bottoms up,' said her companion, downing a generous amount himself after handing her a dripping glass.

A sudden urge to laugh hysterically was driven away by Brad, whose idea of dressing to meet her consisted of donning a pair of the very brief shorts he had worn in the desert and nothing more. He emerged through a curtain of wooden beads and came straight to Vesta with the smile which got him what he wanted every time.

'This is one hell of a moment to arrive. I expected you yesterday,' he greeted, and kissed her as very few husbands kiss their wives in public.

'I expected *you* at Frankfurt,' she retaliated, knowing he was going to get what he wanted this time, too. Brad was the only sign of sanity here.

'I came ahead to fix everything up.' He accepted the full glass offered him by their host. 'Brian knows this area. He was here in '41. The local people respect him and offer every assistance. His detachment is here mainly to deal with local unrest; keeping the peace, it's known as. Now these Japs have been spotted he's been detailed to flush them out and tell them it's all over. See, these guys aren't like Western troops. They live off the land, sleep where they can. Many of them are peasant types without too much intelligence. They've been told to patrol the jungle looking for the enemy, so they keep on doing so until someone says stop. No one has. They don't need ammunition because they use cold steel. Hell, they could stop here the rest of their lives and never know their god-damned country lost the war.' The familiar flush of excitement possessed him. 'What a shock they're due, especially when they learn about the atomic bomb. I can give them first hand –'

'*Brad!*' Vesta cried, unable to handle any more. 'I'm hot, exhausted and the room's going up and down like a . . . like a yo-yo. Can I hear your news and ideas in the morning?' She put down her empty glass on what she thought was a table, but it fell to the ground and smashed. 'Sorry, Mr Chard. It's just that I'm not seeing too straight,' she complained, beginning to sway. 'Thank you for your hospit . . . Which is my room?'

Brad laughed somewhere near her. 'Vic, you're just plumb drunk. I've warned you about the perils of whisky enough times.' She was picked up and carried towards the bead curtain. Brad's voice rumbled from the vicinity of her ear as he bade the mad Englishman goodnight. The room was illuminated by pale light from a lamp on the corner of the hut. Dim outlines of wooden furniture were around the walls; in the centre stood a narrow, iron-framed bed beneath a froth of mosquito netting. The sheets were crumpled.

'Which side do you want?' enquired an amused voice. She knew all too well he would be enjoying this.

She flung her arms around his neck and burst into tears. After that she was aware of very little until she awoke to brilliant light and the raucous call of cockatoos. Her head ached, her mouth felt like sandpaper, and her stomach was rumbling. As she was naked beneath the sheet she wrapped it around her and went in search of aspirin from her bag below the shuttered window. From outside came the sound of a typewriter being pounded. She pushed open the shutters and looked out. Brad was sitting astride a stool, as she had often seen him, attacking the keys with two fingers. He was dressed in brief shorts and an unbuttoned shirt which revealed his hard, brown body, also as she had often seen him. She sighed with relief. This was how it had been during those exciting, dangerous years. This was living in the fullest sense. It was what she wanted; what had been missing since she had let him go to Japan alone.

'Where's the shower?' she called to him.

'This ain't the Ritz, lady,' he responded in a heavy Brooklyn accent, without looking up. 'Wanna cuppa cawfie instead?'

'I'll settle for that.' She smiled and withdrew her head. Then she looked out again. 'How about some breakfast, like bacon and eggs with toast? I'll have the chocolate fudge ice-cream later.'

He glanced up at that. 'You've just missed lunch. Will you settle for afternoon tea and jolly old sandwiches?'

The headache was forgotten as she gazed at him. 'I've missed you. Oh, *how* I've missed you.'

'Who's to blame for that?'

She retreated and hunted for fresh underwear. Brad entered with a cup of what smelled like very good coffee. 'Sober up with this. I've told the water-carrier to fetch you some on the double. That means he'll be at least thirty minutes.'

'Where did you get the coffee?' she asked, sipping it with appreciation. 'That crazy man Chard only had spirits, he said.'

'I brought a supply up from Singapore, along with a load of canned stuff. I knew we'd want more than some British outpost could offer us.'

'How did you find them so quickly?'

'You know me, Vic. When I'm on to something, I go all out for it.'

She glanced up as he stopped in the centre of that basic room watching her. 'Why did you tell Chard I'm your wife?'

'It makes things easier all round.' He had that well-known look in his eye. 'Doesn't it?'

'Yes . . . I suppose so.' She concentrated on the coffee. 'I read your piece on Berlin.'

'I *knew* there'd be something going on behind the scenes. The whole set-up was made for it. A whole lot of guys had to get out in a hurry.'

'Including you?'

'Yeah, but Berlin's dead now. The airlift is no longer news. Even those who did the schmaltz angle on Christmas gifts for orphaned kids living in the city's ruins have run out of copy.'

'But there's a crisis building.'

He shook his head. 'Bluff, no more. The Soviets know they've lost all hope of grabbing Berlin. They're mounting a show of strength to say, OK, I won't do it this time but I could if I really wanted to. The whole business will be over in a month or two, and the biggest losers will be the British. The financial and manpower costs of the airlift will put back their recovery at home several years.'

'You saw Paul in Berlin, you said. At a distance, or face to face?'

'We exchanged opinions.' He frowned. 'He's kind of hot-tempered, isn't he? Invited me outside to settle a few things.'

Vesta was deeply dismayed. 'He *didn't*!'

'When I declined, he socked me on the jaw there in the canteen. I guess it made him feel better.'

'Oh, Brad, how awful! What did you do?'

'Walked out. Rule I made a long time ago – never fight over a woman. I'll hit a guy who lies, cheats or puts the finger on me for something I didn't do, but no woman is worth starting a boxing match for. By the time both guys are cut and bleeding she's found someone else. Socking me did nothing for the Honourable Fitzroy, did it? You're here with me and his ring has gone from your finger. See what I mean?'

'Please don't call him by that silly name. He wanted to marry me.'

'So did I.' He leaned against the wall, arms folded across his tanned chest, regarding her shrewdly. 'Does he still mean something to you?'

'I hated hurting him, that's all.' She left the subject swiftly. 'Brad, I was sick for most of the flight – which was why the whisky had such a violent effect on me – and I'm absolutely *starving*. What's the procedure here for getting a meal?'

'Brian has a batman who also cooks for him. It's a case of opening a few cans and heating the contents. As any fool can do that, I'll substitute for him and rustle up something. Remember the hash I used to do in Italy?'

She nodded. 'I remember everything we did in Italy. Why else do you think I'm here?'

'For a few seconds back there you had me wondering.' He moved forward and pulled her from the chair into his arms. 'I missed out on this last night, and I need incentive to make us a mid-afternoon snack.'

The sheet slid to the floor, and Vesta was very aware that someone could walk past the unshuttered window and look in, but when Brad needed incentive such things went by the board. The sound of splashing on the other side of the thin wall broke them apart at the point when Vesta fully expected to be lifted across to the bed.

'That'll be the water for your bath,' Brad said with faint regret. 'Any other time it takes thirty minutes.' He nodded at the wall. 'Outside, you'll find a wooden stall with a basic shower contraption like those in the desert. As you did there, you'll have to crouch down for privacy unless you want to display these to all and sundry.' He ran a hand lightly over her breasts. 'I wouldn't recommend it. These guys are lonely and very frustrated. Just be thankful you're with me.'

'But you wouldn't defend me. No woman is worth fighting for in Brad Holland's book.'

He grinned. 'That's my Vic! We always made a great team.'

After a tepid shower in what she learnt was water from the river, and dressed in clean, if crumpled clothes, Vesta emerged to find Brad sitting at a table beneath the fan with a glass of whisky in his hand. He always seemed able to drink it in large quantities and at any hour of the day. She did not comment on it, but instead asked about the man who had brought her up from the airport.

'I feel awfully bad about Ahmed. He was very sweet and looked after me so well, then I walked in here and forgot all about him. Never even thanked him.'

Brad waved a nonchalant hand. 'He was very well paid for looking after you, but didn't see a cent until he got you here. I guess he got something to eat in the village then returned to Singapore this morning.' He got up. 'Ready for the hash?'

It was good, but hunger added to its excellence. A sort of stew produced by mixing tinned foods together and adding sauce, it was augmented with chunks of fresh white bread and a bowl of saffron rice.

'Where's our host?' she asked after a while.

'Down at the village. He's got a popsie there and it's siesta time.'

'He's crazy, isn't he?'

Brad grinned. 'Gone native is the polite way to say it. Father was a rubber planter between the wars. Drank too much and the business ran down until he was drowned in debts. Committed suicide. Brian had to leave his banking career, and joined the army for the sake of a job and somewhere to live. This place is in his blood, so he got a posting here as soon as he could. When his time's up next year, he plans to leave the army and settle out here. Didn't say what he'd do. Bum around like so many others, I guess.'

After finishing her first square meal in a long time, Vesta sat back and tackled her companion. 'What are we actually doing here? I mean, if the Japanese have been in the jungle for years the chances of finding them are very slender, surely. We could wait ages and still have nothing at the end of it. You don't propose staying here long, do you? And I can't see what *I'll* find to work on.'

'What about this place? A real outpost of the British Empire, what?' he added with the mimicry he achieved so well.

'But it's no more than a few huts surrounded by jungle. Where's the challenge; the *life*? Even putting a dog in it won't make it fascinating.'

He gave her a straight look. 'I do the words, you do the pictures. Do I ever ask you what to write?'

'What were you typing when I interrupted?'

'Atmosphere, honey.' He put up his hands as if outlining rows of newsprint. 'Straight from the icy wastes of Berlin where a new enemy is on the ascent, to the sweltering back-roads of the Malayan jungle, where an old one is secretly stalking its victors.'

'To get back to my original subject, just how long are we going to be here with crazy Chard?'

'Until a patrol sights the Nips. No one knew they were here until last week, so no one was looking for them. Now these guys have got them pin-pointed to a small area. The headman of each village within it has been told to report any visit by them. Several have apparently tried to explain that the war's over but the Jap troops counter what they think are lies by punishing the people more severely than usual. Headmen have been afraid to report this to the authorities for fear of further reprisals. I guess these Malays just want to get on with their lives and not store up worse trouble by getting involved. A lot of them are unsure whom to believe. Vicious troops march in and take food, rape the girls and threaten to return for more. Then someone like Brian Chard breezes in to say the war's over and the Japs have been totally defeated. Next day or so, the Jap platoon returns, as promised. What the hell is going on, thinks the headman. You can understand his dilemma.'

'Yes,' she sighed. 'Who put you on to this story?'

'I know a guy in Singapore. He heard the rumour but wouldn't follow it up because he didn't think it was feasible. He thought it was for me, and cabled my office. See, I thought it *very* feasible. That time in Japan I got to know a lot about these people. They obey even when it seems ludicrous, danger-ous or suicidal. Defeat is dishonourable; surrender unthink-able. Capture by the enemy is so shaming death is the only course to follow. These guys roaming the jungle will never believe their country's defeat or surrender, so they'll go on for ever out there. I'll bet there are others. Some of that jungle is so inaccessible only a few local Malays know their way around in it. There are tigers and elephants roaming wild, but they're rarely seen. *That's* more in your line, Vic. You won't need a dog in the picture when you can get jolly old jumbo to pose for you.'

'Brad, cut out the humour and tell me what we're going to *do*,' she demanded, lethargy creeping up on her again. The heat was overpowering, the isolation total, and mosquitoes were feasting off her arms and legs. She slapped at another, causing Brad to mention that he had a spray she could use and she to reply that he might have offered it an hour ago.

'We're going to stay here on the spot until one of Brian's patrols calls in to say they've seen the Japs. Then we'll go out there.' He poured more whisky for himself. 'Simple enough. Meanwhile we'll both get "atmosphere", that commodity you've always been so keen on.'

'All right. At least I know the score,' she said heavily. 'The living arrangements are a bit primitive.'

'You should be used to that. You slept in a truck in the desert.'

'That was different. We were on the move all the time. We could be here *ages*.'

'That's the third time you said that. So what, as long as we get the story?'

'*You* get the story, you mean. I was going to paint beautiful people in sarongs, exotic boats on waterways, sunsets.'

He got to his feet. 'Aside from the boats you'll find the rest down by the river. Follow the path beyond the vehicle sheds. You can't miss it.' He stretched. 'I'm going to have me a sleep before dinner. You disturbed me last night, and four hours on top of a table is no joke.' He paused by the bead curtain. 'Brian has arranged for another bed, known as a *charpoy*, to be put in our room. We may need it sometime during the night.'

He vanished behind the curtain, and Vesta soon followed. A sight of his naked body was not what she was after, however, and she very soon disillusioned him. 'If I'm going to see these wonderful things down by the river I'll need a sketchpad and that mosquito spray you have. Get under the sheet, Brad. Four hours on a table are no joke.'

'That's what I love about you, Vic. You never give in too easily.' He climbed beneath the mosquito net and lay back to test the truth of his words. 'The spray is on the top shelf there. Go easy. It has a powerful effect on the nostrils.'

She found it and used it liberally, then had a spasm of sneezing. In response to his 'I warned you', she said, between sneezes, 'See you for a sundowner . . . if there's any left in the bottle when I get back.'

'Watch out for the crocodiles, honey.'

It was more a settlement than a village. Wooden houses on stilts ranged along the bank of a brown, sluggish waterway: no riverside idyll, this. The banks were areas of churned-up mud where crocodiles would not look out of place, and the houses looked dark and deserted. Very little sun penetrated the tangle of greenery, which rustled with the passage of unseen birds and creatures betrayed by their occasional shrill cries. Poultry ran freely between and beneath the raised dwellings; basic nets hung in the dingy waters to catch whatever fish might lurk there. The scene did not inspire Vesta, but she took up her sketchpad and swiftly recorded various aspects if only to satisfy Brad.

Perhaps she should have succumbed and joined him beneath the mosquito netting. Her long, drawn-out journey to get here, and the drastic time change, made her think in terms of an undisturbed sleep starting from that moment. Lack of it probably accounted for her lack of enthusiasm. This was a far cry from her visions of the East. Yet she had seen so little of it and was wrong to make judgements already. Once they had covered this curious story of the Japanese soldiers, they could move on to something with more scope. She wondered how Brad could have imagined this would be of any use to her. Then it dawned on her that he had merely used it as a means to get back together once he discovered she had gone home and Paul was very unhappy in Berlin – so unhappy that he had let fly at Brad. Would her letter have reached him yet? Poor Paul, it was no fault of his that she had come out here. It was what she really wanted to do with her life, that was all.

Overcome with lethargy, Vesta made her way back to the small military post regarding the table top very favourably. Better than the jungle floor as a bed, if she could manage to

404

reach it. Dragging her feet along the path beside the vehicle sheds she was surprised to hear shouts and a suggestion of activity. The place had been deserted since she awoke. The open square bordered by neat army huts was now full of men, and trucks which were being loaded with huge backpacks and radio equipment. There was an unmistakable air of excitement.

A jeep was parked by the steps leading to Brian Chard's quarters. The man himself, now clad in camouflage overalls and a large hat, was ordering the movements of soldiers in similar dress. Vesta quickened her pace. As she reached the jeep, Brad came down the steps in a pair of the overalls carrying several water-bottles over his shoulder.

'What's happened?' she cried, already suspecting the truth.

'We've got 'em earmarked,' he said in brief, familiar style. 'Five minutes more and we'd have been gone. Spare overalls for you inside. Make it snappy, Vic! When they go, I go.' He flung his pack and water-bottles into the jeep, then crossed to Chard who was studying a map.

For a short moment Vesta was tempted to tell him to go to hell, but a surge of warmth then swept through her. She rushed inside to don the overalls. This was how it used to be. This was the challenge and thrill she needed. This was *living*. It was why she had joined Brad and cast aside a settled, secure life with a man who longed to protect her.

CHAPTER NINETEEN

BRAD explained as he drove behind the two army trucks. 'The patrol called in. After three fruitless days they've come upon a village where six different people are prepared to say Japanese soldiers were there yesterday. We're going up to join them.'

'Why so many?' she asked, enjoying the rush of air through her hair as the jeep raced along a road which seemed to stretch forever straight ahead. They had not made a turn since setting out.

'We've got them in a bottleneck. Looking at the direction in which they were heading when they left the village, we can make a pincer move and trap them on three sides. Their only outlet would be the main road. They won't risk walking along that.'

Vesta regarded his profile uneasily. 'You make it sound like a battle plan. Pincer movements and so on. All we're trying to do is make contact to convince them the war's over and they can go home.'

He flashed a glance at her. 'It's not as simple as that. They've been terrorizing villages, raping women and young boys, stealing food. Sure, the war's over, whether or not they're aware of the fact, so they've become virtual outlaws. Your army has just put down the last of the Communist brigands haunting the Malay states. They can't allow these men to go on running wild. The police want to get their hands on them, too. We're not off to do them a good turn. They'll be taken prisoner and delivered up to justice.'

'Yes. Yes, of course,' she murmured. 'I should have thought that out for myself. I'm not at my best right now.' It was pure understatement. She was feeling faint from hunger, stupid from lack of sleep and hazed from the events of the last seventy-two hours.

An elbow nudged her. Brad pointed ahead. 'There's your blood-red sunset.'

The trucks had all turned left on to a mud track leaving a clear view of a great ball of fire. She failed to find any beauty in the sight. If anything, it cast a sinister aspect over this alien scene. The track led through an area of coconut palms far enough apart to give views of native huts liberally scattered amongst the trees. After thirty minutes, the genus of tree changed. They grew more thickly, with fleshy leaves and huge climbing vines. The track narrowed until it was impossible for the trucks to go on. By then it was almost dark. Brad pulled up alongside one of the vehicles from which troops were jumping, and turned to drag his pack from the rear seat.

'This is the rendezvous,' he said, busy with his gear. 'We go on foot from here.' Glancing at her, he added, 'I have a flask of coffee, but we'll need that later. If you want a drink use a water-bottle. But go easy. Once it's gone there'll only be river water, and that'll give you dysentery, dengue fever, or cholera if you didn't get a jab before you left England.'

'I didn't have *time*,' she cried. 'Did you?'

He nodded and climbed from his seat. 'This guy in the hospital at Tempelhof airfield did me a favour in return for a couple of bottles of vodka I'd picked up going around Berlin. Finished with the water?'

'I haven't started.' She uncorked one of the bottles and drank thirstily until Brad took it from her.

'Too much'll slow you down. They won't wait while you spend a penny,' he said, English fashion. Then he smiled. 'Come on, Vic, let's show them what a damn good team we are.'

He helped her to the ground, slung the water-bottles cross-wise around her, then shouldered his pack. By this time Brian Chard was addressing his men; the entire outpost strength judging by the number gathered in that near blackness. Vesta heard a different man. Gone was the eccentric who had greeted her last night. In his place was a brusque, efficient leader outlining the details of a serious operation which consisted of marching to a village several miles further up-river, and there fanning out to form a pincer around their unsuspecting quarry. Vesta had last heard those kinds of words about four years ago. Time appeared to have stood still in this semi-tropical peninsula.

They moved off in single file following Brian Chard, who had a powerful torch. Every fourth man also had one. Brad brought up the rear, guiding Vesta ahead of him. It was comforting to have him behind her, and a large number of armed men ahead. Despite what Brad had told her she still felt uneasy about the warlike aspect of what they were doing. No one had mentioned how many Japanese there were, and if they had been using violence against Malays and raping the women she supposed they wouldn't hesitate to do the same against people they still counted as enemies. Amazing though it seemed, Brad's explanation of their presence made sense. Doubtless, there were others in the jungles of the East who still roamed there in the name of obsolete duty.

It was a fascinating story, Vesta conceded, but she did not presently see how *she* could use it. A painting of men being taken prisoner could possibly register their disbelief and confusion, but could not portray the curious facts behind their capture. Nor did she think the little post at Tanjong Kayu suitable material. It was interesting enough in itself, with its primitive washing facilities and isolation: British efficiency in the midst of encroaching jungle; for King and Country in the outposts of the Empire. She could see Brad's exaggerated headlines, but there was nothing visually exciting, no dramatic overtones. When she had featured such a place in a desert oasis it had been at the heart of the life-and-death battle against Rommel. The affair was ideal for Brad. She could not paint it.

Disappointment settled like a lump on her chest as she struggled through the narrow jungle path behind a tall man with a bulky pack on his back. She clung to its strap while Brad had his hand on her shoulder, but the pace was fast and Vesta was not at her best. This was not at all what she had imagined or looked forward to. She had roughed it many times before; she was not a person to be unhappy without luxuries. Yet this trek had been sprung upon her too soon. She had not yet recovered from the journey, and there had been no time to sort everything out with Brad. Admittedly, she had earlier complained that they could wait for days before anything happened, but the timing was all wrong. It never seemed to be right for her – except Brad's telephone call asking her to team up again. That had come at *exactly* the right time.

She was glad of the desert boots she had brought with her. The jungle floor was slippery and gave way with each step. It was not an enjoyable experience. Tropical jungle after dark was a dangerous, sinister location. Creatures which had been resting during the torpid days came out at night. Poisonous, stealthy creatures which slithered, crawled or swooped. Creatures whose bites were lethal. All at once, Vesta recalled that David had been in a place like this for *seven months*, hiding from men like these they were presently hunting. Men who had performed horrific, bestial acts upon him.

The lump of disappointment then became one of revulsion and fear. This was not living in the fullest sense, it was . . . she could capture no understanding of the emotion which suddenly ruled her, but it was strong enough to make her long to be away from this line of dedicated men; this sinister, dominating place. Compassion, empathy with her brother, told her with overwhelming force why he had changed so drastically after returning to this country only four years after such terror. She now felt it for him. Knew his suffering. She yearned to turn and run back to a road, a house, anything that represented normality. But she was trapped in a line of marching men probing ever deeper into the dense growth. How often had she boasted that she could look after herself? Right now she was fully dependent on them. Even the Vesta Sheridan formula for getting what she wanted would be useless. There was no way she could leave this place until the prey had been caught by the hunter.

Just as Vesta believed her legs would let her down, they reached a village. Waiting there were eight other soldiers – the patrol which had already been out here for three days. Candles burned within several huts. The troops were resting in a sort of store open at both ends. It smelled of dried fish and pungent spices, but it was a haven so far as Vesta was concerned. She staggered in, sank down beside Brad, and immediately fell asleep curled against his body, oblivious to the fact that everyone else was eating and drinking.

At first it seemed a warmly familiar routine, when Brad

shook her awake, to see dim figures of men preparing to move off. How often had she done this in Italy during the northward push: woken after sleeping in her clothes within a tent, a ruin, a heap of hay, in a cave or on a bare mattress in a lofty room of an abandoned château? Men collecting their guns and their heavy packs ready to march on in pursuit of the enemy, unsure whether or not they would be sleeping the sleep of the living that coming night. At first it seemed warmly familiar. Full wakefulness gave her the true picture and heavy-heartedness returned. She took a cup of coffee from Brad without a word.

'Still half asleep?' he teased. 'You went out like a light. Missed the chocolate fudge ice-cream.'

On impulse, she flung her arms around his waist saying, 'Hold me close, Brad. Make me feel human.'

'Hey, what's this?' he asked gently, doing as she asked. 'It's not like you to get cold feet on the job. And it's definitely not like you to throw yourself at me. I usually have to fight for it.'

'*Must* we go on with this?' she begged, gazing up at him in the very faint light from a couple of up-ended torches.

'It's what we've come out here for. I can't believe our luck in arriving just in time.' He held her away. 'You need breakfast. Not that bread stuff you enjoy, real American breakfast. There's Spam and peaches I opened last night, and salted crackers. Throw it in one of those containers and eat it as we go along. No time to stop. Those Nips'll be on the move at dawn.'

He squatted by his pack and fiddled with the contents, then rose and presented her with an aluminium container filled with sliced peaches and strips of the tinned meat which had been the butt of many jokes since its introduction. She began to eat in the belief that she would feel better, but what had been acceptable on numerous other occasions now turned her stomach. She doggedly pushed more into her mouth then went outside to seek a quiet place. The first sight that greeted her was a row of men urinating into the undergrowth. That was familiar enough, too, yet she was loath to seek privacy far into the trees. It had to be done, however, and she then discovered that military camouflage overalls were not designed for women: she had to strip the things practically right off. When she returned, Brian Chard was dividing his force into three and giving them instructions with the help of a map. Vesta thought this ludicrous, and said so to Brad.

'What use is a map? Does it show every tree so that he can point to one and tell them when they reach it to turn left?'

Brad did not find it amusing. He was all tensed up for action. She had seen him this way so many times. 'It shows the network of tracks. No one can move through this except along tracks. It's impenetrable for the most part. Look, I suggest we split up now. Chances are we'll catch them in the pincer, but in case they're not as far advanced as we think we should take a patrol each. I'll go with Sergeant O'Rourke. He's leading the one nearest to where they're likely to be. You go with Brian's patrol, which is forming the centre. He'll keep an eye on you.' He clasped her arm. 'If I miss out on the vital moment, I'll rely on you to give me the copy. You know what I want. Every detail. You've got the eye for it. I'll put it into words. Got that?'

She nodded. 'I've never known you to miss a vital moment. You'll be there when it happens.'

He held her other arm while his dark gaze searched her face with a touch of concern. 'You OK?'

'Of course. Don't worry. I can take care of myself.'

'That's my Vic,' he said with a smile. 'Hair all mussed, great big innocent eyes, and dressed for action. I've missed you like hell. There was never a Rosa or Minnie to touch you.'

His kiss was designed to strengthen those words. Then he shouldered his pack and set off, leaving her with a water-bottle and an aluminium dish filled with soggy Spam and peaches. Vesta put it on a stone and crossed to a trough of water where the men still left in the village were dousing their heads then spitting out any moisture in their mouths. Water was dangerous unless boiled and purified. Vesta scooped some over her face and the back of her neck, then decided she might as well stick her head in it, too. Her hair would not look any worse than it probably did now, and she apparently looked irresistible to the one man that mattered.

Brian Chard came up. 'All ready, Mrs Holland? I'll place you in the middle for maximum protection. You'll be able to keep up, will you?'

'Naturally,' she said with a touch of feminine pique. 'I did last night, and I'll be able to see where I'm going now.'

'Good. Good. Well . . . tally ho, then!'

Vesta treated the troops around her, all very young and probably doing their National Service, to a confident smile and a comment about how different this war was from the North African desert, then set off sandwiched between a baker's son from Glasgow and a boy from Tolworth who planned to be a vet when he left the army.

'There are no end of interesting snakes here,' he told her as they marched through the swift dawn. 'Most of them are killers, but they're unlikely to bite unless you step on them.'

'That's good,' she replied with a cheeriness she did not feel. 'I'll step over and leave them for you.' She was far more worried about one dropping from the trees. With five men in front of her, any sensible snake on the track would be long gone before she came along . . . or he would have bitten one of *them* first.

They stopped at nine a.m. for a ten-minute rest and a drink. By then, Vesta was very definitely one of the boys and felt much more at home. After another hour, however, Brian Chard passed back the word that they would advance silently and with caution from that point on. He was in touch by walkie-talkie with the others, and instructed them all to do the same as the pincer closed in. After that, Vesta trod with as much care as the rest as they followed the tortuous track. She had begun to see a different aspect of this jungle. White cockatoos and large vividly-coloured birds set up a clamour as they approached. Monkeys swung noisily high in the trees. The sun slanted through any opening in the green ceiling to shine on leaves and highlight giant moths resting in the brightness. Her revulsion of the night began to fade. This was no more than a tropical maze housing creatures larger than normal because of the heat. She was with the kind of men she was used to and understood. Her only problems were overalls saturated by perspiration, and legs that would most likely fall off within the next few minutes. Apart from that, this *was* really living.

It happened so suddenly it was a moment or two before Vesta's brain could register it. The Glaswegian ahead halted, she bumped into him, and the budding vet cannoned into her.

Her exclamation was drowned by a blood-curdling yell as the line broke up and spread out across a small clearing beside the river. Men sitting there – she could not tell how many – were starting to scramble to their feet. A deafening fusillade set all Vesta's nerves jumping, and she watched horrified as the Japanese were mown down *en masse*. One threw a machete before he died; another rushed forward with blood pouring from his chest before collapsing with his weapon still in his hand. Others tumbled backwards into the water. One, just one, somehow remained alive to crawl forward, the blade of his weapon held in his mouth, hatred in his black eyes. Brian Chard strode forward, revolver in hand, picked up a machete lying near and beheaded the man with one blow.

'That's for my brother,' he yelled in tones that came from somewhere beyond sanity, then approached the next body with the weapon raised.

The ground came up to meet Vesta.

'They didn't stand a chance,' she cried yet again. 'I *saw* what happened. You told me to. Told me to note every detail. I did . . . until that madman started chopping off their heads. It was murder, Brad, pure and simple. I don't care what you were told, *it was instant murder.*'

They were back in Tanjong Kayu, and Brad was packing ready to drive to Singapore to write his story and cable it to London. Vesta still felt sick, shocked, disbelieving. Brad had missed the most sensational exclusive by five minutes, and was not listening to a word she said. When he and the others had arrived on the scene they were told the Japanese had attacked from their hiding places in the jungle. It was against their creed to surrender, so they committed suicide against overwhelming odds. Every one of the eight men with their CO told the same story. Vesta's was the voice crying in the wilderness, and Brad was deaf to it. He had been all the way back in the jeep. She would not accept his attitude; would not accept what had happened that morning.

She went across and pulled him round to face her. 'Why would I lie? What would I gain? You know me better than anyone. Why would I lie about something so shocking?' As she studied his set face and the resistance in his eyes, she suddenly saw the truth. 'You *knew* this was going to happen. There was never any question of taking them prisoner, was there?'

'You've seen men die before. You've watched wholesale slaughter in tanks and in Italian vineyards. Why get so worked up about this?'

She was more than worked up. She was on the edge of hysteria. 'They buried the bodies in a mass grave. You saw that. Fifteen men who believed they'd died for their country.'

'Better than being branded killers and rapists by a Malay court and sentenced to death. They got off lightly.'

'What about the Geneva convention, the rules of war?'

'The Japs never recognized any rules but their own. You know that all too well. Now, see here. These bastards have been rampaging through this area doing what they've done everywhere in the world they've been. Villages have been burned; women, girls and young boys have been raped time and again; food and possessions have been stolen. The victims have suffered this because they've been so terrorized by this race they were afraid to tell the authorities. They've put up with three and a half years of it they could have spared themselves. That's how frightened they are.' He put a hand on her shoulder. 'Brian's brother was beheaded at Changi along with five RAF colleagues. Their crime was speaking while queuing for rice. Think now! If David had been with Chard, would *he* have walked up to those men, slung an arm along their shoulders and told them in a chummy manner that they could go home and pick up their lives? *Would he?* My guess is he'd have killed them with his bare hands if necessary.'

There was no answer to that because she knew he was right. 'But the war's over,' she protested. '*It's all over.*'

He gave a heavy sigh. 'For some it'll never be over. If you haven't got that yet you've been looking with closed eyes.' His hand gripped her shoulder. 'Come on, I want to get us to Singapore tonight to get my copy off for morning, London time.'

She watched him putting his clothes in a zip bag. He had banished her hysteria with reason, but it was reasoning she did not want to face. All at once she was weary of war; of drama; of human pain. Where was the afterglow, the happy ever after?

Would it be found chasing around the world for exclusives?

'So you're going to print this story the way it's been told, just as if you were an eye-witness?'

He seized the bag. 'That's right.'

Trying to hold on to the man she thought she knew, she said, 'I cast you as the great upholder of truth, however unpalatable.'

He looked hard at her. 'So I am when mankind will be served by telling it.'

'You don't think it would, in this instance?'

'Do you?'

She turned away from that challenge and walked to gaze through the unshuttered window at the peaceful orderly scene. After a moment, she said, 'I loved you for your determination, your courage, and for taking on the world, if it meant good would prevail. I appreciate all you've just said. Most of it makes sense. No, *all* of it makes sense. I just wish I hadn't been there to see it happen, because I can't simply dismiss it as you have.'

He came up from behind and held her upper arms gently. 'Hell, you're tougher than this, Vic.'

She turned. 'I was. War makes us all tougher than we should be. But it's *over*.'

'And?'

She swallowed. 'And I'd think a lot more of you if you killed this story instead of writing a pack of lies.'

'Brad Holland throw away an exclusive?'

'Just for once. *Please*.'

He brushed her lips with his own and smiled into her eyes. 'I can't do that. You know I can't.'

She heard herself say a final goodbye to him. 'Then I don't want to be part of a team.'

He made an impatient gesture. 'You're tired and emotional. You'll be OK when we get back to Singapore and take a day or two off. Right now you don't know *what* you want.'

'Yes, I finally do, Brad,' she told him quietly. 'You see, there's this guy I know in Berlin who gets upset because a little girl living among the rubble might never have owned a doll in her short, tragic life.'

*

The apartment in Fassberg was now occupied by a welfare worker, but the occupier offered Vesta the use of a settee for the short time she would be there. The woman was effusively pleased that Vesta was going to marry the good-looking captain after all, confessing that she had rather fancied him herself except that he had eyes for no one else.

It took three days for Vesta to trace Chuck Peterson, little realizing how lucky she was that he had not yet been sent home for a rest. Using all her powers of persuasion she told him he owed her a trip from last time, and exaggerated the rigours of her days in the detention cell. When he remained resistant, she told him she was trying to reach the man she loved and was going to marry as soon as he could get hold of a licence. To someone who boasted a reputation for wowing the fair sex, that line was irresistible and he caved in.

So another stolen trip on a C-54 took her to Gatow on the morning of a cold, sunny day. The Berlin skyline stood out clearly enough for the demands of any artist, but she had more important things to do than to make sketches. Time enough for that when she was married and installed here with her husband. After coffee and a doughnut with Chuck and his crew, she made arrangements to be picked up for the return flight in six and a half hours. Then she set about finding Paul. The journey from Singapore to Fassberg had taken almost a week, then three further days to find the American pilot she had coerced into again risking court-martial. She was impatient, longing to reach Paul, eager to see his expression when she told him how mistaken she had been.

Armed with the bogus Press pass Brad had given her, and using the maxim that if you look as if you have every right to be where you are no one will challenge you, Vesta walked up to a stationary truck and asked the driver where she would find the RE officers. He was German with poor English, so when Vesta broke into his own language he was so pleased he offered to take her there on his circuit. It meant a wait of twenty minutes, but she made a friend as she sat in the cab with him.

Once several aircrews were aboard the man set off around the perimeter, dropping them off as they reached their designated aircraft. Conversation became difficult against the roar of engines, but the driver went on beyond the aircraft parking bays towards a cluster of huts set aside from hangars and warehouses. His smile and nod told Vesta they must be her destination and, when he pulled up by them, a board identified them as such. She jumped to the ground with thanks, her heart now hammering against her ribs. Paul had told her never to walk in on him unannounced again, but this would be a moment they would both remember for the rest of their days together.

A jeep parked outside showed that someone must be in the main office. She prayed it would be Paul, so that she could say the opening words she had recited so often in her head all the way from Singapore. The door stood ajar to reveal a functional room with a desk, a filing cabinet and two telephones. Paul was standing with his back to the door, speaking into one of them. The sound of his voice was music in her ears as she gazed at his soft brown hair she had ruffled with affection, the neck she had kissed and nibbled, the width of his shoulders she had caressed, the waist, thighs and long legs she had enjoyed on so many nights with him, and she wondered why she had ever hesitated, had ever left him in Fassberg.

She recalled their days in Hanover with Jim, and the laughs they had all had together. She thought of Paul's proposal on the evening he had been shocked by the deaths of people he had unknowingly killed; former enemies. She remembered the bomb in the chimney, and how she had felt watching him high up there, sitting alongside instant death. She relived that morning he had woken her after four days away to tell her he had been half out of his mind with worry, and if he had not known Brad was in Fassberg would have instigated a police search for her. This man cared. He loved her above all things. He had still wanted her despite knowing she had gone off with Brad to Berlin. *He* would provide her afterglow. She finally had it in sight.

'I'm sorry, but that's your bloody problem,' he was saying with some heat. 'I've enough of my own . . . Yes, yes, I know it's top priority. So's everything around here . . . Yes, I . . . Look, I'll do what I can, that's all I'll say . . . Don't thank me . . . And don't expect bloody miracles. We've used them all up, chum.'

After slamming down the receiver Paul wrote something on a notepad then turned towards the door. Acute shock registered in his eyes, his jaw and his stiffening body as he gazed at her across ten feet of a room in the midst of thunderous, hectic activity.

Vesta had to force speech from a throat gone suddenly dry. 'There once was a chap called Jerry Stanstead, whose girlfriend turned him down. Then she realized what a fool she'd been and asked him to take her back. He married her right away before she could change her mind again.'

There was total lack of response from him. His expression did not soften, his mouth remained tight with anger. Then he said coldly, 'You've got the wrong man. My name's Gaynor.' Picking up his cap and jamming it on his head, he walked past her to the jeep, climbed in and drove away.

March, and Berlin had successfully survived the winter. The elements had been kind, for once. There had been a white Christmas but temperatures had not dropped as low as they frequently did in the first months of the year. The airlift had continued almost without a break, but, even as the Allied commanders congratulated themselves, they acknowledged that aircrews must be given a long rest. A few pilots had begun refusing to take off because they knew they were a danger to themselves and everyone else. Others began drinking so heavily they were incapable of controlling an aircraft. One entire American crew went AWOL for a week because the pressures had become unbearable. An RAF Dakota landed safely then taxied into the side of a hangar because the pilot had gone to sleep the minute the wheels touched down.

Plans were drawn up for all those who had been in Germany since the airlift began to be sent home for eight weeks while new men were brought over to replace them. The first batch went amid cheers of relief, but those new to the job inevitably slowed the process which had reached a peak of performance. Amounts being flown in daily grew smaller. If the British and Americans were worried, the Russians were much more so. They had not expected Berlin to survive the winter, and the airlift looked set to continue indefinitely. Their informers had reported the Allied plan to instigate two-monthly rest periods for crews, and this suggested some sort of permanent operation. Short of outright war, what else could be done to gain their desire to rule the whole of the German capital?

David had no wish to go to England and worried over how he could wangle permission to remain in Lübeck. He had spent all his rest periods with Monika, Sonja and Mirjana, including a seven-day leave in the middle of February. His relationship with Monika had entered a new phase since Christmas. He no longer questioned what she did, never showed anxiety or bade her to take care. His concern for her safety was no less, but he schooled himself to keep silent. She had told him there was no future for them, that she was devoted more to her work than him.

He found that difficult to accept. It seemed a reversal of all he had known throughout his life. Men traditionally split their energies between profession and family. Women in his experience concerned themselves fully with the latter. In his heart he felt that was how it should be. He had seen women do all manner of things during the war, but surely they should be allowed to return to their natural role now. He also happened to like the female body enhanced by lace and soft silk; it gave him pleasure to buy flowers and French perfume for women. At least, it had done in the days when girls flocked after him.

Apart from the short period of his marriage, Monika was the first person he had had a long-term sexual relationship with. At the start he had been so bowled over by the reaction her admiration created in him, he had merely been driven to satisfy needs long repressed. Inevitably, as confidence rushed back so did his natural preferences. By Christmas he had regarded Monika as his partner and treated her accordingly. He wanted to be the protective male who gave her all the things life had denied her. She had dismissed that image; she spurned his silks and satins; she needed his scarred body merely as a source of inspiration. Her love was based on his past suffering and his present hazardous endeavours. Yet this girl had given him the brand of intimacy he had never before enjoyed. Prior to 1942 affairs had been brief and wild, with girls as selfish as he had been. His Chinese wife had submitted but never reciprocated. Pat had held him off for so long because of Su, then offered him two hours beneath blankets in empty rooms. Monika had been there when he needed her. She had cleansed him of Kershaw's brutality; calmed his troubled conscience over two alien souls whose lives would be no worse, and probably better, than a legion of children in this troubled world. Monika had restored his sanity and his manhood. He yearned to gather her to him and keep her within his tender guidance, but no man could do that with a woman who risked torture and death in enemy territory and swore to continue her activities for as long as they were needed. When the airlift ended would it be the end of them, too? David dared not risk bringing that threat nearer by going to England for two months' rest. He might not return to Lübeck. So he waited with some anxiety for the next homeward batch to be named.

He returned from two days with his curious family feeling particularly worked up. Monika's Christmas information regarding the latest Russian ploy had been borne out by the new tense situation in Berlin. Massive reinforcements had been moved to Soviet borders in a threatening manner. She had now come back from another brief sortie with firm intelligence concerning a Russian plan to harass Allied aircraft flying through the neutral corridors. If this happened, there could be a number of accidents in the coming days. There were already too many. Weary pilots would be forced into taking evasive action which could all too easily jeopardize the close formations of transports plying those corridors.

There were no orders posted for the second exchange of crews, he noted with relief, but he nevertheless remained troubled as he attended his briefing for the first flight of his twenty-eight hours of continuous duty. Even the now-familiar whistling of 'The Skaters' Waltz' as he entered failed to lift his heavy spirits. Leaving his little family had been harder this time than on any previous occasion. Despite Monika's fervent admiration, he found the prospect of further hour after hour at the controls of a Dakota unwelcome and depressing. He had had enough of flying. Those enjoyable sessions in the little wooden house had lately bred in him the urge for a life like that all the time. No more tricky take-offs, no even trickier landings. No freezing cockpits, no coal dust or obnoxious fishy cargoes. No more painful, blocked sinuses, no sore eyes, no rasping cough. No more orders. He had obeyed orders all his life and was racked by a longing to be free, to spend his days as his own master with people he loved and a little girl bearing his name who seemed like his own child. In addition to this strong reluctance to go through the days he must endure until he could get back to that village was the fear that he would be ordered to England before it was possible to fulfil that longing.

The fear remained as he took off for Gatow on a clear, cold morning. Deep in thought he made the necessary transmissions before reaching his designated height and speed along the corridor, then fell into silence whilst automatically keeping his eye on his instruments and on the other aircraft so close to him.

About an hour into the flight he saw the solution to an unsatisfactory situation. On returning from Singapore in 1946 he had extended his RAF service by a further three years. That time would expire in July. He would not sign on for another three. Wherever he was at that time he would leave the life he had known from the age of nineteen and be free to do whatever he wished. Depression began to lift. Let the RAF do their worst, he had only to obey for another four months. He dearly wished he could take his 'family' back to Tarrant Hall. That would be perfect . . . but he could not, of course. Aside from it being impossible to introduce to the house his mother had occupied for most of her life his father's lover and their child, Monika would never settle for rural tranquillity. He must be the one to settle for less, and find a larger house in Lübeck where they could all live comfortably together. He was prepared to do that. He would do it now if he had not to fly coal, carrots and carbolic to a city full of people he would never see, some of whom had possibly shot down and killed his friends or dropped bombs on British airfields.

Well on his way to the significant Frohnau Beacon, David was shaken out of his daydreaming by a noise he had heard a myriad times before – a noise to put the fear of God into any aircrew. The roar of a diving aircraft spitting bullets from its wings.

'Christ!' he yelled to anyone who might be listening. 'What the hell's happening?'

By way of answer a dark shape flashed past the nose of his Dakota in a steep dive, levelling out at several hundred feet below him over Soviet territory. Then, before he could assimilate the full import of what had happened, there was a repeat performance. Fully alert now, and back in an earlier time, David took in the incredible truth that he was being 'buzzed' by Soviet fighters who were audaciously crossing the neutral corridors with the deliberate intention of causing havoc among the long line of heavily laden unarmed transports.

'Christ, Skip, what the hell's happening?' yelled his navigator.

'I've already asked that,' he snapped, eyes darting in every direction for another fighter and therefore temporarily losing sight of his instruments. 'God, if I was in a Spit I'd teach them not to do that to me.'

'You're wandering off course.' The prompt remark came from someone who did not have the clear view of his captain.

David immediately corrected, saying, 'That's as near to an act of aggression as you can come in my book.' Even as he spoke he spotted similar incidents ahead. There appeared to be an entire squadron of fighters up there with them, darting and diving between the closely spaced transports with daredevil panache. He gritted his teeth. They were bloody well enjoying it! Monika's information had been correct. The harassment had begun. As he watched, lumbering overladen aircraft were attempting to maintain height and distance in the face of this dangerous game. The slightest inaccuracy and there could be an almighty pile-up at any moment.

Gordon McLeod, his navigator, came to take a better look through the perspex and swore softly. The wireless operator then told them, 'There's all hell let loose on these frequencies. They're jammed. It's no use bloody shouting at Gatow control. What can they do about it? How's the situation now, Skip?'

'Seems to have settled down a bit,' he murmured, raking the clear ice-blue heavens with a vigilance hampered by coal dust under his eyelids. 'Sky's empty of the bastards.'

'Oh no, it ain't,' cried Gordon from the seat beside him. 'Take a dekko at this. *Coming right at us!*'

To his horror David saw a formation of around five fighters streaking through the sky no more than two thousand feet above them in the opposite direction. 'Bloody maniacs!' he swore, and caught himself automatically ducking as they raced overhead. 'They'll get us all killed!'

Pete, the wireless operator, appeared looking ashen. 'What's going on? I thought the sky was falling in on us.'

'Five YAKs, that's what,' David informed him, worrying about the ragged line ahead. It was quite obvious the tactics of the Russians were unnerving everyone. Instead of an evenly spaced straight line, the outgoing aircraft now represented an undulating sea. Altitude was being lost, and the space between noses and tails was varying in an alarming fashion. Watching the aircraft ahead while fretting about what the one behind him might be doing, David's attention was again diverted by Gordon shouting in his ear.

'Here comes another lot!'

From a cluster of dark dots in the distance, the fighters enlarged into a threatening, roaring formation much too close for comfort as they raced against the flow of machines in that narrow corridor, and passed overhead with a thunder of sound.

'Is that what they call Russian Roulette?' asked Pete in shaky manner.

'No, it's called the Last Desperate Act before Surrender,' David replied between his teeth. 'We've got 'em by the throat now, and this suicidal nonsense shows they don't know us as well as they should. If anything, it'll make us all the more determined. Get back to the radio, Pete. See if everyone's shut up yet. We'll be coming up to Frohnau shortly. Let's get to the ground before they start sending up the dancing bears.'

David's calm manner was deceptive. He was deeply unsettled by what had happened. While he could deal with the hazards of the airlift, it had been several years since his last combat flying and he was in the wrong aircraft for such tactics. He was even more unsettled by the fact that ahead and behind him were crews just out from England, new to the airlift's demands. Some might never have flown during the war, and it would take only one of them to panic to bring about a disaster. The Russians might well serve to increase Allied determination, but there were a lot of tired men in even more tired machines going back and forth to Berlin. These kinds of scare tactics they could do without.

David's future plans had been forgotten in the face of drama, and they remained in the recesses of his mind as he concentrated on the final approach to the airfield he thought he would surely remember, square foot by square foot, for the rest of his life. He had lost count how many times he had come in to land over the ruined city, but he should be able to touch down with his eyes closed by now. In the event, he decided to keep them open in case some other fool had a similar belief and tried it. He heard Pete, who was a Catholic, mutter a prayer of thanks when the wheels touched down on the runway recently extended, and no tyres burst, no wing fell off, and the tail remained firmly in place. David was inclined to join in. It was good to be down safely.

A marshaller directed him to a parking spot where loaders were waiting to seize the sacks of coal with lightning speed. Within twenty minutes the Dakota would be ready for the return flight. Just enough time for a cup of tea and a bun. He was sick of buns, but they kept him going until he could snatch a quick meal back in Lübeck before the next run. He switched off engines and went through the landing safety check as Pete and Gordon climbed out to drop to the ground in raw, bracing temperatures. When David left the machine, his crewmen, along with a few others, were already in a truck waiting to take them to one of the mobile canteens.

Amidst the thunder of so many ascending and descending aircraft it was still possible for an experienced man to hear something that did not sound right. David turned his head as he walked to the truck and saw one of the civilian transports taxiing towards him far too fast. A marshaller was frantically waving the pilot to slow, but it was obvious the large blue plane was out of control. The hair on the back of David's neck rose in horror as he stood rooted to the spot, watching the machine charge straight at the one he had just climbed from and smack into the side of its fuselage as the loaders all jumped clear. Impetus took both craft forward to where a York was parked half-loaded. The Dakota's right wing penetrated the third plane as the entangled machines slewed grotesquely to a standstill.

David began to run. There would be at least four crewmen trapped inside the wreckage. If it ignited they would not stand a chance. He did not think beyond that as instinct insisted that he help to get them out. He had seen men die in cockpits whose hoods had jammed, or because they were trapped by their injuries, as he had been in Sumatra. He had never forgotten being held by the legs in a Hurricane while foaming sea rushed to the shore all around him. A pilot's first reaction on crashing was to get out. When he saw someone else do it, he tried his best to help them.

Reaching the wreckage he leapt on to a truck half covered with sacks of vegetables, which had been dragged along with the wreckage. Scrambling over the sacks he was then able to reach the cockpit firmly jammed into the side of his own aircraft. One glance was enough to tell him he could do nothing unless he entered his Dakota and brought the men out through it.

Hampered by his heavy flying-suit he frantically began groping his way along the truck's load of sacks to the open hatch where loaders had begun taking off the coal he had flown in. Snatching up one of their grappling hooks he cast a swift glance around to find he was alone. The army of people which had been there was no longer even in sight. This would have to be a solo rescue effort, damn them!

The hammering of trapped men trying to free themselves spurred him into action. As he plunged into the belly of the Dakota he heard, with relief, the bells of rescue vehicles racing over the airfield. The nose of the civilian aircraft had penetrated so deeply, David initially thought it an impossible hope to even reach the cockpit through the scattered coal, but by scrambling up the great black mound he could just see the windows of the larger machine.

It was too dark to assess the situation inside, because coal dust had settled in a thick layer on the perspex, but someone was thudding on the fuselage and he heard the muffled cries of those inside. David did not waste energy shouting back. His breath was already rasping from the effects of the dust as he began attacking the perspex with the grappling hook. When this implement made slow work of it, he thought of the axe forward of his present position in the Dakota. By clawing his way over wreckage, coal and broken sacks, he reached the emergency weapon and returned to apply it with all the energy he could muster.

The thudding from inside strengthened in volume, but it was almost immediately drowned by a deafening thunder of sound all around him. As he hacked away it gradually occurred to him that the noise must be that of gallons of foam being sprayed over the wreckage to prevent any chance of sparks setting off an explosion. In the semi-darkness David then grew aware that he had smashed a way through, and he could now see some kind of movement within the crushed cockpit.

'Everyone OK?' he croaked, doubting if they would hear him above the sound of hoses spraying foam.

A face appeared through an aperture. 'Two of us are fit. Second pilot's badly hurt. Captain's dead. Can you bash away a bit longer?'

David thrust the grappling hook at someone who resembled a chimney-sweep. 'Have a go with this from inside.'

They both made short work of creating an escape hatch, and very soon the first of the trapped crewmen was able to climb free to help David – with the assistance of the fit man still inside – attempt to bring out the injured co-pilot. They were engaged in this tricky business when others appeared beside them. The ambulancemen took over the careful business of handling the casualty, who was moaning in pain and losing blood profusely.

'All right, sir, get these two outside and leave the rest to us,' one said to David, as the second fit man scrambled free. 'There's transport waiting to take you over to sick bay.'

'I'm all right,' he murmured.

'You're not all right. You must be a bloody lunatic to do what you did.'

In the sick bay David and the two civilians were told to lie on couches in the curtained cubicles and wait quietly for the doctor.

'Any chance of a cup of tea, Nurse?' asked the young navigator.

'Later. When Squadron Leader Powell has looked you over.'

'Couldn't you do that?'

'Just lie down, gentlemen,' she returned, used to impudence from her patients.

'Seems a pity to dirty these lovely white sheets.'

The woman's gaze took in their filthy unkempt state. 'None of you looks likely to bleed all over them. A little coal dust won't matter . . . but if you're worried about it you're welcome to wash them for me.'

'Tough as old boots, army nurses,' grumbled the frustrated swain climbing up to lie on a couch alongside David's. 'She might have softened up on the cup of tea.'

'I'll go for a stiff whisky,' muttered the second civilian.

David lay back gazing at the ceiling. He knew there was nothing wrong with him other than airlift fatigue, and was enjoying the chance to rest in a place of relative peace. Even so, after a minute or two he asked, 'What happened out there, for God's sake?'

'Search me,' said the man next to him. 'Everything seemed fine until we actually touched down. It struck me Jim was taking it a bit fast. Martin, our co-pilot, yelled something, and I was on my way to the cockpit when I saw a bloody Dak right in our path. Jim had slumped forward and Martin was pretty near crazy trying to avert certain disaster. I must have fallen and been knocked out on impact. Oh boy, that's one experience I won't want again.'

'I wasn't even aware of what hit us,' said the other man. 'Jim's well over fifty with a war record any man would envy, but he's been overdoing it on this airlift. Saw it as a chance to recapture old thrills and camaraderie. He missed it. Always rattling off anecdotes about night raids and hair-raising escapades. He was one of the Dambusters, so he said. Poor bugger! What a way to go out.'

'What better way?' David challenged, all too familiar with some of the others. 'It was quick. He was doing something he loved, and he didn't take anyone else with him. Was he upset by the YAKs and their scare tactics?'

'Not him,' said the navigator contemptuously. 'He just got flamin' mad. Swore like a trooper, he did, and longed to show them what for.'

'Didn't we all?' murmured David.

After a short silence the civilian said, 'You're a pretty cool customer. Whatever made you come in after us when everyone else was surely haring for the far side of the airfield?'

'That was my Dak you hit . . . I'd flown my bloody coal

427

from Lübeck in nice neat sacks. I wanted to check that you hadn't messed them all up,' he replied with typical aircrew flippancy. 'What was your load?'

'Petrol, chum. Didn't you see the hazard warnings? With your coal it would have made a merry blaze.'

David's eyes flew open with shock. He had seen nothing but the need to free those who were trapped. Small wonder the ambulanceman had called him a lunatic! As he lay taking in the implications of what he had done, he knew he had today used up another of his lives.

'You RAF blokes are *all* crazy, from what I've seen on this airlift caper.'

David began to shake with delayed reaction. They had grown crazy of necessity during those dark, wartime days. No sane men would ever have done all that had been demanded of them. So many of his friends and comrades had been lost. It was now all happening again. The airlift had been mounted because a new enemy was knocking on the door. Jim, with an enviable war record, had died because he had worked too many hours in the desperate bid to keep Berlin free. The Russians had killed him. If they continued their new aerial harassment, they would kill others. He closed his eyes again. How sick he was of death and killing!

In the morning's newspaper there had been a feature by Vesta's old flame, Brad Holland, concerning a group of Japanese soldiers still fighting in the Malayan jungle, unaware that the war was over. They had attacked a routine British patrol, then committed suicide rather than be captured to face terrorist charges. David was certain there were others roaming Far Eastern jungles cut off from news of what was happening elsewhere. He had spent seven months doing it in 1942. Kershaw and a million others like him were still fighting because they had no wish to stop. They would never forget. Further millions were now fighting because they saw a chance to expand territory, gain freedom, settle old scores. David was sick of it all and longed for July to come. He had been a crazy fool today. If that petrol had blown who would have looked after Monika, as he planned to do in some pretty little house where red squirrels leapt in nearby trees and clear water in a brook splashed gently over stones? A pretty little house in a quiet place where he could relax and stop worrying about how many lives he had left. He would then persuade Monika to give up her dangerous work. Her lives would not last forever, either.

The doctor arrived ten minutes later at the first of the examination couches. 'My God, it's "Biggles" again!'

'No, sir, his name's Sheridan. I assure you he seemed no more than slightly dazed when he came in, or I'd have called you sooner,' said the overworked nurse.

'Don't worry. He's simply fallen asleep. How did he get involved in this affair?'

'I understand it was his Dakota they wrecked. He went to their rescue.'

'Bloody fool! He has the Devil's luck. Someone should tell him to give up these heroics before he kills himself . . . which would be a tragic end for a man like him. Remind me to tell you his story one of these days.'

David flew back to Lübeck thirty-six hours later with a cargo of Berlin export goods, ten German children on visits to grandparents in the Western zones, the two civilian crewmen, and the body of their captain. There was no trouble from Russian fighters. The official explanation was that aerial manoeuvres were taking place and the neutral corridors crossed the chosen area. No one believed it would not happen again, and all pilots were prepared for repeat performances until the Russians tired of it.

When David landed his Dakota and taxied into the designated bay he caught himself wishing it was the last time. He had volunteered for this in order to fly himself into exhaustion, which would banish memories; he had continued to do it because a lovely young girl believed he was hitting at the Russians. All he wanted now was to walk away from it and be with her in a peaceful place they could call their own.

After the coffin had been removed, and the children shepherded into the little charabanc waiting for them, David, his crew and the two civilians climbed into a waiting truck to be taken across to Dispersal where they would be given a take-off time and details of their next flight. This allowed David two hours in which to shower, change his clothes and have a meal.

As he turned away wishing the break were longer, the man at the desk called out, 'Sir, there's a message here that says you're to see Wing Commander Forbes when you get back. It's been here two days.'

'Flipper' Forbes, so named by the RFC for his habit of somersaulting his Camel after a kill, could wait, David decided. It was probably to give him a rocket over the Gatow business. Unnecessary risk-taking, should have left it to the Rescue Squad, and so on. He would wash and eat first. With luck, he could take so long over his meal there would be no time to be told off. In his room was a second message marked URGENT requesting him to report to Forbes at his first opportunity. It was dated an hour after he had taken off on Wednesday morning, so it could have nothing to do with the crash at Gatow.

Stopping only to wash his face and hands, David then made his way through a maze of corridors to Forbes's office. After the WAAF clerk told her boss Squadron Leader Sheridan was in the outer office, David was asked to wait a few minutes. At the end of that time the padre entered and approached him.

'You've had some trouble at Gatow, I believe. Glad you came out of it all right.' He indicated the door. 'Shall we go in?'

Chilled by the inference of his presence, David walked through to where Forbes was standing beside his desk. He was not smiling. 'Sit down, David. Sorry to hear about the business at Gatow. Must have given you a hell of a fright to see that thing charging at you.'

'Yes.' What was going on here? The padre had drawn up a chair to sit facing him, and Forbes had perched on the edge of his desk.

'We have some curious news for you,' the churchman began. 'There's been an accident. The local police contacted us yesterday, but you had already left.'

'We thought it best to wait until you got back. No good would have come from radioing Gatow,' said Forbes.

'We were uncertain quite *what* to do, to be honest,' said the other in worried tones. 'There were two ladies in a car which apparently ran off the road and crashed into a tree. One of

430

them was a Madame de Martineau. The police gave us her legal name rather than her famous professional one, Sonja Koltay. The other was a young woman named Monika Szabo. I'm sorry to say they were both killed – most probably on impact.'

'The child in the back seat escaped without injury and is now in the care of the local orphanage, recovering from shock.' Forbes produced a cigarette case. 'Would you like one?' When David humbly shook his head, he continued. 'At Madame de Martineau's house the police found instructions among her papers that her solicitor be contacted immediately in the event of her death. He resides in Paris.'

'Monsieur Rambert revealed that his client had left instructions in her will to contact *you*, David.' The padre frowned. 'He claims the child, Mirjana Sheridan, is your illegitimate half-sister and she is to be placed in your sole guardianship. Did you ... *do* you know anything about this extraordinary affair?'

CHAPTER TWENTY

VESTA was packing to leave home. After a few weeks in a Bournemouth hotel trying to decide what to do with her life, she had reached a decision. She could not take up residence at Tarrant Hall. The atmosphere had changed since the advent of Leo. Her mother had made the place her own after years of being a caretaker hoping David would pick up the reins. Those few weeks over Christmas had shown Vesta it would be difficult to live as a third person in a happy household of two. Her loneliness would be accentuated by their togetherness. She now understood what life had been like for the wife of the brilliant Sir Christopher, who had never been there when she needed him.

Vesta had felt like a dog with its tail between its legs when she telephoned her mother to ask if she might stay for a few days, while looking for a studio. The feeling had intensified when neither Marion nor Leo had bombarded her with questions, because it was all too obvious they guessed she had made a mess of everything and thrown away the best future she had ever been offered. Their tact somehow worsened the humiliation of that morning in Gatow.

Fate had not completely abandoned her, however. Almost immediately she found a beautifully renovated cottage in Tarrant Maundle being let by the owners who were going abroad for nine months. It was ideal for Vesta's purposes. She would be near Pat and the Chandlers, close enough to home to visit occasionally, and in an area she loved. One room in the cottage would make a temporary studio where she could experiment without pressure of commissions. She had no notion which direction to take with her career, and presently had no interest in it at all. Hopefully, nine months on her own in the cottage would get her back on her feet before the owners returned and wanted her out.

In truth, she was bruised and shaken by what had occurred. At Christmas she had been unable to choose between two men. Now she had lost both. Maybe, as Pat suggested with heartfelt sympathy, the red-haired doctor was the best bet. It was only a joke both used to cover their pain, and Vesta had tò lie about her reason for finally breaking with Brad. She was unable to tell even Pat about the slaughter in the jungle she had witnessed, and it haunted her sleep still. Brad had printed the official version of the story, completing her disillusion. Perhaps Leo had been right to claim she was a hero-worshipper? If so, the go-getting, afraid-of-nothing seeker-of-trouble had fallen from his pedestal. Leo himself had voluntarily stepped down in admitting he had married a woman to gain a house. What of Paul? She had stood him on one after the chimney bomb and now bitterly regretted doing so. He had never wanted to be there.

On this bright, blustery day in early April, Vesta was collecting together those things dear to her to take to her temporary home on the following morning. Halfway through the task she sat on the bed, knowing tears were threatening. These possessions told the story of her life; twenty-nine years leading to this moment of failure and isolation. Scattered around her were mementoes of people who had passed through them. Some had been killed, some gone into the mists of a future apart from hers. A Swiss cuckoo-clock; a rag doll; a sepia photograph of a young and happy family on holiday in Provence: an incredibly handsome father, a little boy as beautiful as a cherub, a toddler with a dreamy expression and a woman with her arm around the boy's waist. There was the string of pearls worn at her first ball; the golden lid of a chocolate box presented to her and her ATS friends by a grateful subaltern they had guided to safety on their transmitters, before the other girls had been killed by a direct hit on their hut; a leather stuffed camel from Philip Bream, who had wanted to marry her in Cairo; a crumpled snapshot of a girl sitting at a table beneath an awning in the desert, surrounded by sun-burned, laughing young men in khaki shirts and rolled up shorts. A few names escaped her, but she remembered Jingo, Jim, Tiger, Max. Where were they now? An empty Chianti bottle. What erotic memories of a night in Italy that prompted!

A lace shawl bought by a besotted, homesick American tank commander who said she resembled his girl back home. William P. Myerson the Third. Vesta smiled through her tears. He had died in a field hospital a week later, but he had been so very proud of that name. His family had surely been very proud of him.

As she continued to reflect on those things spread before her, Vesta knew the place for them was a deep cardboard box in the attic, where pictures and possessions of a previous generation of Sheridan, lay preserved. Her past would be inappropriate in a rented cottage from which a new woman would emerge. Yet the past continued to obsess her as she struggled, reluctant to do what was necessary. A carved box, and a silver frame containing a photograph of four smiling people celebrating at the Officers' Club in Hanover. Both were presents from Jim Shannon. Dear Jim. Was he still flitting from girl to girl? A jewelled lipstick case bought in Switzerland as an engagement present. Should she have returned it with the ring to Paul's family? A china pig dressed in breeches and a tail-coat, a filigree brooch, a five-year diary, a rare edition of Shakespeare's *The Tempest*, a Victorian Valentine card, Helena Rubenstein perfume bought off an American who had a large supply – so many things Paul had given her. She had no right to keep them, but could not send them all back. A cardboard box was the only answer. One day a little girl would wander into the attic and be enchanted with what she found – as she and Pat had been on discovering relics of the three handsome, talented Sheridan brothers in a previous age.

The telephone beside the bed rang, making her jump nervously and return to the present. Robson announced from the hall that a gentleman wished to speak to her, then switched the call through to her extension before she could ask who it was.

'Yes, hallo.'

'Hallo, Vee.'

'*David!* Where are you?'

'At Greater Tarrant post office.'

'Good heavens! Whatever are you doing *there*? Why aren't you – David, are you all right?' she asked with sudden fear, remembering Pat telling her he had called in similar fashion after returning from the Far East.

'I'm fine.' A pause. 'Could you come right away? I need to talk to you.'

'Yes . . . yes, of course. But what . . .'

'Don't tell anyone where you're going. I'll wait in the Punch and Judy . . . and Vee, keep to yourself the fact that I'm home. I told Robson to stay mum. I've got to get something straightened out before I come to the Hall.'

'I'll be there in roughly ten minutes.'

Glad of the little car she had bought in Bournemouth, Vesta slipped out of the house and took it from the garage with her mind in a whirl of questions. What was going on? Why was David reluctant to come home? How had he known she was at the Hall? What must he get straightened out and how could *she* help him? As she drove past the foundations of her mother's community project, then the unsightly prefabs, an unwelcome answer to all those questions hit her. David had married a completely unsuitable girl again, and had brought her to live at Tarrant Hall! Bang would go Marion's present happiness, and so would Leo's borrowing of the house he loved. And Pat . . . poor Pat! The girl must be unsuitable or he would not be adopting this tentative way of introducing her. Vesta was filled with instinctive resentment which extended to her brother. How *could* he do this to them all?

By the time she pulled up in front of the café which had been the bastion of the little market town since her father had been a small boy, Vesta was furious at being dragged into David's predicament and certain she would dislike her sister-in-law on sight. Maggie Bates, the elderly cashier who had sat behind the till of the Punch and Judy Tea Rooms for as long as Vesta could remember, greeted her and told her her brother was in the back of the parlour with the young lady. Gritting her teeth Vesta marched through to the snug room they used to frequent in those days before the war, when a large pot of tea and a plate of fancies had cost only one and ninepence. David was sitting in the window-nook facing the doorway. The other two tables were unoccupied. It was too early for lunch and a little late for morning coffee. Vesta pulled up short in utter dismay. There was a child next to her brother on the window-seat, but no sign of its mother. Dear God, had he married a German war widow?

David got up and held out both hands to take hers. 'Bless you, Vee. Thanks for coming.'

'How did you know I was at home?' she asked through stiff lips, ignoring the child.

'I tried your address in Fassberg. A neighbour told me you'd come back to England just before Christmas.'

'You went there?'

'I telephoned – got the number through the army. The woman who answered said you'd come home to be married.'

'She was out of date.' Her lips had difficulty in moving.

'You're *not* married?'

'No, but you are, I take it.'

'Good Lord, no.'

'Then whose child is that?' she demanded, confused even further.

A noise behind Vesta heralded a waitress wearing too much lipstick and not enough dress. The traditional black frock had been cut lower in the neck and higher in the skirt. 'Are yew ready to order, madam?' the girl asked in artificial tones.

'Oh, a pot of tea,' Vesta told her wildly.

'We only do tea between ten and eleven, and from three to 'arf past four. Sor-ree!'

Vesta turned on her. 'Don't be ridiculous. I've been using this place since I was a child and there's never been a limit on when tea can be made. Tell Mrs Bates I'll come out there and make it myself, if necessary.' Turning back to David, she added in angry undertones, 'Did you *have* to do this? Why couldn't you have simply come home?'

'You'll understand when I tell you. Please sit down, Vee, and allow me to put you in the picture. It's a damned tricky situation.'

She sat heavily on the single chair facing him. 'That's nothing new where you're concerned. Why can't you do anything straightforward?'

'That's rich coming from you. I thought you were going to marry Brad, then some other chap you admired in Fassberg.'

Still very worked up, Vesta leaned across the table. '*Whose* is that child beside you?'

'Father's.'

It was so totally unexpected, so impossible, so painful, Vesta could only stare at him in shock. David was serious!

436

'I'm sorry, Vee, but you were determined to shout me down. I meant to break it to you more gently.'

'But . . . how *can* it be. It's so young.'

'Not *it*, *she*. Her mother was pregnant when Father was killed. He didn't know.'

Studying the little girl properly now, Vesta saw a face of immense childish beauty, a mass of red curls and large eyes of violet-blue. But her father had been nearly fifty. How could he have . . .? She swallowed back a cry of protest, remembering again Paul saying how terrible it seemed for one's parents to do such things. Her mind, everything in her, rejected this, and yet reason told her David would not lie about it. The little girl was gazing at Vesta in apprehension, a buttered bun untouched on the plate before her.

The waitress arrived with tea on a tray which she plonked so hard on the table the milk spilt. Vesta hardly registered the incident. The child was lovely enough to be her father's – she could even see David in her expression – but the news was very hard to take. The implications had not even occurred to her when David pushed on.

'You can see why I couldn't simply arrive at the Hall with our illegitimate half-sister.'

'Oh David, how dreadful!' she exclaimed, turning her attention back on him. 'Whatever possessed you to bring her here? Where's the mother? How did she find you? Were you *mad* to let her fob the child off on you? Of course, you can't take her home. You *can't*. You've been cruel enough to Mummy as it is. We both have.'

'Which is why I had to talk to you first.'

Ignoring the tea, Vesta demanded again, 'Where's the mother?'

'I'm afraid she's dead.'

For the first time she noticed the gravity of her brother's expression. He really did look very upset. She took a deep breath. 'The child is *yours*, isn't she?'

'She is now,' came his inexplicable reply. Putting an arm round the little girl and drawing her close to his side, David embarked on a long story concerning their father and the artist, Sonja Koltay, who had conducted an affair for several years unaware that they were both in the espionage business.

'Sonja was given the codename "Mirjana" which she has passed on to their child, and it was only when she was loaned to SOE for a special mission that they came face to face as interrogator and victim.' He gave a heavy sigh. 'The reason he came with me on the night he was killed was because she was the agent involved. I'd dropped her over there a couple of times before, but had no idea about the rest. I guessed that night, when I saw her face after landing. Her pain, added to his determination to get over there to help bring them back, said it all, Vee. She told me at Father's memorial service that she was going to have his baby, and asked that we be friends for his sake. I agreed. We kept in touch for a year, or two, and she wrote that her child had been registered as Mirjana Sheridan.'

He went on to tell how he had met her by chance in Lübeck, and then became a regular visitor to the house whenever he had rest periods. Little Mirjana had been told about her brother and sister and the big house they lived in in England.

'She took to me right away, Vee, and I've grown to love her. Last month Sonja was killed in a road accident. Her will named me Miri's guardian.' His frown contained more than a hint of pain. 'She has no one else in the world, and I'm the only one she trusts.'

'Oh, lord, what a predicament,' breathed Vesta, eyes on the little girl. 'Does she understand what's happened?'

'Of course the poor thing does!' he said explosively. 'She's lost her mother and Monika.'

'Who's Monika?'

'Her . . . her nurse. I've been dragging Miri across Europe with a German Frau in tow trying to settle the legal side of it all. The RAF gave me compassionate leave on top of my back-dated leave. After that, I've got a home posting in Oxford behind a desk until my time runs out in July. I've got to do something about her, Vee.'

'You'll have to pretend she's yours.' It was all she could come up with.

He said wearily, 'I've been through every option I can think of and none of them are foolproof. Her principal language, at present, is German. There's no way I could have duffed up a Fräulein in 1944. Look, Vee, you said just now I'd been cruel enough to Mother already, but it's Father who did this, not me. I've just taken over from him.'

'Poor you! Poor little girl! She looks terrified.'

'I'm not surprised. I told her she was going to meet her lovely sister, and in comes a firebrand who shouts at me, shouts at the waitress, and keeps darting angry looks at her. Good thing she can't understand what we're saying, but she's sensitive enough to know she's not welcome.'

'Oh, David, I didn't mean to fly off the handle. Things aren't going too well for *me*, at the moment, and this *is* a bit of a facer, admit it.' He nodded. 'Why didn't you tell me about this woman a long time ago?'

'She's not "this woman". You've seen her work – Father was mad about it. She . . . she was a cultured, talented Hungarian of considerable beauty and intellect. If you had met her you'd understand why Father fell in love with her. She was the perfect partner for him.'

'Why didn't you tell me earlier?' she insisted.

He shrugged. 'At the time I was pretty well shaken by the events of that night. You'll surely understand that.'

'And later?'

'You'd always put Father on a pedestal – you're inclined to do that with people you love – and I didn't think you'd accept it. Sonja was in Paris furthering her career. The likelihood of something like this happening never occurred to me, naturally. One of the reasons I'd never told Mother about that night was how to explain why he was so insistent on going with me then, but had never gone before. As you said, I've been cruel enough to her without adding to it.'

'I shouldn't have said that,' Vesta told him. 'None of us has been all that kind to her. That's why she's so happy with Leo.'

'He's the other problem. I imagine he's no fool. Whatever we decide to do had better be good or he'll see through it.'

'He wouldn't spill the beans to Mummy,' she assured him. 'He doesn't love her but he protects her like mad.' After another glance at Mirjana – a much softer, sympathetic one – she said, 'You spoke about July. What are you planning to do then?'

'Leave the RAF and come home. I've had enough, Vee. Time to hang up my wings and pick up all the pieces. The war's finally out of my system.'

439

'What about Pat?'

His face changed through several expressions before he cried, 'That's it! Is Uncle Bill at home?'

Vesta was bewildered. 'Yes, why? You don't have to ask his permission to marry her.'

He appeared not to have heard that. 'He knew about Sonja. Father told him everything; they were so close. *He's* the best person to advise us on this. The Chandlers are Mother's dearest friends. They'll be able to tell us what is the best solution to suit her.' He got to his feet. 'I'll ring him now. Get to know Miri while I do it . . . and for God's sake drink some of that tea after browbeating Pouting Pansy to bring it for you.'

Mirjana looked set to cry when David got up, although he told her he would only be away a moment or two. To avert tears, Vesta began to chat to the child in German, still finding it difficult to believe her erudite, self-possessed father could have conducted a passionate affair. Would she be able to see those Koltay pieces now without hating them?

'How do you do, Mirjana. My name is Vesta, and I'm David's sister.'

Calmed by the friendly tone, and by the fact that she could now understand what was being said, the child began to respond in short, sharp sentences. It was then she changed from being an impossible, embarrassing encumbrance into a small, lost human being. Vesta recalled Paul's cry of protest over the little girl whose short life had been so bleak she might never have had a doll. He had said she was about three, like Mirjana. Surely the Sheridan family could not disown this other little soul who was facing tragedy.

Vesta moved to the window seat to sit beside her half-sister and take her hand. Perhaps she had put her father on a pedestal, as Leo claimed, but this daughter had never known him. He would have loved her, loved the beauty of her. With two such parents, Mirjana could not help but be talented. The renowned Sir Christopher Sheridan could do nothing for his child; his family must act on his behalf. He had surely passed on some of his brilliance to her. Mirjana would be *his* afterglow.

*

Marion could not take her eyes from the child sitting beside David in the Chandlers' large airy room. 'Sonja Koltay must have been beautiful as well as talented.'

'She was, Mother.'

'How typical of Chris to die for her,' she mused, lost in other times. 'He rushed into the burning theatre to save Laura, you know, and almost died for *her*.' A faint smile touched her mouth. 'He believed in chivalry, honour, beauty and elegance. It came from reading all the Greek classics as a boy. He lived his life along those lines and must often have been cruelly disillusioned. I was completely the wrong partner for him. What a pity they met each other when it was too late.'

'Not too late, Marion,' put in Bill, puffing at his pipe in a relaxed fashion. 'Like Laura, she made up for the disillusions you mentioned and allowed him to live in his impossibly perfect world for a while. This gorgeous little maid is the result. No, not too late.'

'She really *is* gorgeous,' crooned Tessa. 'I can't wait to take her to Bournemouth and buy her the prettiest dresses they've got.'

'*I* want to do that, Mummy,' said Pat, offering Mirjana the stuffed cat from her bedroom and smiling when she took it. 'She's going to be the most spoiled child around.'

'No, she isn't,' said Marion firmly. 'With her beauty she'd soon become a little madam, and I won't have that. Chris wouldn't want it either.'

'Or her mother,' put in David.

Marion smiled at her son, who had apparently finally come home in a mental as well as physical sense. 'I believe she knew very well Miri would be in the best hands when she made you her guardian. The poor woman could not have expected it to happen so soon; the will was probably made in expectation of her child being a young woman and you a respectable ageing man when it came into force.'

'And you a doting, ancient crone,' said Bill dryly.

For a moment Marion felt a flutter of fear. She would never be that; never see this child, who was as lovely as David had been, grow into a young woman. But, oh, she wanted to have her for as long as she could. How shrewd of Bill to know that.

When Chris had run away to enlist leaving her with a tiny baby, she had been turned out of Tarrant Hall by Roland. From that moment on, she had fought fiercely for her child and loved him more than her life. Sonja Koltay's child had also been abandoned by Chris – not voluntarily, of course – and she must have fought for her child, too. David had been three when Chris took them both to the Hall to live as a family. Mirjana was three. Time she came home where she truly belonged . . . and time David was set free from maternal bonds.

'I want to get one thing straight before we go any further,' Marion told them. 'If anyone's going to Bournemouth to buy her pretty dresses, it's *me*.'

'And me,' added Leo, who had not yet spoken on the subject. He smiled at Marion. 'I've never had a child of my own. I want to enjoy every hour of this one.'

She reached for his hand. 'You can teach her English, darling. And when she's word-perfect, you can start on Norwegian. Chris was fluent in thirty-six languages. This girl is certain to be quick at learning.'

He laughed. 'Oh boy, back to school, eh?'

Tessa gazed around the room, and said quietly, 'This is like old times, isn't it? The Chandlers and the Sheridans all here together again. Do you think we should celebrate, Bill?'

'Sure, we should. Come on, David, help me do the honours and let Vesta have a go at cuddling that little sweetie. You two are the only ones who can communicate with her at the moment.'

'Make that three,' put in Leo from his corner seat. 'Some of the German I learnt is unsuitable for a little girl's ears, but I'm sure I can get along with her on basics. *Do you sell stamps? I need a new toothbrush.* That kind of thing.'

Everyone laughed, and Mirjana surveyed them all with large, wondering eyes which no longer betrayed apprehension. Marion caught Tessa's glance. Her dearest friend raised an enquiring eyebrow, and she nodded reassurance. Everything was all right. They were all here together again – Chris represented by a daughter with a Hungarian name who spoke in German. A worthy child for such a man. Marion's glance strayed to Vesta. She was unhappy, and neither Paul nor Brad seemed to be in her life now. Yet she was lovely to look at, full of courage and immensely talented. Another child worthy of Chris. Her gaze travelled on to David holding glasses while Bill poured champagne. Her son was looking tired and older than his years, but the wildness had gone from his eyes and manner. He had come home and, in July, would take over the running of his property after sacrificing so much for his country. An extremely worthy child for any man.

Only David and Pat could sort out whether they would ever be together, and it would surely take time. It was a precious commodity for Marion now. Surrendering the estate to David would buy her a little more; maybe a lot more. The new village centre was going up fast, and life with Leo was even happier than before. Now there was Miri, as an insurance against not living long enough to see her grandchildren. It would be wonderful to have the child at Tarrant Hall. She had failed Chris during his lifetime, but this was one thing she was capable of doing for him. She thanked God for Bill, who had known her well enough to give her this last delight.

The two men came round with glasses filled to the brim. Bill always said to hell with niceties, let's get all we can in the glass. Marion turned to smile at Leo, and he gave a wink that said all was well with his world.

'Right you are, then, ladies and gentlemen,' boomed Bill from the centre of the room. 'Here's to us all. Here's to peace and goodwill. Most of all, here's to a little beauty who's going to sparkle more than all the champagne in France in the years to come.'

They met on Wey Hill because it was *their* place. It was a perfect April day made for lovers. It should have been ten years ago when David was young and vital, and Pat was full of romantic ideals. Then, he had been arrogant and playing the field; she had believed herself in love with his father. Now they were meeting, scarred and cynical, ideals left by the wayside and a world of pain between them. David had asked Pat to meet him this morning after his return with Mirjana because he owed her an apology and some kind of explanation. That was all.

He had slept deeply and with an untroubled mind for the

first time in months. There had been a sense of peace in that room in which he had grown up. The country silence had never before seemed as blessed. Tessa's words about old times, with Chandlers and Sheridans all together, had affected him strongly, making him sense that he had gone full circle and was back where he belonged.

As he rode through the gentle sunshine, looking out over verdant countryside which was soft on the eyes, they no longer pricked from coal dust or constant vigilance of an instrument panel. His ears were free of the roar of engines. His spirits were surprisingly calm. Fate had decided his future. There was now a wonderful feeling of release from the drive to live up to expectations.

Vesta had painted *The Afterglow* as a tribute to their father. Bringing Mirjana home and caring for her was his. All his obligations would be fulfilled once he had spoken to Pat. He had yesterday made his peace with Marion and Vesta; he had accepted Leo and outlined his plans to them all. This meeting with Pat would remove the last obstacle to freedom of a kind he had never before known.

She looked particularly lovely today in jodhpurs and a thick toffee-coloured sweater over a polo-neck in apple green. A vision of health and energy so welcome after the thin, exhausted, desperate people of Germany.

David smiled as he reached her. 'One of these days I'll get here early and surprise you.'

'One of these days I'll come late.'

'Not you,' he said softly. 'Reliable, loyal Pat.'

They dismounted and tied their horses to the lone tree, then began to walk together along the level stretch above her village. Pat opened the conversation by asking how Mirjana coped with her first night in England.

'Remarkably well. When a child loses two people in her life and finds herself surrounded by an entire group vying with each other to smother her with love, she soon adjusts. It's all wonderfully new, at the moment, but there'll surely come a time when all she'll want are the two she can no longer have. Uncle Bill will step in and help her through that patch. Thank God I asked him what I should tell Mother. She took it so well, and appears to adore her.' He sighed. 'Millions of children all over the world have been through hell and have no Uncle Bill to help. Miri is going to be all right.'

They walked on for a moment or two. 'Leo asked this morning how we are going to explain her presence to the village. We hadn't got as far as thinking about that. Mother surprised me by saying she didn't give a damn what the village was told, but Leo pointed out that the truth, although acceptable to us, would make Miri's life uncomfortable. We've settled on telling half the truth and saying she's the orphaned daughter of a friend of mine, whom I've adopted. I'd already decided that was my next move, anyway. A better arrangement for us all than my being a guardian. Adoption will make Miri a legal Sheridan in the eyes of the world.'

Pat stopped, bringing him to a halt, and faced him wearing an expression he knew so well. 'You're such a wonderful person.'

'No, Pat, just someone struggling through life trying to find the right direction to take.' He reached for her hand. 'I . . . I have to tell you something. Will you listen without interrupting until I've finished?'

'Yes . . . if that's what you want.'

Leading her forward again, he fastened his gaze on the distant hills of that place in the world where he really belonged. 'When I went back to Singapore two awful things happened. I did one of them, the other was done to me. The first made me feel ashamed and guilty; the second took away any remaining sense of worth. I . . . well, I simply wanted to crawl away and hide from those who loved me. Being with them multiplied my shame and self-disgust. I found it impossible to speak about it – even to Uncle Bill – so I warded off questions by making you all hate me. It was easier that way. I hated myself.'

Pat squeezed his hand tightly, and he was conscious of her searching glance, but she said nothing. He continued. 'Living with Sonja in Lübeck was a young Estonian girl whose family had been brutalized by Russians overrunning their country early in the war. Monika had been raped by soldiers when she was twelve, and almost certainly on other occasions.'

His voice thickened with emotion as he saw again that young girl in a doorway gazing at him with such passionate intensity. 'Sonja had told her about me in connection with

445

Miri's father's death, and Monika foolishly saw me as some kind of inspirational hero. She was . . . she was only eighteen and ready for a knight in shining armour. Out of the blue, he turned up.' It was a moment or two before he could go on. 'I was no knight, just a man looking for salvation. This girl, who had suffered much the way I had, offered it. Because her experience of life was deep I could tell her what I had been unable to bring myself to say to you. We became like a complete family in that little German house near the airfield. I grew to love them all and, throughout those unbelievably exhausting days, I kept going on the dream of a new start with them which would somehow wipe out my past. An impossible dream, of course, but I *needed* it.'

'Why impossible, David?'

The quiet question brought him back from that dream to reality on a hillside with a girl he had known all his life. He frowned. 'Admiration for Sonja, Father and me had led Monika to agree to work for a group similar to SOE. She was going regularly into Soviet territory and bringing back information which Sonja put into code and despatched. They both refused to give up the work when I begged them to. You see, they looked beyond the present and saw what most of us closed our eyes to. One war had ended, but another was waiting to start.'

Unaware that he was now gripping Pat's hand with painful strength, he forced himself to carry on. 'The police told me their car had run off the road and hit a tree. They refused to give any further information except that Sonja had been at the wheel. She always drove when they went out together. Monika was . . . was a crazy driver, as I knew from experience. *But Sonja was driving that day.* I . . . I'll never be certain it was merely a tragic accident. One careless word from either of them, one unguarded move, and they could have become targets in the espionage game. I know how it's played. I *know.*' He swallowed back sudden sharp grief. 'The saddest aspect of that possibility is that I suspect Monika would have felt that being murdered by her enemies made her worthy of those who had inspired her.'

He stopped to gaze out at the valley scene whose very peacefulness made his words sound hollow and unreal. Yet he knew there would be other Monikas and Sonjas in the days to come, so far removed from the life he was planning here.

'Did you truly love her, David?'

He continued to study the valley. 'I don't know. I tried to turn her into the person I badly needed at that time, and failed. She did the same with me. She restored my sanity and I loved her for *that*. I'm not sure what I gave her in return. Her youth and dignity, perhaps. I'll never forget her, or Sonja.'

They stood in silence for some time, holding hands, neither wanting to hurry something which must be allowed to take its time now the right moment had come. Finally, Pat asked what he planned to do now.

David turned to her, releasing her hand. 'I'll take over the running of the estate from Mother. It's high time she had a rest, although Leo appears to have coaxed a new woman from her. Such energy! The youth centre project has become a real passion. That's apparent after a single day with her.' He sighed. 'I've been pretty unkind to her one way and another. I'll do my best to compensate, but being the object of . . . well, of almost *devouring* affection was difficult. I sometimes rebelled and hit out. Now she has Leo it'll be easier.'

'She's really happy with him.'

'I can see that.' He began walking again and she fell in beside him. 'Mother sold a set of abstracts to pay for her youth centre. I think I'll sell a few more to cover the annual losses. I've given up the idea of switching to pigs. Things are changing in rural areas. The sleepy old village will be a relic of pre-war days. Mother has the right idea. We have to provide facilities to persuade people to stay with farming, and they have to be exciting enough to compensate for wartime activities. We're all the same, you know. Driving a tank, leading a squadron, chasing a U-boat might have been dangerous but it gave us a sense of great worth. Ploughing, milking, harvesting don't have the same appeal. While I don't advocate giving up our traditions, I do see that dance-halls, cinemas, milk-bars and football matches must also have their place in our local life. I want to be in on building that up. I also want to work the estate up to its former prosperity. The ins and outs of landowning are something of a mystery to me, but I'll soon get the hang of it with the help of Mother and Jack Marshall.'

'Won't you miss flying?' she asked. 'It's been your great passion for as long as I've known you.'

'I'm taking up new passions now. As a matter of fact, the managing director of Airborne Fuels Incorporated offered me a job flying for his company after some idiotic heroics at Gatow, but I turned it down. I'm thinking of becoming one of its directors and investing in the company, however. It's based in Yeovil. Near enough for me to attend meetings and keep an eye on its activities. Aviation is going to go far when the world gets back on its feet, but I want to keep mine on the ground from now on.'

After a moment or two of silence Pat stopped. 'Is that it, your plan for the future?'

Continuing for several more paces he slowed, then turned back to her. 'God knows if it'll work or not, but it's the best I can come up with at short notice.'

She walked to him slowly, her eyes misty with tears. 'Where do I fit into this plan? When you returned from Singapore to make us all hate you, you failed miserably. We continued to love you. Especially me. And I want to know what you're going to do about it.'

He stood before her feeling immensely unsure of himself. Having successfully got through all he had had to say to her, this now threatened his fragile composure. 'Didn't . . . didn't you understand what I told you about Singapore just now?'

'What I understand is that for a long time now all kinds of people have made impossible demands, inflicted unbearable stress and done the most terrible things to you,' she responded emotionally. 'Have you any idea how powerless I've felt watching them gradually change you outwardly and inwardly? When you came back from Singapore that first time you turned to me and made me see that I'd always loved you. I've never stopped. And I don't give a damn what you've done to make you feel ashamed and disgusted.' She brushed away tears with an impatient gesture. 'You say this Monika gave you back your sanity. Well, I must thank her for that, but *I* could have done it if you'd given me the chance, if you'd ever got into your thick head the fact that I've never wanted a knight in shining armour, just someone I love so much I . . . I . . . oh, *David!*'

She flung herself against him while she sobbed with uncharacteristic loss of control. As he held her close David acknowledged with a sense of awe that *no* man could ever feel worthy of such unconditional devotion, but that he was the lucky one to be given it. He stroked her hair with a hand that shook slightly, and told himself he had a great deal to learn as well as a great deal to forget in the days to come.

Eventually Pat grew calmer, and David heard himself say, 'You've known all the people I've been, yet still stayed around. Would you like us to get married?'

She arched away from him with a sigh of relief, her face streaked with tears. 'Of course, you idiot . . . but only if that's what you want, too.'

'You're not getting much of a bargain.'

A wobbly smile broke through. 'Yes, I am. I've never forgotten that morning under the blankets, my lad.'

As he searched her face, her eyes showed him he had almost missed the best thing life had yet offered. Slowly he said 'I've been such a bloody fool. Never let me forget *that*.'

She feathered her fingers across his mouth. 'Please take me to the nearest haystack, darling.'

'I can manage something better than that,' he murmured. 'Mother and Leo are out for the rest of the day buying Miri the prettiest dresses they can find. How would you like to try out all the bedrooms at the Hall and choose which you'd like as ours?'

Although she made no reply he was left in little doubt of her agreement, and the April morning became even more gentle above that quiet valley of home.

It was hot in her rented cottage that summer. On a day late in July Vesta found little air in her studio room, although the windows and front door were open to allow any breeze to come through. Mopping her brow with a piece of cloth, she stood back to survey her canvas. Workmanlike was the word which first sprang to mind. That was how her father would have described it. She abandoned her brushes and went downstairs to make tea.

After four months here she had still not found a fresh direction for her talent. At times she wondered if it had gone for good, and she had pursued the disastrous path of trying to force inspiration when it was lacking. After putting the kettle on to boil she sat on the window-seat with a leg curled beneath her while she watched iridescent damselflies hovering over the small pond at the end of the garden. It had been sunk to encourage wildlife, which it did very successfully. Vesta had tried her hand in that direction, but frogs, field mice, flycatchers, kingfishers, newts and grass snakes remained no more than sketches.

She poured boiling water on the tea, then returned to her window while it brewed. Wild flowers had occasionally appeared on her canvases, but so many brilliant painters of flora and fauna put her efforts into the shade. Scenes from Wey and Longbarrow Hills were effective and competent, but no more than that. The 'on the farm' theme had very swiftly been abandoned. Any resemblance between sunny, romantic haymaking and real farming was laughable, and Vesta Sheridan painted realism. She had tried railways, but her steam engines chugging across country landscapes looked like the posters one found on mainline stations;. In desperation she had brought from beneath sheets her set of airlift canvases. They were still unfinished. Seeing them had been too painful.

Fetching tea in a cup and saucer painted with violets, Vesta settled more comfortably on the window-seat. The blockade was finally over. Berlin had been saved from Russian domination, but not without cost. A large number of men had died before the Soviet authorities accepted that not even scare tactics in the air corridors were going to stop supplies from being flown in. They re-opened rail, road and water routes, but cut off all access to and from their sector, effectively dividing the capital into East and West Berlin, further emphasizing the distrust and aggression between former allies. The airlift had been a tremendous achievement which made Vesta long to produce a worthy tribute to those who had taken part, but her mood was wrong.

David did not want to talk about it. He had married Pat last month and was steeped in the semi-mystery of running his property while discovering the delights of marriage. Far from expecting Marion and Leo to move out, he and his bride had selected their part of Tarrant Hall and all four were apparently

450

living in harmony up there on the hill with a little girl who had acquired parents and two sets of grandparents in her new country. Tessa and Bill Chandler were planning to visit their homeland before he grew too old to enjoy such a journey. As Pat refused to leave David after finally getting him, they had asked Vesta if she would like to accompany them. David also suggested that she return home to her studio when the lease of the cottage ran out. Although she had not given her answers, Vesta did not intend to accept either offer. She felt that David was trying to be extra nice to her, which accentuated her unhappiness.

She was desperately lonely and restless. Work would have been the panacea, but even that was denied her. A sense of failure was with her day and night. Knowing David had overcome terrible events in his life, she longed to talk to him about his strength and determination, his ability to conquer defeat. Afraid of crushing his present fragile serenity, Vesta kept quiet. She had missed her father deeply during the last few months. His advice had always been sound and sincere. Because of this, she spent a great deal of time with Mirjana in the belief that they were both feeling lost and uncertain of what lay ahead – two daughters of a man who had surely passed on to them something of his ability to rise above adversity. The little flame-haired child appeared to be succeeding where Vesta was not.

What would she do when her lease ran out at Christmas? Perhaps she should abandon art and get a job as a telephone operator. She knew about communications, after all. Had she not taken over a transceiver in the midst of a tank battle? Her thoughts flew to that time, and she remembered the camaraderie of those frightening but exciting days. Then Italy. So many faces swam into her mental vision. Americans, Italians, men from home. Laughter, pain, tears but, above all, being part of something vital and recording it. Being one of the boys.

Unable to sit still, Vesta abandoned the tea cup and walked into hot sunshine in the garden. A frog sat beside the pond, large, green and shiny, as if posing for her. Where was the excitement in that? Where the laughter, the companionship, the . . . the *action*? Her thoughts returned to the airlift. The memories those pictures revived were too painful to face, and yet . . .

The frog suddenly leapt into the pond with a great splash, leaving Vesta to gaze at widening ripples on the water. He had had no idea what lurked beneath the surface, yet he had jumped into the green depths to face it because that was where he belonged. He had jumped into the water to do what frogs were meant to do, whatever the risks. He did not attempt to become a kingfisher because life in a pond was unpredictable. Neither did he try to become a snake and meet with failure. He knew what he did best, and got on with doing it.

Vesta returned to the cottage and went upstairs to where her set of airlift canvases stood beneath a sheet. With them were a number of sketches she had done as groundwork for others. Sifting through them she selected a few and placed a virgin canvas on her easel. If a frog had enough sense to know what he was doing, so should she. To hell with flowers, steam engines and merry haymaking. This was what she did best, and pain must not be allowed to stop her. It would surely ease, in time. She was a Sheridan; enough her father's daughter to emulate the example he had set. One which David had risen to with great courage; one he would pass on to Mirjana and his own children.

Vesta worked with great concentration for several hours. Gradually, her mental return to Fassberg overtook all other thoughts and she was lost in the sights, the sounds, the smells of an American C-54 as she sketched Chuck Peterson at its controls *en route* to Gatow. When the light began to fade in late evening, she put down her brushes with regret and discovered that she was hungry.

Rummaging in the tiny pantry she found several tins whose contents could be mixed to make the kind of hash that had been Brad's speciality. She ate it thinking of him. After writing several powerful pieces on the atrocities committed in Changi prison, he had moved on from Singapore to uncover another incident similar to that fatal one in Malaya.

A two-day trek through jungle in New Guinea had led him to a reported 'monster' in an isolated cavern which local people were afraid to approach. Nothing deterred the man forever seeking an exclusive, and Brad had found four people living in desperate circumstances and venturing out only after dark. In 1944 Japanese troops had swept through a village and slaughtered its population because they had sheltered a wounded Australian soldier. Four adolescent boys had fled their huts in terror, and had been in hiding ever since. They were now young men. The weird noises which had kept everyone at bay were the howls of one who had gone mad through fear.

The story had been strongly emotive beneath Brad's talented pen, but Vesta could never read his articles now without wondering if the truth had been doctored. There was a deal of difference between journalistic licence and downright lies. Yet those days with him had been sweet; the nights even sweeter. She knew he would never be alone in his bed, as she now was, and that his dreams would be only occasionally of her. She would never forget Brad, but he would no longer create magic if they met.

After a restful night, Vesta rose early to ring Pat and tell her she would be disconnecting her telephone for several days while she worked. Inspiration had returned, and with it came such strong memories of Germany and Paul she eventually surrendered to the image which superimposed itself on all others. The compulsion to put it on canvas was as strong as the time she had painted *Betrayal*, so she took up a fresh canvas after two days and began to give the vision life. The artist herself was astonished by the clarity of her memory as the tall, broken chimney, the scarred and blackened shell of a factory, and an impression of a crowd gazing in awestruck apprehension slowly appeared beneath her brush strokes.

Vesta worked more swiftly than she had ever done before. It was as if this painting had been so long waiting for creation its patience had run out. By the end of that day the entire canvas was covered by a picture in embryo. Tomorrow she would add the figure clinging to the tower. Perhaps she would then find peace.

Gazing at her work, lost in recollection of her sick fear as she had watched, Vesta did not hear a car pull up outside. Only when the sound of heavy footsteps downstairs broke into her reverie did she grow aware that someone had entered the cottage. Brushes in hand, she went to the top of the narrow staircase. A man in grey flannels and a soft blue shirt stood in a pool of evening sunlight, looking up at her.

'There was once a chap called Jerry Stanstead, whose girl turned him down then went back to him,' he said. 'He had a damn sight more sense than that idiot Gaynor.'

Vesta sank slowly on to the top stair. 'You're not an idiot. I treated you very badly.'

He mounted the first stair. 'I must be a glutton for punishment.'

'I'd be an embarrassment at the colonel's cocktail parties.'

'You'd liven them up.' He took the next stair.

'Your career would suffer.'

'No, it wouldn't. I'm far too good at my job not to get where I want to go.' One more stair.

'I'd want to be alone when I was working.'

'*So would I!*'

She sighed. 'I paid for disobeying. I was as sick as a dog watching you that morning.'

'Good!'

'You'd be jealous of any man who helped me.'

'Probably. No one's perfect.' He was halfway up the stair-case by now. 'I'm on two weeks' embarkation leave before sailing for Hong Kong. There's trouble brewing in China and elsewhere in that part of the world.' He sat on the stair below her. 'I've heard the light out there is perfect for an artist . . . and it's often so hot people have to take off all their clothes.'

She gazed at him for some time before saying, 'I once seduced a man who kept suggesting we did that.'

'Why not do it again?'

'I think I've forgotten how.'

His remembered smile appeared. 'Oh yeah? We'll see about that.'